BET ON YOU

Erin,
Hope you enjoy the
Stories! The book is a
great escape from the
world and lots of fun, too!
After taking care of young
Georgia Grace all day, it'll
really be fun! Hope to see you
both again soon! I have
lots of Sunflowers!!!
God bless you and
family,
Phyllis
Sept
2020

Bet On You

Las Vegas Cocktails and Casino Stories
— Book One —

Phyllis Carver

The Literary Front Publishing Company
Las Vegas, Nevada

This is a work of fiction based loosely on the author's life experiences. Some names of family members are actual; most names, including the main characters, are used fictitiously. Some people, places and incidents are real, but most are a product of the author's imagination and any resemblance to actual persons, living or dead, as well as events and locales is entirely coincidental.

All posted website addresses and contact information were complete and correct at time of publication.

Published by The Literary Front Publishing Company
Las Vegas, Nevada

For additional purchases, visit: PhyllisCarver.com

Printed in the United States of America

ISBN 978-1-64945-175-0

Cover photo by WS Graphics, Rochester, NY

Typesetting services by BOOKOW.COM

ACKNOWLEDGMENTS

There are so many people to thank but first I must thank the "One True Presence and Power" in all our lives. He continues to guide us, thanks to his infinite gift of intelligence, which he shares with all of us. All we must do is accept and practice.

Thank you to WS Graphics for the beautiful picture taken of me when Mr. and Mrs. Wayne A. Sheeler came to Vegas. As they played slots in my section every day, I noticed Wayne always had his camera around his neck. I commented that it was a nice camera and he said, "Stand over there!" He took my serving tray out of my hands, handed it to Mrs. Sheeler, who graciously balanced it on a slot stool while Wayne instructed me how to pose. The results are on my book's cover. I was delighted when they sent me copies of my lovely portrait. I will never forget them! (And I will never look that good in a picture again!) WS Graphics is in Rochester, NY. Wayne can be contacted at WSGraphics@frontier.net.

I lovingly thank my immediate wonderful family: son and daughter-in-law, Scott and Claire Carver and my beautiful granddaughters, Annie, Gigi, and Carmela; and son and daughter-in-law, Aaron and Cristi Carver, my handsome grandson, Clark, and beautiful Grace, my youngest granddaughter. Thank you for loving your Gram and for assisting me through all this! Thanks to my sisters and brother. You are a gift from God! Thanks to ALL my very Italian American cousins and their spouses, and good friends. You mean the world to me. You know it, Joe and Sylvia Yankus. You are always there for me! May God continue to bless all of you with more of the goodness you possess!

A big thanks to Theresa Phillips, my special niece and friend! I mean it when I say, "You are the daughter I never had." You are always ready to assist me with a loving hand. God bless you and your good man, Andy, for fulfilling your life!

Ms. Terri Eileen Liggins (TerriLiggins.com), my editor and friend, you are the very best! I appreciate the authorship world you have opened up to me. Thank you for introducing me to your wonderful daughter, Skye Shepard (socialbutterSkye.com), and now my friend. I love my website, Skye. Continue to make us all proud! Both of you excel in the patience department and the "caring good friend" department, which is rare to find in life. You are blessed!

I must give a shout out to World Renown Motivational Speaker, Mr. Les Brown. Thank you for your endorsement and support! It's obvious you are a man who loves his family and fans. You extend your love to all of them. God blesses you with a truly positive life, which some people will never know exists. Keep teaching and informing the masses. Your voice is a precious gift from God!

Norma DeVries, you are a true friend, my best friend. Always there for me and knowing my true soul. Being the lady that you are, I'm sorry if I freaked you out with some of the stories in this Book One of the *Bet On You* series (more to come!). You hadn't been exposed to that other side of old Las Vegas, but you handled the shock and exposure quite well. (wink) Welcome to my world and your new home. We are lucky to have you in our lovely Las Vegas community. Thank you for your endorsement and all your encouragement. God bless you always!

Barbara Glucksman, you gave me so much encouragement to never give up. You are such a loving, giving spirit! Take care of yourself and your health. You are exceptional, always putting Marc and your family first. I know how much they all love you because you make it easy with your kind and loving heart! Thank you for your introduction to Mr. Ken Sherman, your childhood friend. He was so kind to encourage me, too.

Thanks to my friends and neighbors, "The Brunch Babes"! You girls give me joy and hope for continued happiness in our close-knit community. God bless all of you!

To the cocktail waitresses who I learned so much from, I thank you all! I hope your paths are positive ones. Larry and George, you two bartenders are the best in the world! Thank you for your goodness and kindness. Patti, thank you for always being my friend. Your closeness to the One Presence and Power has allowed me to find peace in the safety of your loving spirit. You are very special, and He knows it. I know it, too, and appreciate and love you.

Having completed over 30 years of hands-on "casino research," I appreciate the fact that God protected me. I tried to stay aware of my surroundings at all times, but it wasn't always possible. For sure, I have a very special Angel watching over me while listening to Eddie whispering into his ear. Please take care of Eddie for me, too!

I want to thank my readers and friends. Without you, none of the goodness, which will result from these stories going to print and beyond, could ever happen. God bless and keep you all! Stay positive and love unconditionally. It's not difficult; it's smart! Teach all the children. They need and yearn for positive guidance. They are the future of our society and all planet Earth! Be kind to each other and to God's creatures who share this space with us.

I am grateful that I can entertain my readers with my stories, giving them a break from the real world and all its unfairness and challenges. We are all united Americans! Let us fight for our beautiful country, the USA.

Contents

Remembering

THE exquisite woman sauntered down the deserted hallway on her way to the largest of the many luxuriously decorated ballrooms in the hotel. The lights of the hand-blown chandeliers caused her blond highlights to shimmer against her long brunette hair, while those same lights caused her form fitting sequin gown to sparkle beautifully against her taut, tall and slender body. She credited her health to the fact she was married to the most wonderful man in her life, Ian, and to the fact that she was extremely physical because of her profession and because she was the only woman on her hotel's four-member ski team.

Her health was no thanks to Tony.

Both she and her job demanded discipline in life. This delicate and refined woman was Cece. She was grateful for this event occurring while she was on a four-month leave of absence. She purposely arrived early, before anyone else, giving her time to think in peace. She wanted to regain her composure after everything she had gone through. She needed to reflect and meditate just to calm down before this "Employee of the Month" event began. Her hotel employed over 4,000 employees.

Tony continued to haunt her memory. He always would, until one of them was dead.

Cece knew her wonderfully good man, Ian, would arrive with everyone else in just over two hours. Ian was her strength, her lover, her best friend, and her husband. They met through a mutual friend when she was 16 and Ian was 17. She always felt that between God and Ian she could accomplish anything. So far that belief was working.

Especially after surviving Tony.

Cece had made a deal with God when she was young. She always remembered praying, "Please God, if you help me through this life, I will be good."

Cece calmly sat at her table, folded her hands, took a deep breath, closed her eyes, and her memories began to flow.... One story after another, until the memories got to Tony, that's when she fought back with Ian's love and help. She knew there was more life to lead no matter what Tony tried to do to her, but Cece was determined to make a good life for Ian and their sons. As thoughts swirled in her mind, she began to relax and remember her young life, Ian's impressive young life events, their two young sons, Scott and Aaron, her wonderful parents, Carmella and Sammie, how she met Ian, and the strange circumstances Ian and she seemed to constantly navigate through.

Chapter 1

Little Ian 1950

Grandma Martha knew what was going to happen that night. She was the one who told her son what was really going on at his wife's North Carolina home while he had been away at war. Grandmother Martha, was not going to let it continue in front of her two grandsons. The boys were going to be stolen away from a preacher's daughter, who could not remain loyal to her U.S. Marine husband, Ian, Sr., while he fought through the horrific battles at Guadalcanal during World War II.

Little Ian was lying on his side of the big bed shared with his mother —she on the other side and two-year-old baby brother in the middle. He was trying not to think about the monsters, but he went to bed frightened every night. Why did God make monsters? He was so tired all the time because the monsters kept waking him up. Why couldn't he just sleep through 'the attacks' like his little baby brother? There wasn't just one monster. There were many kinds of monsters. Some made awful noises and he thought those monsters were really hurting his mother. Ian's Dad said while he was gone to war, little Ian was the head of the house and should take care of his mother and the new baby. Wasn't the war over yet?

He was only 5 years old and couldn't understand what was really happening. Why didn't Mommy just lock the door? Isn't that what other people do to keep monsters and bad things out of their homes at night? Closing the old screen door just wasn't enough!

His childhood thoughts were very confusing to him. It was long past his bedtime when he began to fall off to sleep. He was trying not to think of the monsters who continued to come into their room almost every night. Most children feared monsters in closets or monsters under their bed. His monsters walked into his tiny home through the back door. Why would Mommy leave it open? Then the monsters continued through the kitchen, into the hall, and entered the bedroom and onto their shared bed.

Ian prayed, "Please, God, don't let a monster come tonight. I'm only 5 years old and I don't know if I'm brave enough yet to carry out my plan." Just as he was almost asleep the rickety old screen door squeaked open and broke the night's silence. Ian could hear the creaking noise as he woke up. Oh, NO! not tonight! Was he brave enough yet to carry out his plan? He set it up and knew exactly what he was supposed to do to the monster before it would probably kill him! He was going to protect his mother this time when the monster would jump on her and make groaning noises as it sucked on his mother's face.

The monster appeared in the doorway of the bedroom. He was huge! Most of the monsters were smaller than this one. Oh, little Ian was so very scared, but he stayed still and only peeked out of one eye to watch the monster. Ian had to do something! His dad was brave enough to protect our country and he knew Ian was brave enough to protect his mommy and baby brother.. Ian began to put his gutsy little redheaded boy plan into action. The monster was shedding his clothes. When the monster pulled his shirt up over its head, Ian saw his chance to go unnoticed.

Little Ian quietly slid off the bed towards the dresser. He made it! The monster didn't even see him. Ian waited at the end of the bed. He needed to get between the wall and the dresser into the corner of the room. He had placed a 4-inch-long hat pin in the bowl on top of the dresser near that corner. He scooted down toward the dresser and waited to see if the monster noticed. Ian reached up into the bowl. His little hand searched carefully for his weapon because he had to stab the monster before he got killed. His hand silently nudged the bowl. He felt for the long hat pin. His small hand wrapped around it. He slid back down to the floor and began low crawling towards his mother's side of the bed.

This monster was really hurting his mother because they were both making lots of noises and tossing around. The monster's hands were all tangled in his mother's long hair. The monster was on top of his mommy. Ian was surprised the monster did not know he was there right next to him. Ian began to stand up slowly to avoid losing his footing. He already had his two little fists wrapped around the long hat pin. Ian began to raise the hat pin up over his head, feeling frozen in time, but he had to act now. He held the hat pin tightly and lunged it straight down and deep into the middle of the monster's naked right buttock!

The monster wailed out loud in a bloody scream. He turned to face his assailant. As the monster's contorted face looked down upon little Ian he screamed, "I'm gonna kill you, kid!"

The man could have probably hurt the five year-old child if he could catch him, but the boy knew the woods in back of the tiny home and was very fast. Little Ian ran out of the house by pushing through the old screen door and headed toward the woods to get to his tree house where he could hide, watch, and hear everything.

Meanwhile the man was screaming obscenities, tugging his pants up with one hand, pulling the hat pin out of his buttock with his other hand, and trying to get his loafer shoes onto his feet, all at the same time. He was steaming mad. The woman was screaming to him not to hurt the boy. The fearful boy could hear everything while he tried not to cry. He had to be brave and silent so the monster couldn't find him and kill him. His little brother and mother needed him because he was the head of the family while his dad was gone.

The monster of a man heard the screen door slam shut as the hinges creaked. It was the first clue to where he would begin to look for the boy.

He ran through the house yelling, "I'm coming to get you, kid!"

As the monster man ran into the rusty screen door, knocking it off one of its hinges, a huge fist slammed up into his face. Blood shot out of his dumbfounded mouth. The monster man wondered who hit him, as it certainly wasn't a 5-year old kid! Another fist came crashing down onto the monster man's face as the boy watched them from his tree house.

Could it possibly be him? His dad did tell him once long ago he'd be back someday. The monster was bloody and knocked out after the third punch landed square on his chin causing blood to secrete from every orifice in the man's head.

The boy heard his hero yelling out to him that it was safe and he could come out of hiding now because his dad was home. The boy clambered down the tree.

He ran up to Ian Sr's open arms yelling out to his hero, "Dad, is that you? I knew you'd come back to get us! You knocked the monster out!"

Ian Sr. looked down at his oldest boy and said, "Ian, you'll never be afraid again because you will be able to fight any monster or man! I'll make sure of it. Now, let's go get your little baby brother!"

Ian jumped up into his dad's arms and knew monsters would never hurt them again! They turned to walk into the back of the house as Ian Sr. pulled the old screen door off its last hinge and let it fall to the ground. Ian, Jr. was one gutsy kid. He was going to be just like his dad! Ian Sr. thundered through the house while switching Little Ian onto his back with the boy putting his little arms around his dad's neck. They found the bedroom doorway and Ian Sr. didn't even look at the naked woman in bed.

Instead he picked up the sleeping 2-year-old and said," Now you can have all the visitors you want!"

The three of them turned and walked out of the woman's life forever.

Ian, Sr. and his sons stayed at Grandma Martha's house for a few years. During that time, Ian Sr. met a lady, Mattie, who was single with a little boy of her own. They fell in love, married and created a ready-made family. They packed up and moved away to a place of opportunity. California became their new home. They sang songs and played games all the way to California. The most fun happened when they hit the west. Ian Sr. bought his three sons holsters with play guns that used caps. They each got a cowboy hat and the boys shot at every cactus they saw until they arrived in California.

Chapter 2

LITTLE CECE 1952

THEY were all at the hospital, waiting. Her parents had recently arrived from

New York to Florida to make a new life. Her Uncle Benny was the first to move to southern Florida and the rest of the family followed. Sammie would be the new dad and Carmella the new mom. They already had a 4-year-old daughter, who was conceived before Sammie went to fight in World War II and born while he was away. She was named after Sammie's mama. This one would be a son to be named after Sammie's papa, Phillip.

This happy Sicilian-American family would soon learn this baby had a mind of her own. Everything went along fine but instead of a son, Sammie got another daughter. She was born all shriveled up, wet, and ugly! Sammie couldn't believe his new little girl was so ugly! He wondered how such a terrible thing could happen to Carmella and him.

His first daughter was beautiful. She was strong and full looking. She had big brown eyes and ringlets of long curls that bounced and adorned her cherubim-like face. She personified a perfect angel. Sammie didn't know all babies looked like Cece after fighting their way into the world and Carmella was too tired after the birth to explain it to him. Carmella didn't realize how much his second-born's appearance was affecting him until the next day.

As Carmella fell asleep, she said "Wait until tomorrow!"

Sure enough, the next day, Sammie walked by the hospital's nursery and couldn't find his new ugly baby girl. Someone had made a mistake and put someone else's rather pinkish little blond baby girl into the bassinet marked with their last name, Riccobuono. He stared, really confused.

Sammie questioned, "What kind of hospital is this? On top of everything else that has happened to us, now they lose our baby girl!"

Just then, Carmella walked up behind Sammie and asked, "What's that you're asking? What do you think of your new baby daughter today?"

Sammie was afraid to say anything yet to Carmella about the hospital losing their baby, but he asked, "Where is she? Someone put the wrong baby in our bassinet!"

Carmella laughed and said, "No, Silly. That's our baby girl, Cece!"

Sammie looked at his wife as he grabbed her shoulders and asked, "Do you mean to tell me our ugly baby girl now looks like a beautiful angel? How could that possibly be? And she's blond!"

Carmella smiled and said, "That's what happens, Sammie! They change quickly within one day after they are born. Yes, she's your Cara Mia!"

Cara Mia means 'My Darling" in Italian. She did look like her Father. There was no mistaking it. She had Sammie's fine features and was fair. Cara Mia became Sammie's nickname for Cece. She may not be a boy, but he would make her his tomboy. As time went on, Cece became a novelty in the family. Her cousins would take her to meet friends and show them their blond cousin. Cece learned to live with it but she was embarrassed and confused when one of the friend's fathers asked if the milkman brought her. Cece was only seven years old when she ran home crying to her mother to ask what that man meant.

Carmella said, "Cece, you look just like your Dad. Don't ever worry about the ignorant things said by jealous people! You know the real truth. You must judge people for yourself. If someone says something mean or cruel to you or about you, you know it is not true, so act like it is not true. Hold your head up, be proud, be kind, remain good hearted and other people will soon realize the liar's statement is false. Once people realize the statements are lies they will, also, realize who the liar really is and that the liar is not a kind and trustworthy person.

Gossiping liars will eventually ruin their own reputations. Any simple minded or trusting friends, who they happened to have picked on their way through life, will not remain their friends because they will, also, be scared that the liar will end up being cruel and hurtful to them. It happens to big people, too. Even worse, whoever believes the lies will end up without any true friends. Remember what I've always told you. Not everyone is nice and kind to each other. You must remember there are very bad people who are not nice to little children. There are terrible people who hurt little children. You must always try to protect yourself and not put yourself into any danger. Be careful!"

Cece may have been only 7 years old but she learned valuable lessons constantly from her religious parents. Carmella reached down and kissed her daughter's cheek. She knew how to cheer Cece up.

Carmella asked, "Why don't you go out in our garden and play cowboys with the other kids? All your friends are out there having fun."

Carmella noticed little Cece had toughened up a lot since she was old enough to go to the Saturday cowboy matinee movies with the older children in the neighborhood. Her eyes brightened up and she ran to get her guns, her holster, and her cowboy hat. Cece loved to play cowboys!

As Carmella watched Cece running to join the other children, she called out to her precious little girl, "Be careful!"

Cece stopped, turned around with a great big little girl smile and yelled back, "Ok, I will, Mommy! I love you!"

All the kids were there. They laughed and ululated while they played. Cece followed along happily. Carmella went back to her laundry room.

Suddenly, 11-year-old Tommy from down the street, yelled, "Hey, you guys, look at this!"

Tommy was down at the corner of their street where it met a larger four-lane highway. He was looking down into a ditch that had been dug out on that corner for a gas station. Its financing fell through and was never developed. The contractor had stopped digging the huge hole for the gas tanks, which left the surrounding giant salt pine roots exposed approximately halfway down into the deep huge hole.

None of the kids liked that place because it was full of bugs and biting insects. However, since big Tommy yelled, every one of the children ran to the corner to see why. Cece was the youngest child. She was scared to death as she looked down upon the first intoxicated person she had ever seen. The man was yelling at the children to go away and leave him alone. He was staggering around in the bottom of the big ditch. Judging by his filthy appearance, he apparently had fallen into the hole by accident, but wasn't physically hurt. The children couldn't understand his slurring words. They thought the man needed help because he kept falling whenever he tried to stand.

Suddenly, the drunk spied Cece and sweetly said, "Climb down here, pretty little girl. You can help me. You can make me feel a lot better!"

The bigger boys yelled out, "He wants Cece to help him!"

Cece felt so sad.

Cece called out, "Oh, poor man! Does he need help? I could go get my Mommy. Mommy always knows what to do."

With that thought, Cece turned to leave with the intention of running home to get her Mom. All of a sudden, the wet mud under Cece's little feet gave away and her left foot slipped over the top edge of the pit below her! Daddy's little Cara Mia was sliding down into the huge earthen cavity where a drunk man awaited her arrival. All the children screamed except Cece.

Cece grabbed at whatever she could. Roots whipped and slashed at the bloody little girl as she slid down deeper into the ditch. Cece got lucky and grabbed at an exposed root that both of her little hands could fit around. She did it! She held on feeling for a foot hold. Her tiny right foot found a root stub halfway down into the ditch. Cece's left foot still dangled in midair. The filthy drunk scrambled trying to grab her left foot. He said terrible words to her that she heard some of the big boys say when they thought no one was around to hear. Cece screamed to her friends to help her but they were all too stunned and afraid lest the drunk man grabbed them, too.

Cece cried tears of terror as she yelled at her friends, "Come on, you guys, go get help!"

All the children just stood there as if they were petrified with fear.

Cece knew this was what Mommy meant by bad people who would hurt little children.

The drunk got his hand around Cece's ankle. His hand was too wet and muddy and slid off of his captured prey. Insects kept biting him as he fell to the ground! He tried fighting them off. Once again, he climbed higher up the ditch's side and managed to get ahold higher up on her left leg. This time his hand wasn't sliding off!

Cece thought to herself, "If this mean man was a bad guy in a cowboy movie, what would the good cowboy do?"

With that thought, Cece tried to lift her right foot as high off its root stub as possible while she held tightly onto a branch with both her little hands. He began to slide backwards as he grabbed her left foot with both of his hands. He had a wicked laugh and she could smell his foul pungent breath as he began to pull her down to him.

Cece knew she had to do 'it' soon even though she was crying with terror at the thought of hurting someone. Daddy said it was ok to fight back if someone was trying to hurt her. She had to do 'it' now! Cece raised her right leg up into the air as high as possible. Her bloody painful little hands were slipping down the tree root that she was still holding onto in desperate fear. She thrust her free right foot down as forcefully, and as fast, as a little girl could, right onto the bridge of the pervert's nose!

Blood sputtered everywhere. The drunk let go of her and grabbed at his nose with both of his hands. When he realized he was free falling backward down into the ditch, he began flailing his arms around into the air grabbing for any exposed roots to help break his fall, but there weren't any in the lower half of the ditch. As he hit the bottom, the children could hear the bones in his right arm snapping.

The drunk bellowed, "I'm gonna kill you, little girl, and all these other brats!"

All the children gasped simultaneously. Cece was still bobbing up and down while she held onto the tree root keeping her body from falling along with the drunk to the bottom of the ditch. Cece's legs couldn't seem to find another foothold as she kept looking for support. She was braver because the drunk could not hurt her anymore now that he was injured.

The drunk screamed in terrible pain, which forced Tommy to come out of his stupor. Tommy finally went running and screaming down the middle of the neighborhood's street for help. Cece was still hanging onto the tree root by her two dirty and bloody little hands. She had the courage to still feel for footholds as her hands continued to slide until finding a larger foothold she could get both of her feet up onto safely. Cece waited there for her hands to stop hurting, but her painful hands seemed to bleed even more.

Another mother, who lived at a house closer to the ditch, came running out of her house when she heard the drunk's empathically loud screams from his pain due to his mangled arm. Carmella had been making a pie when she heard the drunk's screams. Now she heard Cece's friends screaming that Cece needed help. Carmella took off running and searching for Cece while she was still holding onto her rolling pin. She would protect her little girl with everything that a mother had. The mothers ran up together to the edge of the ditch where they saw all the children. Carmella saw the dirty drunk at the bottom of the ditch holding his bloody nose with one hand. The mothers saw his badly broken right arm was twisted under his back. He was crying about the nasty little blond girl. Carmella got Cece from the branch and the other mother returned with a wash rag to clean Cece's hands and tears from her face.

Carmella was yelling to the drunk, "You were lucky to only have to deal with my little girl, because if you give anyone else any more trouble, I am coming down there to beat you with this rolling pin."

The drunk began crying, "Look at me, Lady! I've had it! I have a busted arm. I'm full of bug bites and I'm itchy all over. Just keep that nasty little girl of yours, and yourself away from me! Please, I beg you! Please, call the police!"

Cece thought Carmella would be mad at her for being bloody and dirty when Carmella smiled at her and said, "I am proud of you for fighting back."

As other mothers gathered around, Carmella dropped her rolling pin and laughed out loud, grabbing her little girl. She wondered who would protect the drunks of the world from her little girl. Little did Carmella know how prevalent that thought would be someday as she thanked God for the angel who protected her daughter. Carmella realized how strong Cece's Italian Eye and insight must be.

Carmella lifted her girl into her arms and held the crucifix around her little neck. She thanked God for protecting Cece and making her such a spunky child. Other mothers joined Carmella. By that time, the ambulance and the police arrived. Neighborhood mothers were laughing and fussing over Cece, –some washing her little bloody hands and scratches while others stood by with medicine and bandages.

The TV crews showed up right behind the police, with all their cameras set up to film and take photos. They were followed by Harry 'the ice cream man.' Harry loved little Cece. He ran up to her and knelt to check on her. He was so happy she was all right that he handed out free ice cream to everyone there! Reporters gathered information. The TV cameras filmed Harry hugging Cece and putting a popsicle carefully into one of her little bandaged hands. They all happily showed the drunk still in the ditch yelling at the cameras and again as he was being handcuffed to the ambulance's medical stretcher by the wrist of his unbroken arm.

Cameras still rolled as the drunk yelled, "Keep that nasty little blond girl and her mean mother away from me!"

Everyone laughed. The four policemen who lifted the drunk out of ditch posed for the camera. They all smiled and the filthy drunk babbled loudly and stared idiotically at the cameras.

Cece was being interviewed by reporters who asked her if she was afraid.

She said, "I wasn't afraid too much. I was mostly mad because that weird guy wouldn't leave me alone. He's so dirty and he really stinks."

The reporters loved it as they were entertained by Cece's story of bravery.

Then one of the reporters asked Cece how she thought of what to do.

"My daddy said it was all right to fight back if anyone ever tried to hurt me so I just asked myself, "What would the good cowboy do?"

The reporters went wild as they roared, "That's a wrap!"

That night, Cece made the local news in Miami and became the most popular kid on the block where her childhood home stood on East 28th Street in Hialeah, Florida!

After watching the evening news, Sammie seethed with anger and wanted to beat the drunk to a pulp for trying to hurt his lil' Cece. Then Sammie laughed as he thought to himself how he couldn't have done a better job of it then what Cece did! He felt very grateful as he thanked God for watching over his little girl.

One by one, the whole family called Sammie and Carmella about the news. Grandma Angie swore Cece was never in any danger because her granddaughter had the Sicilian-Italian gift of 'The Eye.' Cece's family didn't settle down until very late that evening because of all the talk about the news. The phone just wouldn't stop ringing.

Sammie was so proud of his tomboy as he contemplated her question, *"What would the good cowboy do?"*

"I guess I have a real tomboy on my hands," he thought, "She'd better be, with her looks."

Sammie finally closed his eyes that night smiling while imagining his little tomboy saying, "Watch out, World!"

Chapter 3

AUNT REBECCA

As a young girl, Cece admired pretty ladies. In doing so, she realized many ladies didn't stay pretty for very long. She was young and couldn't figure out why. The women in her family, who were once beautiful, seemed to lose their looks for some unknown reason. When Cece saw pretty ladies, she asked Carmella what Cece would have to do to stay pretty. According to Carmella, staying pretty didn't come naturally. Carmella explained it was a lot of hard work, exercise, food moderation, having a good spirit, and determination.

Then Cece asked, "I have a good spirit, but should I start eating less food?"

Carmella laughed, "Absolutely not! You're a little girl and you eat like a bird already!"

Cece looked quite puzzling at her Mom and tried to picture herself as a Cece bird before asking, "What's that mean?"

Carmella answered, "It just means that you don't eat very much at all. You have a long time to go before you have to begin to think about a woman's weight. As long as a woman is healthy, and exercises, weight is not a problem."

Cece would try on her Mom's old high heels and her old bras, even though Cece never quite got them on correctly. At the early age of ten years, she could not picture herself as beautiful, knowing she was a tomboy. At least everyone told her she was a tomboy.

Cece became determined to be a pretty woman someday. She would watch her mother exercising in front of the TV set where a man wearing a jumpsuit conducted an exercise show. She inquired of her mother if those were the same exercises she needed to do to become pretty. Carmella would laugh loudly and say, "If you keep running around like you do now, you'll always be in shape, and you are already pretty!"

Cece realized how smart Carmella was because Cece already liked to exercise.

Cece was 11 years old when her youngest uncle, Eddie, decided to bring his new bride, Rebecca, to visit his family in Miami, Florida. They were from some small desert town in Nevada. Their city was called Las Vegas. Cece had never heard of it but the older folks in her family acted like it was a shameful place. Then she heard whispers about gangsters, gambling, drinking, and showgirls.

Cece loved all of her family dearly. All were nice Sicilian-American Catholics. However, Cece noticed for some unknown reason, the older relatives were not acting kindly to Eddie's new bride, Rebecca. No one hardly spoke to her. When they said bride, they meant new bride to Eddie. Rebecca had been married six times before she married Eddie. Rebecca was a stunningly beautiful blond, blue eyed showgirl. Her former husbands ranged from every caliber of life with two things in common. They were all filthy rich, and they were all extremely jealous. Eddie was not rich and he was not jealous of Rebecca. He considered himself Rebecca's best friend and loving husband. She was a kind woman and Eddie was determined to make his first marriage last. They were in love. Eddie sadly noticed how his family was reacting to Rebecca. He wanted them to love her as much as he did.

Every time Rebecca went into the kitchen and asked the women if she could help with dinner, the women would tell her, "No, we've got everything under control. Just relax in the family room and we'll be done shortly."

The entire family, women and men alike, were whispering and gossiping about Rebecca. Carmella was taking it all in stride, because she set the example for the younger women of the family, but Carmella noticed that her older sisters and even Grandma Angie seemed unfriendly to Rebecca. Carmella realized they were just worried about Eddie's happiness.

Cece knew everything that was happening. She could move around her Grandma's large house, and among her big family, totally unnoticed by everyone, except her parents. Lonely Rebecca, however, did notice Cece! Cece listened to every conversation while she acted with nonchalance as she constantly moved from room to room. When Cece seemed to float into the family room where Rebecca sat graciously alone, Cece could feel Rebecca's eyes following her. Rebecca could tell the child liked her, too, but that Cece was shy. Rebecca waited patiently.

Cece felt sorry for Rebecca because the women in the family seemed so mean and abrupt to her. Did they fear her because she was beautiful? Cece liked the way her new Aunt Rebecca looked; so pretty. Cece could hear the men talking, too, while they barbqued. They were also afraid to talk to Rebecca—partially because she was so beautifulbut mainly because of what their wives would have to say to them later if they caught them talking to Rebecca. Cece wanted so much to talk to her new, very pretty, Aunt. Cece was sure of one thing. If *she* could figure out how rude her relatives were behaving, so could this pretty grown lady.

Cece moved in, slowly circling Rebecca. She had no idea what to say so she just stopped in front of Rebecca and their eyes locked. Cece was shaking and she wanted to run away but instead she told herself to be brave. She had learned to be strong since she was a little cowgirl. She could do it! With that thought, she blurted out, "Hi, I'm Cece!"

Cece was delighted when Rebecca replied smiling, "Hi, back to you! I'm your new Aunt Rebecca."

The next two things that happened were like a miracle to Cece. First, the bride was so happy someone was actually talking to her. Secondly, Cece was happy she could stop holding her breath in anticipation. They just watched each other as they laughed and giggled like two little girls. No one knew Rebecca couldn't have children. She wanted to grab Cece and hug her and play with her. Rebecca didn't want to chase the girl off with an overt display of affection so she moved slowly.

Cece blurted out, "You are so pretty."

Rebecca smiled and said, "Thank you. You are a very pretty girl, too."

Cece replied, "My parents say I'm a tomboy and that I always get dirty playing football with the boys, but I am better at football than most of the boys."

Rebecca liked that and said, "Cece, all those things are going to change in your life soon. You are at an age now when you'll be growing much faster than the boys. You are soon to become a young lady. Boys take a little longer to grow into young men and, because of that, those same boys will be mean to you and tease you terribly. What you have to remember is, those boys are teasing you because they like you and they think that you are pretty. When I look at you, I realize that you are going to become a gorgeous woman. Look at your long eyelashes. You must have the longest most muscular legs that I've ever seen on such a young girl."

Cece laughed and said, "That's why I am so good at football. I can outrun all the boys."

Rebecca said, "Someday soon you will be changing. You may like to watch football but you won't want to play football with the boys anymore. You are going to like lady things like these earrings I have on my ears. Here, let's try these earrings on your ears."

Cece big eyes opened wide. She watched Rebecca take her earrings off her ears. None of the women in the family would ever let Cece try on their earrings and none of the nuns would like it either. She remembers they sent her home from school one day for wearing pants to the Christmas play rehearsal when she was only eight years old! Carmella had made Cece's outfit. Those nuns could care less her clothes were beautiful and specially made. They called her Mommy on the phone and told her to come and get Cece because she wasn't properly dressed. Cece felt totally embarrassed and dejected just because she happened to be wearing pants. Carmella was even more upset.

Rebecca leaned in close and put the earrings onto Cece's ears. Cece stiffened up. She was waiting for "the bomb" to fall. Surely, someone would be yelling at her soon. Rebecca thought she may have hurt Cece when she stiffened up like that. The earrings hung loosely and felt good. Rebecca leaned back and held Cece's shoulders as she looked into Cece's eyes.

Rebecca asked, "Did I hurt you?"

Cece blurted out, "What makes you smell so delicious?"

Rebecca loved it! This was a very charming young girl.

Rebecca said, "Come on. I'll show you!"

Rebecca grabbed Cece's little hand as they stood up to walk down the long hallway back to Grandma Angelina's guest bedroom. The earrings were swaying back and forth on Cece's little ears as they walked quickly into the room. Rebecca was having as much fun as Cece. They reached the guestroom's doorway and Rebecca told Cece to sit on the bed as she pulled her suitcase out from under the bed and hoisted it up onto the bed. With a sense of excitement, Cece sat there waiting to see what the pretty lady was retrieving.

Rebecca pulled a pretty bottle out of her suitcase and said, "This is called perfume. There are many kinds of perfume. Women like it very much because it smells really nice when they put a dab here and here."

Cece was doused behind both of her little ears with the delicious smelling potent elixir called perfume that Rebecca had on her fingertips. It was cold at first then suddenly Cece smelled the wonderful aroma and felt like she was beautiful, too, just like Aunt Rebecca.

Trying to apologize for the way her family had been treating Rebecca, Cece remarked that she hated it when people were mean to other people when they didn't even know them. Rebecca could see how sincere the little girl was and how she had given the situation some serious consideration.

Rebecca said, "Your family has many good people in it. They just want the best for your Uncle Eddie. Remember, Cece, if someone were to say something cruel about you, act as though it is not true, because it won't be! If you like yourself, and you know you are a good person, nothing any gossiper could say would matter. When you put your head down on your pillow at night to go to sleep and you have no guilty feelings, you'll know you are fine and your world is good. Always know that God loves you! If you respect yourself, you can accomplish anything you want to achieve. Dwell on the positive and let go of the negative. Always try to do better and like yourself. God wants us to learn and do better."

Cece remarked, "Wow, you sound just like my Mommy! And I already know God loves me. He made me strong! He's got some important job he wants me to do when I grow up!"

Aunt Rebecca laughed out loud. They were both totally delighted with each other. Laughter rang out loudly from Grandma's guest bedroom. They were having fun laughing and were so naturally happy with each other, it caused tears to flow down their cheeks. Cece was thanking her new aunt for playing with her and Rebecca was thanking Cece for playing back with her, too.

The women heard the commotion and came running down the hall to see what was happening. The group of women of all ages arrived at the bedroom door lead by Carmella to see if Cece, God forbid, was doing something wrong in Grandma's house. The women gathered by the doorway gawking at Rebecca and Cece, who was still wearing Rebecca's real diamond earrings dangling from her little earlobes. They all looked like their eyes were going to fall out of their sockets.

They were saying, "Cece has diamond earrings on!"

Rebecca and Cece had not heard them coming. They didn't know anyone could hear them in the back bedroom. Rebecca and Cece were having too much fun playing and hysterically laughing out loud when all the women appeared at the bedroom door. Suddenly, a surprised Rebecca jumped from her seated position on the bed next to Cece. Rebecca stared wide eyed at the group.

Carmella was first to the doorway and smiled at Rebecca. Carmella had been completely stoic all afternoon yearning for the family to try to except Rebecca.

Carmella asked inquisitively and most discreetly, "Is everything alright?"

A very surprised Rebecca tried to straighten out her beautiful full skirt with both her lovely manicured hands and answered sheepishly, "Yes, we were just having lots of fun and playing."

Carmella smiled at Rebecca and said, "Oh, good!"

Rebecca said, "You have a wonderful daughter! Cece has been extremely kind to me and we have made fast friends with each other. I wish I could have such a delightful daughter."

Carmella said, "Thank you, Rebecca. Everyone seems to adore Cece."

As the group, headed by Carmella, started back to the kitchen the gossipy older sisters asked, "Can you believe that a grown woman like Rebecca is acting like a child?"

Carmella's family respected Carmella. When Carmella said something, they listened. Carmella stopped and turned around in the hallway to face the women. Carmella felt the women seemed disappointed that someone did not get in trouble.

Carmella eyed the group of female family members of all ages and said, "I like her. Anyone who loves children that much has to be a good person."

Suddenly the group scampered and started agreeing, "Oh, yes, you're right!"

What the women didn't know was Cece and Rebecca could hear their conversation down the hallway.

A wide-eyed Cece turned to Rebecca and whispered, "Did you hear that? Mommy likes you! Watch, now they will all be a lot nicer to you."

Rebecca asked, "Oh, Cece, did you really say that?"

Cece smiled and said, "Yeah, I'm cool! I'm just like my mommy and you!"

Shortly afterwards, everyone was called to dinner. It was a long, and lovingly prepared table set for a huge family of 20 people. Everyone was trying to figure out where to sit down. Rebecca and Eddie looked very confused and a bit bewildered.

Carmella stood up from her seat and offered, “Rebecca, why don’t you and Eddie sit over here with me and Sam?”

Eddie seemed very relieved. He felt he may have been the cause of his family’s determination to ignore his new lovely bride. His big sister, Carmella, had affectionately broken the ice! Eddie smiled and followed Rebecca. After a prayer of thanks, they passed around the wine bottles and the wonderful food. Rebecca was still cautious but things loosened up as the wine glasses were refilled. Carmella thanked Rebecca for keeping Cece occupied. Rebecca replied how delighted she was to get to know Cece. The two women began to talk and laugh. Soon the rest of the family took part in their conversation. Laughter rang throughout the room.

Cece sat at the children’s end of the multiple tables feeling a bit dejected. After all, she was Rebecca’s friend first before the others finally accepted her. Cece felt happy her family was being nice to Rebecca, but at the same time sad that they got to talk to her and not Cece. Cece wanted to continue their wonderful conversation.

Rebecca caught a glimpse of Cece’s sadness and smiled at her. She then winked and gave Cece a tiny wave with her delicate hand. Cece’s face instantly lit up! She waved back, attempting to wink, as well. It was awkward because she didn’t know how. Rebecca laughed at her and pointed to her own eye then threw Cece a kiss. Well, Cece knew how to throw a kiss!

Cece loved her new Aunt Rebecca so much after such a short time! She brought both of her hands to her mouth and threw two huge kisses at one time. Rebecca beamed with joy. Cece knew they would remain best friends for as long as they both lived, and so did Rebecca.

After dinner, Rebecca and Eddie said their goodbyes to the family. They were leaving early in the morning to go home to Las Vegas. Cece began to cry profusely. Cece could hardly catch her breath. Rebecca knelt down, embraced her, encouraging her not to cry. Rebecca told Cece she could come out to Vegas to visit and stay awhile with her and Uncle Eddie. They would go swimming, go to some children’s shows, attend the new Catholic Church on the Las Vegas Strip, and go up to the beautiful surrounding mountains to explore and have a picnic.

Cece cried out, "But, what if I never see you again? Please stay!"

Carmella said, "Don't say that, Cece! Everything will be alright!"

Cece cried, "No, Mommy, No."

Sammie picked his daughter up and carried her to the car. Cece remembered watching her beautiful aunt over her father's shoulder.

Carmella apologized to Rebecca, "I am so sorry. She must be extremely tired. She enjoyed you. Please forgive her."

Rebecca stated, "I have enjoyed her, too! We have made a special connection."

The truth was apparent. They loved each other. Rebecca was trying not to cry, also. Rebecca went to the car's rolled down window and promised she would send Cece a nice gift after she got settled in their new home. They hugged, kissed, and said their last goodbyes. At least, that's how it felt to Cece, because she already knew she would never see her new Aunt Rebecca again.

Cece felt her tears fall onto her cheeks, as she thought, "Why do I have that thing that Grandma Angie calls the 'Italian Eye'? Sometimes I don't want to know what's going to happen!"

A few months later, a box arrived for Cece. Cece was so excited that her new aunt remembered her, but more excited to know her Aunt Rebecca was all right! It was the box Aunt Rebecca promised her!

Carmella couldn't believe it! She thought to herself, "But, when, how? She must have just mailed the box right before 'it' happened!"

They had just recently received a call from Eddie telling them the horrific news. Did he not know Rebecca mailed the box to Cece? It was a beautiful gift! Carmella couldn't believe Rebecca would send such an elaborate gift to her little niece. Rebecca must have sent it right before they were due to move out of their apartment! It was a box of 6 small beautiful bottles of perfume with Rebecca and Eddie's new address and phone number enclosed along with a note for Cece from Rebecca. Carmella had tears in her eyes after watching Cece open the box.

Cece proceeded to find some paper and a pencil. She was happy and was going to write to her new Aunt Rebecca right away. Mommy would mail the thank-you note for her. Cece wrote the note and asked mommy to please take care of it. Cece was very relieved that her favorite Aunt was fine.

Cece asked, "Mommy, are you ok? Are you sad about something?"

Carmella said, "Yes, I'm just busy and have 'things on my mind.' Go play and have fun while I finish dinner."

Somehow, Cece sensed something wasn't right with her Mommy. Cece wondered about that statement. How do grownups put a thing *on* their mind when their minds are inside their heads? She hoped her Mommy was ok. She found her football and reluctantly scurried outside to see what her friends were doing. Daddy pulled up into their driveway and Cece ran to jump up into his arms. Daddy was pure love. He saw the football and told her to be careful.

Daddy continued into the house where Carmella was cooking. He didn't realize Cece had changed her mind about football and decided to follow him inside. She wanted to visit with him because she had the best daddy in the world. She knew she had the best Mommy, too, and Cece wanted to check on her because she was acting strange. Cece knew something wasn't right with her Mommy with those things on her mind. Cece walked into the back washroom when Sammie and Carmella abruptly stopped talking as they saw her entering the kitchen. Daddy was beginning to tell Cece to go back out and play, but Mommy said dinner was ready now anyway.

Soon, the dishes were done, the children were bathed and put into their beds. Cece felt happy to have received her gift from Uncle Eddie and her pretty, new Aunt Rebecca. She loved them so much, but still felt something wasn't right with them. She tried to figure out again 'the things on peoples' minds.

Cece suddenly felt overly ominous and had a hard time falling asleep. She felt broken-hearted and wondered if she, too, had things getting on *her* mind. Maybe, if you are sad, it causes those things to get on your mind. It was as if Cece lost something. Maybe she lost an innocence of some sort that evening. She began to cry. She tried saying her prayers. Talking to God always helped her to feel better.

Her parents must have thought all their six children were asleep, but they were wrong. Cece could hear her parents talking to Grandma Angie on the phone. They told her about the box arriving for Cece. Cece became worried. Grandma Angelina always mentioned that Cece had the "Eye" thing. Then Grandma told Carmella and Sammie in Cece's heart of hearts that Cece already knew 'IT'. They said Rebecca must have sent Cece's gift right before "IT" happened. Cece could hardly believe what she was hearing. They were saying that a jealous ex-husband came into the apartment while Rebecca was alone and finishing up the packing to move into her and Eddie's new home. The man beat Rebecca brutally! He stabbed Aunt Rebecca with a knife many times! Blood was everywhere. Rebecca fought the man with scissors she was using while packing. Rebecca had been slashed over her entire body, but she must have continued to fight back. Blood evidence would show two kinds of blood at the scene!

The fight was so loud that neighbors came running out of their homes as they witnessed the murderer bleeding profusely while trying to run from Rebecca's apartment. Blood spewed from the man as he collapsed in his car. As his car door closed, the man passed out behind the wheel and his forehead hit the horn. The blaring horn brought out more neighbors who started screaming at each other to call an ambulance and the police. Eddie drove up later to a group of neighbors lingering in front of his doorway. Men began holding Eddie back forcefully keeping him from seeing the bloody mess or tampering with the evidence. The police found the killer dead in his blood-smeared expensive car's interior. He was a prominent attorney.

Mommy and Daddy were saying they couldn't tell Cece because she was still too young to understand. It was best she didn't know right now. They should wait until she got a little older to tell her. She curled up on her bed into the fetal position and began crying profusely into her pillow so her parents could not hear. She vowed to herself she wouldn't tell her parents she already knew something was wrong. She didn't want to hurt their feelings anymore because Cece could hear her parents crying when they spoke to Grandma, too.

She asked God to tell her new Aunt Rebecca "Hi" for her because she was in Heaven with Him now. Cece asked God to take care of her Aunt Rebecca until someday when Cece could see her again. She asked God to please introduce her Aunt Rebecca to her Grandpa Phillip Riccobuono so that Aunt Rebecca wouldn't be lonely in heaven. She thanked God very much for listening. Cece began to fall asleep with her hands still in a praying hold.

Before falling off to sleep, she wondered what kind of horrible place was this city called Las Vegas, Nevada? Why would God be sending *me* there someday?

Cece prayed again, "Please, God, don't let anyone I love, or me, ever have to go to Las Vegas!"

But then again, Cece felt 'It.' She once again continued her nightly prayers. She cried herself to sleep that night. She felt guilty for not saying that prayer sooner. If she had, maybe her Aunt Rebecca would still be alive. She would never forget her Aunt Rebecca! She desired to be just like her mommy and her aunt combined when she grew up: Very nice and very pretty.

Through her tears, Cece recited, "Angel of God, my Guardian dear, to whom God's love, commits me here, ever this day be at my side to light and to guard, to rule and to guide. Amen."

As she dosed off, Cece could see a handsome, glowing young male. She wasn't afraid because she saw him often. He was kind and good. She felt certain of that fact. He smiled at her and she smiled back at him. They were both 11 years old.

God was listening for the most part. God is patient. Only He knew Cece's real destiny. God must have decided that Cece had to progress in her lifetime very quickly because He was already giving her many lessons to learn—with more to come! Only God and young Cece knew her soul was already filled with the divine love to handle anything God threw her way. After all, she had a strong Angel.

Cece was a strong girl, and someday she would have a special strong glowing man in her life. She needed his protection. God would be sending the glowing man, who appeared continuously in young Cece's dreams. Her 'Eye' could see him, but the glowing man would need Cece, too. The two of them were destined to become one.

Chapter 4

Young Girl Gone

Cece's parents were working from early mornings to late evenings in their neighborhood convenience store. Cece had to watch the four younger children every day after school and cook dinner. To make matters worse, Carmella had to drive back and forth from the countryside to take Cece's younger brother to a doctor located in the Miami Beach area for breathing treatments. His asthma seemed to be getting worse. There was so much happening. Cece was very confused.

Aunt Rebecca was right! Cece's life was changing and so was her body. When she was 12 years old, she stayed home from school because the whole family had a stomach virus. Finally, by Saturday the family felt like they may be getting over the virus, but Cece felt worse. She had gone to the bathroom when Carmella heard her scream.

Carmella ran into the bathroom and found Cece on the floor. Carmella asked, "Are you ok?"

Cece looked down at her bloody panties and said, "No, Mom, I think I'm dying. Look at this! I feel so awful. What is happening to me? I hate this! I don't want to bleed to death!"

Carmella apologized saying, "Oh, Cece, so much has been happening lately. I'm so sorry. You're ok. I meant to have a talk with you about your body changing. Things have been so crazy with everyone in the family being sick, and your brother's asthma is getting much worse. Don't worry, Honey, you are fine. This is part of becoming a young woman. Come on, we'll fix you up while I explain."

Cece looked up at her mother and said, "I'm just glad to know that I'm not dying."

Carmella said, "Believe it or not, this is a good thing. You have become a fine, healthy, young woman. I'm going to explain everything to you."

Cece often experienced the girls at her Catholic school screaming out the classroom doors to the lavatory. No one was ever allowed to leave the classroom without the nuns giving them prior permission. Cece wondered why the girls stood up, screeched out loud, and then ran to the restroom. She wondered what all the commotion was about and why the girls didn't get in trouble for that. She was finally informed the day that 'it' happened to her. Cece was so grateful her period didn't start at school. How awful for those girls who went through that situation! No wonder all the boys were secretly laughing.

Cece decided to take advantage of this private time with Carmella. She looked at her mother and asked, "Mom, what ever happened to your real Father, Grandpa Salvatore?

Carmella was surprised Cece would ask. She looked at her daughter and said, "I'll tell you as long as you keep it to yourself until after my death. Promise?"

Cece was shocked and looked at her mother and asked, "Why? Was it so terrible? How come none of the family members ever talk about him?"

Carmella answered, "Cece, it is a very private matter. You are old enough to keep a secret. I don't want any of the family to know that I told you. So, you must promise me."

Cece said, "Ok, Mom, I promise you."

Carmella explained, "My father did not attend my 16th birthday party because he was taken away at gunpoint by four mafioso men. They were the brothers of a young woman, who my father got pregnant while he was still married to Grandma Angelina. The young woman's four brothers broke down our front door. Each brother ran into our home with a gun in his hand."

The break-in happened in front of Grandma Angie and her nine children. The four brothers led Grandpa away with their guns in his side. Grandpa didn't know the young woman whom he impregnated was related to a member of the mob. The break-in was a very dramatic time for Grandpa's oldest daughters.

Carmella continued, "We were the same age as the young pregnant woman. We didn't care about our abusive father being taken away, but we never saw men wielding guns around in our lives. We heard about the mob, but we were never exposed to it until that night. The four brothers took our father away from our family at gunpoint to go marry their young pregnant sister. There was no time to waste. She was pregnant and the priest was waiting."

The priest did not know that the groom was already married and had nine children. My grandfather was told not to say anything to the priest, or he would be killed. As soon as those men left with Grandpa, Grandma Angie told the children they were going to have a party to celebrate their father's departure.

The whole family was happy to see Grandpa gone. Grandma took her last bit of change and told the children to go buy some ice cream and hurry back before it melted. She made a cake and some fruit juice. Everyone in the family celebrated grandpa's fortunate 'for them' departure.

Grandpa was a very talented tailor, but also a drunken, frustrated tailor with no ambition. He was abusive to Grandma Angelina and us children. We did not love him. He would come home drunk late at night and tried to beat anyone who he found in the house. The children all had their hiding places so most of the time it was Grandma Angie who was the recipient of his frustrations. Or so Grandpa thought, until the next morning when he woke up. He was the one with black and blue marks all over his body and face. When he asked what happened, Grandma told him she didn't know because he came home that way. Then Grandma would turn around and secretly wink at us children.

Grandpa's new wife's family didn't care that he was not divorced from Grandma. The priest had no idea when he married the couple that it was not legal. His new wife's brothers kept a keen eye on him. He never went out in the evenings to get drunk. He was in church every Sunday and fathered six more children with his new young wife. He never spoke to us, his former family, on the streets or anywhere for that matter. If he passed any of us, he would not acknowledge us for fear of his own fate. His new in-laws wouldn't allow it. He was to become a humble, sober, quiet man, a good husband, or the bottom line was, he would die. Grandma Angie just smiled when she heard the news. She knew he would never hurt her or her children again.

Cece replied, "Wow!" to this sad and revealing background on her grandfather.

Carmela continued, "Your Grandma Angie was tiny and thin, but she was spunky, strong, smart, very industrious, and talented! She was one of the finest young seamstresses in Sicily. She taught her daughters to become accomplished seamstresses, also. I was the third sister. Grandma Angie was said to have, what their Sicilian/Italian family called, 'the mind's eye', like Grandma said you have. She knew what our father was doing and forgot how to care. He became a broken man in many ways, but he never abused his new family. He was much too afraid of his four brothers-in-law and their father, 'the Petrone.'

Grandma Angelina had wonderful talented children and devoted herself to us. She was smart and industrious. During the Great Depression of 1929, we always had good, healthy, and delicious food. She planted, nourished and reaped a good garden. She made homemade pasta and with a little olive oil and bread, which we ate like kings and queens. While so many Americans cried for help, she began to teach neighbors how to grow a garden and make pasta because she couldn't believe their parents hadn't taught them.

Grandma became the 'honored mother' of our small town. Grandma and her two oldest daughters supported their family while working as seamstresses, who repaired and made clothes in a little shop. I helped raise my four younger siblings just like you are expected to do. Grandma was the one who led the drives for rubber tires and metals for the World

War II war efforts. All of Grandma's children became proud and industrious Americans who loved their country. Many years after Grandpa left, we sisters all married and had our own children."

Cece thanked her mother and swore silence. Her parents were starting construction on their new country home. The workmen were eyeing Cece. To be cautious, Aunt Marietta took Cece to New York City to visit for the summer. Marietta thought that Cece was too much of a tomboy. She thought if her niece came to New York she could make her a young lady and dress her like a beautiful doll. Cece was much too young minded for that. She had to run just like when she first stood up at nine months of age. She didn't do baby steps; she ran across a room while balancing her tiny body with her arms. It was in her tomboy blood. She was a runner and a natural athlete. Cece was glad when summer was over and she got to go back to Florida to be with her family and see their newly built home. Carmella decorated Cece's bedroom and Cece loved it.

Aunt Marietta spoke to Uncle Joe and they thought that it was a good idea to make an offer to Carmella and Sammie. After all, Sammie and Carmella did have two other daughters and three sons. Aunt Marietta wanted Cece to come to New York. They offered to take Cece in on a more permanent basis, putting her through all the best schools and refining her into a fine young lady. They would pay for her college education and graduate school or pre-med and medical training if she wanted. Or Cece could go to law school. Aunt Marietta swore that whatever Cece wanted in the way of education, she could have.

Sammie and Carmella couldn't afford college for any of their children because they struggled with their son's medical bills. Families didn't have health insurance in those days. Aunt Marietta and Uncle Joe felt it was a good offer for the family because Cece would benefit from it tremendously and they would love to have her living with them like a daughter, who they could enjoy. People they knew were already offering Cece modeling jobs.

Every time the family went to the beach, model agency owners would approach Cece's parents with offers. They told Carmella and Sammie that Cece could earn her own college money quickly. Aunt Marietta said they wouldn't allow modeling because they could afford college for her on their own. All Carmella and Sammie had to do was approve Cece's move to New York. Cece never felt caught in the middle because she did not know anything was going on between her parents and her beloved aunt and uncle.

Parents should feel an obligation to their children and want the best for them. Carmella was broken hearted because she couldn't do those wonderful things for Cece and was very torn. Carmella knew it was a kind and generous family offer. Sammie got fed up with all the bickering this offer caused. Sammie made the decision that his daughter was going to stay with his family because that was where Cece would get the most love she could possibly have while she grew up.

Cece certainly did grow up. Everyone realized that they all just wanted the best for her. In her heart, Cece really did want to go to school and get an education, but she loved her parents and didn't want to leave her family. She somehow knew that someday she would have two sons, after she found the man with whom she wanted to spend the rest of her life. She promised herself that her sons were definitely going to get educated and that they would become wonderful, kind, loving gentlemen in the future.

Cece loved her home in the Florida countryside. She ran most of the time when she was outside so she wouldn't be bitten by the numerous flying insects. She ran to her bus stop, which was a mile away from her home, twice daily, and she ran at school. Little did she realize that by doing all that running and horseback riding she was shaping up to be quite beautiful and extraordinarily strong. Cece's two main faults were her kindness and her naivete'. Innocence oozed from Cece.

Every day, Cece grew in mind, body, and spirit. She respected everyone until she determined for herself if they deserved it or not. Her future brother-in law, Jake, was a person with whom Cece shared a constant conflict. She didn't like the way he was always watching her. He was even brazened enough to stare at her when his future wife and the family were around. What a creep!

When Cece rode horses, you would have thought she was in heaven. She rode as much as possible. As she was walking up to the barn one day, her future brother-in-law drove up next to her and asked if he could go riding with her.

Cece said, "No, I want to be alone!"

She turned away from him and kept walking.

She didn't know why, but Cece did not like him. She sensed that he had a dark side and that he had cruel tendencies ever since she saw him shoot an innocent bird just for fun. She couldn't quite put her finger on it. She knew she did not trust the man. He was full of himself and she didn't like that in a man. Cece's sister thought she loved him; the only reason Cece tried to get along with Jake. Their pending wedding was right around the corner. Cece was to be the Maid of Honor.

Jake wouldn't accept the fact that Cece didn't want him around her. The next thing she noticed was Jake entering the barn to saddle one of the horses. Cece was already riding by that time or she wouldn't have stayed.

Cece thought to herself, "I bet he had this planned."

Cece's horse went into a trot. It was the first time Cece actually felt her full breasts bounce. She hoped Jake didn't notice. She wondered about it and smiled as she thought it was about that time in her life. Everything else seemed to happen to her right on schedule.

Jake rode up beside her and said," Oh, I see that you felt those babies bounce."

Cece looked at him and said, "You are a crude person. Get away from me and my horse. He doesn't like you either."

Cece didn't know what hate was, but she thought what she felt for Jake was pretty close to it. She was certain she didn't trust him. Grandma Angie told her she had the "Eye" and to pay attention to the subconscious warnings he felt. Cece did most of the time, but today she didn't have to babysit and she just wanted to ride and have some fun–alone. Cece was the sign of Pisces. She enjoyed being alone.

Jake was surprised Cece talked back to him without respect. He would never allow her sister to do that to him. Cece headed back to the barn. Jake rode up hurriedly behind her. She could feel his eyes examining her while she was riding bare back into the barn. Even the horse acted upset. That horse loved Cece and seemed to pick up on her feelings. Cece prepared to brush her horse down. Jake wished that she would coo to him the way she did to the horse. That animal loved her very much.

Jake thought this was his chance. No one was around. He sneaked into the barn. He came up behind her and grabbed her young breasts with both of his hands. Cece yelled out loud but no one could hear her because they were too far from the houses. She was enraged. Jake was very tall, lanky, and strong and Cece could not get loose from his hold on her. He whispered into her ear that he liked virgins. She struggled. She was too angry to cry. Her horse's eyes were crazy and wide open as it looked backwards at Jake. Cece's horse staggered as Jake pulled Cece against him.

Jake kept his hold on her and started to enjoy the encounter. She bent her knees. She twisted around and managed to release her breasts from his hold. Jake grabbed her by her shoulders! She tried to figure out if that was better or worse for her. The horse didn't like the pushing and shoving. It neighed out loud and huffed angrily in place. Jake was trying to push her down onto the hay. He was saying he knew ways to make her feel what ecstasy felt like. She told him to let go of her shoulders. She knew if he got her on the ground, she would have no chance. Her strong legs were holding up, but he outweighed her by 50 pounds at the very least. Plus, he was a strong man.

Cece had to think of something—and quick! She hated him and couldn't stand to live with the thought of him molesting her while he was engaged to her sister. How could she ever explain that to her sister, her parents, and the entire Sicilian family?

Then he made his mistake. Jake said, "Hey, if you act nice, I'll let go of you."

All struggling ceased. Jake looked at her hopefully and smiled, turning her around. Cece realized he actually thought he had a chance.

Cece thought to herself, "The hell with this!"

She thought she had to be very brave to pull it off. He could hurt her. It would be her word against his. He could say that she enticed him. She put forth her best effort. The tense horse shuffled again.

Cece conjured up the sweetest voice she ever heard come out of her own mouth. She looked up into his eyes and said, "Well, stop being so rough and hurting me. Just tell me what you'd like to do, ok?"

She had thrown him completely off guard. He began to look very happy. He immediately eased up. He was interpreting her looks and mannerisms as good signs. She placed her hands on his shoulders, took a deep breath, and used her tongue in a circular motion to slowly wet her lips. Oh, how she hated him. Jake liked watching her tongue. She began to feel his hardness growing as he purposely pressed himself against her. It surprised her. Being a virgin, Cece didn't know what to expect. She had to get it just right because he now had both of his hands on her waist. He smiled deviously. She blinked her eyes sheepishly at him as she tightened her grip on both of his shoulders. He seemed excited at the thought of rough sex being a possibility. He began his move but she moved faster to begin hers. She brought her strong right knee up hard and fast into his groin and quickly backed away from him as he doubled up and fell to the ground.

Jake was whimpering in pain, and yelled, "You little bitch!" Jake struggled to get up. The horse bucked backwards kicking him on both his kneecaps. Jake went down like a falling boulder. It was the perfect retaliation.

Cece yelled. "That'll teach you not to cheat on my pregnant sister! Stay away from me or I'll tell everyone what a piece of shit you really are, and that will devastate both our families!"

Cece ran out of the barn crying profusely. She needed to calm down before she got back to her home. She knew Jake would not be moving for a while.

Her mind was scrambling as she thought to herself, "Why did I say that about a pregnancy. Oh, my gosh, is it true? How did I know? Do my parents know yet? No, they couldn't. There would be total chaos in our big Italian family if anyone knew!"

Jake was still laid out flat behind the horse saying, "Easy, boy, easy."

He could hardly move. He thought to himself, "How could she know about the baby? We promised each other to stay quiet about it. No one knows. The priest doesn't even know. We didn't tell him in confession, how could that little bitch know? I hope that she did not tell her parents! Could the wedding be off?"

Cece didn't even bother running back home. She figured Jake was down for the count and would be for a moment or two. She began to settle down and smiled to herself as she walked down the rocky road toward her home.

Cece laughed out loud with tears in her eyes as she threw her fist up into the air, pulled her elbow back down into her waist and screamed out loud, "Got him!"

She had finally calmed down as she reached the house. Cece looked back toward the barn. Jake was trying to walk in a doubled-up stagger toward his car.

Cece saw Carmella walk toward the kitchen's screen door.

Carmella asked, "Isn't Jake coming up to the house for dinner? I saw his car at the barn."

Cece smiled really big, kissed her mother's cheek, and said, "No, he doesn't feel very well and has to go home."

Carmella said, "That's strange. We watched him following you around while you were riding. Now he looks sick and bent over! It must have come on quickly!"

Cece said, "Yeah, extremely quick."

Carmela asked, "Is tomorrow the day that you are going to the dairy farm to visit Linda?

Grateful for a change of subject, Cece answered, "Yeah, and they're going to take me to the Grand Ole Opry after we all have a wonderful Southern dinner."

Carmella said, "That sounds like a lot of fun!"

Cece said, "Those guys are always fun. They said I would love it. I really don't know what to expect. Linda, her parents, and her brothers are the most wonderful people in the world. I'm excited! They say it's amazing. Charles McCraney teases me, but I love the McCraney family. And don't worry, they said they'd drop me off at home after the night's over."

That night as Cece was getting ready to go to sleep, she thought about her 16-year-old body, "Why me? The last three years were jam packed for me. Was it my fault? I can't control how I am growing and changing. Why would my future brother-in-law lust for me? I never encouraged him at all. My sister loves him. He's such a jerk! What's with this Sicilian/Italian mind's eye thing and me? The baby. I knew. How?"

Cece could tell no one else knew. If her parents did know, they would be confounded and hurt. Her dad would beat Jake. If she tried to tell her parents they would say she was 'high strung'. Cece looked up the word telepathic when she acted like this and began seeing future things! Yeah, they would say she was high strung and didn't know what she was talking about. They would tell her to stop acting that way and grow up! Cece thought maybe she was wrong, but she really did not think that she was.

Tears ran down her cheeks.

Cece continued her thoughts, "What's going to happen when it gets out? All the aunts will be calling Mom on the phone constantly. Mom will be devastated. Dad will want to kill 'Jake the jerk' because he trusted him!"

Cece put her head down on her pillow and thought of the statistics regarding child molestations. Statistics stated that most child molestations are from relatives, neighbors, or family friends. Even after her hot shower, Cece felt scared, violated, dirty, and disgusted while she tried to fall asleep. She needed to regain her control. She needed to stay in control. She didn't want to hurt her parents or her sister. Would he really have gone through with it? She took a deep breath and started saying her prayers. She felt so sleepy and swore to herself she would never put herself in that position again, at least, not on purpose, but what if…*sleepy* …this body…*sleepy*…I have…*sleepier*…I can't help how my body looks.

Cece felt emotionally drained and exhausted, but something in her mind's eye caught her attention. It was a flash. It was him again. His strawberry blond hair was glowing as usual. He looked at her and smiled radiantly. Who was this young man? Was he an archangel? A protector? He was tall and immensely handsome. He looked like he loved her no matter what the circumstances were. She thanked God for the peaceful vision and fell unburdened into a gentle, calm, positive, summer night's slumber.

She dreamt of her glowing man and prayed, "Please, God, let him come to me and help him to protect me because I'm a real handful."

Cece fell into a deep sleep while seeing the glowing man and thinking angelic thoughts all the while saying in her mind, "I love you, too!"

Chapter 5

UP TO MY EARS

CECE grew up happy and healthy like the rest of her siblings, except her little 13-year-old brother, Michael, was struggling just to breathe. The humidity in Florida made it almost impossible for him to survive. Michael looked like a small skeleton with a thin sheet of skin covering his bones. Carmella and Sammie were trying to raise their big family, work, and take care of Michael. He had to go into the Miami Beach area of Florida for weekly doctor visits. The specialists did nothing to cure Michael's asthma. They just continued to inject him with medications that did absolutely nothing to help him.

The Catholic school where Cece and her younger siblings attended had a visit from a good old German doctor. He took one look at Cece's younger brother and told Carmella if she did not get him to a desert environment within 6 months Michael would be dead! Carmella called her brother, Eddie, and asked him to meet her and Michael the next morning at McCarran Airport in Las Vegas, Nevada. Eddie picked them up at the airport and took them to his home. As soon as they stepped off the plane Michael could breathe. He fell asleep peacefully that night after eating a healthy dinner. The next day Carmella settled Michael into Eddie's home. The day after Carmella enrolled Michael in school. Michael ate like he never could before, and the color returned to his face in just those two days.

Meanwhile, back in Southwest Miami, Florida, some innovative folks built a golf course out in no-man's-land. They called it "The Doral Country Club". Cece loved living out in the countryside of Southern Florida.

It could have been because she didn't have to live on a dairy farm, but her best friend, Linda McCraney, did. Linda lived on a dairy farm because her father worked on one. He was in charge of the milking of the cows. Linda was a gorgeous girl. Cece thought of herself as tall at 5'8", but Miss Linda was 5'10" tall, and slender like Cece. She was blond and blue eyed. They were both cheery, well-built 16-year-old girls. Linda had four older brothers, who were tall, muscular, dark, and handsome. The youngest brother was Charles. He was a year older than Linda and Cece.

Cece loved going to the dairy because she got to be around other young wholesome people close to her own age. Linda's parents were exemplary, moral, normal southern folks. Her Italian American family was so different from Linda's southern family. It was fun for the two girls to go back and forth between the two families and their two worlds. Linda and Cece were very much alike in other ways. They were both in excellent physical condition because Linda shared Cece's opinion about it being safer to run through the countryside than to walk. You wouldn't get bit by anything that way!

It was going to be a great day for Linda. She had invited Cece over to the dairy to have dinner and go to the Grand Ole Opry afterwards with her family. Cece wanted to give her money for her ticket, but the McCraneys wouldn't have it. Their Mama would make fried chicken, mashed potatoes, greens, and biscuits for dinner. The fresh milk and the big, soft, homemade chocolate chip cookies were just a bonus. Everyone was so excited about the night to come. Charles teased Cece because she didn't know what the Grand Ole Opry was.

Mrs. McCraney told Linda to take Cece around to see the dairy farm while she cooked. As the two girls left the house where Linda's family lived, Cece asked why the houses had fences all around them. She noticed the grass around the homes was tall and not groomed like her Dad always mowed their lawn. Linda laughed and told Cece that was how it was on a dairy farm. The perimeter of the farm was fenced. The cows grazed wherever they wanted. The people and their homes were 'fenced in' to keep their surrounding areas clean.

Cece was confused. She figured Linda would eventually explain herself, but instead Linda opened the gate and said, "Come on, I'll show you!"

Cece felt like she just wanted to stop time and hold on to her best friend forever. Linda was pure joy and happiness. She was special and good. She and Linda were very much alike, yet so different. Cece couldn't understand why she felt she wanted to hold on tight to Linda and her friendship, but she knew it was impossible to do. She knew she would find out why, eventually.

Cece really didn't want to know at the present. She wanted their friendship to last as long as possible. The one thing she prayed for was that their separation would result into something positive. She loved Linda's friendship because even though they came from different worlds. They had a lot of goodness in common. They were both raised to be moral young ladies.

Cece had figured it had something to do with 'the eye' thing. It usually did when she had those feelings. The feelings sometimes frightened her, but she had learned through the years to handle it better. Cece knew she wouldn't be able to hold on to Linda's friendship for much longer. She knew their destinies were going to be very different.

Linda took off running and yelled to Cece to follow close behind so she could lead Cece on a clean running path. Linda loved the fact Cece could keep up with her. The high school track coach wanted both girls to join. Linda had no interest. Cece would have loved to join 'if' she didn't always have to care for four little children every day after school.

Linda called over to Cece, "If we don't run, we will get insect bites all over us and it'll take forever to see the farm. It's so big!"

Cece agreed, "Yeah, I know! Let's run!"

Both girls laughed with the joy they felt. They finally stopped when they got to the road which ran down through the middle of the farm. They walked on the road when Linda commented about watching where you stepped. Cece laughed and said she noticed there were big piles of cow manure everywhere. Linda said they called them 'cow pies' and you had to be very careful. Linda told her the pastures were worse than the road because the cows crossed the road to get back to the grass. The grass was where the cows liked to hang out. Linda said the cows "went" where they wanted and when they wanted. Hence, the reason the houses were fenced in.

They toured the milking station and got to say hello to Linda's father and older brother. The men were working diligently. They attached milking machines that connected to the cow's udders. After a while they disconnected the machines. It all looked very messy to Cece. The men looked like they all needed a bath. They wore big boots and rubbery looking overalls. They continuously hosed down the cows, but the cows loved it.

The girls went back outside, and Linda pointed out some picnic tables under a tree. The tables had a fence around them. Linda explained this was where the workers ate, but her dad lived close, so he went home for lunch. Linda told Cece her Mama was always cooking and was excellent at it. Cece said Carmella was an excellent cook, too.

Linda said, "Come on, it's a nice place to take a rest."

As they walked over to the tables, Linda settled down on a tabletop to talk. Linda noticed Cece was carefully assessing the cow pies as she walked toward the tables. She did not want to make a mistake of stepping in one.

Not realizing exactly what Cece was thinking, Linda sized up the area and said, "I know what's on your mind. Don't even think about it!"

Cece finally reached the table, sat on a side seat, and asked, "Think about what?"

Cece was thinking dairy kids had to be careful making their own fun, while living out in the countryside with cow pies all around them. She wondered how they could have any fun with cow manure everywhere. Cece had ten acres to run on and never had to worry about where she placed her feet except at the barn or the horse pasture. Cece noticed a 'glazed look' came over Linda's eyes as she looked up in the air.

Cece repeated herself and asked again, "Think about what?"

As Linda stared up, she began her tale, "It's where you put your foot down that matters."

Cece thought to herself the statement was pretty close to what she was thinking about as she was walking toward the tables. From the way Linda was looking up into space, Cece felt she should remain quiet and listen to what Linda was going to say. Linda was recalling a story.

Linda continued, "If you've done it once, you'll never let it happen twice. Not even to your worst enemy. I tried it once, and it was horrific!"

Cece looked at Linda incredulously and couldn't wait to ask, "Tried what?"

Cece could tell the Southerners loved their storytelling, as much as the Sicilians did, as she watched the many expressions come and go on Linda's face.

Linda looked right into Cece's eyes as if she was looking into Cece's soul, as Linda blurted out, "Ok, I'll tell you, but you have to promise never to repeat this story to anyone ever, because I will totally deny it!"

Cece asked, "What story?"

Cece startled as Linda screamed, "Swear on your life as my best friend!" Cece thought to herself it had to be something really horrible to make Linda act like she was crazed.

Cece said, "Ok, don't have a heart attack. I swear as your very best friend!"

Linda spoke, "I was only thirteen years old when it happened. I saw my four older brothers running around and jumping in the cow pasture. They looked like they were having so much fun laughing and whooping it up. They had a stopwatch and everything! I had no idea. I ran up to watch them. They had made a running course in the middle of the cow pasture. The course was a big circle and included jumping over cow pies as they raced to see who had the best times.

You've seen the size of some of those cow pies. They are pretty large. If a couple of those girly cows stand around together to chew the fat, I mean, chew the cud, well some of those cow pies can overlap or at least fall very close together.

I was my brother's little sister and always will be, even though I was already at my full height of 5' 10". My brothers were all over 6'6"'. I wanted to have fun, too. I asked if I could run the course. They told me if Mama ever found out, she would take a switch to all four of them. We all knew Mama never connected with her switches, but you still didn't want to take a chance.

My brothers winked at each other. They said, 'absolutely not', and 'I was a little girl'. They said they could not possibly take a chance on anything happening to me. Then they all laughed at me and winked at each other again. Well, that did it. I got so mad! I screamed I was no little girl. I knew I could get a better running time than they had. Before too long, I was begging to get in on the fun.

I tried everything. I told them I had longer legs than they did. I was almost in tears to get a chance to race them and show them up. I told them they were just afraid I would beat their records and they would never live it down. I think that statement really got to them because they finally consented. They all winked at each other again, so I winked back at them. They doubled over laughing, so I laughed back at them. I said you guys just watch me. I'm going to beat all of you!"

Cece seriously asked, "Are you telling me you all thought running a course with cow pies everywhere was fun?"

Linda said, "I really think the boys thought it was fun. They probably thought I wouldn't really get overly hurt. Finally, it was my turn. Charles got his stopwatch out and said he would time me. I started running. I was doing so good. I guess I got overconfident toward my last turn. I was flying. They couldn't believe I was going to take the record time. They looked like they were in a state of shock. Their baby sister was going to beat all of them! Then it happened!

I rounded the last turn without slowing down at all. Now you know how slippery the wet grass in Florida can get. Well, shit's even much more slippery. The combination of both wet grass and wet cow pies is much more deadly slippery! Plus, not to deny, it is downright stinky! I rounded the last corner. My foot hit the edge of a huge one. As I was flying up into the air, all I could hear were my four brothers laughing hysterically. I came down into three gigantic, super smelly, grosser than gross cow pies. My ass hit first, right into the middle of a cow pie between two other cow pies. I felt like it was all happening in slow motion. I could hear a big squish sound as my butt settled into the middle cow pie. As I was listening to the squishing sound, I could see both of my sneakers descending into another pile of shit. I knew the worst was yet to come. I quickly closed my eyes. What I never saw, thank heaven, was the back of my head going down into the third cow pie, which had to have been from a bull, because it was rather large and extremely thick. There were squishing sounds everywhere around me.

I felt frozen in time. I couldn't move. I guess it was like being in a state of shock. When I finally opened my eyes, I realized I was up to my ears in shit! My eyes were at the same level as the top of the third thick cow pie under my head. The fact that cow pies are extremely soft is what probably saved me from really getting hurt.

Could you imagine how I felt watching my four brothers laughing so hard with tears running down their cheeks? It finally hit me. I burst into tears and started screaming. Well, after having four sons, a Mama recognizes her daughter's screaming. It was like some miracle because we weren't even close to the house. You could hear her. Big Mama was on her way! My Mama is 5'10" and weighs about 230 pounds. There's no way to escape her. If you did get lucky enough to get away from Mama, you still had to deal with my Papa! You know he's much bigger than my Mama.

All of a sudden, the boys went dead quiet and turned to see Mama waving a switch in her hand. Charles commented Mama had to have been in a big hurry because the big switch still had leaves on the tip.

The boys didn't move. They knew if they moved, Mama would really get even with them. Meanwhile, I was still stuck in piles of shit crying and screaming. No one offered any help because they didn't want to touch me! Apparently, my Mama didn't want to touch me either, because the next thing I saw was Mama grabbing the boy's ears. Mama's switch was just a-flying around in the air as fast as Mama could swing it. She was gathering them up, and she was herding them home. I felt sorry for them for about five seconds. Then I remembered I was the one still stuck in shit. I was being completely abandoned by my family! I'm not sure what happened after that because I couldn't turn my head to watch and there was too much shit in my ears to hear what she was screaming at them. They were just all gone at once. Even Mama was gone. I was alone. I cried some more."

Cece's eyes were huge as she declared, "Oh my gosh! They left you there?"

Linda loudly said, "Yes, they left me there, all alone helpless and up to my ears in shit! After crying for about 15 minutes, I figured I better help myself because no one was coming back to help me. I finally stopped crying and screaming and tried to think of the best way to get out of my sticky and shitty position. Now, come on, there's no easy way out of a shitty situation involving cow pies! I figured my face, my hands, and the front of my clothes were the only clean parts of my body that I had left.

Since I was covered and in a sticky way, I figured if I could roll over onto my elbows. I could push my body upwards. Wrong! It seemed like an excellent remedy until my elbows slipped out from under me. The clean front of my body was free falling towards more shit. I arched my back and went down on my side, but I figured that was better than getting it on my face. It seemed like it was taking me way too long to get out of shit. I slipped a bit again and the tip on my chin got coated with shit, too! I couldn't wipe it off because my hands were now all full of shit, too. It was going from bad to extremely worse. I started thinking it was the worst game in the world to play and how could I have fallen for it?

I couldn't believe my own Mama chased my brothers all the way home and never came back for me. I knew it was getting late because the sun was setting. Well, I guess I finally decided to stop rolling around in shit and got mad enough to somehow get up and out of it. I pulled my head up first and then I lifted my feet up. There I was, balancing on my ass. My stomach muscles ached while I was trying to figure out what to do next. I noticed the second cow pie had spread over to the first cow pie while the third cow pie spread backwards into the middle one which had spread out tremendously when my ass landed in it. There wasn't any clean ground near me. Shit was everywhere! Shit was dripping down my hair and out of my sneakers. The only clean part of me left was the front of my face from the chin up.

My stomach muscles started to spasm and I couldn't take it anymore. I almost slipped again but was determined not to get anymore shit on my face. I had to release my current position because my stomach hurt so much. There I was, flat on my back and up to my ears in shit once again! By then I was covered with manure. I finally sat up and managed to get my legs up under me without slipping again. What did it matter? There wasn't anything clean with me but my eyes, my mouth, and my nose. My chin itched, but I couldn't scratch it, so I tried to wiggle it around but had to stop because small droplets of shit flew sideways through the air. At least I could still see, even though I didn't like what my nose was smelling and what my chin was dripping. I carefully stood up and shit gushed out of my sneakers. Ew, it was dripping everywhere.

I figured I had about enough shit for the day until I began following the farm road home. I was amazed to see how much shit was squishing out of my sneakers every time I took a step. It just kept coming out of my shoes! I was trying to hurry home so no one could see me, but I didn't want to slip again and be in a similar situation. I couldn't start running because of the slipping hazard. You know you can't do much when you are covered with shit and your shoes are full of shit, too."

Cece was laughing so much she felt like she could lose her breath and her stomach muscles were contracting to the point of extreme pain. Tears were rolling down her face.

Linda continued the story, "Then I saw the fancy car leaving the milking area and heading right towards me. I wanted to die right there. It was the dairy farm owner driving and his gorgeous sixteen-year-old son, Johnny, was sitting in the front passenger's seat. Johnny was so handsome and nice. I hoped they wouldn't recognize me because there wasn't a place to hide. Cows had eaten all the foliage and all the bushes.

The car drove up beside me. I wanted to keep my eyes down, but I was afraid shit would get into them. I just kept looking straight ahead. Johnny leaned out of the window. He kept the straightest face I ever saw. I knew he wanted to burst out laughing. His Dad was doing the same thing. They calmly said hi to me and asked how I was doing and then they asked if maybe I slipped in shit. They said they were sorry they couldn't give me a ride home because they had an important errand to run.

As they drove away, I could hear their loud nose snortin' laughter. It was horrible! Someone had told them because their timing was perfect. That's when I realized Mama must have sent my brothers to the milking station to help my Papa for their punishment. That meant the universe would know by now. I was so embarrassed I started crying again, but then I could only imagine how angry Mama was still going to be.

When I got to the house, Mama was at the front door. She must have had some time to calm down because I could tell she was trying not to laugh. Mama said I wasn't coming into her clean house in my condition. She told me I would find everything I would need in Papa's outdoor shower. She told me to hurry because the men would come home from the milking for dinner soon. Mama said I didn't have much time to clean up before they could all see me naked, but it wouldn't be anything new since I was the foolish baby of the family. It took three years for the 'up to my ears' story to die down. I truly never thought it would."

Linda didn't seem to mind the looks of horror and laughter coming from Cece. They were best friends after all. Linda didn't know they had only a short time to be together, but somehow Cece did. Johnny Cash and June Carter were the stars that night at the Grand Ole Opry. Cece thought it would probably be the most fantastic show she would ever see. Then Minnie Pearl walked out on the stage with the price tag still hanging off the front of her straw hat and the laughter soared through the roof. All of it happened within feet of Cece because the McCraney Family had bought front row seats. It was one of the most wonderful memories of sensory overload Cece had ever experienced. Then Johnny sang 'Ring of Fire' right in front of her while the audience screamed and clapped.

Only six months later, Linda announced she had met a dairy worker 'up north a-ways' in central Florida, and they were going to be married. Brett was tall, blond, strong and handsome! He was 18. Linda wouldn't be graduating high school. She and Cece had both just turned sixteen. Cece couldn't believe anyone would get married at the age of 16. They were very moral people, and they said it was normal in southern families to marry young. Linda was totally in love, but so was Brett. Somehow Cece knew when she said goodbye to Linda that day, they would never see each other again. Cece's family didn't know they would leave Florida for the west soon after Linda married. Cece never forgot the McCraney Family and Miss Linda and teasing Charles.

Six months later, Cece's family packed up and headed out west because Cece's younger brother's health and his asthmatic condition had improved while he lived with their Uncle Eddie in Las Vegas. Michael blossomed into a strong young healthy man. Carmella didn't want to raise her family in Las Vegas. Sammie and Carmella bought a home in Southern California, after all it was only 300 miles from Las Vegas. Sammie oversaw moving the rest of the family west. Cece would be his designated co-driver.

Cece asked God, "Is this what you want? Will you please help me figure this out? Is it Las Vegas or not?"

That night, Cece dreamt of her glowing man.

Chapter 6

Across Country

It all happened quickly. Within months, Michael regained his health in the Las Vegas desert. Carmella realized she would have to go on ahead of the family to purchase a new home out west. She knew just how much would be put onto Cece's shoulders again. She, also, realized what an exceptional young woman Cece had become in her sixteenth year. Carmella knew Cece could handle anything life put in her path. Cece was still pure and naïve, but God made her child strong.

When Carmella returned to Florida after her first trip to Las Vegas, everyone in the entire family asked her about fabulous Las Vegas.

Carmella replied, "It's the most God forsaken place on the face of the Earth!"

Carmella's youngest sister rebuked, "But it's Vegas! It's exciting and glamorous!"

Cece listened to the two women and prayed, "Please, God, don't make our family ever have to go there!"

The last few months flew by, and it was one month before summer break! Cece was listening to her Mother and Aunt talking while Carmella was packing to go back to Las Vegas to retrieve her healthy son, Michael, and take him on to Los Angeles, California to buy a home.

Sammie would move the family as soon as school ended.

Carmella said, "I don't want to raise my children in Las Vegas. The schools are overcrowded and financially burdened. Eddie told me the State of Nevada and the casinos had made deals long ago. In exchange for them not having to pay high taxes, the casinos were supposed to take care of the roads. But they don't! The casinos were supposed to take care of the schools. They don't! The casinos waste electricity and water. They do! Yet the communities are asked to save electricity and water. The communities carry the financial burdens. The deserts are full of trash. There are rumors gangsters were buried everywhere because of the mob influence. Las Vegas was not family friendly!"

No one realized Las Vegas would go through many transitions and become a desirable place to live in the future.

Cece's ailing and aging Aunt and Uncle put in a special request to Sammie. They hoped Grandma Jerolma, Sammie's Mother, who had been living with them for many years, could go on the cross-country trip with Sammie and the children. Sammie could deliver his Mother, Grandma Jerolma, to Sammie's oldest sister in California. An immigrant from Sicily, she was still a very strong Sicilian lady even into her early 80s.

Grandma Jerolma only said a few words in English, but she could make anyone understand her. She was loving and kind. She was soft but tough. Cece and Grandma hit it off as soon as they met. The relatives told Carmella and Sammie Grandma would be a big help to Cece with the young children. Cece had just obtained her driver's license, and if she had help with the little ones, she could help Sammie drive across the USA. It was settled. Carmella and Sammie thought it was an excellent idea.

Five months had passed. Michael had gained 50 pounds and grew 4 inches taller. He couldn't seem to get enough food. Carmella planned to fly out west, meet Michael at McCarran Airport and then connect into Los Angeles, CA. Carmela and Michael would stay with Sammie's sister while Carmella bought a home. The timing should work out perfectly. Sammie and Carmella thought the LA area would be a better place to raise a normal family.

Little did they know what a mistake that was, except for Ian. Who?

Sammie planned the family's route from Miami to LA. They would be taking the famous two-lane Route 66 across the south toward the west in the summer's heat after they left Florida. Cece was still Sammie's tomboy, but now she was a beautiful Sweet 16. She was gorgeous, but she didn't know it. She was long legged and slender. Sammie couldn't believe his own eyes. She was still naïve and pure, but exceptionally optimistic. Cece put her family first. Her young parents needed help. Cece was an old soul trapped in a young body.

Grandma Angelina was right when she told her Cece had 'The Eye'. Cece knew her parents had so much to handle. Cece would always be there to help them and her siblings. Their second son, Steven, had the chickenpox when they left Florida. He sat in the middle of the front bench seat of the family's 1961 Pontiac. Whoever wasn't driving was used as a pillow for the sick child to sleep upon. Steve could lean on Cece all he wanted. When Carmella came home from the hospital after giving birth to Stevie, she presented Steve into 7-year-old Cece's arms as Cece's birthday gift. Cece always figured Stevie was hers. Cece loved him dearly.

Grandma Jerolma was in the backseat with Sammie's two youngest children, ages 7 and 6. She was kind and a soft pillow of a woman for the two little ones to snuggle with, but she was 'bulldog tough' by nature. She knew how beautiful her granddaughter, Cece, was. Grandma Jerolma could not speak much English, but she got her point across. Plus, Sammie could speak Italian and converse with his mother freely without the children knowing what they were saying.

There were no navigation apps in those days. It was the summer of 1963. You had to read maps and estimate mileage. You had to watch for road signs and to follow those signs. It was almost like a young adult puzzle game, only more exciting! You had to be quick and alert because your car was going through traffic and sometimes it was going fast. Cece learned from Sammie to look for and to read the road signs. She was a fast learner. Sometimes the signs were big, and sometimes the signs were tiny. Soon, she was navigating quite well during the daily car trips crossing the southern portions of the greatest country on Earth, the U.S.A.

While falling asleep at night, Cece would see the lines in the center of the roads coming at her closed eyelids. She was excited to make the trip across the United States, eager to learn and to see. She really wanted to see Route 66 as it unfolded from the southlands to the deserts across America's southern states and into California. She loved the early TV show series called 'Route 66' and 'Rawhide'. She was told California was beautiful, like Florida. She thought it would be fun to live there. It had beaches, too. She definitely thought it would be better than living in the desert of Las Vegas. Little did she know California beaches were cold and polluted, containing globs of oil. And there were strange men speaking strange languages, trying to pull young girls into their cars while the girls walked to school.

There were no public rest stops on highways in 1963. Gas stations, restaurants, and motels offered the only restrooms, and most of the time those restrooms were filthy, and many were out of order. If you didn't buy something, some businesses would not let you use their restrooms. Cece thought those people were unbelievably crude! She couldn't believe people would be so ill-mannered toward other people. What you give is what you get.

Restaurants charged way too much to feed a growing family. Little children only ate a few bites. Theirs was not going to be an easy trip. Grandma did help immensely with the two smallest children. They would have the whole backseat to themselves with soft Grandma Jerolma in the middle. The two little ones took naps on Grandma's comfortable plump body. It was a good thing Cece had been a tomboy, and she learned to roll with the punches that life threw in her path. She would need it on this trip just to keep her mouth shut when she saw adult business owners acting cruel. Their trip was just beginning, and Cece was amazed at what she saw!

When they made it to central Florida, it was all wilderness. Everyone in the car had to have a restroom break. There were no gas stations or restaurants around. Sammie stopped by the side of the road and told everyone to stay together until they were told to take turns. They had to wait until Cece returned. Sammie had to guard his family, their belongings, and the car. Cece went into the Florida Pine forests alone. She scouted around for a safe, clean spot. She wanted to find an area where she didn't find poison ivy, bees, wasps, dirty shallow water where alligators or water moccasins could lurk, quicksand or anything else could harm Grandma or the children.

Cece grew up in the wilds of the dairy land areas surrounding southwest Miami. That area was located between Miami, dangerous marshes, and the Everglades. She was cautious. She knew the dangers from the wildlife, weeds, and the people.

Cece saw human defecation everywhere. She was appalled, but Cece finally found a safe spot for her family. She started with the females first. She got them back to the car. She told Sammie and the 2 boys how to get to the spot. It was Cece's turn to guard the vehicle and to be with her Grandma to help her with the babies.

Cece saw Sammie coming back.

She cheerfully looked at her Dad and said, "This is not going to be as glamorous as I had imagined."

Sammie agreed, shaking his head in disgust.

Cece thought to herself she was just happy it wasn't her time of the month. Things could have been worse than now. She was ready for modern technology. She wondered why there were no public restrooms along the highways. Then she realized there weren't many people traveling by car. However, whatever amount of people were traveling, restrooms and conveniences should still be put up because they are essential. Cece kept thinking someone needed to sell bottled water, and something to wipe hands clean.

Everyone got back into the car because Sammie stayed on a tight schedule. No one ever heard of tailgating in those days. Cece figured her Dad discovered tailgating. Enough people saw them doing it. If they needed to buy food to cook, Sammie would go to a grocery store first.

After, Sammie would drive on until he found a clean place. He pulled the car off the road and organized everything to cook. Sammie would pull out his ice chest, water jug, and gas camping stove. He gave orders in both Italian and English. Grandma would be washing the faces and hands of the little ones. Cece would be cooking. Sammie would be protecting his family when people would walk up saying how delicious everything smelled and asked if they had any extra food.

Cece couldn't believe how many poor people she saw in the south along the way. Any extra food was always given away by her father. Sammie was a generous man, and he remembered when his parents first arrived in the United States as legal immigrants from Sicily. His family knew what hunger was. There was no welfare in those days. People were expected to find jobs and work. He remembered his junior years. He couldn't stand for children to be hungry.

The trip was a real eye opener for Cece. She was like any other well cared for teenager. She thought all children had decent housing, food, and wonderful parents. Not all the roads were highways. They drove through areas where folks lived in shacks, and they looked right through the wall boards to see outside. They wore ragged, torn clothing. They looked hot and bored. They fanned themselves as they sat on the wooden porch steps of their shacks while swatting at bugs. The children looked so sad.

Sammie explained to his family these folks were very poor. It was how they lived. They were of every creed, color, and persuasion. Poverty is a terrible thing for anyone to endure. Even motels, along the way in those poorer areas, were run down. Sammie would ask to be shown the rooms before he would rent one for the night. The next morning Sammie had everyone up at sunrise. They would pile into their vehicle and begin driving. If the little ones started to fuss, Cece would break out in song and get all the little ones singing. Grandma didn't know the words, but she could hum her lovely tunes and smiled all the time.

Cece had never seen her grandma upset. She was always in a good mood and loved being with Sammie's family. Mornings lightened up and Sammie would find a breakfast spot. People walked by smelling bacon frying and eggs cooking in another pan. Poor folks came around again and Sammie shared. Folks would comment about what a brilliant idea it was to make your own food while traveling. Many travelers said they would try it.

That day they planned to cross the Mississippi River. Sammie had filled up his jug of water from the motel where they had spent the previous night. They were packing up the breakfast mess when one of the small children asked for some water. Cece poured some water from the jug and handed it to her sibling. The little one cried. She asked what the problem was, and the child said the water tasted funny and smelled bad. Cece tasted and smelled the water, and she agreed. She told Sammie. Sammie tested the water. He agreed. He told her they could have milk instead.

When Cece was done, Sammie took the carton of milk over to a mother sitting on some wooden steps of a shack, and gave it to her along with bacon, eggs, and bread. He told her he didn't have room to carry the food. She thanked him profusely. Cece knew her Dad had a big ice chest with lots of room in it. Sammie was the reason Cece learned to be such a giver. She knew what her father was doing, and she loved him dearly because he was a kind, good, God fearing, and generous man.

Cece thought, "Will I ever be fortunate enough to find a man as good as my father, with whom I can share my life? Is the glowing man good?"

That night she saw 'the flash of a vision from her mind's eye' before she fell asleep. He came to her mind often before she slept. She called him the glowing man. It was as if he was looking for her, too. Who or what did she see? She wanted and needed to know him if he was to be part of her destiny. He looked like an Adonis God created just for her, but he had to be good, too, like her Dad. Cece was sure of it. Cece smiled and fell asleep.

The next day the family was on the road only a brief time and entering onto the two-way old Mississippi River bridge. The car started having problems. Suddenly Sammie's car stalled. It was miserable and humid. Bugs were biting. People in other cars were hot and frustrated. Car horns began blaring. The babies were crying for fresh water that wasn't smelly and nasty. People couldn't get around Sammie's disabled vehicle! Sammie got out of his car to look under his hood. Cece prayed.

Suddenly everyone around Sammie's vehicle jumped out of their cars to help Sammie. It was like an army of angels. Cece was amazed as she thought, 'When you give, you will receive'. They got Sammie's family to the gas station on the other side of the Mississippi bridge by pushing and towing the car across the big River. Everyone was so nice when Sammie was thanking them. It felt like they were all good friends. Cece saw them as angels.

The gas station owner fixed their vehicle. They were about to leave when she told her Dad to ask if they could get some fresh water. Sammie was telling the gas station owner how horrible the water was from their motel. The gas station owner told them his water was the best water around those parts and they could have all the water they wanted from the faucet around the side of his gas station. As they were driving away Cece again told her Dad companies needed to bottle water like they bottled soft drinks and root beer. Sammie agreed stating, "It's a good idea, but I doubt anyone would pay for water."

They traveled about 10 miles down the road when one of the babies wanted water.

Grandma handed a paper cup to Cece. Cece poured the water into the cup and started laughing. They got the same smelly, nasty tasting water they had before they crossed the Mississippi. Cece told Sammie they better find a store that sold milk soon. Thirty minutes later, after listening to the small children screaming, Sammie found a store. The well water in their Florida countryside home was so clean and delicious in the early 1960s. They took it for granted.

They were all happy when they made it into Texas, but there were hardly any trees on the country two-lane highways. The big cities were jam-packed and busy, but the countryside was desolate for long, hot, and flat distances. The family didn't see poor folks anymore. It was too hot to live in shacks there. Texas was booming with oil businesses.

Everyone was getting hungry. Sammie had bought supplies and spotted shade up ahead but couldn't make out what it was. Was it a mirage? It didn't look like trees. As they got closer, they realized it was a brand-new overpass bridge. Everything in Texas was spotless! Cece loved Texas. She thought she would be happy if her family could live there, after all it had desert land. They stopped under the shady bridge for lunch. They cooked, ate, and cleaned up without another car passing by for the entire time they were there. When they left the bridge, the weather was getting hotter. The family wasn't used to the dry, scorching desert heat. In those days, most cars did not have air conditioning.

As they got closer to the next town, the children kept seeing motels with pools. People looked like they were really enjoying themselves in the beautiful Texas sun. Cece asked her Dad if they could stay at a hotel with a pool that evening. All the children got excited. Sammie said he would look for a place that wasn't crowded. The children were delighted when Sammie stopped early that evening at an empty motel with an empty parking lot, but a beautiful swimming pool right on the highway frontage. Sammie went to check to see if they could get rooms. The sad motel owner told Sammie he had lots of empty rooms and no bookings so he could have his choice of rooms. Sammie commented they wanted quiet rooms because they would take off early the following morning. The owner was very nice and grateful for the business. Then the owner spotted Cece and became extremely friendly.

The family got settled in their rooms and changed into their bathing suits. Cece's suit was considered a two-piece. It was a 'hand-me-down' from one of Carmella's adult friends who couldn't fit into it anymore. There were bikinis in those days, but Carmella would never allow her daughter to wear one. A two-piece was a top with a full bottom. It was what Cece's 'hand-me-down' bathing suit was supposed to be until you put a girl who looked like Cece into it. It should have been outlawed, but Carmella didn't realize Cece would grow that much in a few months' time. Carmella was thinking of more important things. The bathing suit was red with ruffles across the top and ruffles on the bottom's sides and backside. It was very feminine and alluring. The suit would not look right on just any type of body, but on Cece's body, it was spectacular! Innocent Cece didn't realize how stunning she was.

Grandma Jerolma had her black dress up to her knees and was sitting on the pool's steps playing with the babies, when Cece came walking out of her room. She spotted Cece and started in on Sammie, speaking Italian quickly. Sammie was trying to explain Cece fit into the suit just a few months ago. Grandma's voice got louder. He explained Cece did not realize how she looked because her body was changing so quickly. He was sure Carmella would not have purposely let Cece wear a bathing suit looked like that bathing suit looked on his daughter.

Sammie said in Italian, "Please Mama, there's no harm. It's only our family, and this motel is empty."

That was when Sammie and Grandma looked up and saw two cars going 5 mph crashing head on into each other in the parking lot as Cece was walking by them on her way to the pool. Grandma started in on poor Sammie again. Cece stopped and looked behind her. She thought to herself she really liked Texas, but the men here sure did not know how to drive. How could they hit 'head on' doing only 5 mph in an empty parking lot?

The "Desert Rose" motel owner ran out of the office to see what the noise was and saw two cars had hit head on. And then he saw the reason! He watched Cece walking toward the pool. He stopped dead in his tracks. His eyes flew open. His jaw dropped, causing his cigar to fall from his lips. He ran his hand through his hair, puffed up, and smiled widely when he saw three other vehicles do sudden 'tire squealing' U turns off the highway and right into his parking lot. He was very grateful as he eyed Cece. She was a gorgeous creature and attracting business! He realized she was oblivious and innocent of the accident being her fault as she continued into the pool's gate. The drivers asked for a phone to call the police. The owner kept staring at Cece while he pointed towards the office.

Both drivers walked by him asking, "Can you believe that girl?"

His office became very full! Keys to the rooms were flying off the pegboard. He wished he could hire Cece just to walk around the pool 'around this time of day' every day. He couldn't believe it. His motel was in a decent location on a major highway, but it never had this much business in the middle of the week. He designed the motel to have the pool area on the highway frontage to attract visitors, but it never worked until this girl showed up. However, the customers were all men, but they were spending money.

The owner watched the young beauty walking around the pool deck and playing with her family's little ones. Cars were slamming on their brakes to make more turns into his parking lot. His rooms were being rented right and left. Men started heading for the pool area. Some didn't even have on bathing suits! They wore their Bermuda shorts or cutoffs. It was strange. No families were turning in to book a room, only single businessmen, truckdrivers, big handsome men on Harley motorcycles, and diesel drivers, who were parking along the highway.

The owner's mouth fell open once again when he saw a cab pull up with 6 foreign oriental businessmen saying they all wanted their own rooms. They wanted to know if he sold bathing suits. His business was booming! He entered the pool area and walked up to Sammie. He asked if everything was satisfactory. Sammie looked at him strangely and told him the rooms were nice and clean. The manager asked Sammie to please tell him if his family needed anything and that he appreciated their business. The owner offered Sammie a serious discount if he and his family would like to spend a few extra days at his motel.

Grandma watched the manager talking to Sammie. She couldn't understand what they were saying, but she did not like the way the manager was looking at Cece. When the manager hurried back to the office,

Grandma started speaking Italian quickly to Sammie again. She was getting upset. Lots of men were coming into the pool area. The children and Cece were having too much fun playing in the pool to notice, but men started getting into the water with beers in their hands.

Cece noticed Grandma's fury. Grandma never got upset, but now Grandma kept looking at her. Cece wondered what was wrong and got out of the pool to talk to Sammie. A soaking wet Cece asked Sammie if Grandma was upset with her because Grandma kept looking at her and was rambling on in Italian. Sammie just shook his head "No".

The police finally turned into the parking lot to speak with the two men who hit each other head-on at 5 mph. The police asked them how in the world could that happen. The two men pointed to Cece talking to Sammie at the pool. Both policemen turned to look. As they turned their heads back around to face the drivers, the police said they understood, but they weren't too sure the insurance companies would understand.

None of the children had any idea what was happening, not even Cece. They were still cooling off from the hot Texas weather as she re-entered the water to play the little ones. Cece never gave all the commotion a thought except to think she was unhappy because more people were crowding into the pool. She was disappointed her family didn't have the pool all to themselves like they did when they first arrived. She was totally ignoring everyone around except her family.

Grandma kept telling Sammie things in Italian, but Sammie only shrugged his shoulders and said in Italian, "Let the children play. She's in the water. What can they see?"

More men started to come into the pool area, blocking the children from playing.

Grandma was getting more agitated. All the children had looked forward to this play time all day, and they were enjoying it tremendously. Cece wondered why the pool was getting so crowded. She then noticed the men, who were standing around in the pool, were drinking beer. She thought the men were strange. She went to the pool steps to sit next to her family.

Grandma kept getting more and more agitated. Sammie kept shaking his head. Now men were gathering around the entire pool area, the pool steps, and the pool's gate entry. The family couldn't play in the crowded water anymore because men were everywhere. The two guys, who just ran into each other, were standing in the pool next to Sammie's family. They were smiling at Cece and sucking in their bellies. Cece frowned. She thought men looked stupid trying to hold in their bellies. They weren't even enjoying themselves. That's when men started moving in on Cece.

They began to speak to her. She looked at them strangely. She didn't know how to talk to men whom she didn't know. Cece became frightened when she realized there were no other wives, children, or families anywhere.

Grandma saw Cece's face and became extremely agitated and was telling Sammie they had to go because she didn't want Sammie to get into a fight. There wasn't any room left in the pool, anyway. Grandma said she didn't want Sammie to get hurt protecting Cece. She warned Sammie it would happen if they didn't leave.

Suddenly, Grandma jumped up off the pool steps and started flinging her chubby arms up into the air at the crowd of men. Grandma blurted out loudly in broken English, "Enoughfa, Enoughfa!"

She wasn't going to wait for Sammie to make a judgement. She was Sammie's mother and he would do whatever Grandma decided. She waved her hands to insinuate her whole family was to get out of the pool. Grandma looked at Cece, and Cece knew it was time to leave. Why didn't her Dad just tell her? Oh, how she missed Carmella. Dad just didn't know how to handle girl things.

Cece helped the little ones when Sammie told her, "No, Cece, wrap a few towels around yourself and quickly go to the rooms NOW with Grandma. I'll take care of the little ones."

Cece was confused. Was Grandma mad at her? Was her Dad mad at her? Sammie handled it by saying they had to get an early start in the morning. Sammie didn't know how to deal with the situation. Cece got out of the pool to go grab two towels when all sound ceased. Every man in the crowd stopped whatever he was doing or saying to turn and watch Cece get out of the water in a dripping wet bathing suit that clung to her taut sculptured body that she filled out beautifully. There was complete silence. Men were stepping apart to get a better look while they admired her. They were blocking the pool entrance while holding the gate's latch.

They were planning on controlling the pool gate. They wanted her to move as slowly as possible so they could stare while admiring her figure and those long legs. Or so they thought.

Suddenly, here came Grandma's short little plump body. It was amazing how fast she charged towards Cece. She had already grabbed two towels and started helping Cece to wrap her body. Grandma was pushing Cece toward the pool gate and yelling at approximately 40 men at once, "Enoughfa, Enoughfa!"

Grandma lifted her leg while holding on to Cece and forcibly kicked the pool gate open with her foot. It made an intense, loud banging noise as it snapped open. Big burly men backed right off to get away from Grandma! Grandma was walking Cece to her room while Grandma excitedly charged and jabbered at men in the parking lot if they got too close to Cece. Men dashed away from the Grandma like she was going to bite them! Grandma led Cece to her room's door. She thought her Grandma was wonderful.

Cece started crying. Grandma gave her a big protective hug and kisses on top of the teardrops on both of Cece cheeks. Grandmas knew how to make things better, too, just like Moms did, because they had more years of girl experiences.

Grandma came back out of Cece's room still waving her arms at all the men, who disappointedly continued staring at the room's closed door, saying, "Enoughfa, Enoughfa!"

She wanted them to go. There would be no more Cece that evening. Men were backing off in all directions. The police officers were finishing the accident paperwork.

The two policemen laughed as the senior one commented, "We could sure use that grandma on the force. She made our jobs a lot easier this evening. It looked like there might have been a fight brewing in the pool area, but now we should be free to go. It is amazing to witness the control of a beautiful young woman has over men. Sure, was fun watching Grandma protecting her pretty granddaughter. Got to admit I was getting a little concerned when the men started breaking out those beers. I was worried we may have needed backup. That young girl was sure a looker, though!"

The police were glad peace was restored because of the chubby little Italian Grandma, and 'what a Grandma' she was!

Enoughfa!

Grandma told Cece to shower. The pool was completely empty 10 minutes later. The show was over. Men were still walking around stupidly in the parking lot with looks of dejection. Sam came in with the little ones.

Grandma ran out the door waving her arms in the air still yelling at men standing anywhere near their room's door, "Enoughfa!"

The police left after they made sure the men stopped lurking around the door.

Cece was falling off to sleep while she was praying, "God, why did you give me this body? Who was 'it' for? I am still only a kid inside. Who will be the man to handle life with me? Please, God, make the glowing man be special! But what is special about me? Who would want to be my man? Who could handle being my man?"

As Cece continued to drift off, Sammie watched his Mother watching Cece's lips move as she was praying. The tears still rolled down Cece's face. Grandma bent down and kissed Cece's wet cheeks with love while she adjusted the blanket covering Cece and tucked her in for the night.

In her mind's eye, Cece saw him again! Were those wings? No, he was shining more brightly. She could see him much better than she ever did before. He looked like a beautiful archangel. He was tall and well built. His mane of strawberry blond hair glowed. Cece never saw hair that color. It wasn't red. It is strawberry blond. He had the most beautiful blue eyes and the kindest radiant smile. She saw him more clearly for the first time in her life! Why was she seeing this person more and more clearly every time she was trying to fall asleep lately? Was their meeting time close? Who was he? Where was he? Who could he be? Was he even real? He was much more handsome than she noticed before, but he was still rugged. Why were these things happening to her? Cece finally fell into a deep rest. "Enoughfa."

Chapter 7

THE DANCE

CECE, Grandma, Dad, Stevie, Rosanne, and Philip arrived in Los Angeles in the late summer of 1963. Carmella had a delicious dinner waiting for her hungry family in their new home after their cross-country adventure. After dinner, they all collapsed into their beds. The movers arrived 3 days before Sammie, Cece, and the children got there. It gave Carmella and Michael time to set everything up.

Cece spent the rest of the summer making outfits to wear to school. Carmella made her some, too. Before they knew it, school was starting. Cece was in the eleventh grade and got whatever classes had vacancies. She tried catching the city bus to school, which never came, but ended up walking miles to the high school. Cece felt dirty by the time she finally made it to school. To make matters worse, it was hell trying to walk to school. Men pulled over to the side of the road and tried to catch Cece and pull her into their cars. They spoke in many foreign languages. She could outrun them easily, but it was awfully frightening! Cece hated California! She missed her peaceful countryside of Florida.

Finally, a girl, named Trudy, pulled over one morning, while causing a traffic jam at the bus stop, and told Cece to jump into her car. Cece didn't know her but her car was empty and Cece was scared standing at a bus stop for a bus which never came, but where perverts were always prevalent! Plus, this girl spoke English!

Trudy said, "Jump in! I've been watching you every morning trying to catch the bus that never comes, while all the perverts are screaming at you. My folks just bought a house a few blocks from here. You are welcome to ride with me!" Trudy and Cece became fast friends. They were nothing alike, but they liked each other very much. Trudy kept talking about some guy she knew from her old neighborhood. She wanted to introduce Cece to him. Trudy was sure they would like each other. His name was Ian.

Cece was finally getting the feel of the California high school. It had an outside nutrition area because the California weather was nice most of the time. Trudy kept telling Cece she had to go to a dance with her after football season was over around Christmas time. Trudy said there was a football player, Ian, who she wanted to introduce to Cece. Cece didn't pay much attention to Trudy or her talk of boys.

One beautiful evening, when they finally got to their seats at their high school football game, Ian was tackling the opponent high school's running back. Trudy was bigger than Cece and grabbed Cece's arm, yelling that he was Ian, the boy who she wanted to introduce to her. Cece was more concerned about having a huge black and blue mark on her arm from Trudy's grip. The guy was dressed in full football gear. Cece couldn't tell what he looked like.

Trudy said, "Cece, you have to meet this guy! That's Ian!" Cece shined her on, "Like, ok." Then she forgot about it.

Trudy was with Cece in the open nutrition area soon after. Cece was staring at something and Trudy asked what she was looking at.

Cece said, "Oh, nothing."

Trudy said, "Don't tell me that! I see you watching something. What is it?"

Cece finally said, "Something glowing caught my eye. That's all."

Trudy said, "Oh, no, you don't. I want to see. What is it?"

Cece said, "Just forget about it."

Trudy got behind her to see what Cece was looking at. Trudy spotted Ian.

Trudy yelled, "That's the guy I told you about! He's my friend, Ian, who I want to introduce to you! Come on!"

Trudy grabbed Cece's wrist. Cece's couldn't get loose from Trudy's firm grip. Cece yelled, "Let go of me!"

Trudy said, "No. Come on. I really want you two to meet. He'll love you and you'll like him. Trust me!"

Cece yelled back, "Come on, Trud, you're hurting my wrist!" Trudy said, "No, you come on."

Trudy started pulling Cece through the patio area like they were little girls. An embarrassed Cece could not hold her own with Trudy. Trudy was a big sturdy girl, and she was determined! Trudy finally pulled Cece threw the crowd of kids and stopped in front of Ian and Jimmy. Between the time Cece first spotted Ian and the time it took to pull Cece over to meet Ian, another 'obsessed' girl had intercepted Ian.

Trudy stopped in front of Ian and Jimmy while still holding Cece's wrist captive. Trudy was trying to introduce Ian to Cece, but Diane went after her prey full force. Diane had Ian backed up against a pole. Ian was holding his books in front of him as he tried to protect himself from Diane. Diane was mad at Trudy and Cece for daring to interrupt her advance on Ian. Diane's face was not pretty, but she was very well endowed with big boobs! Most guys loved that, but Ian wasn't one of them. Jimmy was watching the whole thing unfold. Trudy was trying to introduce Ian to the new girl in school, who was reluctantly trying to make Trudy let go of her wrist. Jimmy watched and admired Cece. Diane was captivating Ian's full attention by rubbing her breasts up and down his chest. Then Diane turned to pretty Cece and snarled like an animal at her.

Cece thought, "Oh my gosh, this girl is so ugly in every way! No woman should ever belittle themselves and their body parts in front of a man like she is doing."

Diane snarled at Cece again.

Diane continually would say something to Ian as she put her big breasts onto his waist and pushed her breasts up his chest towards his chin. Every time she got her breasts to Ian's chin, he would jerk his head backwards and banged his head on the pole behind him. The guy was cornered! Jimmy was even getting frustrated. He wished any girl would do those 'things' to him!

Cece was embarrassed to be around the interaction and told Trudy to give it up. The bell rang and everyone went to their last classes before the Christmas Holidays began. Ian finally came out of his stupor.

For weeks before the dance, Cece really didn't want to go. Trudy just kept asking her and wouldn't leave Cece alone. Finally, Cece gave into going with her just to get some peace in her life. Cece never had such a chatty and persistent friend. Trudy even had Carmella excited about that night's dance.

Carmella went into Cece's room to see how Cece was doing, expecting to see her getting ready. Cece had been thinking the last dance she attended was her own Sweet 16 birthday party back home with all her friends in Florida. It was a wonderful party. All the kids showed up and brought all kinds of records. Carmella and Aunt Harriet made the cake and all kinds of food. Everyone in the family came and danced. Young and old had a wonderful time. Everyone enjoyed it tremendously.

But tonight Cece hadn't even got ready. She was feeling very melancholy.

Cece thought no dance could ever be that much fun again. Cece didn't even notice Carmella had walked into her room.

Carmella stopped inside the doorway and asked, "What's wrong?"

Cece loved Carmella more than anything in the world and didn't want to burden her with silly things that couldn't be changed.

Cece answered, "Oh, nothing's wrong."

Carmella knew better. "I know there's something on your mind, Cece, what is it?"

Cece just looked so sad. Carmella's heart felt like it was going to break because she loved her daughter so much. Cece was such a lovely girl. She was a loving daughter and sister.

"Tell me, Ce."

"It's stupid. Really, Mom."

"So pass it by me and let me see if I think it's stupid." Cece's big eyes watered.

Carmella said, "Don't start crying! You don't want to go to the dance with red eyes!

Everyone will think you're smoking that weird stuff they have out here in California. You know that stuff that they sneak in from Mexico."

That broke the ice! They both started laughing.

Cece said, "Oh, Mom, I didn't know you knew about that stuff! I don't even know that much about marijuana. I never heard of it in school in Florida, but they show us scary films about it here at school in California."

Carmella said, "You'd be surprised to know what I know. Come on, tell me what's wrong? Whatever it is, we can find a solution between us."

Cece looked down gloomily as she sat in front of the pretty vanity Carmella and Sammie had set up for her.

Cece began, "Well, Mom, everyone's getting dressed up and I have no clothes to wear that are kind of, you know, classy, but a little sexy, too. They dress differently out here in the west, Mom."

Suddenly Carmella's eyes lit up as she asked, "Is that all?"

Cece looked bewildered and said, "That's a lot, Mom!"

Carmella smiled warmly at Cece and said, "Well, I have an early Christmas gift for you that would solve all of your problems."

With that, Carmella jumped up and quickly left the room yelling back, "Wait, I'll be right back!"

Cece said to herself, "It's not Christmas for another few days. Or is it?"

Within minutes Carmella was back with the most beautiful outfit Cece ever saw. It was a pair of long baby blue tights and a hand knitted soft pink angora sleeveless sweater top that Carmella handmade for Cece. No one else would have an outfit like Cece's. It was a 'one of a kind originals' by her Mom 'Carmella Theresa Muscare Riccobuono'! It was so exquisite!

Carmella said, "One other thing is for sure! No one else would look like you will in this outfit, Cece."

Cece's eyes sparkled as she commented, "Oh, Mom, it is the most beautiful outfit I have ever seen! I'll be so proud to wear it tonight!" Carmella smiled brightly and said, "Put it on and let's see how it looks".

Cece couldn't put everything on fast enough. The tights fit her long, firm, slender, and muscled legs like a glove. The pink angora sweater accented her femininity to the hilt.

Carmella was thinking, "My daughter is beautiful to begin with, but, Wow, this outfit is gorgeous on her!"

Carmella smiled because she was sure Cece would look lovely in it.

Cece turned around to look into the mirror at her reflection, and even Cece couldn't believe her own eyes.

Cece saw a flash in her mind's eye and thought to herself, "Tonight I'm going to meet my future husband!"

Her second thought was, I'm just 16, and I'll only be 17 in March! What am I thinking?

The glowing flash disappeared.

Cece asked, "But how did you know how to buy these tights, Mom?"

Carmella told her their new neighbor helped her shop. They had become good friends, and they wanted to surprise Cece, which they truly did.

Cece kept repeating, "Oh, thank you so much! It's such a pretty outfit. I'm so excited now!"

They both laughed out loud because they were happy to have each other in their lives. Cece was excited. She couldn't believe this was happening to her. Maybe there was hope for this dance after all.

Carmella said, "You make the outfit look good, Cece. You are such a beautiful girl in your heart and soul! Any outer beauty is just a bonus!"

They hugged and laughed together.

Finally, Carmella said, "You better be ready before Trudy gets here or she'll follow me around and talk my head off!"

Cece laughed and said, "She won't tonight because she wanted to leave right away and get there early. She is very excited about this dance. I just don't get why!"

Cece just finished getting ready when Trudy's car pulled up in front of her home. Trudy came into the house and took one look at Cece.

Trudy staggered backwards and said, "OH, WOW! Cece, you look fabulous! Stay close to me tonight because I want to catch all of your fallout! I can just picture all the guys following you around all night."

Cece said, "Look in the mirror, Girl! You look great, too."

Trudy always made Cece's family laugh, but that night Sammie was stoic and concerned.

He really took a good look at Cece and realized his little girl wasn't a little girl anymore. Cece was all grown up. Sammie didn't know what to do or say. Sammie stayed quiet, trying to act like he was reading his newspaper until Cece gave him a kiss and the two girls left.

Sammie felt like someone was twisting his heart inside his chest as he asked Carmella, "Are you really going to let her go out tonight looking like that in her new outfit?"

Carmella answered, "We can't keep our girl locked up forever. She's a good moral person with a good head on her shoulders. Besides that, Sam, all the girls dress like that in California!"

Sammie shook his head and picked up his newspaper again and said, "I'm not going to get any sleep tonight. I thought the pool in Texas was 'enoughfa'. Good thing Mama's at my sister's house!"

Carmella laughed and smiled happily.

While Trudy was driving, Cece was telling her how Carmella surprised her with the new outfit.

Trudy said, "Your Mom could surprise me anytime!"

The next memory Cece had was her walking into the entrance where the dance was to be held.

Two handsome men held the entrance doors open for them and smiled while they said, "Welcome."

Cece thought, "Wow, how nice!"

Tons of guys were inside of the 20' by 20' entrance foyer room, but they stood in a shoulder to shoulder circle around the walls like they were waiting. Everyone was very excited, including Trudy. It seemed like it was mostly boys were already inside the entrance. It was then Cece realized the nice handsome doormen were only letting unescorted girls enter the large foyer. Cece suddenly felt trapped.

Cece yelled over the commotion to Trudy, "Why are these boys standing in everyone's way. Why won't they let us go into the big hall? More and more girls are entering. It's getting crowded and hot. We can hardly move. Stay close to me! What if they start grabbing us?

Everyone's getting close and mingling shoulder to shoulder in here! People are bumping into me!"

Trudy had to yell while she asked, "You're kidding, right?"

Cece looked at Trudy wide eyed and asked, "What are you talking about? I'm talking about all these boys blocking us from going anywhere!"

Trudy said, "I know. You're a slow learner, or you truly are a little Miss Innocent."

Cece was very confused and asked, "What are you talking about? Please make sense to me!"

Trudy continued, "These are all the boys from the football teams, Silly! Coach allows them-in-first. Then when unescorted girls arrive, the assistant coaches at the foyer doors only let them in this foyer, like they just let us enter. The main dance hall is behind those other bigger doors that the boys are blocking. This is like a reward for the guys on the football teams for practicing and playing hard all season. They get to see who the single girls are first and get to see which ones they like best. Then they know who they want to pursue, and who they want to dance with. They get first picks. Mostly they are all talking about the new girl in school.

It's you they are talking about, Cece! It's you, who they are all looking back at for a second time, and a third time! Don't worry, Coach warns them, there's no touching the girl's bodies, or else!

Cece, it's ok. You look scared. Don't be! It's fun. Enjoy it! Coach purposely has the big hall's door locked until 'ALL' of his players are done looking at the girls. Some players haven't even arrived yet. They are intentionally blocking the doors to the hall to keep us locked up and surrounded by this circle of guys so that all the players can check us out. They don't want Coach to open the hall's doors yet. Did you understand everything I just said? I know it's noisy here.

They are enjoying this! They're all looking at you!" "CECE, CECE, CECE!!!!!!"

Cece nodded with a confused look and said, "These guys are calling me by my name, and I don't know any of them. No one introduced me to them."

Trudy said, "I know them, and I've already told all of them your name and that we are best friends. That's how they know you. There are no introductions here, Cece. Just pretend they are all your friends and smile, Cece! They are all really nice."

Bodies shuffled between them as Cece asked, "Why did you tell all of them my name?"

Trudy yelled, "They asked! Listen, they're chanting your name because you made a big impression on all of them!"

Suddenly, crowded bodies swept a smiling Trudy away from Cece. Cece became frightened. Trudy smiled back at her and winked. Cece felt like she was going to panic. She felt vulnerable. She would run, but she couldn't move an inch.

"CECE, CECE, CECE!"

Then the noise got louder as more guys kept surrounding her and started chanting, "CECE, CECE, CECE, CECE!"

All of a sudden Coach got on the loudspeaker and said, "Ok, Guys, settle down. I see her, too. I can't blame you, but let's keep our manners now or else you know what will happen. Thanks!"

It continued only the chanting was lower while guys would walk up to her and say, "HI, Cece. I am 'so and so'. Save a dance for me."

Others were saying, "Hi, Beautiful!" Or "Hi, Pretty Woman!" Or "Save me a dance or two!"

It was continually happening over and over. Cece was so self-conscious. She forced herself to smile as graciously as she could manage. She thought she would never remember all those names. She wished she had been warned. Many of them asked if they could have a dance, but Cece thought there could not possibly be that many dances allowed for this celebration.

She thought, "What am I going to do? There are too many of them! They said they were glad to meet me. They are all very polite and nice but there is absolutely no room to move around, and I feel faint!

Suddenly, Cece felt naked. Like she needed to run to safety, but she still couldn't move. Ecstatic young men having good clean fun surrounded her. Cece told herself to calm down and relax. She saw Trudy at the other end of the room. It looked like she was floating away on a sea of young men. Trudy was laughing and pointing at Cece. Trudy smiled and waved at her while she showed Cece a thumbs up! Then she waved at Cece and winked again. She didn't know Cece felt scared to death. Cece was trapped and on her own. People's bodies were all touching and bumping into each other. Boys were all around her, smiling at her and talking to her all at the same time. She began to smile and nod. That seemed to do the trick, even though she couldn't understand half of what was happening or being said to her.

Ian looked at Jimmy and asked, "WHO IS SHE? What is the guys chanting?"

Jimmy said, "I can't believe you! You could have had first dibs on her, and you blew it away today at lunch! She's the girl Trudy brought over to introduce to you while Diane had you backed up against that pole at lunch. Every time Diane crawled up your chest with her cow boobs rubbing all the way up to your face, your head banged on the pole, but she continued rubbing her big boobs all over your chest and she was rude to Cece. Shit, I saw her snarl at Cece like a monster with her captive prey. Cece's so beautiful and you completely ignored her."

Ian asked, "Do you mean to say she was the girl in the big coat?"

Jimmy replied, "I know it was rainy and cool today, but, Yes, that's her! I got a really good look at her face."

Ian asked, "Do you mean that body was under that coat?"

Jimmy yelled, "What?"

Ian just stood there staring at Cece like a little boy who wanted a toy as he said, "Jimmy, look at all the guys swarming her! She's breathtaking. I've never seen a woman as gorgeous! What else do you know?"

Jimmy replied, "All I know is she is new in school and she's Italian American. Actually, I think Trudy said Sicilian American. That's her first name, Cece, all the guys are chanting her first name. SHE is CECE!"

Ian panicked saying, "I've got to clear this up right away! Let me get through to her!" Ian took off after her, but all of his good friends surrounded her, talking to her at once and he couldn't get through the crowd fast enough.

Cece was in a complete whirlwind. She tried to remain calm but didn't know how much longer she could maintain. She felt lightheaded and dizzy!

Cece heard Coach saying, "Ok, Guys, we have all seen the girls, now that Ian and Jimmy have finally graced us with their arrival. Remember to be polite and have respect for all of them. You better or you will deal with me. Have fun. It's time to open the doors to the hall and start this Christmas celebration dance!"

All the guys cheered.

The big hall's doors flew open. The crowd seemed to all enter at once. Someone grabbed Cece's hand, and he was dancing with her before there was any music. Suddenly the music started. She couldn't remember if he asked her to dance, or if he asked while they were in the entrance. Then another boy cut in and she wondered all the same things about him. She felt like she couldn't get her bearings. It was one handsome boy after another. Cece saw someone who she couldn't recognize because he was behind her dance partner, but she saw a glow. The glowing young man began tapping the shoulder of the boy who was dancing with her. Her dance partner handed her over to Ian. Ian took her into his arms gently. She looked flustered. Then she saw his beautiful face and his glowing mane of strawberry blond hair.

Ian said, "I'm Ian! We met today. I'm sorry that we weren't able to talk." Another young man tapped Ian's shoulder, and Ian asked him for a minute.

Cece innocently asked, "Were you the guy at lunch today with that strange girl crawling up your chest while you kept banging your head on a pole behind you trying to get away from her? Doesn't your head hurt? You sure hit that pole behind your head a lot. Are you ok?"

Ian laughed, "Yes, I'm afraid that was me. I am so sorry. I was raised in a family of five men except for my mom. I didn't know how to handle that very uncomfortable situation. A guy is easy to throw off, but when a woman does something like that to a guy, he's not allowed to touch her. If a guy tried to throw her off, he'd get in a lot of trouble. Diane had me trapped. Guys from the Southern United States are taught to be very polite to women, or else. I never had a girl doing something like that to me in my life before today! I was really embarrassed!"

Ian looked seriously at Cece and asked, "Are you alright?"

Cece looked up into his baby blue eyes and said, "I think all of this is a lot for me to absorb. I feel very faint."

Ian immediately said, "Come with me!"

Ian put his arm around the beautiful girl's waist as he assisted her trying to get through the crowd. Cece felt like she was staggering. Suddenly, Ian had her outside.

Ian took Cece to the cool entrance steps as he took off his letterman's sweater and threw it on top of the tallest step and sat her down.

Ian asked, "Is this better?"

Cece replied, "Oh, yes, thank you!"

Ian told her he would be right back. Ian ran through the hall to get some iced fruit punch for Cece. He ran quickly back through the crowd of dancing people and outside where he placed

Cece in the cool California night air. He sat next to Cece and handed the fruit punch over to her. Cece drank the juice and took a deep breath.

Cece said, "Thank you."

Ian asked, "Do you feel ok now? Can I do anything else for you? Where are you from?"

Cece replied, "The beautiful countryside of Florida about 30 minutes west of Miami by car and before you get to the Everglades. It is all dairy and farmland, but now some people are building a beautiful golf course and homes near to where my home was. I miss it. A lot of very happy memories were made there!"

Ian said, "I loved Florida, too. My family lived in Jacksonville before we came west."

Cece said, "I loved Florida. It's so different out here. Everything's very fast, and in a hurry, with crowds of people everywhere! Men try to pull me into their cars. I can't even walk down the sidewalk two blocks to my aunt's home without it happening. It's very frightening. I hate it! I was a runner in Florida so I can get away, but it's ridiculous having to be afraid to go for a walk. Women shouldn't have to go through those kinds of things every time they want to walk. I really can't imagine how those guys would act on Miami Beach. What would they think of bikini-clad women? They would have to arrest all the men. To make matters worse, I don't understand any of their unfamiliar languages."

Ian admired her as she spoke. He smiled and thought to himself, "This is a very gentle person with a gorgeous body."

Ian softly smiled at her and said, "You're such a lovely girl. They would love to catch you. You have to be careful here. It is different. You should always be with someone."

Cece said, "I'm a regular person. I can't hire a bodyguard."

Ian said, "I'll be your bodyguard!"

Cece looked surprised and smiled at Ian. He liked her and returned a beautiful smile of his own.

With that said, their love story began instantly. Ian asked Cece for her phone number and her last name. Cece told Ian her last name was Riccobuono, and it was very Sicilian-Italian.

Ian asked, "RICK A WHAT?" Cece laughed, "Riccobuono."

They both started laughing. Cece said her last name was pronounced 'Rick-o-bone-o' in America to make it easier for people to say. She said to just call her Cece. They stood up to go back into the dance when Ian asked her to save her last dance for him. She said she would. Now she was having fun! She noticed Ian glowed in every noble way a man should. She felt like she had known him from her dreams for all of her life. He was exceptional, kind, attentive, and utterly handsome!

Cece asked God, "Is he the glowing man? You really sent him to me?" She felt like she had always known him.

Boys swarmed to her when she walked back into the hall as they asked where she had been. Everyone was telling Cece and Ian they had just missed seeing Rowdy Yates from the TV series Rawhide, and the couple singing "I got you, Babe."

Cece was very disappointed. She grew up in love with Rowdy Yates and liked that song, but she finally got to meet the glowing man. He was everything she thought he would be in all her younger years.

She looked at Ian and said, "You know, you look a lot like Rowdy Yates. Were we outside long?"

Ian beamed and grabbed both of Cece's hands into his own.

As he looked into her eyes, he said, "I guess so. It didn't feel long. Please save the last dance for me."

Cece was sure he was her glowing man from her mind's eye as she answered Ian, "Ok, I will!"

Suddenly, Cece was swept away by a circle of boys as she looked back at Ian and smiled at him. Ian had a look of panic on his face, but Cece kept looking back at him and smiling.

Cece thought to herself, "How could a man be so handsome and so kind?" She felt like she knew him somehow because of her dreams, the flashes, and "The Eye".

Coach walked up to Ian and said, "Ok, you monopolized a lot of the young lady's time.

Now give the other guys a chance."

Ian smiled at his coach, but he looked apprehensively back at Cece as Cece was watching his reaction. She felt disappointed the coach interfered.

Jimmy just looked at Ian as the guys started asking Cece for dances all over again. Both of them noticed how disappointed Cece looked as guys took her hand to dance.

Ian said, "It's ok, I have the last dance reserved. After that, she's my girl alone, forever.

We'll be driving her home tonight."

Jimmy said, "I can't believe you pulled it off!"

Ian said, "I didn't pull anything off. I'm already in love with her. I'm going to marry her. She's got me wrapped around her little finger forever and she has no idea. I can't help myself!"

Jimmy said, "Some guys have all the luck!"

Ian replied, "Jimmy, it's not luck. I'm going to marry her someday!" Jimmy said, "I just can't get over you! How did you do it, Ian?

Ian answered, "I don't understand it myself. It's like it was meant to be."

Cece anxiously saved the last dance for Ian. It was a slow dance. He couldn't dance and she didn't care as long as they got to hold each other. Cece decided she had an amazing time at the dance. It was exciting, fun, and it was all because of Ian. Ian drove her home and politely asked for a first kiss. When their lips touched it was like magic, with a flow of many wonderful sensations through both of their bodies. After that night, Ian informed all the guys Cece was his girl.

Cece was almost glad when the dance was over. She was exhausted. She couldn't remember being that wearied. She recalled how Ian catered to her, after their talk on the steps, and for the whole evening. He kept coming by while all the guys danced with her. Ian kept checking on her to see if she was doing ok, or if she needed more juice punch. Cece noticed Ian did not dance with anyone else. He was watching her the rest of the entire evening.

Cece liked that about him. He was very attentive, protective, handsomely well built, and he glowed like an archangel, just like in her dreams. Cece could tell he was a strong man in many ways. Most importantly, Cece could tell he was a good and kind young man with manners.

As Ian was falling to sleep that night, he smiled and thanked God for making a woman like Cece for him to love. As hard as Ian wished for it, he never really believed his ideal woman could actually exist. Cece was everything he had prayed for, and she was even more than he ever expected. He knew he already loved her. Now he had to convince Cece to love him, too. All Ian could think about was Cece. He was preoccupied with thoughts of her. He found his woman. He would do whatever it took to gain her love and keep her love. Ian adored Cece, and vice versa!

The next 4 months of their lives were bliss. They didn't have lots of money, but they had fun by just being together and talking. They would take a blanket and walk down to the beautiful park every Sunday afternoon after eating Carmella's traditional Sunday dinner of meatballs and spaghetti. They would sit and talk for hours on end. There was never a lack of anything to say. They spoke non-stop for hours while getting to know each other's hearts and each other's souls. They spoke of their wishes and hopes for the future. They held hands like young sweethearts do and shared innocent kisses. They were respectful of each other and became more deeply in love because of that respect. Cece remained virtuous. Ian loved the fact she had good morals. It assured him his future wife would be an exemplary faithful woman.

Then, four weeks before Ian's high school graduation, the bad news hit. Everyone was shocked. Ian was told Cece was to be pulled out of his life because her brother suffered a severe asthma attack and had to be rushed to the hospital. Cece's parents put their house up for sale the next day. It sold the following week.

Cece's parents again uprooted their family to finally move to the small desert town of Las Vegas, Nevada. The new Western High School in Las Vegas would be Cece's fourth high school in four years. The family knew

Michael thrived there once before, and Carmella and Sammie didn't have a choice. Constant moving caused Cece to lose many friends. Ian had become her best friend. She learned to live without friends, but she cried terribly while regretting living without Ian. They were young and very much in love.

Luckily, Cece's aunt and uncle agreed to have Cece finish out her high school year in California with them and her cousins. Cece was so grateful because she could see Ian and be with Ian for a few more weeks at least before she had to go live in the god-forsaken desert of Las Vegas, Nevada. The thought of it was pure hell for the young couple. Little did they realize their fate yet to come.

When the family moved to Las Vegas, there was a bad financial depression in the city. Cece's family noticed the casinos weren't suffering, but the city was. Home builders built too many homes, and the homes were not selling. People were moving out of Las Vegas because of the depression in the local economy. People had stopped moving into the small town. Sammie and Carmella could have their pick of new homes at low prices. They found a home right next to where the desert started and where the homes ended on the west end of Las Vegas near Fremont Street and Torrey Pines.

Ian and Cece feared they would miss each other terribly. Las Vegas wasn't the only one in a depression. Cece's heart was breaking, and she hated thinking of having to live in the ugly desert without Ian. Cece was due to leave for Las Vegas on Ian's graduation Day, June 4, 1964. It broke her heart, but Ian was in love and determined never to lose his Cece.

That summer was a lonely one for both of the young lovers, but after summer ended Ian met a new friend, Rod, in their first year of college. Rod's Dad had lots of money and bought Rod a brand-new red sports car. Rod loved driving his souped-up car to Vegas on weekends and needed company on the rides. The good times began to roll ('em dice).

Chapter 8

THE BROOMSTICK KILLER 1965

THE desert was next to the Riccobuono home. Little animals wandered into the front garden from the desert to drink water and eat grass. Cece loved the bunnies and desert tortoises. She never realized the desert was home to so many birds, animals, and insects. It was pleasant to see the pretty outskirts of Las Vegas compared to the flying sand and trash on Las Vegas Blvd. South, nicknamed "The Las Vegas Strip". As September came, the desert felt tamed. The fall weather was anticipated with joy by the locals. Winters were very pleasant in Vegas.

Cece remembered her first impression of the Strip. She thought the city was filthy. Papers and plastic bags clung to sagebrush and cacti on the undeveloped lots along the Strip. There were cans and bottles everywhere. Hot winds were blowing. Ladies were trying to hold down their hairstyles and their skirts, while some of them were completely unsuccessful on both counts. Fine silty sand was flying in front of the car's windshield. Cece instantly hated this ugly place!

Except for right around the hotels, landscaping was almost non-existent in the Las Vegas valley. It certainly was not like Florida or California. When Cece arrived, Sammie had to go get his Clark County Sheriff's card in the downtown area of Las Vegas, Nevada. The sheriff's card would allow him to work in any business involving cash. Sammie's photograph and fingerprints were taken, and a background check was completed. Once everything was done and checked out, Sammie could start a new job. Employees in Clark County, Nevada, who wanted to work for a business, when handling cash, had to have a sheriff's card to secure employment. It was a good system because if you turned out to be a thief, the Sheriff's department already had your photographs, your personal information, and your fingerprints on file. They would find and arrest you. They got rid of possible unsavory citizens quickly. Plus, the system had all your information on file in case you were to turn rogue, steal, and flee. The authorities 'would' find you! It was still a good old fashion Cowboy town, as well as a mob influenced town.

When Sammie was done at the sheriff's office, he began walking to his car, which was parked on a gravel lot next to Fremont Street. It shocked Sammie to see a familiar face from his long ago past. His childhood playmate looked up and saw Sammie looking at him. They both smiled and laughed. Sammie grabbed his old friend, Vito. They were from the same neighborhood in the Bronx, New York, in the late 1920s. Vito ducked his head and asked Sammie if they could go into the coffee shop next door to talk.

Sammie said, "Sure, Vito!"

Vito led the way. Everything in Las Vegas was new to Sammie. Vito seemed very familiar with downtown. He picked the far end booth, and selected to sit in the booth seat facing the back wall. As Vito faced Sammie, Sammie realized Vito's face was very scarred. Vito was acting extremely nervous, as if there was trouble brewing. After they exchanged familiarities between the two old compadres, they began to talk quickly.

Vito told Sam, "I was so far in debt to the mob I had to run away from New York. What better place to hide than Las Vegas?"

Sammie was dumbfounded as he looked at Vito incredulously.

In those old days in Vegas, locals knew unscrupulous people could hide amongst the crowds of tourists in the Las Vegas areas. As long as street people had no need for health cards, Sheriff work cards, or driver's licenses they could hustle on the streets to survive, while remaining anonymous, unless, of course, they attracted attention to themselves, and were fingerprinted. Sammie was appalled! Sammie realized Vito's story was too horribly far-fetched to be false. He could tell Vito's circumstances were the truth because of Vito's nervous and frightened demeanor.

Vito looked into Sammie's eyes and said, "I had to run away, or the Mob would have killed me. My own family doesn't even know where I'm hiding."

Sammie hesitantly asked, "You left Marge and your children?"

Vito admitted, "I have a horrible gambling habit. The mob was leaning heavily on me to pay back my debts with higher interest daily. I had to run for my life or they would have been beaten me to death. I had to leave New York without telling my wife and children where I was going. I didn't even say goodbye. I figured my family couldn't tell the mob where I was if they didn't know. You can imagine how many beatings it took for me to get these many scars."

Sammie was starting to realize Vito's speech was badly slurred.

A wide-eyed Sammie said, "You left your family to the mercy of the mob?"

Sammie thought it was terrible to just leave your family. What kind of man would leave his family? Sammie mentally answered his own question. Only a worthless man with no gumption, who loved his bad habits more than he loved his family, would leave them. Sammie realized Vito was mentally sick.

Sammie asked, "So you sacrificed your wife and children? Won't the Mob hurt them?"

Sammie remained quiet and listened.

As Vito spoke, Sammie began to grasp his childhood friend was much more demented and unbalanced than Sammie could have imagined. You didn't have to be a medical expert to surmise Vito's condition was probably the result of many beatings, which he endured from the mob's collectors over the years. Sammie realized he could be in danger for just talking to Vito. Sammie had his own family to protect. Sammie definitely did not need Vito's problems in his life. Vito was beyond help if the mob was still pursuing him heavily.

Vito answered, "I don't know. My children are pre-teenagers. My wife, Marge, moved out of our apartment and is living with her elderly parents in another city and state. She is using her maiden name. The last time I saw my wife she told me she was done with me forever. I don't think the mob will find them. Marge is a good lady who did not deserve to fall in love with me. We were only 16 and 17 when we met."

Sammie said, "The mob can find people anywhere!"

Sammie knew his old friend was messed up, but this was ludicrous! The mob would eventually find anyone who they really sought diligently.

Sammie thought to himself, "Why is the Mob so passionate to find Vito?"

Sammie realized Vito had not told him everything. There must be much more to the story. Vito watched Sammie's expressions.

Vito could read Sammie's face and confessed, "So, ok! I was involved with some High-level Mobster's girlfriend. She was beautiful and spoiled. They beat her until she admitted to the affair. Then they knifed her breasts, her face, and finally her genitals until she bled to death. I was there. The confrontation was loud and horrible with a lot of screaming, but none of the frightened neighbors called for help. I was hiding on an outside ledge of a six-story building around the corner from her bathroom window!"

Sammie thought to himself, "What a piece of garbage!"

People involved with the mob learned quickly 'no piece of ass on Earth' was worth death, especially the mob's own Molls and Dolls. Vito knew that fact, but Sammie realized Vito was mentally deranged and obsessive because of his bad gambling habits, his lust for gorgeous women, and his own sordid beatings over the years. Vito hid for his life when he heard the mobster's girlfriend being killed right under his nose for 'fooling around' with him, especially because she named him before she died!

Sammie was shocked hearing this kind of news as his thoughts flew through his mind, "What did Vito think was going to happen to him if the mob killed the woman right away? Of course, he was going to be next. What a mess! The mob would have done an equally horrible number on him until he died! Vito is a cowardly jerk with no balls and had to be a 'sweet-talking son of a bitch' to let the girl be killed under his nose. If the murderers caught Vito, within minutes he would have been tortured to death in much the same way as the woman was killed. The police would have found his sliced-up body, castrated, with his genitals stuffed deep down into his throat, causing him to finally die from asphyxiation as he bled out! How awful! I have to get away from this jerk!"

Vito admitted, "I know I wasn't a good husband or father. I had a reputation of being a wife beater, but Marge was always complaining we never had enough for the children or for food. I know I'm a compulsive gambler. I drink. I do drugs. I am a womanizer. I am completely broke, living on the streets, and scrounging to exist, but I still want to 'have' young pretty women."

Sammie was having a difficult time comprehending the information overload Vito was throwing at him. Sammie could tell Vito was setting him up for a handout.

Sammie stood up and said, "Hey, I got to go!"

Vito and Sammie weren't close in proximity after they had reached the age of fifteen because Sammie's family moved to another neighborhood. Sammie didn't know what happened to Vito until this accidental meeting. Sammie had good childhood memories of them, as young boys playing in Central Park, and going to the Bronx Zoo. Later in life, Sammie had heard through family members Vito had changed into a person with a sketchy background, but no one ever elaborated on the subject. Now Sammie knew!

Sammie's family members did talk about Vito's mother, Maria, and her husband, Vito, Sr., who was shot by the mob. Vito, Sr. was killed in their poor neighborhood. No one had a telephone in those days to call the police or to call an ambulance. People were too fearful to look outside after the killing shots were fired. They were too frightened to go out to find a phone booth. The neighborhood had their own families to shield from mobsters. Vito, Sr. was left to bleed to death in the street gutter located right in front of his own apartment. Maria claimed the mob murdered an innocent man, but Sammie's family did not believe it. The mob usually knew what they were doing. Maria and her three sons fled to another state and luckily were unharmed. It was 25 years before this meeting between Sammie and Vito, Jr. The Mob never gives up, but in Maria's case, she didn't work, drive, or speak English. Wherever she fled with her children, her unknown relatives probably took care of them and made them untraceable.

Vito, Jr. pleaded with Sammie, "Please don't let on who I really am, in case someone might be watching us and asks you!"

Sammie threw money on the table. He became very uncomfortable and wanted to wrap up this crazy conversation. He didn't want to be seen with Vito, Jr! Sammie was thinking of his own beautiful family and protecting them.

As Sammie turned to leave, Vito grabbed Sammie by the wrist and said, "I think my major problem is the fault of all those beautiful young whores, who I lusted for in our old neighborhood. I have the same problems my father had. I realize I am not anywhere as handsome as you are, Sammie. The only way I really could ever get beautiful women was to have money. Money is the reason I gambled so heavily. I wanted those beautiful women, whether I was married or not, and that's the reason I needed money. Even when I had many chances to pay the mob back, I didn't do it, because I continually wanted to entertain gorgeous young women. I will forever hate women of disrepute because they caused my downfall. The beautiful whores tempted me! They were the reason my family had to suffer. Can you lend me a few bucks? I'll pay you back."

Sammie stood looking down at Vito in wonder at his stupid rationalizations. Sammie knew he would never get any money back from Vito. Sammie tried to pull his wrist out of Vito's hand, but Vito held on tightly. Sammie undoubtedly knew Vito was mentally unbalanced.

Suddenly, Vito realized he had told Sammie too much because Sammie was looking at him strangely.

Sammie said, "It's late. I really must go now! Just to let you know, I am currently out of work, and any little bit of money I have is a lot to me."

Sammie didn't want Vito to know anything about his family! Sammie didn't want him involved with his life in any way. Sammie wanted to get away from this perverted past acquaintance as quickly as possible. Vito was no longer the nice little boy, who Sammie knew from their childhood years. Sammie pulled forcefully enough to break his wrist away from Vito's hold.

Vito said, "Sammie, I'm sorry. I'm just scared! Please do not talk to me on the streets or call out my name. If we see each other again, let's just nod at each other, ok?"

Sammie shook his head in an affirmative manner, turned, and hastily walked away. Sammie understood Vito's fear of the mob! They still ran Las Vegas, and Vito was hiding right under their noses.

A year later Sammie had finally obtained his barber license. Cece worked and helped Carmella support their family while Sammie was going to a barber college in Arizona. Sammie had to struggle to go back and forth to Arizona and come home on weekends. Eventually, Sammie was working in a downtown casino and hotel's barbershop. Sammie spotted Vito every once in a while on the streets through the barbershop's big plate-glass window overlooking Fremont Street and Casino Center Blvd. Sammie noticed Vito was looking old and gaunt. Vito's badly scarred face was extremely drawn and pale. Vito made himself scarce. It was apparent Vito was living a difficult life on the downtown Las Vegas streets.

Sammie couldn't believe how his young childhood friend had turned out!

When told about Vito, Carmella said, "Sammie, please make sure you keep Vito away from our family. I would be frightened to have him anywhere around Cece or the children."

Sammie assured her, "I will never talk to him again. He's a walking dead man! He's going to screw up sooner or later. He will be found!"

Murders in the depressed area, between downtown Las Vegas and the Boulder Highway, were increasing in the 1960s. The area had several old boarded-up motels built in the early 1920s to house the Hoover Dam workers and their families. Las Vegas officials 'hushed things up'. They didn't want any bad publicity for downtown Las Vegas, which had the only department store in Las Vegas, one of the two movie theaters in Las Vegas, and many small miscellaneous shops for locals and tourists.

Local rumors started spreading around Las Vegas in the 1960s. It was said Las Vegas had a horrible woman killer. The killer would rape and torture 'bound and gagged' young prostitutes to death by inserting a broomstick handle into the vaginal area of their bodies. The killer would push the handles up a little at a time, while he enjoyed watching the life drain from their eyes as they bleed to death! The newspapers were threatened they would lose advertising revenues if they elaborated on the story because the good Las Vegas downtown reputation would be ruined. The tiny published articles regarding the mysterious murders were tucked away in back obscure corners of the local newspapers. The newspaper articles stated the women were "prostitutes".

Somehow, the good mothers in the small town of Las Vegas used word of mouth to warn each other to protect their daughters when their daughters would go downtown for any reason. They told each other in churches, grocery stores, pharmacies, real estate companies, doctor's clinic, dental clinics, hospitals, dry cleaners, and even at school bus stops. Carmella found out the terrible news about the "Broomstick Killer" from the mothers picking up and delivering their children to and from schools. Carmella thanked God for her neighbors.

Mothers were praying the Popular Cowboy who was running for Sheriff of Clark County, Nevada, would win!

Meanwhile, just outside of Las Vegas…

Lia's family members couldn't speak English. They were illegal. Lia was 12 years old and the oldest child. She needed to care for her four younger siblings and her aging parents. She learned to speak some English at the convent school south of the border. Lia's family needed food. The children needed milk. They prayed.

There were several families brought into the U.S.A. in the back of an overcrowded semi-tractor trailer. They were bribed by unscrupulous people, who told them they could obtain legal citizenship and a lucrative life in America. They had to pay money to be secretly brought to this wonderful new life. After starting their journey to the United States, Lia's family realized they, and the other families, were in trouble. None of the families understood what was happening. The food and water, which was supposed to be provided by the transporters, was insufficient for all the families. They had been living in the back of the dark locked trailer for 4 days. They were scared, hungry, tired, dehydrated, and living in filth.

Circumstances changed when the truck driver made a stop along Boulder Highway outside of Las Vegas. He was cheap and parked off the highway on an empty dirt lot. He needed food and a restroom break before sunset. Being the fool who he was, he forget about the darkening skies because he was too busy flirting with a waitress. The waitress was constantly serving him drinks because he was playing a loose slot machine that was paying off enough to pique his interest. The Sun set and thieves broke his trailer's locks. The thieves threw the trailer doors wide open in a rush. As the thieves climbed into the back of the trailer, the hijacked families grabbed their children and their meager belongings and rushed out into the desert to hide. It surprised the thieves to see people rushing out the back of the trailer. The thieves weren't interested in the hijacked families. They wanted easy money. The thieves went deeper into the cargo area to see if there was anything left to steal, but the thieves quickly left, too, because of the filth and stench inside the trailer.

The truck driver was furious when he returned from his break. Someone at the truck stop had called the Nevada Highway Patrol. The driver had to explain why the back of his trailer looked like people had been living in it for quite a while. The driver was arrested, and his tractor-trailer was impounded. The families would have been worth a lot of money to the driver once he had delivered them to their final destinations. They were to become pickers for orchards in some northwestern destination of the U.S.A. The families had been told that the orchards would sponsor them.

Who knows if that wouldn't have been a far better situation for Lia?

Lia had to think. She had too much responsibility for a 12-year-old girl. Her family needed food, and they needed milk for the babies. They began to follow the highway by walking through the desert far off the two-lane Boulder Highway. Lia's family spotted Las Vegas after sleeping that night in the desert. They walked up Boulder Highway where it met the end of Fremont Street, and where a very popular teenage hangout, called 'The Blue Onion', was located. It had the best food in town. All the Las Vegas teenagers would cruise in their cars on Fremont Street every weekend, East to West, and back again when they reached the Blue Onion. The teenagers found their friends by cruising Fremont Street, or at the downtown movie theater. After the teens would meet up at the Blue Onion to eat and listen to the latest rock-and-roll music.

Lia's family bought as much food as they could at the Blue Onion and began walking up Fremont Street. Her parents found an opened cheap motel in between other boarded-up motels two blocks west of the Blue Onion. Lia's father paid for the food with the little money he had hidden in his boot. When they showed the money to a motel clerk, the clerk took all the money from them and handed them a motel room key with the number 13 on it.

Lia's first day in Vegas was frightening. She walked up and down Fremont Street during the day asking people for food or money. By following the noise of fun and music like most teens would do, Lia, once again, found the 'The Blue Onion'. Since she couldn't get food or money on her first days try on Fremont Street, Lia found some leftover food scraps on car trays at the "Blue Onion". Lia went to the Blue Onion because it was close to her own motel room. Las Vegas teenagers frequented the 'best hamburger place in Vegas' every night, but especially on weekends.

Lia was a beautiful and innocent 12-year-old girl. Lia was walking the streets of Las Vegas alone at night.

Meanwhile:

Western High School turned out to be an interesting experience for Cece. She missed Ian. However, after the summer ended, Ian visited Las Vegas almost weekly because of his new college friend, Rod. Rod and Ian enjoyed making weekend trips to Las Vegas with the money Rod's busy single father continuously gave to Rod, along with Rod's brand new beautiful red Pontiac sports car.

Downtown Las Vegas was so much fun, but Carmella continually warned Cece she was not to go there without an escort or a friend. Carmella required Cece to wear a dress like a proper young lady if she went downtown. Cece asked Carmella why she couldn't wear jeans. Carmella said that there was someone killing young women, who may have looked like cheaply dressed prostitutes. Cece was appalled, but undoubtedly complied with her mother's wishes. Ian and Ron would take Cece downtown to the movie theater and shopping, but they would, also, frequent Lake Mead, the Valley of Fire, Red Rock Canyon, and drive up to the surrounding beautiful mountains around Las Vegas. Mount Charleston's young snow skiing area was where automated tow bars pulled people up the mountain so they could ski down. They saw all the pristine lands surrounding Las Vegas, Nevada, which would eventually become national parks.

Ian wasn't coming to Las Vegas on one weekend Liz and Cece decided to go to a movie downtown. Cece and her friend, Liz, pulled into the Blue Onion to get a chili dog after all their friends had left the movie theatre. Going to the Blue Onion for a chili dog and French fries was their treat at the end of the week. They were waiting for their order when Cece saw a very young pretty girl asking other teenagers for food or money. Those people were yelling at the girl and telling her to get away from them.

Cece called the young girl over and asked her, "What are you doing out on the streets of downtown alone at night? What is your name?"

Lia shrugged her shoulders and said, "Lia."

Cece told Lia, "Ola, Lia. Are you hungry?"

Lia said, "Si, mucho!"

Cece said, "Get into the back of my car now! This is my friend, Liz. I am Cece. Ok?"

Lia got into the car without even thinking about it. Cece gave Lia the chili dog and fries that Cece had just ordered. Lia couldn't eat it fast enough. Cece ordered more food.

Cece said, "Liz and I will take you home after you eat because we have to leave downtown soon. We have school tomorrow. Where are your parents?"

Lia only pointed down Fremont Street because her mouth was full of food. They could barely understand each other.

After they all ate, Cece and Liz pooled the rest of their little bit of money and took Lia to a mini-market to buy food before going to Lia's motel room. In the 1960s, you could get a lot of food for fifteen dollars. Cece stocked up with milk, cheese, sandwich meat, bread, and whatever else they thought was a necessity. They drove where Lia pointed. When Lia got out of the car, the family opened the door of their motel room and came running out to meet her.

Lia's family grabbed at the bags of food, milk, cheese, shampoo, and soap. They thanked the two ladies profusely, "Gracias, gracias, Senoritas!"

Cece and Liz carried in a foam ice chest full of ice with food and milk.

The family entered the motel room to eat while a toddler carried a loaf of bread into the room behind everyone.

Cece looked at Liz, asking, "Do you believe this?"

As Lia went into the room, Cece bent over, grabbed her shoulders, and Cece looked into Lia's eyes while she warned her, "Do not go out alone in the dangerous areas of east downtown Las Vegas at night or even during the day. There are a lot of boarded-up motels. See, like the ones over there. Stay away from them because bad people could be in there. Do you understand me?"

Lia shook her head affirmatively.

Cece continued, "There is danger! Be very careful. Take this note to the church rectory straight down this street tomorrow morning. Do you understand me?"

Cece pointed to the street and to the address on the note.

Lia was so happy, but she didn't pay enough attention. Lia just kept smiling and saying, "Si!"

Cece continued as she pointed, "Make sure one of your parents, Madre, Padre, goes with you. The church is about one-half mile down this street. Understand? They will help your family. Like I already said, I have to go to school tomorrow for 5 days and cannot go out again until next weekend. Do you understand me?"

Lia smiled as she stuffed the note into her skirt pocket and said, "Si! Gracias, Bonitas Liz Y Cece."

Cece gave Lia a hug and once again warned her, "Be careful."

Cece was forlorn as she watched Lia go into the motel room. Cece kept having a strange feeling about Lia. Cece rode home while worrying all the way. She prayed Lia would take heed of her warning.

The little family ate in the motel room and wondered about what they would have to do after the next few days for food. Lia smiled and thought she could trust Cece and she would find the Padre in the morning. Lia fondled the note in her skirt pocket to make sure it was there and safe. She was determined to find the Padre the next day. Lia's toddler sister watched everything Lia did. She loved Lia. As Lia removed her hand from her skirt's deep pocket, the folded note caught onto the button of Lia's blouse long sleeve's cuff and fell out onto the floor. Lia didn't notice. She felt so thankful. She shared in her family's happiness and the good fortune of an indoor picnic dinner. Lia's little sister picked the note up off the floor, wadded it into a ball, and played with it.

Lia's father, Jose, handed Lia a sharp steak knife he had confiscated off of an empty table at a restaurant where he went in to look for work earlier that day. He told Lia the knife was for her protection. Lia frowned, but her father insisted. He told Lia to put it into her skirt's pocket. Lia did not want to comply, but she appeased her father. Lia did not notice the note was no longer in her pocket. The large family fell asleep on the two small beds and on the dirty floors of their motel room. Their stomachs were quieted, and their dreams of America were great.

The next day was Monday. It came and went. Cece was exhausted from her weekend and from helping with her small siblings. She was still constantly assisting Carmella with the four younger children. She kept herself busy with her hectic schedule. Not realizing Cece forgot about Lia. Cece didn't mean to forget, but her plate was so full at home. Cece was far away from Lia's Eastside motel room, and without a car of her own.

Cece came back to reality when she heard a TV announcer saying, "People shouldn't trust just anyone downtown. There has been another killing."

Cece was thankful she gave Lia the note for the priest.

Monday Lia went one way toward where she thought the church would be even though she couldn't find the note. Jose went another way to look for work. Lia never found the church and Jose never found work. The babies would have food only for a few more days!

Four days had gone by and the food Cece and Liz helped Lia buy was nearly gone. The foam ice chest Cece filled with ice, food, and drinks was almost empty. The motel room was a mess. Lia left the motel room the next afternoon to go look for the church again, thinking maybe she could explain her circumstances to a priest. She searched until she was tired. She drank water from a garden hose. It was getting dark, and she was angry with herself for losing the note. However, the knife Lia's father, Jose, gave to Lia was still in her skirt's pocket. She frowned at the thought of the knife but dismissed her thoughts quickly as she continued to look for the church. Lia had no idea why her father gave her the knife. Lia didn't realize her parents were afraid for her protection. When Jose insisted Lia should listen to him, Lia thought nothing bad could happen in the United States of America. After all, American teenagers went out every weekend and had fun at the Blue Onion.

The next day was Friday, and Rod and Ian were coming into Las Vegas. Rod was going out on his own, but Ian was coming to pick up Cece after dinner. Cece was excited. She knew Ian would buy her a box of chocolates after they saw a movie and then they would cruise Fremont Street while just having fun being together. They would see their friends again and be able to visit. Cece would look for Lia. All the valley's teenagers constantly cruised up and down Fremont Street on weekends to greet each other in cars through opened windows. Cece asked everyone about Lia. No one had any information. Ian drove through the brightly lit casino corridor off Fremont Street. It is now called 'The Fremont Street Experience' and closed to traffic. When they arrived at Main, they would cross over into the railroad station's entrance, which is now the Union Plaza, and use the circular drive to make the loop back around to Main Street and cross back over onto Fremont Street. Then they headed east towards their favorite hamburger hangout, the Blue Onion. Happiness, good food, and the latest best rock-and-roll music reigned at the hamburger joint. Time just went by too quickly when Ian came into Las Vegas from Los Angeles for weekends. Cece planned to ask him to drive by to check if Lia's family was still at their motel. Cece figured Lia's family was already gone but wanted to be sure. They couldn't tell which motel it was because no lights were on at any of the very dark motels. Ian said they could try again the next day.

Saturday:

The broomstick killer tied one stocking to the filthy bed's left front bedpost. Then he tied another stocking to the opposite side of the bed's right front bedpost. He was demented. He didn't know or care. He was preparing. He was doing the world a favor by getting rid of human trash. He saw enough of this type of woman in New York's older neighborhoods all his younger life. He escaped to Nevada. Now he was seeing loose, beautiful and very young women coming into Las Vegas, and unsuspecting abused American teenage runaways. They were very pretty, but desperate. They were fragile, hungry, and easy prey.

He smiled and thought, "They are still beautiful, helpless, and young."

No one could have ever realized how Lia felt. She felt there was no other way out for her family's situation. She had nothing else. No other way to drag her family out of poverty, but to beg the rich Americans for money. She was too young to work. Her parents prayed all the time, but they were still poor. She had to help them. Since she was the only family member who spoke any English, the responsibility fell on her shoulders to ask for food and milk money. Her father was trying to learn English while he looked for work every day.

Jose didn't realize he needed to obtain both 'work and health' cards. People tried to explain it to him, but he didn't understand. Lia's mother, her baby brother, and her small sisters were all still in the one-room motel with nowhere else to go. Their electricity was turned off for non-payment. They were hungry. They were tired. They were sickly. They were illegal, but most of all, they were poor. They needed to pay the rent for the next day or they would be evicted from their only home, which was the tiny dirty motel room where they all waited to anticipate their father's and Lia's daily returns.

Lia walked on Fremont Street asking people for money. Most people looked at her strangely and told her to go home. Some people just ignored her. Then Lia listened to passersby.

She saw a man walk up to a young woman, who was leaning on a building and waiting on a corner next to where Lia stood.

The man asked the woman, "How much?"

The young woman said, "One hundred dollars."

The man said, "Ok."

They began to walk away together when Lia saw the man hand to the pretty girl a hundred-dollar bill!

Lia thought, "ARRIBA!"

While the family was waiting for Lia and her father to return, her mother prayed they would be back soon with some money for their motel, food, and milk. Time ticked by slowly. The little ones cried softly.

Lia's mother cried more. Lia had left once again that same afternoon after her first return without telling her mother she was going out to try again.

Lia's mother cried out in Spanish, "Will God ever help us? Time is going by quickly and my oldest child is not returning."

It was getting late. Lia's mother prayed some more.

An older man walked up to Lia as she waited on the corner of Fremont Street and Main. The man asked Lia a question.

The scarred face man asked, "How much?"

Lia was frightened but said, "One hundred dollars!"

The man waved for Lia to follow and said, "Si. Follow me and I'll go get it."

Lia woke with a terrible pain in her head. It was throbbing as blood rolled down onto her neck. Her eyes flew open, but she stayed very still. She couldn't remember exactly what happened. She vaguely saw a shadowy figure reclined in an old straight-back chair in a corner on the other side of the room. She thought her eyes were impaired because of the terrible pain in her head. She couldn't see much movement. She thought it was safe to try to move. She felt her wrists were tied in opposite directions. She instinctively fought to free them as quietly as possible, but her arms seemed to be stretched in a wide-opened position.

Lia moved slightly. She was careful not to let the sleeping figure notice she was awake. She felt her ankles were, also, bound to the bed's bottom posts. She looked. Yes, she was right. She was tied to the four bedposts. She had something stuffed into her mouth. She was having a difficult time breathing. She was coming around more and began to think. She was bound but still fully clothed. She couldn't scream and move. She glared at the figure across the room. It never moved. She thought the figure was the man she was following. He must have fallen asleep in the chair after he had apparently tied her to the bedposts. Lia felt she was about to be harmed, but she didn't even know why he would want to hurt her. Why did he hit her and tie her to a bed? She could feel blood seeping out of the side of her head and running down onto her neck again. Why couldn't she remember? She had to think. She needed to remember. She had to get out of this place. Where was she?

The last thing Lia could recall was she was standing on a corner of Fremont Street in downtown Las Vegas.

A man with a badly scarred face walked up and asked her, "How much?"

She answered, "One hundred dollars, por favor."

She hoped it was the correct answer. These Americans had lots of money.

He answered, "Si. I'll go get it. Segura."

She was happy he quickly agreed to give her money. She knew she wasn't a good beggar because she had tried for two days and no one gave her any money. She wondered how much money a hundred dollars was. She followed. He left the brightly lit areas of downtown and headed towards the dark, frightening areas of East Fremont Street where the cheap run-down motels were boarded up for many blocks. They walked for a long time. Lia was brave. She had to get money. She realized their current location was one block from her family's motel. They were near Boulder Highway, where eventually the evening would light up again once the Blue Onion would shine brightly.

In the early 1960s Fremont Street between Main Street and Casino Center Boulevard was where most of the hotels and action were located, but approximately a mile down Fremont Street, the area still harbored old boarded-up filthy motels and deserted buildings. Lia was frightened following him through that dark area of town, but she was fast and kept a safe distance behind him while she walked down Fremont Street. Lia could tell the man was old and not healthy. Lia knew she could outrun him.

She heard scary voices as the man passed through alleys and he became distracted. The female voices were trying to lure him into the small dark passageways behind the old broken-down buildings. The man acted like he had to be careful. He was preoccupied with a worried look on his ugly face. He didn't see the police squad car with its lights off. The car was slowly and carefully being driven by a policewoman when the vehicle passed behind him as it slowly entered the dark alley. The man was preoccupied with watching Lia. Lia did see the police car and worried about them finding her family hiding only a few blocks away.

The police vehicle was cruising the area because it was where many of the tortured bodies of the dead young women had been found. The policewoman and her fellow officer spotted little Lia following a man at a distance. They weren't sure if the little girl was following her father. They continued to watch as their cruiser exited the alley.

Suddenly, a shot was fired from another dark alley on the other side of the street. The police cruiser went toward the shot, but the female officer did a worried doubled back look toward Lia.

Lia knew when she saw drunks turning into the back alleys, that they were being robbed, rolled, and beaten. She could hear them being struck violently. It frightened her to hear their cries. Lia saw the man looked frightened, as well. She still followed behind him against her better judgement. She kept thinking of how much one hundred dollars might do for her family. Her parents could still have their motel room for a while. The manager would turn their lights on again. All the little ones could have needed food and milk. Maybe they could even find a nicer place to stay if they had some money. Then Lia thought maybe Cece would come back to check on her family this weekend. Cece could show her exactly where the church was located.

Lia wondered, "Where is this man going?"

It was getting very dark, but in the distance, Lia saw where East Fremont Street ended at Boulder Highway. Lia realized she had been following the man for a long while, but she was smart and kept her distance. Lia knew she was close to her family's run-down motel room. Lia recognized the teenage hangout 'The Blue Onion'. She saw the brightly lit Showboat hotel and casino beyond the teenage hangout! Lia saw all the teenagers at the Blue Onion hamburger joint sitting in, and on top of, their pretty cars. Some of them had what they called "convertibles". She watched the car hop waitresses' roller skating back and forth between the parked cars and the restaurant's kitchen takeout window. The young rich teenagers were listening to rock-and-roll music while they ordered milk-shakes, french fries, hamburgers, and cokes after they had slowly cruised up and down Fremont Street. Lia was hungry and smelled the delicious food. The teenagers were all laughing and having fun. Now Lia and the old man were a few blocks away from the Blue Onion. Lia was mesmerized as she watched the beautiful young people from the distance. Lia thought American teenagers were so fortunate, and they took it all for granted. Lia knew it was a weekend night and the teens would be having fun. Lia looked through the groups of teens talking. Lia looked to see if she could see Cece or Liz's car. They lived in a great country. They were never hungry. They had all the food they wanted. Lia wished for just a little of the same for her family. Suddenly, Lia saw Cece and reached out her arm as she prepared to yell her name.

Lia did not realize she had taken her eyes off the man, who she was supposed to be watching and following because she was daydreaming about the young lucky Americans. As Lia tried to scream Cece's name something hit the right side of her head. Lia felt her knees buckle, and she went down as she blacked out.

He had to hurry. He was close to his boarded-up motel room, and he needed to get the girl inside before someone saw him. He picked her up and held her as if she were his sleeping daughter on his shoulder while he hurried to the boarded-up motel. He worried if he didn't hurry her blood would dip onto the sidewalk. Her wound was bleeding.

Someone in the distance at the Blue Onion did see something.

Cece had planned to check to see if Lia's family was still in the area. Cece figured after a week the priest would have made other arrangements for them. Suddenly, Cece had one of her feelings and had turned around quickly. Cece saw an older 'stooped over' man picking up a limp girl off the sidewalk about two blocks away. All Cece's friends were talking happily at once. The area was dark but Cece was amazed because she recognized the skirt the girl wore. It was Lia! The old man was not her Father.

Cece grabbed Ian's arm and screamed, "Did you see?"

Ian turned to her and asked, "See what?"

Cece said, "Over there! A strange man has Lia! She's hurt!"

Ian could tell instantly Cece was extremely upset. He turned to look but saw nothing. Cece started running towards the darkened motel. Ian ran up behind her and grabbed her. Ian told her to go back to the Blue Onion and call the police, and he ran towards the boarded-up motel. Ian yelled for her to direct the police. Cece was shaking and yelling at Ian to be careful.

The police cruised the Blue onion often, because of all the teenagers! Cece started screaming for help. Ian turned around when he saw the police vehicle. A small group of frantic teenagers flagged down the slow-moving police car. It was being driven by a female officer, while her partner jumped out to talk to the group of teenagers. Cece couldn't talk fast enough to the police. Cece explained she saw a strange man carrying a young girl who Cece recognized. The man carried the listless girl down a walkway towards a big boarded-up motel complex. Cece was too far away to know exactly which room they would have entered, but she could point out where to start searching. The police yelled at Cece and Ian to get into the back of the police car and they headed towards the last place Cece saw Lia.

The police called for backup. The female officer confirmed she, also, saw a young girl walking behind a man the policewoman thought was her father.

Lia heard a noise. The figure had stirred awake. She closed her eyes and pretended to be asleep. The figure rose from the chair and walked over to Lia. He unzipped his pants and pulled himself out. He held his penis in his hand and urinated on Lia's arms and face. She felt like she wanted to vomit but fought back the urge because she had to continue breathing with a gag in her mouth. She remained very still. He smelled horrible. He removed his trousers along with a gun he had tucked into his belt behind his back. He put the gun at the foot of the bed. He could see the young girl was acting as if she was asleep. He knew it was not possible after he had just violated her, but she kept her eyes closed. He lifted her skirt and ripped her panties off her little body. Her eyes flew open. He laughed and mounted the bed. He straddled her small hips. He untied one arm and grabbed her hand and placed it on his penis. He was erect.

He laughed, "I know you are awake. I am going to rape you now until your tears of pain roll down your cheeks."

He was enjoying frightening her as much as possible before his violent brutality would begin. He ripped her blouse open and chewed on her skin, leaving his teeth marks on her chest. Lia painfully gagged for breath. He brutally felt inside her small vagina. He laughed that she was a virgin. She bled and tried to scream in pain, but the gag was still stuffed into her mouth. She had to make herself breathe if she still wanted to live.

The perpetrator told Lia it was useless. He untied three of her bonds. He left one of her legs tied so he could turn her painful little body over on the bed. He said no one could hear her. He laid down on top of her backside and planned to sodomize her, but Lia fainted. He wanted her awake. He waited. When Lia woke again, she prayed this would end quickly. She was so little and suffering violent pain. The man was off the filthy old mattress and walking across the room looking out the windows. He did not want her to die yet. He wanted to enjoy himself. The man reached for something in the room's corner. He wanted to enjoy torturing her before he continued to sodomize her. Then he would torture her to death with the broken broomstick. He wanted to enjoy watching the blood leaving her body and seeing her eyes go blank as her death approached.

Suddenly, the man jumped. He heard something outside. Lia heard it, but she was too frightened! When he pulled the ragged curtain back to look out the window, the glass was so dirty that he couldn't see anything. He tried to rub a circular spot clean on the glass to look out, but the glass was still filthy. Lia was awakening again. It excited him so much he did not notice he had rubbed some of Lia's vaginal blood, which was still on his hand, onto the windowpane.

Someone noticed the curtain being pulled back, and the side of a man's hand rubbing the dirty glass as he smeared something red onto the glass.

The perpetrator remained still, but he was so caught up at the moment he decided the noise was nothing but a stray animal. He wanted to carry on with his exciting plan. He would again proceed with his pleasure of tormenting the awakened young girl.

Lia was sobbing in unbelievable pain while she prayed. He turned her body back over again, exposing her bloody chest so she could watch him. She saw he was holding a dirty old broomstick. He cracked the broomstick over his knee.

Someone heard it, as well. They ran for backup!

Lia could barely move. Lia felt she was getting weaker from her loss of blood. He was parading around the room while he held the broom's jagged handle up into the air. He unconsciously laughed out loud. He was much too boisterous with his exhilaration! Lia forced herself to slowly reach down into her skirt pocket. He walked over to the bed as she was sobbing and shaking her head back and forth to say 'No'! Her fingers folded tightly around the knife in her pocket.

The monster laughed. He sat on the bed next to the fragile little girl. He placed the rounded top of the broom handle between her tiny little legs, barely touching her vulva. Lia's eyes opened wide as she prayed frantically. Lia was only a little girl, but she was smart enough to know this was a very evil man. He would harm her more and then he was going to kill her. He was too excited to notice Lia slowly pulled something out of her skirt's pocket.

He began to insert the broomstick slowly into her vagina and enjoyed the show as he pushed the stick up a little. He desired seeing this young trash die from bleeding to death before his eyes. It was the same way he had killed the other girls. He laughed, watching the weak little whore suffer in anticipation of what he was planning to do to her. He wanted to take his time tormenting her even more. It excited him tremendously.

By some unknown miracle, Lia gathered up all her strength and sat up as high as possible as she plunged the knife into the monster's neck. He looked shocked. He gazed at her in a stupor. His shock showed in his wide, bewildered, and surprised eyes. She must have hit his jugular vein. Blood erupted from his neck. He grabbed at his neck as if he could stop the blood flowing from the jagged knife wound. Lia suddenly realized she had a chance to survive. She didn't want to kill this man, but she definitely wanted to survive. Lia jabbed the knife again into the man's neck a second time. Then Lia threw the knife across the room. Lia kicked the broomstick away. Blood was spurting out from the pervert's neck even more. He continued to try using both his hands to stop the flow of blood. It was useless. His eyes and face looked like he was in shock because of what the little girl had accomplished.

The pervert thought, "How could this be possible? I tortured grown women who couldn't fight me. This is only a little girl."

Blood continued spurting from his neck.

He screamed out loud, "You little bitch! I'm gonna kill you!"

Wrong.

Lia could see the pain on his face as he gagged for more breath. Lia kicked at him. Lia tore a dirty rag off her head and pulled the gag out of her mouth with her free hands. She wanted to untie her other leg, but the pervert kept getting in her way as he jumped around trying to slow the flow of blood from his neck.

Lia gathered up all her strength and screamed as loud as she could, "Ayuda! Ayuda! Ayuda!"

The dying killer looked at Lia and thought, "What the fuck?"

He tried to scream at Lia to shut up through his coughing and suffocating pain, which would soon relieve him at Satan's door. No sound emanated from the fiend's mouth except his gurgling noises. He tried to regain control of his broomstick weapon, but it was futile because Lia managed to kick it off the bed. The man's blood continued to gush and flow freely as he doubled over. He realized he had to stand up. He grabbed for the gun he had placed on the foot of the bed. His right hand held his neck. His left hand found the gun.

In a rush of blood streaming from her own body's wounds, Lia's weakened torso fell backwards onto the bed.

Lia resigned herself to it being the time of her death, too.

Suddenly the door of the sleazy motel room was kicked inward as it slammed open and hit the wall behind it with a ferocious impact. Lia could see the armed male police officer who had abruptly kicked the door open, while a female police officer ran in and planted her feet in a shooting position as she scanned her gun across the room. The policewoman saw the pervert aiming his gun and fired off a shot at him, as the weakened pervert tried to point his weapon at the male officer. The male officer made sure the perpetrator was restrained and disarmed as he bled to death. The female officer ran to the aid of the child. The officers were worried they may have been too late. They had called for backup, and a silent ambulance had already arrived. They gave the child reassurances, but she kept frantically screaming Cece's name.

A police helicopter flew overhead as Ian held a sobbing Cece at a distance back by the police car. Other police were securing the grounds of the boarded-up motel. Street people started coming out of all the doors of the abandoned motel to see what was happening. More police stormed the motel and began lining people up against walls.

Because Cece wanted to follow the paramedics, Ian kept explaining to Cece the professionals had to have space to assist Lia. As the paramedics brought Lia out of the room, the dazed little girl spotted Cece and reached out her arms towards her. The paramedics asked for Cece's help to calm the child. Cece got into the ambulance with Lia as they hugged each other. Ian ran to the car to follow them to Southern Nevada Memorial Hospital's emergency entrance.

A few months before Lia's abduction:

The big headlines of the cowboy sheriff's election had hit the front pages of the newspapers. People were excited and hoping crime would go down especially the whispered woman killer's crimes. The new sheriff was big, mean, and out to clean up downtown Las Vegas. The situation with Lia and her family was covered up. The community officials came together to aid Lia's family. It would have been devastating news to the community if the truth got out. The Las Vegas community would have been outraged. Lia was only a little girl. Two weeks after Lia's abduction, the police found one more female body decomposing in another motel. Apparently, the coroner determined the other murder was committed one week before Lia was tortured, and in the same manner as many other young women had been mutilated to death in the recent past. The sheriff realized the broomstick killer had been getting bolder right before the police had to defend themselves against him to save Lia, but the fact that Lia fought back was outstanding for such a young girl.

The new sheriff figured they got their man when a flustered motel desk clerk stated a scarred face man gave him cash money for a three-week stay. Vito must have gambled and was lucky. There were abandoned casino chips all over the motel room's floor. Police thought Vito had to get away fast for a reason or just for his own paranoia. The scarred man had told the desk clerk to prohibit anyone from 'disturbing his honeymoon' until he notified the clerk they were leaving. When the man didn't notify the clerk of an extension or pay anymore rent, the clerk went to the room's door and smelled a horrible stench emanating from the room.

There was no DNA evidence in the 1960s to be collected and saved, but they had the pervert's bloody fingerprints at every scene where the female bodies had been recovered. They caught the dying maniac red-handed with Lia. The sheriff knew it was miraculous Cece saw the girl being carried away and Ian sought the police.

Cold-blooded politicians, casino owners, and business owners repeatedly asked, "Why would anyone even care if the girls were only prostitutes?"

People were silenced to 'protect' the community's reputation.

Las Vegas had elected their new tough cowboy sheriff in hopes the pervert would become frightened and leave Las Vegas. After most of the killings, spaced approximately one week to one month apart, the horrible murders finally stopped. No more bodies were found. All motels and hotels were put on notice. Every boarded-up hotel and motel room was checked and searched. The new Sheriff insisted on the demolition of the rundown motels or holding the owners responsible for hiring a security company to guard them constantly. Crime went down tremendously. The sheriff was sure they got their man, but in the Las Vegas community, people weren't sure if the 'peaceful time' would last.

Because of the cover-up, the pervert seemed to just disappear into thin air. No one ever found out who the murderer was except the police and the mob. The speculation was the murderer may have been murdered by some girl's pimp. Other people said the murderer may have been put in prison for another crime and was behind bars. That news frightened the women of Las Vegas even more.

Women thought, "Would the murderer start again when he got out of jail?" Some people thought mobsters got him because he was destroying the reputation of Las Vegas. Many in Las Vegas community thought the murderer feared the newly elected 'Cowboy Sheriff' and maybe he left town because the new Sheriff figured out who he was. The sheriff became even more popular!

Unknown downtown businesses and city benefactors made sure Lia and her family were well cared for and hushed up. Whatever Lia or her family needed, they got. Cece visited Lia every day in the hospital and was considered a good family friend.

* * *

The new Las Vegas Sheriff sat behind his desk with his arms crossed over his chest as one of his teams entered his private office. He stood up and smiled at his officers, and he especially smiled at the one young female officer and her male partner. They were all very proud of themselves.

The Sheriff said, "I take pride in all of you and the highly honorable teamwork every one of you put into this case. It was a real son of a bitch! Remember, we should strictly keep all of this between us. You are never to talk about any of this information to anyone else, at any time, for the rest of your lives. Do not even talk amongst yourselves, or else you will have to face me. I would like none of you to ever forget what I just told you. Can I have your word?"

Every one of them smiled and agreed to gladly give their word. In those days, their word meant something, and they liked their new gutsy sheriff.

Sammie never saw Vito again. He was relieved. How could someone go so wrong? Sammie figured Vito moved on to a different town or just died as an unknown vagrant on the streets. As far as Sammie knew, Vito had never been fingerprinted. It was better Sammie didn't know the truth.

Las Vegas enjoyed their town's good reputation for better protection. Everything seemed to settle down as soon as the new 'Cowboy' sheriff got into office. No more tortured female bodies turned up. The new sheriff did have a reputation for being a mean son of a bitch! No one ever heard of the broomstick killer again.

Vito's body rotted in a deep, secret, well hidden, hard-packed dirt grave outside of the Las Vegas Metropolitan area. They buried it in an unmarked place far up into the rugged forest of the high steep Sheep Mountain range north of the City of Las Vegas. Only one person knew where the grave was. That very trusted person would tell no one where the body was buried, or else he may have to answer to the newly elected sheriff of Clark County, Nevada, and his Petrone.

It hasn't yet been estimated how many mountain hikers have walked on the trail above the grave, and it never will be, because the person who buried the body finally died himself. There was a huge mob funeral.

Meanwhile across the United States:

Unfortunately, an innocent wife and mother was murdered by mobsters for not revealing information she did not know. If the mob had gotten the information on Vito's death a little sooner, Marge probably would have been left alone. The mob got the information a day too late to stop her retaliation murder. It seemed things in Vegas were immediately 'Hushed Up'.

Marge's body, also, rotted in a similar unmarked grave back in the eastern United States. Marge's parents and Marge's children would never know what really happened to Marge or Vito. What Marge's parents suspected could never be proved. The mob had been convinced Marge really didn't know where her husband had gone. It was too bad and too late. Marge was murdered for nothing. The local mobsters were satisfied after they heard from Las Vegas Vito wasn't a problem anymore. They enjoyed the news about the way he died and how he was buried.

When it came to the subject of Vito's wife, Marge, the mobsters' philosophy was, "Well, that's what the stupid bitch gets for marrying a piece of shit."

Marge's two elderly parents and her two children were allowed to live. The mobsters thought them to be innocent. They liked old folks and young kids. Besides, someone had to raise them. Who could do a better job of raising children than their own grandparents? The mob made sure that unknown benefactors sent money and gifts on a regular basis to Marge's parents for their grandchildren and for their college funds. No one ever figured out who the benefactors were, but the mob knew, and the 'High-level Mobster' was finally satisfied.

* * *

Lia survived her terrible initiation to Las Vegas, Nevada. It was a difficult time, but she was a strong-minded, beautiful young lady with a determined inner spirit of strength. She grew up to be a scholar and a fine young woman. Her family knew God. The city of Las Vegas helped her family and Lia to gain legal access to the United States of America with their citizenships. Lia won a scholarship to the University of Nevada, Las Vegas. Lia became one of the first Spanish American female police officers in Las Vegas, Nevada. Lia and her entire family still live in Las Vegas today and proudly call Las Vegas their home.

Chapter 9

YOUNG LOVE

CECE's parents had finally settled permanently in Las Vegas. Cece felt four high schools in four years was enough for anyone to go through. She prepared to start her last year of high school. Carmella gave her materials to sew five different outfits for school. When school started Cece could tell which students had parents who worked in the casinos. They had new vehicles to drive or were picked up and dropped off at school in expensive cars. The boys were well groomed and nicely dressed. The girls had designer outfits for everyday of the month with different purses and shoes to match! Cece couldn't help but wonder how big their closets must have been. Many of the high school girls wore makeup while she had no makeup and only five outfits. One outfit for each day of the week. Sammie bought an old jalopy of a car from a desperate gambler for $50.00 for Cece to drive. Cece prayed daily she would make it safely to school and back home.

She thought, "Why me? Why do strange things happen to me?"

God must have thought Cece was strong.

Cece made it to school her first month ok. She was especially happy because her recent friend, Lia and Lia's Family, were in good hands. She was now in her second month of High School. She prayed everyday her jalopy would make it home again. She had an ominous feeling as she walked to her jalopy after school. She excused the thought by telling herself she would be careful driving home. Oh, it was still a sweltering day even after summer ended! Cece got in the jalopy, and of course, it didn't have air conditioning. She rolled both jalopy's front windows halfway down for airflow and took off for home.

A new friend, Randy, pulled up beside her as they were leaving the school parking lot and yelled, "Hey, Cece, want to drag?"

It seemed her new male classmates loved her old jalopy, or maybe it was Cece. The guys were all very friendly with her. Cece didn't understand the girls. They gave her dirty looks and acted very conceited. Randy befriended Cece quickly and told her not to say anything about what he was going to tell her. Cece told him that whatever it was, she would be discreet.

Randy said, "All the girls are afraid of you. The senior guys think you are really nice, smart, and pretty, but those guys don't want their girlfriends to be mad at them for being nice to you. The guys think your jalopy is cool, too!"

Cece was thinking, "How could this jalopy possibly be cool!"

She smiled at Randy and told him, "I've got a boyfriend in California. The girls don't have to worry about me. I've got to get home so no dragging for me. See you tomorrow, Randy, and thanks for being so nice to me!"

Randy yelled back, "Hey, it's my pleasure, pretty lady! See you tomorrow."

Cece drove to the corner of West Fremont Street and South Decatur Blvd at the front side of Western High School. She needed to turn right to go home, which was just under 2 miles away. Because of road construction, there were concrete barriers on both sides of the cars going into the right turn lane heading west. As Cece came to the stop, she heard a huge POW! Another car was behind her and had followed her into the right turn lane with many more cars behind it. Cece immediately looked up into her rear-view mirror. She saw a young couple who were maybe 10 years older than her. The POW sounded like a huge gun went off. It scared her so much. Cece started shaking. She was, also, thinking of what she would have to do after a tire blowout. There were no phones anywhere near her. No one had cell phones in those days. She was in a strange city with no one to help her. Randy had already left in the opposite direction. She thought of her beautiful Aunt Rebecca being at the mercy of just anyone. Cece was so exasperated she put her forehead onto her hands as she held onto the big hot steering wheel and said a little prayer. Just then a man walked up and used his knuckles to rap on her passenger side window. She didn't expect him to be there. He realized he had startled Cece.

The kind looking stranger said, "Don't be afraid! Everything's going to be alright. I need your keys. I am going to unlock your trunk and get what I need to change your tire. You had a blowout. Please give me your keys. You can just sit where you are and wait. We have lots of traffic behind our two cars waiting to turn right. No one can move because there are these concrete barriers on both sides of all our cars. Until I fix the tire, we all will be stuck in this traffic jam. It won't take me very long. Everything's going to be alright. Don't worry, Miss, please."

Cece managed a questionable and weak, "Thank you very much."

When the strong young man spoke to Cece, he was a very matter of fact, but his voice was authoritative and extremely calming. She could feel herself beginning to relax. Cece felt a bit embarrassed as the incident made her upset, frightened and very hot causing droplets to form on her temples.

There was a gentle knock on the front passenger's side window! Cece was apprehensive. She was grateful this wasn't happening in California. She turned to look. The young man's very sweet wife was getting into Cece's car.

The woman said, "Hi, I am married to the man who is changing your tire. Don't be afraid. Everything's going to be alright. We can just wait right here. In the desert it is wise to always carry some extra water. I brought you a cup of water from our car. Drink it. It will only take my husband a few minutes to change the tire!"

Cece was looking strangely at the big oversized glass of water but drank it down gratefully. It wasn't the normal water in Las Vegas, and water wasn't bottled yet. It was so cool and delicious! Cece felt instantly better.

They waited in an awkward silence because Cece was too bewildered to speak. She felt the whole situation was somehow too surreal. These two people were exceptionally kind! Why? It almost felt like a dream. She was thinking of the dilapidated vehicle. It was such an old car. The young husband quickly put everything back into the trunk. He approached the passenger's side door, opened it, and held his hand out for his gracious wife to exit the old jalopy. When the wife got out, the couple closed the door. The husband put his other arm through the half-opened window and held out Cece's keys.

Cece smiled and turned to look at them as she said, "Thank you both, very, very much!"

They leaned down together to look in at Cece through the half-opened passenger's side window.

They both smiled and said in perfect unison, "Ok, young lady, you're welcome! You are all set to go. Drive safely."

Cece kept saying thank you to them as they walked away. She watched them get into the car behind her car. Cece waved to them. Through her rear-view mirror, she saw them waved back to her. She had particularly noticed their perfect manner of calm unisonous speaking. Cece thought it was quite strange. It was almost as if they just went around helping stranded people and were well practiced at it!

Cece thought, "Wow, how odd! They were so COOL! It was nice to meet them even though I was apprehensive! I wish I wasn't so upset and could have spoken more to them. I guess after California I was a bit afraid. They were both very kind."

Cece smiled and waved a last time into her rear-view mirror as they both smiled and waved back to her in return. Cece felt like she was in a fairytale. Cece thought the couple was too good to be true. It was almost as if they were heaven sent. Cece thought, "What kind of wonderful people lived here in Vegas?"

Cece thought, "Did all this really just happen to me?"

As Cece started to make her right turn. She looked into her rear-view mirror. The kind couple was completely gone! They had disappeared. Their car had disappeared, too. There was an unfamiliar man in the car behind her. He was alone. Cece couldn't believe it! Shocked, Cece slowed down to 5 mph.

That man behind her yelled out his window at Cece's slow-moving vehicle, "Are you ok, Miss?"

Cece yelled out her window, "Yes, thank you! What happened to the couple behind me?"

The gentleman answered nicely, "I've been behind you for quite a while now. We all have been waiting to turn right. I haven't seen any other people except you in front of me."

Cece could feel her eyes grow wide. Cece thought, "Oh my goodness, where did they go?"

Cece waved thank you to the man and sped up. Cece thought, "Did that really just happen to me? Their car couldn't have jumped the concrete barriers on both sides of them. There were cars lined up behind them! Where did they go? We were all waiting to make the right turn. They couldn't have all backed up because that would have taken an hour. The kind gentleman did change the tire quickly. Did I even really have a blown-out tire? This man behind me did not see the kind young couple! Please God, tell me this just happened!"

Then Cece felt a mental flash of wings and smiled. She was sure she had an encounter with two wonderful spiritual beings.

When Cece got home, Sammie was there, which was unusual. She told her Dad what had happened. Sammie checked the trunk. He confirmed there was a blown-out tire inside the trunk. Sammie asked her for the keys. He said he'd take the tire to be replaced right away so she would have another safe spare. Cece watched her Dad leaving.

Cece thought to herself, "They really did help me! I could not have imagined them. I had a blown-out tire! Oh, good, thank you, God! Now I know, for sure, God is with me! This Las Vegas 'place' isn't going to be so bad after all. There're angels here! I met them today! Thank You!"

Cece originally thought Las Vegas was going to be a dreadful city, but so far, she had encountered above normal people. At least there weren't any men trying to pull her into their cars while speaking foreign languages. Cece almost felt like she was leading a charmed life. Her parents were exceptional, and so was Ian. Sometimes the things that happened to her seemed so wonderfully bizarre. Ian felt almost surreal to her, too. It was as if Cece wanted to hold on tightly to him forever and never let him go. She missed and loved him. When Ian was with her, she felt completely safe and loved.

You can imagine Cece's delight when she was getting ready to leave for school the next morning. It was a Friday. She opened the front door to leave as Rod and Ian were pulling up to her front door ready to take her to school. It was Friday. That made Cece happy because she missed Ian so much over the summer. Ian and Rod both had Fridays offed on their college schedules so they could really enjoy weekends in Vegas.

Carmella saw how happy the three of them were and fed everyone a lovely breakfast. Carmella announced Cece was getting straight A's so she could have the day off, too, and they could all go explore the Las Vegas community together. Cece couldn't believe Carmella gave her the day off to go 'run and play'!

Carmella said, "Why not, Cece? You've earned it. You've just started school, and you're carrying all straight A average in your classes. I checked. I know I can trust you. You are a responsible young woman. You know right from wrong. Most of all, I know I can trust Ian to take good care of you and to protect you. Now he's got a backup with Rod. Go have fun!"

They did just that. Ian loved to take good care of his girl.

They took off toward Mt. Charleston. The Rolling Stones were singing "I can't get no satisfaction" on the car's radio. There still wasn't any snow. Cece's first sight of those vast Pine trees thrilled her. She thought she saw a beautiful bulletin board and pointed for the guys to look! Instead, it turned out to be a large buck leading his herd of deer. Rod stopped the car and the big buck led his herd across the road right in front of Rod's car. Cece kept commenting on how very beautiful they were. It was the first time she ever saw a deer. Rod and Ian had huge smiles on their faces as they watched. They saw new clean beautiful campsites with bar-be-ques. Ian said maybe they could return to camp or spend a restful day there. The birds were gorgeous, too. There were small shanty cabins in what was called "Old Town", but they were tiny, locked, and private. There was an elementary school, a library, a fire station, and a ranger station nearby. Up the road was the Mt. Charleston lodge. It was large and had a restaurant and bar. They hiked around the Deer Creek area. That creek was flowing. It was so pretty at Mount Charleston. Cece understood why Vegas folks affectionately called it Mount Charlie.

Time seemed to pass quickly for Ian and Cece! They were both so naturally high on life and being together. It felt like 'someone' was always timing them. Cece would look over at Ian and pray to God she would have him in her life for as long as possible. She wanted him to be the father of her two sons. Ian was a very handsome, intelligent, kind, fun, good, and fearless man. No one told her she was going to have two sons in the future. Cece just knew Ian was a man who would father sons. Just like she always dreamed she would have someday.

On the way back to Vegas, the three of them were talking about the layout of the city. The west end of town was a newer area and a desirable place to live, but also the most expensive. They asked what areas went to her high school. Cece told them about the more industrial area North and along Bonanza Road. Teens, who lived in that area, also went to her school. Ian asked about the Moulin Rouge and Cece got all excited. She told them how it was a place where Afro-American performers, singers, musicians, and dancers performed. Cece said every cool kid she spoke to about it said the place was a great 'Hot Spot' and they all wanted to go there, but people didn't go there unless they got an invitation. Cece loved gospel, blues, and rock-and-roll music since she was the young blond child sitting on the steps of the little white church waiting for her Dad on Sunday mornings in Florida many years ago.

Cece said almost everyone seemed nice at school. Ian and Rod were saying they were thrilled at college. Mondays always came fast. The boys left at noon on Sunday to go back to LA to get some sleep for college the next day.

Cece felt exhausted. After sleeping Sunday night, Cece somehow managed to get out the door at 6:30 a.m. on Monday morning. School started at 7:00 a.m. She drove the old jalopy to school. She saw a school bus and felt compelled to park next to it. She got out of her jalopy and gathered up her things to bring to class. Cece began walking towards the school's entrance. She was oblivious to what was happening.

After walking only a few yards passing in front of the bus, Cece heard screaming and yelling. Cece looked up and saw the school bus still had lots of young Afro-American men inside of it. Lots of boys on the school bus were yelling at her to get out of the way. Cece had stopped so close to the bus she could talk to the guys on the bus. They weren't exiting the bus. They kept telling Cece to get out of the way. It seemed all the girls had already debarked the bus and went into school. Cece began to look around because there was yelling behind her.

Cece saw white boys behind their cars as they were facing the side of the school bus. The white boys began yelling for Cece to go inside and get out of their way. Cece noticed no girls with them either. Cece did notice one skinny 'Puny Guy', who kept throwing his arms up into the air and trying to agitate all the guys on both sides, to start fighting. He didn't have a gun, but he had a totally negative mouth full of hatred.

The Puny Guy looked excited and happy to stir up trouble as he was yelling, "Shoot! Shoot! Shoot!"

While standing still and looking around trying to figure out what was happening, Cece saw two police cars pulling up into the school parking lot. Their sirens were on and their lights were flashing. She saw two TV news cars pull in behind the police cars. The TV newsmen jumped out and were setting up cameras. Police were yelling on loudspeakers at everyone and telling them not to get close to the school bus. Cece felt frozen in place. She realized something was terribly wrong and she was standing right in the middle of it.

Cece thought, "Please God, send your angels to help me!"

A frightened Cece had already learned what to do, but she didn't realize it.

The TV cameras were pointing at the school bus. Cece realized this was a dangerous problem when she saw all the boys, on both sides, had handguns. They were pointing guns at each other with her right in the middle of their confrontation! She stood dead in her tracks. Cece got mad! Cece always seemed to get along better with boys than she did with girls. Now she would have to prove it!

Cece threw her arms up as her books fell to the ground and she screamed out, "What are all of you guys doing? Are you crazy? Don't you recognize each other? You better stop and think! Do you all want to die today? I don't, but it could happen!"

The wide-eyed Puny Guy crouched down and sort of slivered away through their parked cars towards the school's entrance. All the guys were watching Cece. Cece 'would' remember Puny Guy, the agitator, but Cece had more important matters at hand to consider.

Cece screamed, "Most of you are on the senior varsity and junior varsity football, baseball, and basketball teams. Some of you are on the track teams. You're each other's best friends. Who put you up to this? Some cheap talker? Is it the Puny Guy, who just ran away scared towards the school entrance? Where is he now? He's smart enough to get out of here, I need to talk to him after I finish talking to you guys."

Cece stopped while all the guys looked and saw 'Puny Guy' running for cover toward the school.

Cece could hear all the boys saying, "Yeah look over there, Man. He's running away! He didn't even bring a gun and he organized all this mess! We 'are' friends!"

Cece continued, "Who's going to win this week's games if you guys kill each other? It's for sure not going to be the stupid knot-head who started this fight! Hey, Terrance, what about that winning touchdown last Friday night? That was big, but you would have never made it happen if it wasn't for George defending you! You guys are all teammates, and each other's best friends. You work together, not apart! What are you all thinking?"

The police Sergeant saw his chance and ran up to try to pull Cece out of the middle of the boys' confrontation. She saw him running up to her. Cece immediately sat down on the parking lot pavement between the bus and the boys behind their parked cars. It upset her thinking she might have a big grease spot on her skirt bottom all day at school, and she could lose one of her five outfits, but this was more important. These guys were her classmates and her friends, too.

Cece yelled out, "Well, okay, if that's the way you guys want it. Start shooting. Kill a girl. You are all a bunch of big bullies! See which ones of you will be heroes tomorrow for killing a defenseless girl. Embarrass your parents while they agonize over their sons losing their lives for nothing or going to prison! Wait until they find out all you stupid idiots used your father's guns to kill each other! They are going to be broken-hearted if you all go through with this fight! Do you really want to break your mother's hearts and shame your fathers? Wow, you guys are real men, huh? You better start thinking and stop acting like the girls in this school act!"

All the noise stopped. No one said a word.

Cece yelled out, "What's wrong? Maybe it's too much testosterone! Dying for no good reason is ridiculous! Just think of how awful this will be for your fathers. They will know you guys stole their guns for this awful fight! They will want to die, too. Your mothers will suffer and cry. Is that what you really want?"

The Sergeant saw his chance. He ran forward with his arms up in the air.

The Sergeant called out, "All right, you guys, I know you don't want to hurt this pretty young lady. I heard you all saying to get her out of the way, but she's stubborn. She's not going to move. You all know her, and she certainly knows all of you. So, what are you guys going to do?"

Everyone on both sides could be heard saying things like they didn't want to hurt Cece, they were only into the beginning of their school year, and they were good friends.

The Sergeant pointed and said, "Ok, Guys, half of the police officers are going to get on the bus and collect your weapons, and the other half of the police officers will collect the weapons from you, Guys, behind your cars. Your parents can redeem the weapons after school at the police station downtown. Do all you, Guys, on both sides understand?"

Cece could hear affirmative mumbling from both sides. The boys really didn't want a gunfight that some idiot talked them into.

As the Sergeant gave Cece a hand to help her up off the pavement he said, "Young lady, I certainly don't know who you are or how you did it, but you stopped a situation here that could have been very devastating to many families, the Clark County School System, the Las Vegas community, and to the State of Nevada! We almost made it on the national news today! When this call came in, we didn't know the severity of the situation. We weren't prepared for a disaster. You are a very strong-willed young woman. Your parents should be proud. Come on, I'll walk you to your class and away from the cameras."

Reporters were yelling they wanted to interview the young woman, who stopped the gunfight, but the police sergeant waved them down. The cameras kept filming Cece as she walked towards the entrance of Western High School.

Cece replied to the Sergeant, "Sir, I don't know how this all happened. I just felt compelled to park there next to the bus. These kinds of things just seem to happen to me and have happened to me throughout my life! Their parents are going to be very mad at them. They really are all a bunch of nice guys. They are friends. I'm sure when their parents find out they brought their Dad's guns to school; it will set things on both sides. If the boys are smart, their parents will be, too. Hopefully today will help end whatever has been happening around our community. They are all on the athletic teams. I think if a police Sergeant talked to their team's coaches, it would definitely help nip 'all this' in the bud, Sir!"

The Sergeant agreed with Cece, "Good idea! I will take care of that, too, Miss."

They walked into the school building. When they arrived at her classroom, the Sergeant stayed in the hallway and told Cece to please quietly tell the teacher to meet him out in the hallway before she went to her desk.

Cece told the teacher and went to sit down.

As soon as the teacher left the room, she heard a boy announce to the full classroom while pointing at Cece, "This is the dumb girl who walked right into the middle of the fight making it impossible for us guys to fire our weapons like we had all planned to do."

The Sergeant and the teacher in the hall, also, could hear the boy telling the news to Cece's classmates, but the police Sergeant put his forefinger up to his lips as he held the teacher back. The Sergeant wanted more information.

Cece rolled her eyes as she recognized the boy was the instigator. He was the 'Puny Guy'. He was the one who ran into the school building after setting up the confrontation.

Cece stood up and looked right at Puny Guy and said, "I thought you were the Puny Guy, who I saw running into the building as the guys were all getting ready to shoot! You're the stupid knot-head organizer who started the confrontation! Why did you run away and hide? Why are you hiding in here and acting like a big shot now? You are a coward! You talked all of them into bringing guns, and you didn't bring a gun, why?"

The police Sergeant heard Cece finish and came around the classroom door as he looked at Puny Guy and said, "I'd like to know that information, too, Son, and I could absolutely bet your parents need to know as well! Come with me!"

Puny Guy sat down and shut his mouth, but the sergeant curled up his index finger and said, "Come here, Boy, now. You're coming with me."

That night, Cece told Ian over the phone about what had happened at school. Ian was concerned and told Cece to be careful. He said anyone could harbor ill feelings over her involvement. He wanted to know who the Puny Guy was.

Carmella and Sammie watched Cece on the news again eleven years after her first time on the news in Miami. They asked why she didn't leave.

Cece said, "It wouldn't have been the right thing to do!"

Carmella said, "Ian's got his hands full with you, Cece! You must really have a very strong Angel!"

Sammie just smiled and quietly shook his head as he said, "She definitely does, maybe even more than one!"

Cece nodded her head, thought about her blown-out tire, raised one eyebrow, smiled at her parents, and said, "Maybe, two other angels, and that's not even including Ian and you both!"

* * *

Ian and Rod arrived in Vegas the following Friday afternoon because they were delayed by college tests. They were out in the parking lot in front of Western high school with the hood up on Rod's new souped-up car while they waited for Cece to come out of school. Randy had a bunch of jocks looking under Rod's hood when she finally walked out of the school. Ian spotted her immediately as he admired her from afar.

Ian thought, "She's my girl!"

Puny Guy knew nothing about Ian.

Puny Guy saw Cece walking out of the school, too, and yelled out loud for everyone to hear, "Hey, everyone, that's the stupid girl who stopped the gunfight last Monday morning!"

Cece froze in her tracks. The crowd went completely quiet. Cece's eyes searched out Puny Guy. All eyes were on them. Ian caught Cece's eyes looking at Puny Guy. Ian was getting angry. Ian's protective mode kicked into gear. He was already on his way to the guy who Cece was watching. Rod was his backup, followed by Randy and all the guys on the football team. The crowd around Puny guy was stepping back away from him. Cece hurried over towards Puny Guy. She knew Ian was somewhere waiting to pick her up, and she didn't want Ian to hurt the wimp. Everyone was staring at her.

Suddenly heads turned through the crowd as people heard Ian's forceful voice saying, "Excuse me. Excuse me, let me through, please, NOW!"

Puny Guy had a cocky smile on his face as he sneered at Cece with contempt. Cece didn't know what Ian would do to Puny. Puny spotted the tall man walking toward him as Ian asked the crowd to excuse him. The glowing man was big, tall, muscular, and in a hurry. Puny cringed. He realized he was the target of the big man's stare. Puny knew he was in trouble. He felt weak-kneed. Cece grabbed the glowing man's muscular arm and whispered into his ear. Puny Guy felt weaker.

Ian reached for Puny's elbow in front of the large captured crowd and loudly said, "Cece belongs to me. Do not harm her. Protect her with all your might, or else I will find you and I will take care of you myself! Be nice to your classmates. Grow up! Do you understand me?"

Puny thought he felt a warm trickle running down his leg. He grabbed his lap with one hand and covered himself with the books he carried with his other hand. He put his head down and hurried off in quick little shuffling steps towards his parent's car. But Puny's parents saw the whole encounter. Urine was running down Puny's legs and into his shoes. Kids started laughing and pointing at him. Ian lifted his head up and started looking around at the crowd. Everyone immediately became quiet.

Ian announced to the crowd, "None of this is funny! It's time to go home."

The crowd quickly dispersed.

Puny Guy knew to leave Cece alone after meeting Ian. He would try to respect her. Everyone else watched and everyone else learned. Because of Ian's emphatic mannerism toward Puny, he eventually apologized to everyone. Puny's exasperated parents decided to send him off to military school.

Ian and Rod had driven up to Vegas on weekends for approximately five months before Ian's dad couldn't take it anymore. His wife was complaining about Cece. A family fight broke out, and Ian was given an ultimatum. Ian was to quit going to Vegas to see Cece or to leave home. Ian said he would rather die than lose Cece.

Ian told his father, "Cece is the most moral person whom I have ever known. She is kind and loving. Cece is my life and the best thing that ever happened to me."

Ian didn't say anything else. Ian went into the kitchen and got a big paper grocery bag. He took it upstairs and put his few things in it. He walked down the stairs and out the front door and never looked back. His three little brothers were crying. His parents accelerated their argument.

When Ian arrived in Vegas, he went directly to Janey's boyfriend's home. Cece's friend, Janey, had a boyfriend whose mother, Mabel, had a room for rent. The room for rent was near downtown Las Vegas. Ian eventually got a job at their favorite downtown hotel and casino hangout. Ian was too young for the casino work, but not too young to go to war and die. He got a restaurant job on the graveyard shift. Ian was 18. He made friends with the casino and hotel owner. The lonely owner ate at the coffee shop very late every night. The owner loved to tell his good ole cowboy's life stories and Ian loved to listen to his adventures. They became fast friends. The owner told Ian someday he would give Ian a job as a dealer if he wanted the job when he got back from his service duty. Ian had just enlisted in the United States Army. The Army recruiter told Ian he could get him into the Army's new computer division because of his high IQ. The Army would not remember their promise. Ian scored high for shooting every type of weapon.

The casino owner 'would' remember his promise.

Before they knew what was happening, Ian was getting ready to leave. Cece was beside herself with worry. The Army put Ian into clerical work to train in the Army's new computers department. Ian was amazed because he had never had any training or experience with guns or rifles. The Army doctors asked about his origin. When they found out he was from the Southern United States, they put it all together. They told Ian men from that region of the country were experts with guns and rifles. Southerners, because of their keen eyes and their good coordination, were able to feed their families by hunting squirrels during the Civil War. Ian was a descendant of Southern folks. Rifle proficiency meant the difference between starving or surviving for Southern families during the Civil War. Ian was suddenly very important to the Army. There weren't many American sharpshooters with the natural abilities of seeing enemies waiting in tree camouflage to ambush Americans soldiers. Before Ian knew it, his basic training was completed. They assigned him to Fort Bliss in El Paso, Texas in an Army personnel office, but the U.S. Army had to decide. Ian's high IQ with computers or Ian's Sharpshooting.

Ian wanted Cece. He needed her. He loved her. She loved Ian. They got married and Ian brought Cece back to El Paso, Texas. Cece remembered Texas from passing through it on her family's trek west from Florida to California. She loved Texas. They had to find a place of their own. It was difficult because soldiers and their families were continuously coming and going at Fort Bliss. Most vacancies were rented within a 24-hour period. At the end of a day of exasperation, they spotted a tiny 'Trailer for rent' sign on Dyer Blvd. It was a dump, but Cece made it spotless!

Ian had lots of work at his recent assignment. He loved it and looked forward to computer training courses. Ian had to bring in his new bride for processing. When Cece walked into the Army office all the men instantly stood up. Cece was amazed at their manners. It was the way all men should learn to be. Ian was very proud of his bride. The personnel office gave Cece a new social security card with her new name on it. The soldiers continued to smile and stare at her. Cece was a little self-conscious while they all made small talk and joked around with her. They all stayed around the camera while they took her pictures.

Finally, Sergeant Johnson said, "Ok, men, everyone back to work."

Sergeant Johnson led Ian to the corner of the office, "You did good, Son!"

Ian just said, "Cece is a wonderful person. She loves me very much, and I love her even more. Her appearance is a bonus."

Sergeant Johnson just smiled proudly, "Not to mention she's gorgeous!"

Ian blushed and said, "Thanks."

Ian and Cece's first ten months of marital life was bliss turned into a prolonged honeymoon. Time passed like the wink of an eye. Cece and Ian expected to be transferred to Germany because of the talk in Ian's Army personnel office. Ian had been told he would probably go to Germany. Cece wasn't so sure about Germany, but she just wanted to be with Ian no matter where he went. Fate changed the Army's plans.

Suddenly the President of the United States ordered an all-out offensive in Vietnam. Ian came home with the news on a Friday. Cece broke down. They had only been married for ten months. She didn't want to lose her husband now. He was her life. What would she do? She cried for the entire weekend. Ian held her tightly in his arms. Ian told Cece he knew why he was being shipped out.

Ian said, "Lots of soldiers had high IQs and could learn computers, but few soldiers had the eyes of a sharpshooting squirrel hunter."

Cece looked at her man in a puzzled amazement and asked, "What?"

Ian explained to Cece everything he was told. She looked at him and asked what it meant. Ian explained computers were new to the Army, but sharp shooters were rare, and what the Army needed right then were sharpshooters to fight in the jungles of Vietnam.

Ian was shipped out to Vietnam within 10 months of their marriage date. Ian arrived in Oakland, California. Ian immediately called her. Cece and Ian were together those last three days in Oakland. Ian told Cece they would meet in Hawaii in six months for 'R and R', which meant, Rest and Relaxation, or as laymen called it, vacation.

Cece wondered, "How could anyone rest and relax when they knew they were going right back into the hellhole of the Vietnam war?"

After Ian's plane left for Vietnam, Cece left Oakland broken-hearted. She learned to really respect the armed forces of the U.S.A. Cece's beautiful young man was being shipped out to go to war in a faraway country, but American people could not understand why. They were told the reason was to fight communism. Cece prayed she would see Ian again. She loved him dearly. Ian was her life. Ian did not run away like many young men. Soldiers were supposed to be good upstanding Americans, who stood up to fight for our country, and died doing what President Johnson commanded.

Cece would awake in the middle of the night and know something was amiss half a world away from her. Ian was involved in the crisis! She got her former job back at a doctor's office. Cece and Ian sent gifts to each other. Ian bought china and jewelry for Cece to have in their future. Cece and Ian both had small tape recorders, and she sent music to Vietnam as soon as it came out. Because of Ian's high IQ and office experience, Ian got a special clearance, Ian worked in the General's underground radio room directing the troops when Ian wasn't out on a field assignment. The General allowed Ian to play Cece's music tapes on the loudspeakers so the entire base could hear the songs. The base could hear the latest hits from home or abroad.

There was the group from the Netherlands. Golden Earring's latest hit, 'Radar Love' was extremely popular with the soldiers. There was another song by the Box Tops quoting, "Give me a ticket for an airplane, ain't got time to take a fast train, LONELY DAYS ARE GONE, I AM GOING HOME, MY BABY WROTE ME A LETTER." Amazing 60s' wartime songs!

All the soldiers, doctors, and nurses on the base went crazy for the music from their free world.

After a year, Ian almost didn't get home from the war. His return plane was under fire as it was leaving Vietnam. Several planes didn't make it out of the country because they were shot out of the sky as they were leaving. Those honorable, brave soldiers spent their time in Vietnam and never made it home in the end. Their remains were in the ocean. Those times were very hard.

Returning soldiers needed jobs. Women had received equal rights during Vietnam and had filled a lot of the jobs the soldiers had prior to the war. The men were at war trying to do the right thing for their country. The soldiers stood up and did what their country asked them to do, but when they got back to America they were booed at, instead of honored. They returned to hostility instead of appreciation. Even the United States Government began compensating employees' salaries if companies would hire the refugees and women. That certainly didn't help the soldiers. Plus, the U.S.A. Government was sending child refugees from Vietnam to the U.S.A. to school. They received a free education. Our government didn't do that for our own children, unless their parents abandoned them. Times were very difficult. Families were monetarily challenged and refused loans to buy homes because the wives were of childbearing age, which was totally prejudiced against women! The lawsuits flew. Cece got pregnant.

Ian tried to find work in Las Vegas, but it seemed impossible. Ian turned to his old casino owner and friend for work in downtown Vegas. Once Ian got a casino job, they were able to purchase a home. Cece was so thankful because their first son, Scott, was born. When Scott was a little over a year old, Cece got pregnant again. May 15, 1972 Cece was the mother of two sons, just like she knew she would be someday. She was so happy. Ian and Cece had their own family. When the baby, Aaron, was four years old, Cece realized she would have to return to work. They wanted to give their children everything they didn't have, including a good education.

Ian started dealing 21 in casinos seven years before Cece returned to work. She tried several types of employment. Times were still difficult. People were bitter. Jobs were scarce. Cece didn't have a choice but to return to work. Ian didn't want her to go to work in a casino but Cece decided on a job in a casino cage. From time to time, she checked in with the head cocktail waitress about a cocktail server job at the same casino. She heard the hotshot new owner had big plans to develop a new hotel and casino on the Las Vegas Strip!

What they called the "Casino Cage" is actually the casino's bank. Cece was good at math, but the woman in charge of the casino cage lied when she hired Cece. She promised Cece, if her banks balanced daily, Cece would get a raise every three months. Cece's banks balanced every night. The first three-month period ended. The Casino Cage Manager wouldn't even look at Cece.

Cece was getting frustrated. She was already supposed to have received her first raise. Cece checked with the head cocktail waitress again. She was told to go to the union and register. She was already registered from her Slot cashier days at the Hilton. It was a good sign because the head cocktail waitress didn't say no. Cece couldn't get an appointment with the Casino Cage Manager. She kept trying. Cece wanted her promised raises. The woman wouldn't call Cece back.

The second three-month period ended and she still did not get her raises. The Cage Manager thought she would 'fix' Cece. She put her on the graveyard shift to get her out of the way. Cece was furious! Was this Cece's reward for being an exemplary employee? Cece's third three-month period ended without a raise.

As if it was a sign, Cece had an unexpected customer that night. She had her head down at her station on her graveyard shift counting over her bank when someone approached her window at approximately 3:00 a.m. Cece raised her head up when she saw a 'very feminine see through black lace negligee' opened to the waist on a very skinny and flat chested person. As a frightened child would do, she looked up slowly from there. The person's chest had a couple of long black hairs in the middle of the breastbone. This was a first for Cece. She had never experienced anything like this before she worked in a casino. She didn't know cross-dressers existed. The timid person was extremely happy. He was smiling broadly at her. Cece smiled back, but she felt afraid. She saw red rouged lips as she looked up and into his eyes. His eyes were darting back and forth as if he was worried someone would approach him.

Cece thought, "This isn't a woman!"

Cece could only see the person from the waist up. She wondered what showed on the bottom of this person's body. Cece didn't mean to, but she stared blankly into the boy's eyes. Yes, Cece figured he was a pubescent male teenager. She wondered what was about to happen. As Cece took a deep breath and calmed down, Cece looked at a mulatto skinned handsome young male teenager with a very thin mustache over his upper lip. He still had coagulating gooey creamy white stuff around his mouth and in his mustache. He continued to hold his big smile while he looked at Cece, but he was constantly fidgeting and looking around as if he was scared and thinking he may have to run.

Cece hesitantly asked him, "What can I do for you?"

He put two black chips in front of Cece's desk's window, but he never spoke. He only continued to smile, point, and fidget. He slid the chips all the way across and under the window's protective bars. He smiled and withdrew his arm. Cece thought maybe he couldn't speak English. He pointed at the chips again. He wanted cash for the chips.

Cece realized his 'John' had just paid him for his 'service performance' with the casino chips. She wondered where the "performance" had taken place. He kept looking around as if he was frightened. His eyes seemed to implore Cece. Cece handed him his $200.00 in two one hundred-dollar bills. The very young man snatched the money up, looked quickly to both sides, and took off running towards the casino's exit.

Cece stood there in awe.

Again, she thought, "Did that just happen? Please, God, get me out of here!"

Cece realized God was really listening to her prayers because every time she prayed, things really did change in her life. She thought maybe she led some sort of charmed life, or if God had a great sense of humor. Could it have been she had exceptional parents and grandparents, who taught her to be a proper young lady? They had all always loved God and cherished their children, no matter where they hung their hats. Cece thought they still did, even in a hellish place like Las Vegas.

The next day a phone call from the local culinary union awakened her. The woman apologized. She had an opening in Cece's same hotel, but it was a 'bottom of the barrel' position. However, it was full time! After six months she would be able to 'bid out' of her starting shift and she would have full benefits for her family! Cece was being told she had the cocktail job if she wanted it. YES! She wanted it! She was to report that evening to the head cocktail waitress on day shift.

Cece said, "Yes. Yes!"

The rest would be history!

Cece immediately hung up and called the casino cage. She told whoever answered the phone to tell the Casino Cage Manager she quit. Within minutes the Casino Cage Manager called Cece right back. She offered Cece a $10.00 a day raise. She refused and hung up. An hour went by and the casino cage manager called her back again a second time and offered her a $20.00 a day raise. Cece refused and hung up again. Immediately the Casino Cage Manager turned around again and offered her a $30.00 a day raise and a day shift schedule permanently. Cece knew better than to trust her or to believe her again.

Cece asked, "Why haven't you ever returned any of my calls in the last ten months? This offer is what you had offered me almost a year ago when I was hired. Meanwhile, I have lost all that income for my family and have endured the difficulties of a graveyard shift so you wouldn't have to face me."

Cece hung up the phone on her manager. She now knew the casino cage manager was a despicable and a strange woman. She wouldn't talk to Cece since the day she hired her. All of a sudden, all she wanted to do was talk. Cece knew how the woman could lie. She refused the casino cage manager a fourth time and hung up. The Cage Manager called back and got sharp with Cece. That was it. She told the Cage Manager what she thought of all of her lies and her not answering any of Cece's messages for appointments to speak to her in person. The Cage

Manager told Cece she would never make any better money than she was now being offered.

Cece said, "Oh, Yes, I will!"

The Casino Cage Manager asked, "Where?"

Cece answered as she hung up the phone for the fifth time, "Watch!"

The next evening Cece worked her first day as a cocktail waitress in the fancy plush coffee shop of the hotel where she had just quit her job as a casino cage cashier. Cece had no idea what she was supposed to do as far as cocktails went. She was just thrown into her new job. Cece was very nervous, but you would have never known it. She was promenading constantly through the pretty restaurant in her dainty short sexy red uniform. It was as if she was a ballet dancer pirouetting on stage. Her moves were so graceful. Then Cece spotted 'HER' but did not act as if she did.

The Casino Cage Manager was steaming mad. She spotted Cece. She saw Cece in her pretty red cocktail uniform. The cage manager was entering the coffee shop to eat lunch with her entourage. The cage manager's face turned a shade of blood red. She couldn't do a thing about Cece having this new job. Cece now had a union job. She would have to work hard, but she would get all her benefits, her raises, her shifts, and time off when she deserved those benefits. The cage manager was staring intently at her and mumbling to her entourage. They acted afraid of the manager.

Cece and the whole restaurant full of people knew the cage manager was there because the manager stumbled over four dining room chairs. Instead of watching where she was going, she was watching Cece. The manager was trying to get out of sight before Cece could see her on the floor, but it was too late because of all the noise created when the heavy dining chairs were tumbling over each other. The entire restaurant was startled and went quiet. Everyone stared at the cage manager on the floor trying to free herself of chairs.

Cece smiled at the Cage Manager. The embarrassed manager turned her face to the side and put her nose up in the air and tried to leave with what little dignity she had left. The manager's entourage were all staring at Cece in awe. They tried to help the casino cage manager stabilize herself through the maze of chairs. Cece 'almost' felt sorry for her, but Cece was a firm believer in the fact, "What you do to others, will come back to you several times over! Even if it does not 'always' come back to you from where you would expect!"

The next week 'The Word' got around the casino quickly. The person who the Cage Manager hired to replace Cece, made an excuse that she had a medical appointment. She said she had to leave work early to go to her appointment on her lunch break. The new cashier told everyone she would be back as soon as possible. After three hours went by, the other cashiers were complaining they needed their lunch breaks, too. When their shift ended, they all realized the new cashier wasn't coming back. The Cage Manager finally opened the new cashier's cash drawer, and $50,000.00, in one hundred-dollar bills, was missing. They surmised the new cashier took all morning to do it. She stuffed all the ten stacks of 'wrapped one hundred-dollar bills' down her pants, one $5,000.00 stack at a time, and no one ever noticed. The Casino Cage Manager was fired the next day. She didn't blame herself. She blamed Cece for quitting.

The casino owner asked her, "What? Are you crazy? I don't blame Cece for quitting her cage position because you did not give her what she deserved and earned. I blame you for not recognizing an outstanding employee because you're cheap. Now I'm out $50,000.00! My insurance rates are going to go through the roof! You ARE fired!"

The casino owner wanted to know why cameras were not in the casino cage. He was determined to find out more about getting cameras installed throughout his hotel and his hotel's grounds.

The escaped casino cage teller, whose social security number, photograph, and fingerprints were on file in the Clark County sheriff's office, was hunted down along with her husband. Eventually they were put in prison after their arrival at their Southern Family's home. The casino owner had insurance for theft, but he thought his higher insurance rates were not worth it. The casino owner decided to look into getting cameras throughout the hotel, its grounds, the casino cage, and anywhere else where cash was handled in his business. He wanted everyone who handled money filmed on camera and he wanted no one in security leaking information about his intentions to install cameras everywhere.

Cece and Ian would go on with their lives and the raising of their two young sons. The former cage manager never found another job in Las Vegas. She left town broke. Times were changing, which times should. Cece always strove to be responsible, productive, and to help others. She felt this positivity would lead to others doing the same.

She remembers an example of this during the 1992 LA riot that happened as a result of police being acquitted of their charges in the excessive beating of a drunk driver, Rodney King. One innocent, naïve truck driver passing through the rioting neighborhood was pulled out of the cab of his truck by thugs and beaten almost to death. A 'fine upstanding neighborhood lady of dignity' stepped in literally saved him from being killed without thinking about her own life at risk. When other decent neighbors saw this, they helped her. That heroine and the other good people of that neighborhood stood up for what was right and for the honor of their city, Los Angeles!

Later, to help diffuse the rioting, Rodney King asked an especially important question, "Can we all get along?"

Raising a family during that time concerned CeCe because of all the greed and drugs polluting the country. Scarier still was that it seemed greed and drugs would never fade away. Drugs have infiltrated into every family in our country, even if only with a distant relative.

When Cece was a teenager in the 1960s, she remembered seeing a cartoon of two Russian soldiers talking while they were watching Americans through binoculars. The caption of the cartoon showed one Russian soldier telling his comrade, "Don't worry. Soon they will all be on drugs, and we can just walk in and take over." DUH.

The military only takes our best and our brightest. They don't even want the rest. Addicts make themselves useless to our society, their spouses, their children, and their families, not to mention their country. Now with terrorism and cyber-attacks, our nation better wake up. Our military's best and brightest were being killed. "Do you really want to reduce the gene pool?"

Our forefathers gave their lives for a free world, and for our free country in the Revolutionary War, the Spanish American War, two World Wars, the Korean War, and Vietnam. Our ancestors would expect us to insure a peaceful, prosperous nation where everyone could live and raise their good, educated, and healthy children!

What have you given? Have you raised good children? Are you good for our country? Children, honor your parents. Parents, honor your children. Spouses, honor each other. Honor our soldiers, our firefighters, our educated health professionals, our dedicated law enforcement officers, and our wonderful USA military. Be the best person who you can possibly be, and you will raise the 'Best Children' to carry on this great American Philosophy. Freedom will honor you, love you, and care for you when you are old! Citizens will honor each other! Citizens will honor their home, the United States of America, as well as, honoring our planet, Earth! Teach your children well. Love them well! Teach them to honor each other.

For all our sakes and the sake of the young, support good and shun evil. Negative people only destroy. Negativity never wins. Drugs are negative. BE POSITIVE, for the sake of all our futures on our beautiful planet, Earth!

CeCe believes there is only one God, no matter what one calls Him. He wants us to love, live happily, be good to our children, and each other. He wants us to be kind to the animals, and especially to our planet Earth. God blesses us all unless we throw God away. God gave us everything to earn our way back to Him, our planet and each other.

WAKE UP AND THINK, WORLD!

Chapter 10

Cece's New Life

When Cece's "Head Cocktail Waitress" first dropped her off at the entrance of the coffee shop, it was like she was living in a real-life nightmare. She felt almost naked in her tiny uniform. It totally freaked Cece out. She was praying she could make it through the first evening without being fired. She had 'white-lied' her way into her job by telling people she had cocktail experience. Cece did it because Ian and Cece needed to pay their bills. They were proud people who didn't want to have to collect unemployment. They couldn't qualify for financial aid because they had a home, which they didn't want to lose. Plus, they were married, and they had a beautiful little family.

Cece was ashamed for the citizens of the United States of America, who acted so cruelly toward the returning Vietnam Vets. They didn't welcome the Vets home with opened arms, instead chanted in demonstrations against the returning soldiers. Those men, and the world, were told the USA and their Allies were fighting communism. The Vets were loyal citizens and soldiers, who did what they were told to do by their country's highest elected officials, and the armed services they had joined. The War Vets went through Hell and lucky enough to live to get back home! They were the best of our best! It seemed only the families of the Veterans were the ones who welcomed them home and were glad they were still alive. Cece prayed for a time when US citizens would appreciate their soldiers again.

After the war ended, the US government was bringing in refugees and training them for American jobs, while educating them with US taxpayers' money. However, the United States' own returning Veterans and their families continued suffering without jobs to support their families! Cece couldn't believe what was happening! It seemed sometimes even the US government forgot the Veterans. There weren't many jobs. Many women held the jobs the veterans had to vacate to go to war in Vietnam to do their unappreciated war duties. Those women demanded to keep their jobs.

There were a lot of things happening in the US in the late 1960s and early 1970s. Some veterans were even forming motorcycle clubs just to survive. At least, that way they could help each other find construction jobs or servile work, and travel inexpensively to and from those jobs. The Vets believed in God, Family, and Country, but were extremely disappointed the USA government had forgotten about them, their wives, and their children! The US government should learn valuable lessons about how to honor their Veterans in the future. Divorces ballooned after the Vietnam war ended, because many families had a difficult time learning to adjust when the odds were against love.

Ian was upset with Cece because he didn't want his wife to become a Las Vegas cocktail waitress. She was distressed because every job she ever had in the past had a pervert who sexually harassed her. There was no help for sexual harassment in those days. Businesses were ignorant about acquiring Human Resource Departments. No one had even heard of sexual harassment lawsuits, but the time would come. She didn't have a union to protect her until she became a cocktail waitress which meant she would be protected from advances she didn't want to be the recipient of constantly receiving. Cece wondered if she would ever be safe because some men just never gave up!

When she first saw Franz, the assistant Food and Beverage Manager, Cece didn't know who he was. He was a little man, who ran around in the back halls of the restaurants and bars. Franz was very nervous and hyper. It was as if he was afraid to speak to anyone. He ran up beside

Cece while she was ordering her drinks through a lounge back window into the hallway. Franz loudly ripped a very large price chart off the wall right next to where she was ordering. He frightened Cece because she did not know him. She jumped back startled and looked at him. He ran away without even introducing himself to the new employee.

Cece thought, "Who was that man?"

She then said out loud to herself, "He scared me to death! How am I supposed to know the price of all the different cocktails when he ran away with the price chart?"

She had to have this job so she and Ian could afford the essentials of life. They needed food, housing, and clothing for their two little boys and themselves. Cece wanted her two sons to go to college and continue onto graduate school. They needed the medical and dental insurance for their family that Cece's latest job would provide. They needed to make money for their house payment, or they would risk losing their home, like so many veteran's families were going through after the Vietnam war.

Cece wondered why all this was happening to Ian and herself, but she believed in God. We are all part of God, and if they wouldn't give up. She was sure God wouldn't give up on them and would help them.

Cece made a promise, "God, I'll always be good and as strong as I can possibly be, if you will please help us get through all the strange things we'll encounter along this journey."

God kept her strong because she knew Him. Cece realized there were many unscrupulous people in the casino world. Those people did not care how many people they hurt, if they could advance themselves, and that included her fellow cocktail waitresses.

Cece's Sicilian American family had a lot of pride. No one in their family would ever think to go on government assistance. They worked. Her grandparents came from Sicily with nothing. As soon as they reached the streets of New York, they went to work. No one helped them. They had to help themselves. It was never even discussed or an option. They were very proud people. Cece reassured Ian everything would work out for them if they just worked together. You could be sure she wished she could have stayed home and raised her children on a full-time basis, like any normal mother wanted. Ian and Cece agreed to raise their children together with each other's help. They thanked God that Carmella and Sammie were there for backup in case of an emergency. Cece and Ian agreed that if more fathers got involved with raising their children, the children would be better off, and society would have much less crime. Being two good young parents, Cece and Ian were destined to work opposite shifts to handle raising their children. Genuine love finds a way!

Cece never had to wear a short skimpy uniform in her life. She was frightened. She actually looked more like a tall, real life doll. Her uniform was bright red with a peek of a white lace slip barely showing below her skirt's bottom. She was also wearing red dancewear panties under the slip. The uniform skirt and lacey slip were flowing and full. The top of the uniform had a V neck surrounded with white lace and short sleeves with the same delicate white lace around the bottom of the sleeves. The uniform was short, but it still covered all of Cece's most private assets and showed off her long slender muscular legs. Cece quickly learned to never bend over. She gracefully bent her knees. The uniform had a nicely shaped brown peasant belt. The belt went around her tiny waist and laced up into a point in the middle of the uniform's front, right under and between her breasts.

Cece was self-conscious and frightened on her first day. She felt a little dizzy and short of breath. As frightened as she was, Cece knew she was completely covered where it mattered. Her bathing suit showed a lot more. As far as her legs were concerned, they were gorgeous! People saw more around pools and at beaches, where women had a choice of what they wanted to wear. Cece had no choice. She needed this job and its benefits.

The plush coffee shop restaurant had more sophisticated food than she could have imagined. It was a very busy place. The hotel and casino owner knew how to get business into his gourmet restaurants, his beautiful hotel, and his fabulous casino. It was a decent place to be for her first cocktail job. Cece knew the owner had plans to build a beautiful Strip hotel and casino. Her new boss had already gained the land because of his parent's endeavors. The land had mobile homes and campers parked on it at that current time. Plus, the best burlesque show in town was still performing at the old Silver Slipper on that land. Her boss planned to build a spectacular Hotel and Casino on the "Strip" land. He was an intelligent and industrious man, who had hard-working parents, who taught him well.

The plush coffee shop's very busy and fast-moving hostess, Jazel, came up to meet Cece, when the Head Cocktail Waitress dropped her off at that restaurant's entrance. Jazel seemed to take over and gave Cece instructions. She told Cece where to go to order her drinks. Eventually, Cece's ordering station would be changed into a 'back of the house area' that would serve six restaurants and Cece. It was in an extensive room behind all the restaurants where the public was prohibited. That huge crowded area was where all the chefs and preps worked preparing and cooking food. The dishwashing section was in a far back corner of the massive room, and the cocktail service bar was at the far front corner.

Cece had liked the window ordering station where she first worked because the bartender was a kind man, who was very patient with her. Plus, he was an honest gentleman and taught her a lot. He kept asking her if she had any experience because Cece did not know how to order. She learned enough from him to get along on her own by the time the back of the house bar would take over making drinks for her.

Then the adventure began:

Cece's new bar was inside a compact room, but her bar's large entry had no door and faced into the huge crowded prep and cooking area where the chefs and their helpers were constantly working. Dishes were always washed, food was beautifully assembled onto plates, and large cleavers were constantly chopping. When the 'back of the house' bartender saw Cece walk around the corner and into his bar, he acted like a horn dog gone wild. He jumped straight up off a stool he was not supposed to be sitting on and started huffing while sticking out his chest. He was used to working with older, sophisticated waiters and waitresses from the very formal specialty restaurants.

The first question that came out of his mouth was, "Are you married?"

Cece answered, "Yes."

His second question was, "Do you fool around?"

Cece could feel her eyebrows knit together as she answered, "Of course not!"

Suddenly, there before Chas, stood a goddess of unmentionable proportions. She was tall and slender. She had a muscular, but feminine, build. Most of all, she was stunningly gorgeous. Most times women had one thing or another that wasn't quite right, but this unbelievable woman had it all. The bartender tried to catch his breath and introduce himself. The harassment began.

Chas said, "Wow, Girlie, what might your name be? I tell everyone to call me 'Fat Chas' because I'm always eating, and I weigh as much as two of them put together."

Cece thought, "Yuck!"

Cece introduced herself. She could never tell Ian about Chas' demeanor. She cringed to think what Ian would think or do. She would set Chas straight herself and let him know how it was going to be.

Cece said, "I am happily married, and I love my husband very much."

Fat Chas said, "So what? I'm married, too. I love my wife, but when she's at work, my neighbor lady comes over and swims naked with me in our pool, and we do the nasty thing in the jacuzzi. We 'get it on' as often as possible. Food isn't the only thing that I can eat really good! If you know what I mean. Why do you think all the girls love me and do not care about my appearance?"

Cece thought, "Oh, gross! How could any woman ever let this man touch her?"

Cece was repulsed. She couldn't help herself! Chas had a filthy mouth, a filthy mind, and a constantly perspiring filthy body! She definitely did not want to imagine what he just told her about his neighbor lady, or why all the women loved him! She tried not to let on that her sensibilities were shaken. Chas and his demented mind infuriated Cece. She called out her order. Chas filled it.

As she finally gathered up her wits, her thoughts, and her drinks Cece said, "Chas, I could tell if my man was cheating on me. Don't be surprised if your wife hasn't already figured it out for herself and doesn't care!"

Chas answered, "She already found out about me, and she doesn't care."

Cece thought to herself, "He's absolutely disgusting! What could the neighbor woman possibly look like or be like?"

Cece didn't blame Chas' wife for not caring because she was married to a sloppy, vulgar scumbag. No wife with sight and smell would care what Chas did, as long as it wasn't with her!

As Cece was walking out with her order, Chas took advantage of her full hands. He started coming around the corner of the bar with his arms extended towards Cece.

Cece suddenly screamed out loud, "What do you think you're doing? Don't get anywhere near me! I'll tell my husband if you so much as touch any part of my body! He is a Vietnam Veteran and an ex-Army Ranger! He will kill you, and he will enjoy it! If you don't stop this, I'll report you to management and the culinary union!"

Chas replied nonchalantly, "There are no witnesses. You can't hurt me."

Cece screamed out loud again, "Why do you think I am screaming out loud? There's no door on this bar! Do you hear people working or the cleavers at the chopping table? No, you don't, but 'They' are all listening to me screaming at you and telling you not to touch me! Go look! There are many witnesses! The 'Head Chef' certainly will not let himself be caught in a lie! The hotel needs him, but they don't need you! I'll fill out charges at the union tomorrow if you do not behave around me! They are all out there listening right now! People like you dig their own graves!

Just make sure you keep away from me! Do not ever touch me in any way!"

Cece held on tightly to her large tray of drinks and backed out of the bar's doorway. Everyone in the cooking and prep room had stopped working. They were staring dumbfounded at the doorway to see who the unfamiliar pretty girl was when she backed out of the bar and turned. Then the murmuring started.

The head chef, also, faced towards her doorway. He could see what got Chas all riled up.

Cece stopped to return the head chef's gaze when he gave her a nod and said, "I've got your message, young lady. Let me know if you need any further assistance."

Cece smiled at him and replied, "Thank you, Sir. I will let you know for sure."

As she was walking away toward her restaurant, balancing her heavy tray, she and the Head Chef could hear all the comments the men were making, "Wow, where did they find her?" "What a looker!" "Yeah, she's a keeper!" "No wonder Chas got all turned on!" "Awe, do you believe that one?" "Yeah, she's pretty!" "I never thought there was a perfect woman, until now." "Did you hear how she told Chas off?" "She's something!" "I like her!" "Chas is a jerk."

Cece didn't feel beautiful at all. She felt like she was working so hard for nothing. Her tips were almost nonexistent. She had to put up with a disgusting bartender. As Cece was about to enter her plush coffee shop, she paused with her heavy tray to catch her breath. She was too mad to cry, but she had to regain her composure. Cece smiled as if she were truly happy and walked into her restaurant.

Time went by and Chas didn't touch Cece, but his filthy mouth never gave up. The head chef threatened Chas to make him stop because some employees complained that Cece seemed so upset, and she needed some backup. He finally gave up but was then bitter towards Cece! He got back at her by stalling around while making Cece's orders. She figured that was some form of harassment, too, but she just kept telling him to hurry before her customers didn't want the drinks anymore. Chas ignored her. She really didn't want to get someone fired. Cece payed no attention to Chas, unless when she had an order. That seemed to set him off more. All Chas wanted to do was to continuously eat on the job and talk about sex.

That's when Cece would tell him to put a fork in it. He disgusted her. She made him wash his hands constantly before she would place her orders because he was continuously eating while he worked. On crowded evenings, returning food carts stood outside in front of their bar's doorway. The carts were full of expensive uneaten trays of food and discarded food on dishes that were being brought back to the dishwasher after people were done eating. The carts were waiting to be unloaded, and those dishes were being scraped. The leftover food was sold to the local pig farmer.

Before the dishwashers emptied all the backed up waiting carts, Chas would sneak up to the carts and peruse the leftover food. Then he would bring the food that he selected into his little bar and eat it. When Cece walked into the bar with her orders, she was appalled at the sight of Chas eating peoples' leftover food.

Cece said, "Chas, it is against the health department's rules for you to eat while you are working! Stop it! You don't know if someone coughed, sneezed, or spit on that food. You could become ill, or get caught eating on the job, and you could be fired. It's disgusting!"

Cece could see the mashed food being chewed in Chas' mouth as he answered, "Mind your own business. They need me. I'll do what I want. I'll never get fired. The Health Department's personnel have gone home for the day by the time we start our shift!"

Cece prayed for another cocktail position to open soon. The beautiful hotel and casino was booming in popularity. Then she could bid out of the coffee shop. Cece had a grueling time balancing Chas. He just didn't give up. However, one day, what some people call 'karma', or 'justification' caught up with 'Fat Chas'.

That fateful evening, the main 'High Limit 21 Pit' had a 'High Roller'. She was a wealthy oriental Lady. They called her the 'Hat Lady' because she always kept her head covered for privacy. She didn't want anyone to see her face while she gambled in casinos. She was particularly superstitious and rich! Hat Lady was very generous when she won! She thought she would have good luck when she was generous to employees! Plus, it worked! Management was forbidden to give out her name. She preferred anonymity. She ordered a specialty frozen drink from her cocktail waitress, Missy.

Missy was an older lady and was one of the sweetest women to ever walk on the face of the Earth. Missy had to go into Chas' back restaurant bar to get her Hat Lady's frozen drinks because the floormen did not want to sign comp slips for the drinks at the front casino bars. They were too afraid that some accountant would come down on them, six months into the future, about signing comp slips, and they wouldn't remember why they signed them! The corporate would fire them! It happened unless you owned the joint, but the owner never got involved. That's why he employed experienced people to run his casino, but his Italian Mama was always watching. It was her hotel and casino, too.

Missy explained to Chas that the Hat Lady was tipping her a $1000.00 chip for every frozen drink Missy delivered to the winning Hat Lady. Missy was a very generous waitress. She tipped her bartenders 10% of what she made. Missy tipped Chas a black chip worth $100.00 every time Chas made Missy a cocktail for her Hat Lady. Chas already had $1000.00 of his own from Missy tipping him, but Chas was a glutton in many ways. The $1,000.00, which Missy had already given him for the 10 drinks he made for her customer, was not enough!

Cece was in shock. She could not believe the older cocktail waitresses could make that kind of money working in a pit station, even if it may happen only once in a lifetime. Cece was lucky to make a small amount of tip money each night where she was working so much harder!

Meanwhile, Chas got all agitated and very angry.

Chas yelled out loudly, "I'm going out into the casino and get a yellow thousand-dollar chip of my own! After all, I am the one making the Hat Lady's delicious drinks! I'm the important one."

Cece pleaded, "Chas, I have a large order!"

Chas left his station, which is a big NO in the business, unless it's an emergency or a fire. Cece couldn't get any of her orders because he left!

Chas was still ranting and raving as he ran out, "I'm the important one."

Chas left his bar unattended to go out on the casino floor to hustle the Hat Lady for his own thousand-dollar chip. He left a very perplexed Cece standing at his bar's ordering area waiting to get her order. Cece didn't know what to do. She stood and waited at her ordering station. Cece knew that her customers would be mad at her and blame her for the poor service!

All kinds of important casino people were watching the Hat Lady while she was winning.

Cece said to herself, "How am I supposed to explain to my waiting customers that my bartender left his workstation to go hustle a customer in the casino?"

Customers can't possibly imagine what goes on behind the scenes in casinos, and hotels, and especially in bars and restaurants.

Chas walked to where the Hat Lady was gambling. He leaned on the Hat Lady and her barstool like he was an intimate old friend and hustled her for money!

Chas said, "How do you like your drinks? I am the best bartender here! So, I am your personal bartender, and my drinks are the best drinks in any Las Vegas casino! Don't you agree that your drink is delicious?"

The Hat Lady looked at Chas like he was insane.

The big bosses went wild asking each other, "Who is this jerk? Is he wearing a bartender's uniform? What the hell does he think he's doing? Is he hustling her for money? Oh, no, this can't be happening! She better not be chased away by some stupid idiot. We need to get our money back before someone pisses her off and she decides to leave when she's this far ahead!"

Chas wanted a yellow chip and was determined to get one. He did, and more! Chas wouldn't have to share it with anyone else. He was in the Hat Lady's face for so long that she threw up her arms in exasperation and gave him a yellow chip just to get rid of him. The bosses went wild! What Chas didn't realize is that one of the owner's family members and other top casino VIPs were all watching him hustle the Hat Lady!

Meanwhile, bosses were running around trying to find out who Chas was!

Someone important knew who he was, because she knew everyone who worked in her Son's casino, because it was her casino, too! Every night she hung out in the casino just for fun and brought her favorite family members, or friends. She gave them all money to play the machines. She was the Big Boss's Mama.

Chas came back from the casino. He was holding his yellow chip up in the air. He was parading the chip around the kitchen prep and cooking room, and showing off his tip of a $1,000.00 yellow chip to all the other poor employees, who did not make tips, so they could see it, stare at it, be in awe of his good fortune, and envy him.

The Head Chef kept yelling repeatedly, "Everyone, get back to work!"

Chas would be sorry that he ignored the head chef's orders, but for Boss Mama, it was too late for Chas, anyway. He left his station attended. He hustled an important customer! Chas was totally 'out of line'!

Cece was still nervously waiting at her station to get an order she took 15 minutes prior to Chas' return. No one was filling in for Chas. He saw Cece still waiting to order and ignored her while he showed off his yellow chip even more.

The head chef kept yelling, "Everyone get back to work!".

Cece thought, "Now, what am I supposed to do? All of my customers are going to be so mad at me and they are all going to blame me for taking too long!"

Cece heard a loud 'BOOM'.

She jumped back thinking, "What was that?"

Just then the prep room's second set of double doors burst open!

The 'BOOM' sounded again.

It was the hotel and casino owner's Italian Mama, followed by a security team of four gigantic men dressed in black and fully armed. Boss Mama was first generation Italian American, but she could bellow like 'an old school mama'. You could tell that she knew what hard work was. She saw everyone standing around Chas while they were admiring his yellow chip. Boss Mama heard the head chef yelling and saw everyone still around Chas. Boss Mama, also, looked over into Chas' bar and saw a worried Cece waiting in her ordering station to get her customer's drinks at an unattended bar! Boss Mama went into a rage. Boss Mama got right in Chas' face. The surrounding workers were scared to death but couldn't help their curiosity!

Boss Mama loudly yelled, "Chas, I hope that tip made you very happy because it better last you for a long time! Everyone, who is important, saw you hustling our VIP customer. You know that you are not allowed to leave your workstation without permission. Get your things. You are to go with these four security guards to clock out. Do not come back. You're FIRED. The rest of you stop standing around. Go back to work now! Listen to your head chef or you will be next to go! Got it?"

All the workers scurried back to their stations!

Chas' mouth fell open and his belly quivered. He was petrified. After one of the security team members retrieved Chas' belongings, two huge security guards took him by his arms and the 4 security guards lead him away.

Boss Mama looked over to Cece as she smiled and said, "Someone get this young lady a 'real bartender' immediately."

Within one-minute Cece had a new bartender. She went out to deliver her drinks. Some people said rude things to her because she took too long to get her orders. Tears came into her eyes. Some nicer folks just took the drinks and thanked her, even though they no longer wanted the cocktails because they had already finished their dinners. No one even attempted to tip Cece. They left money on their tables, but the food waitresses kept taking all the money, and not taking care of Cece.

Cece wanted to cry. What had she gotten herself into? She silently prayed for help. Her first day in the plush coffee shop had been a complete disaster and each day after that, it seemed to get worse. She did not want to come back the next day, but she had no choice. Cece had a family!

She came to work and wondered if she would make it out alive. Cece didn't realize how close to reality her thought really was!

Cece asked herself, "Well, girl, what do you think they'll do to you today?"

It seemed to be going fine until about halfway through Cece's shift. The 'high class' oriental restaurant's head chef got pissed off at the assistant food and beverage manager, Franz, for some unknown irritating reason. Cece knew this wasn't going to be good. Here it goes again!

Cece came out of her bar with a full tray of drinks, which seemed to take her forever to get from a substitute bartender, who was unfamiliar with the tiny bar. Boss Mama wasn't responsible to report to Beverage Management she had fired Chas. Cece watched in astonishment as the oriental chef chased Franz around his enormous chopping table while waving a giant meat cleaver at the back of Franz's head. A wide-eyed Cece had to get by them! She tried but couldn't escape the commotion! Cece stood there helpless again, trying to rebalance her full tray of drinks.

All Cece wanted to do was to get by the flying meat cleaver without spilling her full tray of drinks. The two men were running at full speed around the big chopping table. Cece was amazed at how fast they both could run. Because Cece had a full tray, she didn't have a chance to regain her tray's balance each time they passed. Just as Cece would regain her tray's balance, they were there again, coming at her. The huge meat cleaver was flying around in the air between the two crazed, screaming, running men. She prayed that it wouldn't slip out of the chef's hand and hit her or her tray. She wasn't too worried about Franz. The guy could run! Cece guessed he was used to it! She remembered the first time she saw Franz. All Cece could do was to stay still and lean tightly into the wall behind her and hope they didn't hit her.

The oriental chef was constantly yelling. "Chop, chop! Me gonna choppy you!"

Cece was freaked out. She didn't want to get in the way of the huge meat cleaver, so she pressed herself against the wall again and again. Cece was in shock thinking the prep area was such a crazy place to work. Once again, everyone was ignoring the oriental head chef's screams. A female supervisor of one of the fancy restaurants was walking by very casually along the far side of the area. She was ignoring all the screaming and yelling.

Cece called out to her, "Shouldn't someone call the police, please? Someone could get killed!"

The supervisor nonchalantly called out, "No, this happens quite a lot around here."

A wide-eyed Cece stood in shock as the supervisor just walked away from there and entered an office door. Cece was astonished. How was she supposed to serve her drinks in a timely matter when she worked in this 'crazy back of the house' place? Customers have no idea what really goes on in kitchens, prep areas, or behind bars.

Cece yelled back to the fast-moving supervisor as she closed the office door, "What?"

The supervisor disappeared into a back office. Franz was losing ground. The meat cleaver came closer to his head. The oriental chef was gaining on him.

BOOM! Cece thought the sound was a gunshot, but then she remembered!

Cece squeezed back against the wall behind her, once again regaining the balance of her tray for a fifth time. She was so angry at the way she was expected to work. She felt tears welling up in her eyes.

BOOM! Someone hit the second set of double doors into the 'back of the house' restaurant prep area! As those double doors blew opened,

Boss Mama was back and yelling, "Franz, get out of here and go clock out! No one is allowed to piss off our oriental chef. YOU'RE FIRED!"

The chef immediately stopped running and grinned! He won.

Franz was grateful for the rescue and to still be alive. He ran out fast!

Mama looked around the prep room and saw Cece staggering with a heavy full tray of drinks and trying to rebalance them.

Mama smiled warmly at Cece, as Cece regained her composure, and asked, "What's your name, young lady?"

Cece looked up flustered and answered, "I'm Cece."

Mama said, "You're doing a good job, Cece. Soon you'll be out in the casino!"

Cece answered, "Hopefully, Ma'am."

Cece hustled out the exit into the coffee shop. Once again Cece thought regular people would never know what really happened behind the scenes! Literally, heads could go flying!

Cece said to herself, "God bless all people who serve the rest of us from airplanes, restaurants, to huts on beaches, and Mommies and Daddies! Just be glad you are not in casinos or restaurants where heads could really fly! Ask the oriental chef! He'd love to tell you the story." Cece realized that you never knew who would be working the next day in her crazy place of employment!

Customers would just blame the poor waitresses anyway, right? Well, they did!

Nine months after Cece began cocktailing, a shift opened in the casino area. It wasn't much of a shift, but anything would be better than the coffee shop!

Cece thought to herself, "At least my life will be safer!"

Or would it?

The new shift was a slot section that began at 7:00 p.m. and ended at 3:00 a.m. Cece's little 5 cent slot section emptied after the buffet closed at 10:00 p.m. and show break came out at 10:30 p.m. Cece's new slot shift, also, included the one hour baccarat cocktail waitress' lunch break between 10pm and 11 pm. The Baccarat cocktail waitress was newly married and asked Cece to give her early outs often. It turned out to be beneficial. Otherwise, Cece had only four hours to make any money. Many times, the baccarat waitress left at 10 p.m. for the night because business was so slow. Cece could easily give her an early out and watch Baccarat and her 5 cent machines. She asked Cece for early outs often so she could be with her new husband. Cece couldn't afford to go home, but other waitresses always wanted early outs. That fact enabled Cece to 'pick up' extra areas occasionally. It was not easy, but somehow Cece hung in there and left with a little money every night to buy enough food for her family's next day, and to buy enough gas for her old truck to get back to work the next night. Little did Cece realize what was around the corner for her!

Ian and her boys were happy, healthy, and content. They were home safe in their beds, sleeping. That made Cece proud, even though she and Ian had to work separate shifts to make things work! They never knew when Ian would be laid off again because casinos wanted to hire female dealers.

Their love would continue to make it through the tough times, as stressful as they were, which genuine love always manages to do.

One evening Cece took the back roads, through the industrial areas, because there was a fatal accident on the 'I 15 South Freeway' causing cars to sit waiting for hours to get off. The South 'I 15' Freeway was under construction where it would meet with the South '215' Freeway which was normally Cece's way home.

Cece headed for the industrial area. She was driving down South Valley View Avenue as she looked right. She saw a big beautiful SUV coming down a dark alleyway at a high rate of speed, but it at least had its headlights turned on. It didn't seem as though the driver even noticed Cece's old truck approaching his exit. The driver pulled out right in front of her without stopping! Cece changed lanes and missed hitting him. Cece thought, "Who the heck drives drunk at 3: 30 a.m. after working all day in an industrial area?" She decided it had to be a frustrated owner or a boss!

Cece stayed well behind the SUV driver because she had to make a right at West Russell Road. The SUV DUI driver went straight through his red light at Russell. He managed not to hit anyone, but another approaching vehicle, who had the right of way on Russell, slammed on their brake in the intersection! After the screeching stopped, Cece turned right. She drove about a fourth of a mile down West Russell Road when she saw another car flying out of Hammer's Bar's parking lot, at a high speed. Cece knew the car was not going to stop because it was speeding so she once again had to adjust, slamming on her brakes.

The seemingly intoxicated woman driver didn't look right or left for cars. She bounced her vehicle out of the parking lot, over a sidewalk and onto Russell Road, going straight across the 6-lane road and finally turning East. The woman turned at the last second, bounced along on the sidewalk awhile, turned to get back onto Russell Road, and lost her back fender on a fire hydrant as she was traveling away. The good thing was her license plate was still on the fender. The bad thing was the fire hydrant was shooting water about 30 feet straight up into the air. No one had cell phones in those days. When Cece got home, she called 311 to report it. After Cece told them what happened, they told her that she was required to go through the inconvenience of going to the downtown police department the next day to make out a report. She had to work the next day!

Cece thought, "Only me, these things happen to 'only' me!"

Cece remembered thinking, "Gee, how stupid of me to think I would be safer on this new shift because I am NOT working in the kitchen prep area! Now I have to drive home with the night's drunks!"

Chapter 11

DEADLY BACCARAT

CECE was working on her new casino shift. The hours were 7:00 p.m. to 3:00 a.m. She was grateful to be out of the restaurant prep area's service bar! Her latest shift was quite boring; it included the Baccarat room waitress' lunch break for one hour starting at 10:00 p.m. It was the same time the show let out. When her lunch break was due, the Baccarat waitress begged Cece to give her early outs often so she could go home to be with her new husband. Many times, the high rollers coming out of the show frequented the Baccarat room during Cece's hour there, but the room usually emptied by 11:00 p.m. Sometimes that was the only good money hour in the Baccarat room for the entire night. Even though money was hard to make in Baccarat, a waitress never knew when it could happen.

The girl who worked the Baccarat shift didn't need to worry about making a steady income because her new husband had a very good job as a hotel and casino engineer. He was also industrious enough to make money on the side. So, when she wanted to go home, Cece had to take over watching the Baccarat room area and her own area. Most times after that Baccarat lunch break was over, there was no more action there for the entire night. However, you never could tell when someone would come in for middle of the night gambling just to be alone and unencumbered.

Cece remembered one very early morning as two young men came into the room with a rather large leather satchel and announced that it was full of cash. They looked rushed as they tried to settle down. Their casual clothing was extremely disheveled. The potential customers put their satchel on one of the plush chairs surrounding the beautiful ornate Baccarat table. The Baccarat bosses had to count the cash, so they started rushing about the room getting ready for the two big gamblers.

Cece would usually ask the players quickly if they wanted a drink while the bosses prepared, but that night she sensed something about the two nervous customers and waited patiently. She watched them hovering over their satchel while closely talking. The Baccarat bosses told one of the customers to open the satchel so they could start the count.

He obliged and suddenly there was a popping sound. Immediately, powdered purple dye shot up into the air above the satchel and spread all over the money, the two men who had been carrying it, the beautiful chair, and half of the very expensive Baccarat table. The dye came close to the bosses, but they jumped backwards! As the satchel continued puffing out dye, the shocked table dealers jumped up from their seats and backed away from the dusted table in time to prevent getting covered with dye.

The Baccarat security guard immediately drew his gun and yelled out, "Put your hands up and keep your hands up where I can see them. You are under arrest!"

The security guard called on his radio for backup. He told the dispatcher to inform the Head of Security and call the police.

Cece was amazed! She was thankful for her intuition not to serve them. The satchel was full of money from a robbery. The dye pellet, strategically placed by whoever they had robbed, was set to explode as soon as someone touched the money.

It was quite exciting when the police arrived. They put the thieves in handcuffs and read them their rights. The two men looked hilarious with dye all over their faces, hair, clothes, and entire bodies. Cece repressed her laughter. It looked like she was watching a funny movie, but it was real life! The not so funny part was she and the Baccarat staff all became witnesses.

Cece thought, "Oh great! Another day downtown at the police department making out reports before I have to go to work tomorrow evening because of this crazy job!"

Many a night came and went when the high limit Baccarat room had no play at all. The hotel and casino owner made a lot of income from that room when there were players. It indeed made enough money to pay for its plush environment and the three shifts of staff to man the room, while still giving the owner lots of extra income.

Cece's new casino shift was the first time she would be working out of the main service bar. It would force her to get to know many cocktail waitresses and their different personalities. The entrance to the main service bar had a sign over the bar's doorway where customers couldn't see it. The sign read "You are now entering the Twilight Zone". Cece laughed and thought to herself how appropriate those words were, but she still thought nothing could top her coffee shop shift. Little did she know.

The older, more established cocktail waitresses had the busier and more lucrative high limit pit and slot areas. They didn't want to take care of any other sections because they were able to make good money nightly, hardly had to work for it, and got to stay near the service bar. They smoked, talked, and passed the nights away. They didn't have to carry out heavy trays full of drinks or walk far.

No other cocktail waitresses ever wanted anything to do with Cece's nickel slot section. Therefore, no one would ever give Cece an out early. Cece bid on her new shift because she had no choice if she wanted to get out of the crazy back-of-the house coffee shop's prep area. Those people were all nuts! She had to admit that the real crazies had all been fired by Big Mama. Cece hoped it would not be as difficult on the next new girl as it had been for her. Cece always seemed to be a trailblazer. Sometimes she actually wondered if the crazy things that happened at work only happened to her.

When Cece got out onto the casino floor, she heard lots of things from the other cocktail waitresses. It was her first time working with so many cocktail waitresses in the small main service bar. Waitresses constantly walked in and out of the small bar's two side doorways. Cece could not help hearing the girls gossiping while she was waiting in line to order her beverages. The women talked about all kinds of things, from men to their periods and BEYOND!

The two bartenders were behind the bar listening to the girls ordering and gossiping. The bar had low hanging tray racks over the bar's two ordering sections. Every inch of space was utilized in the small bar. The girls could hardly move around! But it was really a luxurious real estate. It was easy to forget about the bartenders being behind those glass racks. Cece immediately thought the girls should beware! Bartenders were worse gossipers than cocktail waitresses!

The girls heard one of the lounge cocktail waitresses was going up to rooms with men to make extra money on slow days. They thought her bartender must have been covering for her. The 'Johns' didn't care what the girl looked like. It was against the rules and termination was certain if the girl got caught. It made it difficult on the rest of the good moral women because some customers, unfortunately, took it for granted all cocktail waitresses were the same way. Cece worked with a lot of good moral women, who did not deserve to be in that category.

The women knew everything about everyone. Even though they did not partake in breaking the rules and risking the loss of their good positions, nothing could stop the women from talking. They didn't think much of it because they figured the gossip was only between them. Cece wondered why they spoke in front of the bartenders like they did. Cece knew the bartenders could hear them. Why didn't the other women think?

There were a few male bartenders who were very attentive and listened to everything the girls mentioned. Those bartenders repeated things the girls would have never said if they realized someone would actually go around repeating them. Plus, those bartenders dropped the names of the girls spreading the gossip, which caused many a cat fight. The important thing to remember about gossip is every time someone speaks, the story changes. Any moment a fight could occur!

Cece kept her mouth shut, especially not saying anything, about her private life. Cece did not want to be blamed for repeating anything because terrible repercussions could easily happen to the participants. There were many mandatory leaves of absence pending investigations because of fights. Frightened women thought they could lose their jobs. She seemed to remember learning those lessons when she was a preteenager. She wondered why it was taking so long for some older women to figure it out—not that it differed greatly from what happens in any profession.

On Cece's new slot shift, if someone wanted to leave early on slow nights, she might have a chance to 'take them out', which meant, to let them leave and work their shift along with her own shift. Some girls were older, some were alone, some were married, and some were single mothers. It seemed there was always someone who wanted to go home early for some reason. Some women had commitments the next day. Many of the unmarried women had children and went to parent-teacher conferences or appointments, just like any other parent. Cece loved her new shift because the service bar was too busy for the girls to get into too much trouble, if they could learn to keep their mouths closed.

However, there was always an attention getter with a big mouth or a jealous nature, who did not have enough to do, or was having a bad night. One of them may be suffering from a hangover and thought you were prettier than her. Cece knew she had to be careful. A few girls were just downright mean and nasty, and they loved being that way; and the good meek girls were afraid of them. Some girls used the filthiest language, knew all the extreme curse words, and could back it up better than a hardcore biker. Some of them were as big and as frightening as a man. Others were just downright sluts, drinkers, druggies, or angels. The most dangerous ones were the educated girls and the manipulators, especially if they were union shop stewards, because they could control girls' lives and incomes if the girls went up against them.

It would have been wonderful if employers hired only honest people, but that is impossible in any profession. There seemed to be excessive greed in some casino employees that could not be quenched. Greed always found a way to backfire on those employees, eventually. Cece was so glad she didn't have to work with them or near them, but it could only be a matter of time.

Cece made sure to ring all her orders because it was the honest thing to do, and she would never want to lose one of the best jobs she ever had. Orders were rung up for tax and inventory control. Some people didn't want to be taxed. Some lazy bartenders just didn't care. One bartender kept his book on his glass rack right in front of his face. He got perturbed if you interrupted him while he was reading, and especially if you asked him to make an order of drinks for you. Cece kept her mouth shut, but she was honest! Cece also realized that if your bar was busy and you rang up all your orders, you had a proof you were an essential employee which would secure your position.

One afternoon, the hotel's newly installed outdoor cameras caught a cocktail waitress on film while she was climbing out of a window and onto the fire escape. She had gone to a guest room and did not want to be caught.

Cece thought, "How humiliating for her!"

When Security finally rescued the cocktail waitress off of the fire escape, they confronted her in the presence of the casino owner and his host. The woman was badly shaken. She began to cry and apologized.

The gruff old casino host yelled at Security, "So what? I live here. It's my home away from home. I can ask anyone I want to come up to my suite. What are you going to do about it? She was my guest!"

Nothing happened to the girl, except a lot of teasing. The bartenders, who overheard the girls' gossip, gave the waitress a nickname, 'Spider Woman'. She was laughed at and made fun of by the bartenders until that news got so old that everyone was tired of listening to it. The gossip took years to die down.

That host brought so much money into the casino, the hotel and casino owner told Security to drop it. The next day the cocktail waitress was called into the cocktail department and asked if she would please change out of her uniform the next time she went to visit the host in his room, and to please use the regular hallways and elevators instead of the fire escapes. She never visited the old host again.

Hence, 'Spider Woman' did not lose any respect from the girls because they never judged each other morally, in any way. So many of them were always doing something morally wrong. They partied with management. Some did heavy drugs. Some fornicated with the hotel owner and higher-up management staff. Most of the girls considered those girls to be unpaid hookers. No matter what, the women would cover for them. They considered themselves to be a sisterhood of sorts and always looked out for each other! All of it was undeniably strange, because the majority of the women were good moral wives, mothers and respected ladies. Being a woman herself, Cece kind of understood their rationalization.

There but for the grace of God, go I. Once your morals slip, they are hard to recover. Just like water and words are hard to recover. Be careful!

It was almost like a protective mother would think. Mothers love their children no matter how bad those children are! The waitresses felt like a family or rationalized they were on the same team.

Some of the older women, who had terrible habits, but good stations, were heavy drinkers and gamblers. They gambled every night after work and sometimes stayed up the whole night partying. They didn't go home. They would show up for work like they were staggering zombies. They had not gone home to eat, bathe, or sleep in an entire 24-hour period! They were intoxicated, smelled of alcohol, were disheveled, and still were wearing their same dirty uniforms from the prior day. Of course, they couldn't possibly work because they stayed up for over 24 hours, and drank alcohol, took drugs, and smoked! The other girls covered for them and told them to go home and go to sleep. The girls who covered their shifts liked the extra income and never reported them. They certainly didn't care about customer service. The girls who covered the shifts made very good money for doing them a favor. So, they were happy to cover. Many of the old waitresses died penniless because of their destructive habits.

There was a certain camaraderie amongst the girls where they didn't judge, and they did not want to be judged. They covered for each other because they knew that anyone could have a weak or trying moment, but some of them just incorporated their awful habits constantly into their daily lives. When the girls covered each other's backs, it allowed the lost souls to continue their bad habits, but it did keep them from being fired.

Cece wondered how people got away with being so terrible to their employer. She couldn't believe the women got away with some of the things they were doing. Cece realized some girls were partying with the hotel owner, the higher-up hotel and casino staff, and the owner's relatives. If they were doing it on their own time, that would be their own business, but if they were doing it on company time, it was their employer's business, and a perfect setup for future sexual harassment lawsuits against management, which eventually happened.

* * *

One night, things were as boring as they could be on Cece's late swing shift! Cece was standing in Baccarat because she had just checked her slots and there was not one person in her entire area. It was 11:00 p.m. and Cece didn't get off until 3:00 a.m. She had four long hours to go. The regular Baccarat cocktail waitress asked Cece for an early out when Cece was due to give her a lunch break at 10:00 p.m. Cece happily agreed because it was a very quiet night.

Cece was in the Baccarat room waiting for any possible business, when a real creep of a relief boss decided he was going to be clever and harass Cece because he thought she was beautiful.

He walked up to Cece and looked her up and down lustily as he stated, "Wow, Girl, you sure are healthy!"

He continued on by saying he remembered seeing her centerfold in a man's magazine. He was all smug with himself and smiled widely at her. His chest was all puffed out. He looked like an ugly peacock! Cece took advantage of this situation. She had nothing else to do, and she wanted to set him straight.

Cece started acting fidgety and terrified. Her eyes were quickly darting around, as if to see if anyone was watching them. The relief boss was watching her, and he wondered what she was doing. Then he started looking around to try to figure it out.

Cece thought to herself, "I'll stop this harassment right now!"

Cece grabbed his bicep, went right up onto her tiptoes, and spoke into his ear in a tiny whisper, "Oh, please, don't say anything to anyone. No one's supposed to know about that magazine, and management told me they would definitely protect me from any gossip about it by getting rid of anyone who mentioned it!"

Cece had totally insinuated that anyone who was talking about her would be fired! You should have seen how nervous the floorman became.

The boss whispered back to Cece, "I... ah...I... Oh my! I'll be sure to protect you, Miss!"

He stood back, very erect. His eyes were looking back and forth to see if anyone in higher management saw him talking to Cece. He looked utterly frightened thinking someone might say he spoke 'out of line' to Cece, or maybe someone important had seen him whispering in her ear. He wondered who this girl knew in top management. He wondered who would give her a job, and who was protecting her! He thought she must have important connections, or maybe she was a daughter of someone high up in management. He never thought such an innocent-looking young lady could have been a centerfold! He was just 'coming on to her'. He didn't realize that he could get fired for flirting! He was using the centerfold thing as a come on line. He thought he was an idiot to talk to her like he did. He never thought Cece could have been "juiced" into her job and trying to start a fresh life. He began to sweat profusely. He couldn't afford to be fired. He had a wife and four children. Soon he asked for an early out because he said he didn't feel well. He got the early out and practically ran out of the casino.

Cece thought to herself, "That fixed his goose! No more sexual harassment from him."

Cece didn't want to be mean, but she definitely didn't want creeps flirting with her, whispering in her ear, and she didn't need to have to endure rude sexual comments from unwanted sources. She wanted to laugh when he left but forced herself to keep a straight face. That boss never spoke to Cece again unless it was about business. He was always polite and business-like afterwards. She was glad. Another jerk down!

Surveillance cameras were installed in the Baccarat room as soon as the perimeter of the hotel's exterior was completed. The Baccarat room was ready to go if they got a customer.

* * *

It was getting to be close to 2:00 a.m. when they showed up. You could hear them coming. They were two tall dark-skinned foreign looking handsome men with wild looks in their eyes. A warning flashed in Cece's mind. It frightened her. The woman hanging on the second man was a cheap looking local hooker wearing a wig. She acted like she didn't get paid enough money for her services. She was obnoxious. She had a look of money hungry greed in her eyes as she watched every chip the leader handled. Sometimes prostitutes were hard to spot, but not this time. Especially because of the way she was dressed. In the olden days, they dressed beautifully, but this woman looked outright trashy. Her makeup was askew. Even her wig was smashed straight up on top of its back side because she had been lying down on it for so long. She didn't speak out loud. She looked shifty-eyed, like she was going along for the 'money ride', and she was determined to get more!

Their mannerisms and their wild eyes suggested the three of them were on some serious meth. The bigger of the two men was definitely the leader. He had a look of sexy evil. Mr. Leader was controlling a large amount of casino chips in his massive hands in every denomination the hotel furnished. The second man was more timid and more submissive to the leader. Cece noticed Mr. Timid was afraid of Mr. Leader. She confirmed Mr. Leader was the boss. The hooker was always whispering in Mr. Timid's ear.

Chips went back and forth on the Baccarat table between Mr. Leader and the dealers. His two companions just watched and cheered Mr. Leader on! They shouted and screamed out loud, drawing much attention to the Baccarat room and to themselves. Mr. Leader was very lucky and winning big! Their cheering caught the attention of everyone, including security. The Hooker and Mr. Timid Man acted like they were messed up, but not Mr. Leader. He seemed to be in some serious control. He was extremely concentrating; he was quiet, and he was determined. No one could understand the language the men spoke, but people could pick up on their moods.

The prostitute only spoke English. Mr. Timid seemed to understand the hooker, and she seemed to understand him. He spoke broken English quietly back to her. Chips were flying everywhere. Mr. Leader continued winning, but never spoke to anyone besides the prostitute. Cece noticed that only Mr. Leader handled all the chips, and he did not tip the dealers. The dealers weren't happy with his winning because the house was losing so much money. Mr. Leader was a stiff!

The dealers were thinking casino management would make sure they would be hearing about this loss for the whole next week. The casino bosses would continue complaining about the loss for a long time to draw attention away from themselves and put the loss on the dealers. It was a stupid game casino personnel played. No one had control of the cards except fate. There were 6 decks of cards in the card shoe.

Cece never understood how the dealers could be responsible for the casino's loss if it was obvious they were not cheating. No one wanted to be responsible for the casino losing. Cece figured they just passed the blame down the line. It only stood to reason someday someone would truly get lucky and win. After all, the casino won every night. It is all about winning! They didn't build multibillion-dollar casinos and hotels because they were losing money. However, people never knew who could be the lucky one to really win big. It happens! Your life could completely change because you did win! You just never knew.

Cece was happy to get the tips Mr. Leader threw onto her tray. He did not flirt with Cece at all. Every time she brought them an order, the leader would turn to her and gently throw a black $100.00 chip onto her tray. She was so happy the Baccarat waitress wanted to go home early! Cece never thought twice about the leader having other intentions on his mind about her. He did not seem to notice her. He was honorable to her, and she thanked him politely for the tips he had given her after each delivered order.

Cece never made eye contact with the leader, but toward the end of his betting spree his aura and a sudden change of mannerism frightened Cece. She suddenly felt different about him. His dark eyes were checking her out as he probably was doing the entire time.

He had won really huge amount of money and was getting cocky! There was something evil about him suddenly. Suddenly everyone in the room, and now even Cece, noticed Mr. Leader's eyes as he lustfully watched her work. She never acted any way other than professionally towards him.

Cece took pride in her work and in the beginning of Mr. Leader's betting spree, she genuinely thought he was tipping her for her excellent prompt service. This would have been a bad night for tip money if she didn't get a lucky customer who was winning! Winners, who tip that much, do not happen often, and Cece knew it.

Mr. Leader started acting like he had other ideas for Cece. After winning huge money, and tipping Cece generously, the staff figured Mr. Leader wanted Cece to leave with him. Mr. Leader thought he could have any woman he wanted, or maybe, in his actual life it was a reality for him because of his wealth.

The dealers and the bosses watched him eyeing Cece as she worked. Cece was unaware of Mr. Leader's intentions. She just kept working. The dealers and bosses heard Mr. Leader commenting to the man with him. They surmised Cece was a big distraction to him while he was finishing up gambling. He was constantly looking over at her and making comments to his partner in their language as he was sorting his chips.

Then Mr. Leader started to smile as he looked over at Mr. Timid and they both looked at Cece. The staff noticed the prostitute looked relieved to think another girl could take over for her. Cece just kept working.

Cece watched their drinks closely and continued to get their drinks while they finished up being huge winners! She was right there with the best service possible. They won every time Cece delivered their drinks. Cece made money. She was grateful.

The dealers and all the bosses were taking everything in and watching Cece's reactions. She was being most professional. The dealers were happy for her, but they did not like these people. The dealers and the bosses wanted nothing bad to happen to Cece. The dealers and the bosses figured Mr. Leader was going to ask Cece to leave with him, which many cocktail waitresses did under those circumstances. No amount of money would ever ruin Cece's life with Ian and their sons.

The group had a total of five rounds of drinks. Finally, the leader of the group started to pick up all his high limit chips. He had handfuls of chips. It was apparent that Mr. Leader was counting his chips quickly with his back towards Mr. Timid and the hooker. The hooker and Mr. Timid were huddled together, speaking to each other. They didn't realize Mr. Leader knew exactly how much money he had won.

The hooker looked determined.

The leader turned around and faced his male counterpart and the prostitute. He called to them. They looked up, surprised, and came out of their huddled position. He spoke to them in broken, quiet English.

Mr. Leader said, "Take these chips to the casino cage. You are to wait for me to get there before cashing out."

He asked them if they understood him. They both said they did understand. The leader said to go to the cage and wait for him there because he wanted to speak to the cocktail waitress.

Cece thought to herself after Mr. Leader had stated his orders, "Who doesn't he trust? He had finally spoken in English! I didn't realize he understood me thanking him. He does speak English! It is the prostitute he does not trust, of course! He wants to make sure they wait for him to cash out. Why does he want to speak to me?"

Mr. Leader then turned around to Cece in front of the staff of the Baccarat room and ordered her, "Come on, Let's party!"

Cece smiled at him sincerely and innocently answered, "I'm married!"

Cece continued to look into the face of a devil, even though she was scared to death. She knew the armed Baccarat security guard was protecting her.

She could see the hatred on Mr. Leader's face. He felt insulted. His whole face became contorted. He was so angry with her. He couldn't understand it. He gave her tip money and wanted a return. He looked around at Security. Mr. Leader knew he couldn't do anything about Cece in front of everyone. There were a lot of people watching him. Cece could feel the fury in his demeanor. Suddenly, she could read him like a book. Cece felt she would have been badly hurt if they were alone. She was frightened! He gave her one of his cruel looks. She felt his evil spirit. You didn't need "the Eye" to know he was selfish, deadly, and frightening. A woman was nothing to him. He felt a woman was to be used.

Cece felt he had never been refused! Cece was very protected by cameras and the top undercover security team who started walking up into the Baccarat room as they watched him with Cece. The armed security guard had secretly called the security team, warning them the customer was acting irate even after he had won. Baccarat security told the security team that Mr. Leader wanted the cocktail waitress to leave with him, and she was refusing.

Mr. Leader looked around at all the armed security guards and gave Cece one more horrible look as he left. Cece finally read him like a book, and so did everyone else working in the Baccarat room. He stormed off towards the cage to get his money. She turned towards the cage and watched him walk up to the prostitute and Mr. Timid. The hooker spoke and looked wide eyed at Mr. Leader as he pushed her. Mr. Timid looked confused.

Cece thought the prostitute must have tricked his friend into cashing out before Mr. Leader got there, because his friend didn't speak very good English. Mr. Leader gave them both a horrible look. He roughly shoved the prostitute to go towards the exit. The leader looked angry, because they didn't wait for him to do the cash out like he had told them. Cece felt a deep ominous fear. Her inner warning flashed through her mind. She would not want to be that hooker, not in a million years!

Cece felt nauseous and wanted to scream to the prostitute, "Stop, please, give him back the chips you stole. Don't go with them!"

But for some strange reason the prostitute smiled happily as she walked away. She looked very smug, like she got away with it.

That's when Cece felt it. The woman definitely stole some chips and probably slipped the chips into her clothing. She had Mr. Leader's stolen chips to cash out at a later time.

Cece suddenly saw a hideous dead woman walking away. It scared her.

Some Baccarat staff didn't know Cece because she had just gotten her new shift. She turned and faced them, noticing they were speaking about her and looking at her. She smiled at them. They told her they were very glad she didn't go with the customer, because they had seen waitresses go in the past. Cece told them she had a family and would never consider going anywhere with a man. She told them she would not especially go out with any man who treated a woman like Mr. Leader did, no matter what her life's situation was. One of the bosses said he thought there was something evil about them. Cece and everyone else completely agreed.

Cece was overly intuitive. She had been perceptive from childhood. Her sensitive insight had protected her since she was a child. She had Grandma's 'Eye'!

The next day Cece had to pick up the boys from school before 3:00 p.m. She would take them home and get dinner for her family. She would clean up the kitchen and start to get dressed to be at work by 7:00 p.m. She had to leave the house early to have time to drive through traffic and then look for a place to park. She didn't have a chance to see the news or look at Ian's newspaper. She barely had time to help the boys with most of their homework before she left the house. Ian just got home from work as Cece was leaving. Cece kissed Ian and the boys good night and told Ian that he was in charge of the math homework after he finished eating his dinner.

Ian smiled and said, "Oh, thank you for leaving the best for me!"

Cece smiled at her handsome man, leaned into him, and said, "I'll always leave the best for you, Ian. I love you!"

Their young sons both smiled and giggled. Children feel love.

Ian grabbed her slender shoulders with his hands and brought her towards him as he looked deeply into her eyes and said, "I love you, too, Cece!"

They kissed a long time. Their sons giggled again with happiness!

Cece kissed her sons, too, and told them all to be good men and ran out the door. Cece drove downtown, parked, and hurried into the employee's entrance. Cece didn't hear anything about what had happened until it was time for her Baccarat break.

When she walked into the empty Baccarat room to do the Baccarat cocktail waitress' break, all the dealers called out to her, "Cece, did you see the news?"

Cece looked at her new friends and told them she had been too busy with her sons. One of the bosses told Cece to go over to the desk where the pit clerk was sitting and check out the newspaper. Cece looked at them like she suspected something was wrong. Cece walked over to the desk. There she saw the paper. Even though she had felt "IT" before she reached the opened newspaper on the desk, it was still a horrible shock to her. She stepped back and put her hand up to her mouth. She was wide eyed. All the dealers and bosses were watching for her reaction. She looked at the newspaper with a blank look on her face, and her hand was still covering her mouth.

There was a picture of the money hungry prostitute who had accompanied the two foreign men. Her face was not impaired, but you could tell she had suffered in death. There was a look of anguish on the lifeless face of the woman. Next to the picture was another picture of her dead, twisted, and crumbled body. Blood surrounded her lifeless, unrecognizable mangled body's remains. She was lying like a pile of garbage on the ground in a filthy alley. Five $100.00 black chips from Cece's employer's hotel were on the ground next to her half-opened hand. Cece wondered when newspapers would stop printing pictures like these on the front page. It reminded her of the live newspaper camera shots of American soldiers dying while fighting in Vietnam! Children could see these terrible pictures in newspapers if their parents weren't careful.

The police were asking for help from anyone who had seen the woman the last night before her death. Cece could feel herself turn white as the blood left her face. She felt so sorry. She was sick to her stomach, and she felt dizzy. Cece leaned on the desk and took several deep breaths. She felt a little steadier.

She walked over to the dealers and stood there saying, "Oh my, how could they do that to her?"

Then Cece put two and two together as she said, "The lead guy had to know how much money he had won. I saw him counting it. That is probably why he killed her like he did. He would let no woman, especially a whore, hold out on him!"

How many other women had Mr. Leader abused in his lifetime?

Cece remembered seeing him turn his back to his associates while he counted the chips. Cece thought he must be an intelligent man because he counted all those chips quickly. Cece heard him tell the other man and the woman not to do the cash-out until he got to the casino cage. If Cece could understand his English, so could the prostitute!

Cece thought she was right. The woman must have talked Mr. Timid into cashing out quickly because the prostitute thought Mr. Leader did not have a chance to count the value of the casino chips. She had been holding out on them! There were five black chips next to the dead woman's hand. She had to be grasping those chips tightly in her hand, and at the moment of her death, her hand must have opened up enough to drop the chips on the ground next to her hand. The woman talked

Mr. Timid into cashing out before the leader got to the cage. The prostitute was planning on stealing extra money from them all along, just like Cece thought when she first saw the hooker.

Cece thought, "Oh my goodness, that's why Mr. Leader shoved her to go out the exit of the casino quickly! He already knew she was holding out $500.00. The prostitute looked so smug, turning away from Mr. Leader as she smiled and walked towards the casino exit. Was $500.00 worth her life?"

The bosses and the dealers told Cece management had called the police. The police were going to interview all of the employees who were working and dealt with the three people. If the police ever caught the two men, any of the staff could be asked to testify against them. Cece's information was included in the names the police collected. The police took a copy of the tapes the "eye in the sky" filmed of the action in the Baccarat room from the previous night. The detectives had the information they needed, but they had not yet found the two men.

Cece sighed, thinking, "Was the other guy still alive? Maybe he didn't know the prostitute was holding out on them. If he knew, he probably would have already been found dead with the prostitute, but it was a big desert out there. They didn't know if someone saw them killing her and they didn't have time to cash out five hundred dollars' worth of black chips before getting out of town… or… MAYBE… they were still in town holing up somewhere."

Cece felt her body shudder just thinking they may still be in town, but something told Cece they had already fled. Why would they put themselves in jeopardy by hanging around Las Vegas after committing a murder?

However, the Baccarat staff thought differently, and so did the Baccarat security guard and the police. They thought this was a woman killer. They all thought Mr. Leader may want to get even with the cocktail waitress, too! They didn't want anything to happen to Cece. They assigned her a security escort to her car after work for the next 3 months.

Cece tried to tell the police and the staff the woman was killed because she was holding out on the two men.

Cece thought, "Oh, no! My life's going to be pure hell for a while and no amount of money would be worth that happening!"

Chapter 12

Finally Busted

THE hotel and casino owner were wondering why bar inventory was costing so much and why the return wasn't coming back as profits. Inventory was not showing up. How could inventory just disappear? There were empty bottles and glasses in all places! Employees were serving drinks. Customers were drinking cocktails and beers everywhere. The owner was determined to find out where his inventory was going.

To top matters off, the owner's business was booming! The hotel owner needed to find out where his bar profits were going. He ran around himself looking, watching, and even spying between slot machines. He couldn't find out anything, especially because he didn't know what he was searching to find in the first place! He needed professional help. The owner went up to the 'Eye in the Sky' for help and suggestions.

In the early days, the 'Eye in the Sky' was originally a casino's security watch area, which was built over, and into the ceilings above a casino's live, big money, and high limit areas. Those areas were called casino 'Pits'. The "EYE" was camouflaged by see-through mirrors. Originally 'The Eye' had catwalks and keen-eyed experienced men watching the live gaming tables below on the casino floor. They watched for card sharks and any other suspicious behaviors, such as card markers, counters, and just about anything else a thief could imagine including working with a crooked dealer.

The 'Eye in the Sky' progressed tremendously when electronic surveillance devices were installed, however, devices were only as good as the people who manned them, as well as the people who watched the recordings made by the devices. After hiring a top-notch Head of Security and four security shift managers, the owner bought much of the latest state-of-the-art security equipment requested by his new Head of Security. The owner had already installed cameras on the outside of the hotel for security. That's how 'Spider Woman' was apprehended on the fire escape. Security started inside the hotel's casino with cameras installed in his high limit baccarat room, which proved to be very successful.

The happy owner wanted cameras everywhere possible and not only in casino areas. The security team members would eventually watch recordings until their eyes felt like they were going to cross. Some of the first recordings would be saved because the recordings could contain incriminating evidence against employees. The Owner was not even close to being ready to do a 'sting' in all the different departments, but he knew he wanted security to organize and have the correct tools.

The Owner was very eager to start with his busiest and non-profitable beverage department. He was determined the security devices would be placed anywhere he wanted, except the guest rooms and restrooms. It was his private property! He was responsible to pay bills, to answer to the stockholders, and to Uncle Sam. Essentially, the Eye in the Sky, gaming security, hotel security, grounds security, and all manned surveillance equipment became one huge department. It would be called just plain, "Security".

The first step the owner took was to fire anyone in the security department, who the new security shift managers said was not carrying their own weight. He wanted the most intelligent, security masterminded surveillance personnel. He got them. His security force would grow to be one of the most renowned and largest in Las Vegas, Nevada. He managed to under pay many of the most brilliant young minds, who were hired as security team members. They had young families. They needed insurance. Jobs were scarce. Many of them were smart, but inexperienced.

His new security managers wanted to train their own new security team members to work on the newest state-of-the-art security devices. The owner wanted his security teams trained, also, to watch for inappropriate employees and guests. Some new security team members would regret selling themselves out by settling for less pay while learning. However, if they became the best, they would have guaranteed jobs with excellent benefits and promotions. Those benefits could be in the owner's future employment, or in any hotel and casino organization in Las Vegas, Nevada, U.S.A., or the World.

The owner worked hard. He expected his employees to work hard, too. He was a fair employer who took care of his good employees for whatever length of time they choose to work for him. He was an asset to his stockholders, his customers, his employees, and his community of Las Vegas, Nevada. However, you never wanted him to be angry with you, even if it took an awful lot to make the man mad. He was meticulously clean and wanted everything he owned spotless, secure, and accurate.

There were many meetings between the hotel owner, the head of security, the assistant head of security, and the Eye in the Sky security shift managers. Each of the four security shifts would have a different shift manager and his own security team. They designed the fourth shift to give days off. The relief shift had to have the knowledge of all three shifts, if things were to work properly. Theirs was the toughest of the shifts because they had to become comfortable working different hours. They had to be strong, healthy, straight, and adaptable. All security members were hired knowing they could be drug tested whenever. Security managers were called into private meetings without their teams. The meetings only included the head of security, his assistant head of security, the four shift managers, and the owner. The owner did not want to appear as ignorant as he was regarding the equipment and procedures. He just kept repeating what he wanted done with the security project, and the team leaders were expected to carry out his orders. It took a while to prepare, but the security managers were finally ready to begin.

They organized everything they needed and carried out the owner's orders. The owner finally finished furnishing his security staff with the rest of all the finest state-of-the-art security equipment. His entire building had been expertly wired. It was not an easy project because much of the original casino area was built in 1947 and added onto a little at a time. Expert engineers with spelunking abilities accomplished everything they needed to do for the job to be successful! After the equipment would be installed, and in perfect working order, they would be ready to call in all the security team members from the four distinct shifts to show them what was at their fingertips. Security became a huge and very important department. The Security department even had holding cells in with their high-tech offices. Security was almost ready to break all Hell loose.

* * *

Cece was working in a beautiful central casino lounge on day shift. As she approached the cash register, she heard a terrible rumbling above her head. She looked up but could see nothing extraordinary. The lounge was usually a quiet spot to work. Cece noticed every sound.

Later a very handsome, strong, wiry looking, muscular blond man walked up to Cece and said, "Hi! I feel like I know you."

She was surprised by his statement and replied to the disheveled man, who was wearing a heavy work belt, "I'm sorry, but I don't think we have ever met. I'm pretty sure I would remember you."

The tall, curly headed man pointed up and replied, "I'm Hal. Do you know what a Speleologist is? I've been spelunking in all the cavernous crawl spaces above and through this old ceiling's parts, which was built many years ago in 1947. I am a private contractor who is installing equipment for the hotel's security department. I have an electronic degree and an electrical engineer's degree, too. I can see you, but you haven't been able to see me. Recently I've been working directly over your station."

Cece smiled and said, "I thought I heard noises above my station in the ceiling."

Hal said, "Yeah, it was me. I saw you, too! You're a lovely woman! I wanted to stop by and introduce myself on my lunch break."

Cece replied, "Well, Hi, Hal. I am glad to make your acquaintance. What's spelunking?" Hal explained and told Cece about the surveillance wiring being put everywhere in the hotel and casino for hi-tech security purposes. He told her everyone was going to be watched. He explained the original building was very old and had many built-on additions over the past 40+ years. Hal explained a spelunking expert had to be hired because of the hazards involved with the many added on structures to the original building's connections. No one in security had the skill or ability to crawl through the many compact spaces within the hotel's original ceiling's skeleton. It was like hobbyists exploring mountain caves.

Hal's job was to get the security wiring through the tough areas to the hidden cameras. It was right above Cece's Pickup station and her bartender's station's cash register. Hal said his company was temporarily hired to accomplish all the wiring and camera installations for the hotel and casino's new security department. Hal said only few people could do what his company did.

Cece was amazed as she said, "Wow, I can't believe what you do. It's fascinating. Don't you ever feel claustrophobic? You must have excellent job security!"

Hal laughed, "I've been in mountain caves, which are much worse than these old buildings. It's a strange business, sport, or hobby, I realize, but I've always loved it! I have seen places people don't know exist, like hidden mountain caves, their secluded garden areas, crystal waterfalls, beautiful birds, and animals. Plus, it keeps me in shape!"

Cece added as she asked, "Do you see spiders and bugs, too?"

Hal laughed, "Yeah, lots of them and bats and reptiles! I did it for fun growing up. Now, I plant wires and cameras, and I make a very good living because of my skills. No one else wants to do what I enjoy. It's actually funny."

Cece giggled, "I can see why! Spiders, reptiles, bats, and bugs can freak anyone out."

Hal laughed out loud and finally got around to the main purpose for his visit, "So, are you single? If you are, I would like to know if we could go out sometime."

Cece didn't expect him to ask that question. Cece always wore her wedding ring. She was enjoying his company and didn't think their conversation was leading to the conclusion regarding her matrimonial status. Cece felt melancholy to say goodbye to Hal's kind and delightful spirit.

Cece nicely replied, "Yes, I married very young to my teenage love. We have two sons and a lot of love in our home."

Hal replied, "My kind of luck. You are such a beautiful woman, Cece. You are normal. That's why I wanted to meet you. You're nice to everyone, too. Always stay that way. Be very careful in the near future. I am not supposed to tell anyone, but this whole place will be loaded with cameras. Security will have cameras for recording all the employees' actions. Please, don't say anything about what I just told you. It's sort of top secret, ok?"

Cece looked at Hal and said, "Ok, sure. I promise. I don't do anything wrong. That way I don't have to worry about looking over my shoulder to see if someone is watching me. I like honesty and having honor. Life's a lot easier and much more comfortable."

Hal added, "Yeah, a woman, as pretty as you are, should have those qualities, but you'd be surprised just how many beautiful women don't!"

Cece laughed, "You don't have to tell me! It's from an Italian American upbringing. I was more afraid of my Mama than the Nuns! No, I am never surprised about women! All I have to do is look around at my fellow employees. Pretty is as pretty does! It has been so nice to meet you, Hal. You are a very interesting person. Be careful up there and in those mountain caves. Always have a partner with you, please!"

Hal smiled and said, "I am always careful, and we only go spelunking as a group. It was very nice speaking with you, Cece. Hopefully, I'll see you again. Bye."

Cece smiled and said, "God bless you, Hal! Bye!"

* * *

Cece did not realize how many terrible employees were going to get fired.

* * *

Tiny little pen cameras were discreetly installed into ceilings and other imaginative locations like decorative planters. Those tiny cameras could spy on employees or whatever the owner had an interest to inspect. The cameras were so tiny they went unnoticed by the employees and customers. All employees were going to be watched and recorded when handling cash anywhere in the hotel.

The owner wanted honest employees and even more, he wanted employees with integrity. He wanted his employees to be as dedicated to their jobs as he was dedicated to overseeing his beautiful hotel and casino. Cameras were installed in elevators, guest room hallways, the back of the house hallways, bars, bar storage room areas, restaurant areas, every cashier station, the casino cage, the pool areas, pool bars, the entire back of the house work areas, and in the hotel's surrounding gardens.

There is a 2,000 plus year old Taekwondo meditation stating, "An honest man never had to worry about watching over his shoulder to see if 'The Man' was watching him."

It was one of Cece's favorite proverbs.

It is a much more pleasant way to live your life.

* * *

Immediately, Hell opened its gates!

* * *

Many times, daily, customers getting off the guest room elevators, would go up to Seria's lounge, which faced those elevators, and buy a beer with cash to carry around while they gambled. Seria was their cocktail waitress. Seria worked one side of the lounge with her bartender, JD, while

Cece and Larry worked the lounge's other side. Unbeknownst to Cece, Seria made deals with her bartender. Cece watched them divide lots of small denominations of cash money daily and split the money at their shift's end.

Cece was perplexed, thinking, "How can they make so many tips in one day? This lounge is not that busy!"

Cece later figured Larry must have known what was going on when JD worked the lounge with Seria, but Larry never said anything to anyone until the bust was over. Larry was as honest as Cece, but Larry minded his own business, and because Larry had his own stock room.

Seria would repeatedly use the same cash beer receipt JD had given her from her first 'cash' beer sale of the day. Most customers didn't want to carry a receipt for a cash purchase. Those customers would leave their cash receipt on their tables for Seria to throw out! Once Seria and JD got a current dated cash receipt, they were good for the entire day. Eventually management would get smarter and time stamp the already dated receipts. Using one receipt afforded Seria and JD a very good living. JD and Seria only rang up one cash beer receipt on their entire shift. By the end of the day, they had a bundle of cash money to share, but only one cash beer was rung up. It seemed Seria and JD made very good money at the lounge, even when they did not have seated customers. JD and Seria hardly showed any receipts, except for room charges and credit cards. They got too greedy. Bookkeeping started to notice.

Seria did very well money wise. Whenever there was a bachelor party visiting, JD would inform the male customers Seria was available. Customers could be seen making deals with J.D. Soon after, Seria took her purse and coat from behind JD's bar and headed for the elevators.

Seria would call out to Cece as she left, "Hey Ce, keep an eye on my side. I have to go to the office."

JD would cover for Seria if anyone asked where she was. JD had just about a million excuses for Seria not being on her station. Seria and JD were scammers and had ways of making money illegally anyway you looked at it.

* * *

Peggy was the main head cocktail waitress. She worked on day shift. Peggy had lots of power for the last 30 years. She did the cocktail staff hiring, all the paperwork for cocktails, and the firing, but there was a 'sort of code' that 'cocktails' protected each other. There was very little firing in cocktails. New girls weren't hired unless other ladies left or retired, which didn't happen often. Cocktails was a well sought-after job ever since it had become a union position. Before that, it was a wild department which employed boss' girlfriends and even some prostitutes to service the customers in more ways than one. In the early days before the union was formed, the more moral women didn't want to be employed in a casino cocktail waitress position.

* * *

The primary values of the union were beneficial for family security, but the union had corruption in different ranks of management during its years of existence. One of the worst crimes was when the top executive for the culinary union left with the union's entire retirement fund. The money and the executive were never found.

Many of the union's department managers got away with determining what happened to hotel and casino employees whether it was right or wrong. Sometimes corrupt casino employees, who were union shop stewards, would work with a union department manager to get what they and their friends wanted. Those shop stewards would do anything they had to do to convince a union department manager to accomplish what the steward wanted them to do. In exchange for the favor, shop stewards would even go into the union hall on their days off, to do the union department manager's work for them. Instead of showing the shop stewards were being corrupt, the union managers acted like the shop stewards were their best friends. Those crooked union shop stewards were actually hurting good workers and helping their own friends get the results they wanted. Meanwhile, the union made sure your dues were taken out of your paycheck before you got it. Being deceitful, also, enabled the shop stewards to have control over their fellow employees, their workstations, their pocketbooks, and the employee's bidding rights on shifts. Those corrupt people would gang up on a person and gain their shift or station with the union department manager's blessings.

That's pure corruption.

* * *

Peggy, the senior Head cocktail waitress, worked on day shift. There were two other assistant head cocktail managers/waitresses. Gerri was to manage the swing shift. Mitzy was to manage the graveyard shift. They were the three main 'Queen Bees'. They each worked a main casino pit on the shift they managed.

They had a lot of power and a regular waitress dare not cross them in any way or she could be fired on the spot. When the 'Bees' had their days off, there were junior assistant head cocktail waitress managers, who took over the manager's duties. Gerri and Mitzy answered only to Peggy. Peggy had the power to do just about anything, especially to cocktail waitresses. She only had to answer to the hotel and casino owner. It was not easy to get into the cocktail service in those days because the Beverage Managers only wanted experienced cocktail waitresses. Cece got hired because no one else wanted the coffee shop bid.

There was a sign on the new East Sahara Avenue I I5 freeway off ramp in the mid-1960s. The sign read there were approximately 140,000 people who lived in Southern Nevada. That was true for a very short amount of time, but the Las Vegas population always doubled on weekends when tourists hit the streets of Las Vegas to party.

Beverage management picked the most beautiful girls in town to be cocktail waitresses. If a girl were related to someone involved with a casino, or knew someone important, she could get a job, but she still had to be pretty. The town started growing so quickly the freeway population sign had to be removed soon after it was installed.

Beverage Shift Managers were mostly men, but upper management had enough brains in those early days to put women in charge of cocktail servers. It afforded some kind of assurance the women would not use special means to control the male managers, but some evil women still got away with it for years.

Some women will do anything to get what they want, and they did, when male personnel were put in charge of cocktail waitresses. The most proficient female liars were amazing because they could use their lying tongues to achieve what they wanted from the men and never had to bed them. It was fascinating to watch, and even more amazing to pity the female liars. The liars would even manipulate other women into doing things for them and get the women to 'gang up' on a fellow waitress. Many times women can control men with the wicked lies that easily roll off their tongues. The less intelligent male managers could be easily charmed and corrupted. Fraternizing caused many a fight, because certain women could control male managers, just like they had a hook in their nose.

Most of the women were kind enough to each other, but there were always a few who would lie and hurt the other girls, after they had pretended to befriend them. When nice girls would let down their guard, those witches attacked once they weaseled into a person's confidence! Soon all the other girls got wise. Weasels lost respect and many good potential friends. Girls didn't understand why, but they thought it was usually out of jealousy, envy, bitterness, or insecurity. It was sad when the girls named a troublemaker a 'Weasel', because that was how they saw her, that was how she truly was, and that was how they treated her.

Fool me once, shame on you. Fool me twice, shame on me.

NEVER AGAIN!

A weasel's greed, her jealousy, or her sick money lust would hurt only herself. Cece was sure those women were psychopaths. The liar could take a harmless innocent statement or act, and turn it around in her sick mind, to make the other girls hate an innocent girl. However, eventually the girls figured it out, and the lair was permanently labeled a "Weasel".

After the lying girl did 'whatever she wanted' to more and more of the girls, the women spread the word to beware of the weasel. Since many of the women make a profession out of their union cocktail jobs, once the women spread the word about a liar, the weasel is shunned. No one, except new innocent girls or other weasels, wanted to be in her miserable company. Weasels burnt too many bridges. Keeping their lies straight was a problem which was even more interesting to watch. Female bullies learned as little girls to be cruel and conniving people.

When a woman tells you, "she had very horrible fights with her own sisters, or they had not spoken to them for years", BEWARE!

* * *

Workers continued to install cameras in the service bars, the front bars, pump rooms, and everywhere else right after Cece got her first casino lounge bid and met Hal. If anyone asked what the installers were doing, they were told the casino and hotel's old wiring was being replaced. Cece kept her promise to Hal to be quiet.

It was truly interesting! Security was finally ready to go. They had been filming and watching mainly the head cocktail waitresses, and some high profile bartenders. The security viewers always watched for thieves. Not one of those surveillance people realized what was happening with employees. Security wanted to see if there were patterns involved. There definitely were.

The lying 'Head Cocktail Waitress', Peggy, on day shift, was called into the beverage office. No one knew about the new cameras. Management wanted to know why she hung out of the service bar instead of at her casino station. The beverage manager mentioned Peggy was in corners whispering with other girls as they passed in and out of the service bar, instead of looking out for customers in her station. Peggy said the pit bosses on the floor would call her if customers showed up or requested drinks. The bar manager told her that was unacceptable. She was to remain on her station. Peace reigned in the service bar for quite a while after her visit from the office. She actually had to work.

Honesty was Cece's best friend. She was the new cocktail waitress on the casino floor and did not need any added attention. Just getting along with the women's different personalities, walking around gracefully in public wearing a tiny uniform, and diligently working in high heels, was enough for Cece to accomplish daily.

* * *

After the recordings were started and viewed, employees was called in to the beverage office, security office, or worse, to watch their recordings.

Employees began to lose their lucrative positions.

After 30 years of being a day shift head cocktail waitress, Peggy got fired for disclosing confidential medical information out of an employee's private personnel file. She gave personal medical information to a disgruntled 'soon to be ex-husband' of a beautiful, hardworking, young mother of two little girls and one of Peggy's best cocktail waitresses.

Peggy knew the 'soon to be ex-husband' personally for years before the couple was married. Well to do, and very handsome playboy the husband was trying to divorce his young wife 'and' his two little girls. He wanted to get out of paying alimony to his wife or any kind of support for their two little daughters. For that reason, he wanted to dig up dirt on his ex-wife to use in court against her. The husband had already gone to the girl's medical doctor to get confidential medical information from him, but the doctor refused to give the husband any information. The husband had a thriving business. He didn't want to be bothered supporting his little daughters, when he could use the money to escort beautiful women. He wanted his freedom and convinced Peggy to give him the personal information out of his wife's personnel file. He felt his little girls would just get in his way of enjoying what he would like to do in his single playboy future.

Peggy was seen for approximately one hour talking, hugging, and flirting around with the soon to be ex-husband. Peggy totally ignored her busy high limit 21 pit customers for the entire hour as she spoke to the playboy. What Peggy didn't realize was the young wife's medical information would not help the playboy or his lawyer in court. They both would lose.

The young wife's lawyer called the hotel's owner directly and told him what Peggy had done. The husband's lawyer tried to use the information in court against the wife. The judge threw out the non-admissible medical information. The hotel and casino owner became enraged! He did not want to be held liable or get sued. The hotel and casino owner promised the young wife a job for life, as long as she wanted to continue to work for him, if she would not sue him. Security went back into the head cocktail waitresses' recordings to view the films. The owner wanted the film of Peggy talking to the ex-husband. He called Security.

One of the best security film viewers remembered seeing something about Peggy holding a file and talking to a man for a very long time, when Peggy was supposed to be working. The young security viewer finally found that recording! The girl's lawyer arrived at the hotel owner's office just in time to watch.

The owner called the young wife to his office. The owner called Peggy at the main casino service bar and told her to immediately report to his private office. He told Peggy to cover her station and he would send someone to get her. She did.

The owner did, too!

The special young security viewer who found the recording got a $1,000.00 bonus check as a 'good job, thank you'. The rest of the security viewers paid attention. Bonuses became an actual possibility in their future! The incentive made for more diligent security viewers.

Peggy was escorted, like a common criminal, through the hotel and casino by a team of four fully armed huge men dressed in black combat uniforms. One guard walked in front of Peggy. The two guards, at her sides, each had one of her arms above the elbow in their adjacent hand. The last guard walked behind her. Peggy was embarrassed, humiliated, and perplexed. Everyone in the casino knew Peggy. Everyone was confused. Peggy was taken right off the casino floor, put into a plush elevator, and escorted into the owner's gorgeous private office, which contained his own surveillance equipment. Peggy saw her recordings, heard the charges against her, and was fired by the hotel and casino owner in front of the young wife and her lawyer.

The wife's lawyer and the hotel and casino owner's lawyer confronted Peggy for divulging confidential medical information from the wife's personal file. It was apparent the hotel and casino owner was furious when he told Peggy she was to be immediately removed from his property. Peggy was to take any belongings she may have with her, and to never come back onto any of his properties because, SHE WAS FIRED!

For 30 years Peggy was the powerful head cocktail waitress of the hotel and casino. It was a shock for all the girls to watch Peggy gathering her things and being taken away in disgrace by four armed security guards. The guards escorted Peggy to the front door of the hotel and casino. They were not letting her leave by the employee exit. They took all her hotel ID information before she walked away. She would be charged for the uniform on her back and the cost would come out of her last check.

When Peggy got fired, it was a disgraceful situation because of the serious allegations against her. Peggy was somewhat fortunate she did not get in any worse trouble than she did, or get the company, for which she worked into a more serious legal situation.

When you work for someone, they are the ones responsible for you, your behavior, and your actions. The owner wanted Peggy forever gone, and she was from his employment, anyway!

* * *

A few months after Peggy got fired, she showed up in the hotel and casino as a union steward. The union employees were all appalled. The union received many complaints because they hired a disgruntled employee even after what she did, but many union stewards were corrupt!

The girls were saying, "Peggy paid union dues all of her working life, plus she wasn't going to honestly tell the union what happened, and incriminate herself, or would she, and if she did, would that incriminate the union?"

Hush, someone could be listening!

* * *

Since the husband of the young lady who was the cocktail waitress and mother involved, couldn't get any dirt on his wife, he made himself penniless on paper. Then he wouldn't be obligated to pay anything to his ex-wife or support his daughters. He signed all his business, financial accounts, and assets over to a trusted family member.

He continued to be a womanizer. He caught a serious sexually transmitted disease. His 'trusted' relative took him and his lucrative business for a ride and blew all his money gambling. They both were broke. The IRS moved in on the ex-husband's business, him, and his relative. Charges were pressed. They both paid Uncle Sam until they died, which wasn't long after the IRS served the ex-husband and his untrustworthy relative. The ex-husband would not go to doctors. He was in denial of acquiring a serious venereal disease. He died young, penniless, alone, and in great pain. The relative died very soon after from a heart attack.

The devastated young cocktail waitress, ex-wife, and mother continued to work hard. She supported her two little daughters for the next four years. She kept herself healthy and dedicated to her two little girls. The cocktail waitresses banded together to give her all the early outs she needed. Some even helped to babysit. They were a sisterhood after all.

One day, when she least expected it, a wonderful man walked into her life. They fell in love, married, and had another baby. The baby was a little boy. The girls were delighted to have a baby brother. No one would ever abuse her or her children again. They were all very much loved and cared for by her good new husband!

* * *

In cocktails, the excitement never ends.

* * *

The graveyard head cocktail waitress, Mitzy, was compared to a scum bucket by the women with whom she worked. Mitzy never seemed to get caught no matter what she did. She knew how to be a crude mouthed person and liked it. Her appearance was sloppy and ugly. She appeared threatening to the other women. The more feminine women were frightened by her, what she could do to harm them, fire them, or physically hurt them. For that reason, all the other women, who worked on her shift with her, only whispered about her escapades between each other and no one else.

Before the cameras were installed, all head management personnel were on their honor, even if they had none. The new cameras showed Mitzy, ordering her vulnerable pit partner, Candy, to work her section all night for 8 hours, along with Candy's own section. If Candy refused, it would be a regular girl's word against Mitzy's word, and Mitzy would win. Upper management would believe the word of the head cocktail waitress in charge. Mitzy was a girl's worst nightmare. The women were frightened continuously by Mitzy because, to put it nicely, she was a mean hag! She could make your life miserable, and could beat almost any man in a fight. Mitzy was huge, tough, and ominous. Even Mitzy's wig looked like a filthy petrified combat helmet.

The graveyard shift security cameras filmed Mitzy, while she was 'on the clock'. She was in uniform, taking her purse, her coat, and leaving to go across the street to a neighboring hotel and casino where she gambled and drank alcohol. Plain clothes security followed her for her 8-hour shifts while she was at the adjacent casino. Mitzy would return to her job one hour before the day shift women were due to arrive. She would act like she was working on cigarette inventory, while Candy continued to cover both stations.

For three weeks before the beverage sting occurred, plain clothes security had documented everything Mitzy was doing. They had her on film doing everything wrong. Security had her walking out the front door, while in full uniform, with her coat and purse over her arm, while she was on the clock. They filmed Mitzy returning an hour before clock out. Thanks to films made on precisely dated and timed portable camera equipment, she was filmed in full uniform gambling and drinking during her work shift at the casino across the street.

After security documented Mitzy's recordings on the owner's new state-of-the-art security equipment, they were ready for 'sting day'. Mitzy was getting paid for eight hours of work, receiving union benefits, and getting medical and dental insurance, while she was not even working in the hotel and casino.

On the morning of the sting, Mitzy began her last hours routine after coming back to her place of employment. The only reason Mitzy would ever stay at work was if she had a very generous 'high roller' in her section, which was rare on the 3:00 am to 11:00 am graveyard shift.

Mitzi returned to the service bar, while discreetly followed by four plain clothed security guards. They spoke to the 'Eye in the Sky' through tiny mikes pinned to their uniform collars. The 'Eye in the Sky' began more in-house filming. To make matters worse, Mitzy was seen on camera in the service bar taking half of the tips Candy had made in the last seven hours and putting the tips into her own large cloth bag. Mitzy still ordered Candy to work her section for the last hour of their shift, which enabled Mitzy to stay in the service bar and 'work on' the free cigarettes reserved for only high limit gambling customers. The cameras showed Mitzy stealing two cartons of cigarettes daily and putting the cartons in her huge bag. Mitzy went over to the coffee area. She removed a 10 lb bag of the hotel's most expensive Colombian whole coffee beans. She took the coffee beans over to her bag and put the coffee beans under her two stolen cartons of cigarettes so the cartons would not be crushed. Mitzy took another half of the last hour tips Candy just had finished making before they would leave the casino floor to dayshift.

When Mitzy's shift was ending she was escorted as Peggy was into the security office to view her recordings. She was told charges would not be filed against her if she resigned and did not get unemployment. Mitzy started screaming vulgarities at the security officers. She was a big tough woman, who could go up against any man, but Security helped Mitzy uncomfortably leave through the casino's front door after retrieving the two cartons of cigarettes, the bag of coffee, and her hotel personnel ID card from her bag. It was all recorded for the future, just in case of repercussions.

None of the graveyard girls were surprised because they had been watching Mitzy for many years. Those women knew what Mitzy was doing, but they were completely afraid of her and the 'hell' she could do to them. They rejoiced when Mitzy was escorted out of the hotel by armed security guards as she continued to scream, yell, rant and rave. The other two shifts of girls were totally surprised by what Mitzy had been doing for years and how she 'blew away' a grand job.

* * *

Nothing happened to the head cocktail waitress on swing shift, Gerri. The only things proven about Gerri was she was trustworthy, kind, caring, and fair to all the girls and to the customers. Gerri received a big promotion to Head Cocktail Waitress without a raise, if you call that a promotion!

* * *

Security continued on to the bartenders. The alternative security system was eventually installed everywhere possible. The cameras were aimed at the cash registers, the front bars, the bartender's customers, the service personnel and the storage and pump rooms behind all the bars. The best thing about the pen cameras was they were tiny, portable, and could be placed almost anywhere. The cameras were placed at many angles. The owner's orders were no employees were to be told about any of the cameras. The order included some upper beverage management personnel, who were caught sleeping their shifts away in back pump rooms while completely inebriated.

The casino pit personnel, on 21 games and in Crap pits, had been on camera for years, but that's another story. Cece was amazed by the results security was finding. Everyday Cece wondered how many more bar personnel would be gone at the day's end.

Many of the security team members worked 10-hour shifts to watch the recordings being played back to see what all the bartenders were doing during their eight-hour shifts. Those security personnel watched every customer transaction whether it was cash, check, credit cards, debit cards, or a room charge. The honest employees had nothing to worry about because they would just go on with the normal business of their day. The security teams came up with many more revelations in the days that followed. Some findings were vulgar, while some findings were downright stupid.

* * *

JD and Seria were called into the owner's office. They were shown their films and how they stole from their employer by not ringing up inventory and kept the cash money customers paid for bottles of beer. They showed them using the same cash receipt for many more than just one beer, and how they did it daily, repeatedly. They had all the evidence needed against Seria for prostitution, and JD for pimping and covering for Seria. Seria was recorded going up in guest elevators with hotel patrons. The guest hallway cameras caught her willingly entering different guest rooms. Many times Seria was recorded leaving a guest room while tucking a wad of cash down into her bra. Apparently Seria was even holding out on JD.

All the cocktail waitresses weren't surprised, except for Cece, who had wondered why Seria was gone from her station so much. The girls had been talking about a lounge waitress involved in prostitution, and a bartender covering for her. JD did a remarkable job covering for her because he got a cut of her action. Security got two birds with one stone when they were filming Seria and tied JD into her action. All of what Seria and JD did was right under Cece's nose, but Cece did not even know prostitution was occurring. Cece did wonder why JD and Seria counted a lot of cash money at the end of their shift and split it when they hardly worked! Cece did not constantly watch them because she had different hours than Seria, and her own customers to serve. When it was over, the puzzle pieces fell into place for Cece, but Larry had figured it out on his own.

The Bartenders

* * *

There were many other recordings. No one knew there was a sting ordered on a certain weekend day, except the Eye in the Sky. The day security picked was a perfect weekend day. It was a day everyone, who was suspected, was scheduled to work. Security made sure things went exactly as planned. Security could not believe employees with such good money-making jobs would do the things these employees were doing. Security realized many of the employees were old timers, who got away with so much for so many years, that they were used to doing whatever they wanted to do. There are always a few bad employees, who seem to slip through the cracks for so many years and not get caught, but things would catch up to them finally. Let's see, with whom shall we start?

* * *

Harvey was a quiet bartender who looked so clean-cut and straight, you would never think he could do anything wrong. He looked like a perfect older clean-cut gentleman but he was not what he appeared to be. Harvey worked one hour in each of the best high limit bars on day shift doing other bartender's lunch breaks. It was the most envied day shift bartender position. Harvey made excellent tips. The only nasty break he had for tips was Tex's back of the house keno service bar where he worked with Cece. His other bad break was, Harvey was cheap! He hoarded his tips.

Harvey had been harassing Cece, while she was working on her newly acquired keno bid. Harvey didn't think Cece tipped him enough. The keno players hardly tipped Cece because Harvey kept leaving his workstation, making it impossible for Cece to get her drinks in a timely manner. It was her new shift, and she needed to prove herself to the players and let them know she'd be there every day. Harvey felt Cece disturbed him constantly while Harvey was giving Tex his lunch break. Cece was only trying to get her orders made promptly and keep her customers happy. Keno was next to the Race and Sportsbook. Many hotel executives hung out there, including the hotel and casino owner. Sometimes the Race and Sportsbook boss would ask Cece to take a round in his area, but only when he gave her permission because the players had to be betting. Many times, people would sit and watch the action all day and not bet.

Harvey thought Cece made him work too hard. Cece began working in the very busy keno station at the time of the bartender's ongoing sting. Keno was a tough place to make tips and Cece had to constantly carry out a heavy tray full of drinks, or the customers would get upset and report her for not working diligently and continuously.

Security watched Harvey frequently leaving Cece's work area, while he was supposed to be giving Cece's regular bartender, Tex, his lunch break. Harvey was a spoiled 64 years old break bartender. He had the most seniority of all the bartenders, and the best break shift in the house. Harvey feared nothing. He had been in the union for over 30 years and had a false sense of security.

Harvey's work bank was always short the odd amount of two dollars a day. Most of the time, management would overlook such a minor discrepancy, but Harvey's 'discrepancy' never went away. It had been on Harvey's record since before the new owner gained the property.

Harvey was leaving his one-hour keno break, by walking out the dark back service hallway, and into the casino. Harvey left the keno workstation unattended for 10 to 20 minutes or more at a time. Security suggested looking into Harvey. The owner agreed because Harvey's daily shortage intrigued the hotel and casino owner.

Harvey's shift was only six hours long. All the bartenders wanted his shift. Harvey was cocky because he was top in seniority and only had to stay in the different bars giving lunch breaks for one hour at a time. Harvey's own break was his last break. He could stay his sixth hour and get paid for having his own lunch, or he could sign out early after working only five hours and go home. If Harvey signed out early, he did not get paid for his own lunch break. He could just work only five hours a day if he wanted. Harvey worked in five different bars. Four bars were the best bar areas to make tips on day shift. Harvey's keno break was not a lucrative station.

The back of the house Keno bar was Harvey's next-to-last break. It was adjacent to the dark back service hallway. The Race and Sports Book bar was in front of the back service hallway. Harvey's last break was for Dave, one of two bartenders who worked in the Sports Bar. When Harvey worked with Cece in the keno service bar, he took four to five 'falsely called' restroom breaks in one hour to go check out the horse race action and info.

Dave watched Harvey leaving his keno break unattended to go out to the casino's race and sportsbook. Dave knew Harvey was cheap. Harvey wouldn't risk his own tips to make a bet! Yet Dave saw Harvey constantly going in and out the back-service hallway behind the sports bar and across from the keno bar. That hallway went out into the casino's race and sportsbook out area, keno area, and slots. Everyone knew he was supposed to be making drinks for Cece. Harvey was hooked on the horses. Cece was too busy to continually watch Harvey, but she figured Harvey was taking generous time advantage of his employer. Cece was just thankful she didn't have to work with Harvey over one hellish hour a day.

Cece would heat all her coffee mugs enabling her ordered coffees to stay hot because Harvey took so long to get back to her service bar. Normally, Cece took an order every 10 to 15 minutes in her busy keno area. During Harvey's absences, Cece would go behind the bar and get her ordered bottles of beer ready to be opened. She would gather the needed amount of iced glasses for her order. If he still didn't come back into the bar, Cece would make all her coffees. Usually by then, Harvey would come back into the bar. If he still didn't come back, Cece would have to go out into the race and sportsbook and find him. The cameras had it all recorded, including Harvey yelling at Cece for bothering him.

There were many times when Dave would look at Cece and point at Harvey looking at the horse racing screens. Cece would just look back at Dave, shake her head negatively, hold her hands out with palms up, and shrug her shoulders. Then she would go get Harvey. Cece had done all the rest of his work except take the caps off of the beer bottles, pick up the faucet guns to pour the mixed drinks, and ring up her order. Many times Harvey would tell Cece he was going to report her to the culinary union for doing his bartending work.

DUH!

Cece knew she would not report Harvey for doing his job improperly. Who would the union and the 'DON'T BOTHER ME BOSSES' believe? A relatively new cocktail waitress would not be believed over a bartender with 30 years of experience and top union seniority. Yes, Cece made Harvey's job easier, but it was only out of desperation. Cece learned to wait for Harvey meant the customers would be mad at her for taking too long to get their orders. It gave customers a perfect excuse not to tip Cece.

Keno was turning out to be another 'coffee shop nightmare'. Even though it wasn't her fault, Cece's tips suffered. The tips weren't good to begin with in keno, but Cece would rather have Harvey bitching at her regularly than to be late getting her heavy orders out to her customers. Harvey always tried to put her on the defensive, but she knew better. Cece didn't take abuse lightly. She spoke back to Harvey, while stating the truth and always maintaining a professional attitude.

Yes, Harvey would get mad at Cece for going behind the bar and doing his job, but Cece would tell him she was under a lot of pressure to get her orders out to her customers speedily.

Cece said, "My customers will blame me, and not a bartender, for my tardiness. It's not fair, Harvey!"

The cameras watched and recorded.

Cece told Harvey the customers would never understand the fact he was in the race and sportsbook watching horse races. That actually shut Harvey up... for a while! He didn't want to work! Harvey continued to threaten Cece telling her he was going to report her to the union for doing a bartender's work, which was, and still is, a serious allegation. She would tell Harvey she would not have to do his job, if he stayed on his station and did his own work.

Harvey became very mean, frightening, and threatening to Cece. He knew she wasn't a fink. Cece didn't know what Harvey was 'really doing' and had been 'really doing' for many years. Cece always made sure Harvey rang up all her drinks even though he didn't want to bother. Harvey would have preferred to hurry back out to the race book instead, without ringing up any of her drinks. Undercover security really got an eyeful watching when Harvey was supposed to be breaking the keno bartender.

Cece was an honest employee who had a family to raise. She needed her job, which included excellent benefits for her family, and retirement for her future. A bartender or an employee could get fired if they didn't ring up all their orders. It was considered theft by their employer. Ringing up drinks was a stringent rule. It was for IRS tax information, for inventory control, for category control, etc. It was morally the right thing to do for the company. Plus, once again, ringing up her revenue showed Cece was working hard and was 'needed' in her area, which was good job security.

Many bartenders were very lackadaisical about doing the ring ups for the drinks they poured because they were just being 'lazy'. Security cameras were catching several bartenders not ringing up any of their drinks, but if they weren't doing anything worse, they were given a onetime written warning notice. They were not fired unless they did it a second time.

However, if bartenders continued after their first warning notice was given, the next procedure was to be terminated for noncompliance. Most importantly, having a written warning notice on their records meant the bartenders were ineligible to bid on a better money-making station for six months. Bartenders made sure their total drink ring ups were done and accurate.

Suddenly, revenue and the counts were showing up. The owner was very pleased, but the owner was also very pleased with his employees who showed honest work habits. He watched! He remembered!

Theft is a horrible thing to have on a work record. In those days employers told the truth about an employee's character, when someone called for an employee reference. However, in the very near future, most managers would become very diplomatic about what they said on phone calls pertaining to an employee's past work performance, because of 'defamation of character' lawsuits. Those former terrible and dishonest employees were threatening lawsuits against the hotels, casinos, and owners, even though they did not deserve a good recommendation! Thieves cheated only on themselves because there were no benefits stacking up for their future. An honest employee never had to worry because they did an honest job. There were several employees, who apparently had been dishonest, or worse, for many years! The owner and security were astonished!

Security cameras began making employees honest, and the more busts, the more honest 'the luckier' still working employees became!

The owner asked many of the terrible employees if they would like to resign or would rather go to court and air out their dirty laundry in front of everyone, including their families. They resigned and didn't ask for unemployment. Many new positions would open up because of the amount of dishonest people involved in the firing spree, and that was just in the beverage department!

Cameras would change everything in all locations of hotels and casinos in Las Vegas in the 1980s.

Dishonest people learned "honesty did pay".

* * *

Harvey's bank continued to be two dollars short in his register's daily count balance. However, $2.00 short every day when he worked for the last 30 years was on his record and was ridiculous! The owner wanted to know why Harvey's bank never balanced, and why it was always only short $2.00 a day for over the last 30 years. Harvey was next! It took a while, but Security cameras finally caught everything.

Harvey didn't care about the keno customers getting their drinks in a timely manner. He didn't care about ringing up Cece's ordered drinks. He didn't care about anyone or anything, and that included his employer. Harvey only cared about the horses. He figured with 30 years of union seniority; he would never get fired. Cece could not understand Harvey's addiction to the horse races, because he was so bad at it. She never saw Harvey win.

The front sportsbook bartender, Dave, was getting disgusted watching Harvey taking advantage of him and Cece. When it was Dave's break time, Harvey would ask Dave for an actual restroom break before breaking into his sports bar. Dave needed a restroom break after being on the floor for 5 straight hours, and Dave was looking forward to sitting down for his lunch hour. Dave thought it was downright rude of Harvey to expect Dave to short himself on his break, especially when Dave had to work two more busy hours after his break. Dave knew Harvey had many opportunities to walk thirty more feet from the race and sportsbook to the restroom when he was breaking the Keno service bar. However, obsessed Harvey couldn't pull himself away from the Race and Sportsbook screens.

Cece was the only girl working out of the keno service bar, except on weekends. It was a Saturday. The two Sportsbook bartenders and the keno bartender kept their two back doors opened into the back-service hallway on busy weekends. When those two back doors were opened, everyone could see in and out of the gaming areas, including the entire race and sportsbook, the sports bar, the keno desk, keno seating areas, the slot areas, and beyond into the whole busy casino. Plus, all those same casino areas could see into the back-service hallway. Customers could see Cece ordering their drinks at the back of the house keno service bar.

Many of the employees would sneak peeks at the sportsbook scoreboards, dog races, horse races, and sports. It got so prevalent that employees were not allowed to look up at the screens or events shown, unless they were off the time clock, but Harvey seemed to get away with it, or Cece thought.

Harvey figured if Cece ever did say anything, it would be his word against her word. Harvey had a lot more seniority than Cece had in the union. Harvey figured if he ever got called into the beverage office for leaving his station, he would just confirm what he said in the past to the managers. Harvey would just say he had a fragile heart, a weak bladder, and needed restroom breaks often. However, there were cameras now, and no one knew… except Cece, Hal, the Hotel and Casino Owner, and Security!

It would do no good to report Harvey as a poor employee because many of the bar management staff wanted no more problems to solve. They didn't think they made enough money to deal with personal or personnel problems on top of all the other things they were responsible to accomplish. Eventually they would be sorry. If someone tried to go to bar management for help, they were labeled a troublemaker.

All things are subject to change and no one should ever forget… it happens. Harvey would never tell the bosses the truth. He certainly would not say he took up to four restroom breaks during his keno break hour when he wasn't really going to the restroom. He would never say he was going to the race book to figure out his daily bet. Cece tried to get along with everyone. If it was not possible, she would speak directly with the fellow employee and tell the person what they needed to hear. Cece told Harvey like it was. Harvey didn't like Cece. She suffered from his verbal abuse, but she could handle that even if it were not fair. She never got Ian involved. She was right, and she was strong! Thanks to Carmella and Sammie for making Cece stealth and an honest person of principle.

The Race and Sportsbook crew and the Keno crew knew Harvey was perpetually checking out the race action. All the bar doors were open, everyone could see him, and the cameras got an eye full of many angles! The extremely busy Race and Sportsbook was a different department and minded their own business. Cece assumed Race and Sportsbook employees erroneously thought Harvey was on his lunch break when he made bets.

Harvey did not realize Dave, the bartender in the sports bar, was watching everything Harvey did. Dave could see Harvey peruse the race and sportsbook daily while he was supposed to be doing his keno break. Dave knew Harvey kept leaving his keno station. Dave knew Harvey had plenty of chances to use the restroom while doing the keno bartender's lunch break. Dave wondered why Harvey kept asking him for a restroom break when he first arrived to do Dave's sports bar break when he could have gone during his keno break.

No one spoke of gambling addiction and obsession in those years.

Harvey really loved Dave's sports bar because he could watch all the big screens and not get in any trouble. Working in the sports bar, Harvey would never have to worry about explaining any breaks, because he never wanted to leave. Harvey would make good tips at the Sports bar and he watched all the electronic information boards, the gigantic screens, and discussed odds with customers. Harvey should have been looking over his shoulder, but he never would have seen it coming. It was set up perfectly.

When Harvey got to the sports bar, he would surround the cash register with all his things including his bulky jacket hanging over his arm. Harvey awkwardly changed out Dave's cash drawer and handed it to Dave, which Dave would take on his break. Then oddly, Harvey would grab his jacket as he was clumsily inserting his own cash drawer into the cash register. Suddenly Harvey would tell Dave he would be right back because he needed to use the restroom. By the time Harvey got back from a restroom break, Dave had already lost ten minutes of his own one-hour lunch break. You could almost see the steam coming out of Dave's ears. Dave was getting tired of Harvey taking advantage of him, especially because he could have been going to the restroom while he was breaking Cece's keno bartender, instead of watching the race and sportsbook's screens. Harvey was 'cutting into Dave's lunch break time'. It caused the two bartenders to argue.

Security watched Harvey and Dave switch out their two banks, but Harvey's jacket always seemed to be in the way while he installed his own cash drawer into the cash register. Then Harvey put his jacket on and ran for a real restroom break.

Security managers wondered, "Why was Harvey always carrying his jacket when they switched banks. Wasn't it summer? Who needs a jacket in Las Vegas in the summer? Why did he carry a jacket year-round?"

Security was suspicious of his jacket dangling over the cash register until they installed tiny pen cameras at varying angles aimed at that cash register from the planters surrounding it. Security had become very suspicious of Harvey leaving his keno service bar station as often as he did. Security wanted to know what Harvey was doing. The day of the sting, Security knew how many times Harvey really entered restrooms during his six-hour shift. The total was zero. Security knew everything five days prior to Harvey's predicted termination. Security was set to go! They just needed that final film.

Security had Harvey on a lot of recordings. In the past, the camera shots were not clear because Harvey's jacket was blocking the views. As Harvey arrived in the sports bar, he once again dumped his belongings all around in the cash register.

Many pen size cameras had been readjusted in the sports bar's planters surrounding the cash register area the night before the actual day of Harvey's sting. For two weeks prior to the sting, the cameras filmed Harvey's arrival in the sports bar as he fumbled his jacket around the cash register, but the cameras caught nothing. It looked like Harvey would make an excuse to leave the sports bar for a real restroom break before the regular bartender, Dave, finally got to leave late on his own lunch break. Security saw Dave getting angry with Harvey.

Dave, Cece, and the Eye in the Sky had watched Harvey taking constant breaks while doing the break for the keno service bar. Security wanted to know why Harvey was on the casino floor and always out of his keno service bar's break. There were many films labeled with Harvey's Info. The security viewers wanted those bonuses and stayed diligent figuring out Harvey's actions. They teamed up and finally did. They were glad to share their bonus tip!

Security realized the sportsbook bartender, Dave, didn't want to cut his own break short every day to give Harvey a 10-minute restroom break. Especially after Dave saw Harvey hanging out in the sportsbook area for an hour, on and off, while he was supposed to be breaking Tex and serving Cece in the keno service bar.

Security was having a revelation!

Two bartenders fighting daily didn't look right to the sharp-eyed security people watching Harvey's recordings.

Finally, the hallway cameras in front of the restrooms picked up some info.

The day of the beverage department sting, Harvey brought his jacket and other things over to the cash register area of the sports bar. Angry looking, Dave grabbed his own bank register out of Harvey's hands and left. Harvey was surprised by Dave. Harvey looked like he worked, or so it seemed. He fumbled around in the cash register area once again. A set of pen cameras caught something!

Harvey quickly left the sports bar unattended, put on his jacket, and went around to the far side of the race and sportsbook betting windows, where a second camera over the restroom entrance was aimed toward the back-betting area. Harvey placed a $2.00 bet and quickly returned to the sports bar. The new Eye in the Sky cameras picked up something very interesting after watching Harvey for those last five minutes. In that period, Harvey had been recorded fumbling in his cash drawer by a set of five mini cameras hidden in the planters behind the bar. Security got a perfect shot of what they had suspected Harvey was doing everyday he worked. Security finally saw everything for the first time. Security needed to be sure before they proceeded with their plan. They waited and waited for backup.

An undercover security enforcement team of 15 armed men dressed in combat black moved into the very dark back service hallway. They stood outside of both the Sports Bar and the Keno bar's two back doors. From that black hallway, the Security team watched the two bar's back doors. They held long black shields in front of them. The security cameras already had what was needed on film. They just had to confirm if they got their picture.

From where Cece exited her bar, you could see into all the casino areas, but when she turned to walk out the dark back service hallway, it was painted black, so customers would not accidentally walk into it. It was very dark and Cece always had to be careful, but it was her last round before going home and she was anxious.

The security enforcement team waited and listened while the film processors finished. The security manager and his team couldn't be seen in the dark. Cece took her full tray of drinks into her arms and walked out into the black hallway leading out to the gaming areas. She walked right and almost into the 15-man Security team, because everything was so dark, and everyone was dressed in black with big black shields. She didn't even see them until they were right in front of her. Cece almost slammed into them! She looked very startled to them because they scared her! They were fully equipped. They had weapons and guns! She must have looked frightened because they smiled at her, put their forefingers to their lips, and silently waved her forward.

Cece was very confused. She had never seen so many fully armed security guards in a group of 15 men at once. They looked like they were ready for war. Then the team's lead guard put his index finger over his lips in the 'shh' position. Cece realized she was not to speak or make noise. Some guards were whispering to Cece to be silent as they gently helped her find a path through their group of armed men and out to the casino. Cece was bewildered but knew all the guards. They were her friends.

As Cece arrived in the keno lounge, she handed out her ordered drinks. She tried not to act bewildered. The cameras kept recording Harvey. Security listened for the 'go ahead' orders. Apparently, security wanted everything perfect on Harvey's recordings, or it would have all been called off, if the recording was not perfect, especially after they worked so hard putting it all together. Clark County Metropolitan Police department had their own team of men coming in from the other end of the back hallway. Once the 'Eye' was sure they had the perfect shots on film, they gave the ground team the 'go ahead' orders.

The security enforcement members knew who Cece was and knew how Harvey had been treating her. They all respected Cece because they knew she was honest and hardworking. They didn't like the way Harvey ridiculed her when she was trying to do her job and trying to do Harvey's job for him. Security's eye in the sky recorded what Harvey had been doing when he and Cece were working together and it showed how Harvey mistreated her. The 15 manned security enforcement team waited for the 'go ahead' order. They had what they needed on film. Harvey was giving the last break of his career when Cece served her last round of drinks for her day.

Cece walked back towards the keno service bar. She saw the enforcement team moving as they joined up with the team of police from the Clark County Metropolitan Police Department coming in to see Harvey. She could hear a lot of commotion and many male voices because the police were following the security team into the back door of the sports bar. She wondered what was happening. As Cece got back to the keno service bar, she looked through the sports bar's opened back door and saw many policemen behind the sports bar with the security team reading Harvey his rights as they were trying to handcuff him in front of a huge crowd of spectators. It was time for Cece and Tex to get ready to clock out because it was the change of shifts. Cece asked Tex what was going on.

Tex came around his bar to look and said, "I have no idea! But I don't think Harvey's going on his lunch break because he is being handcuffed!"

Cece told Tex, "I almost walked right into the security team on my way out to deliver my last order. They waved me through with my order and said to be very quiet."

Dave was dumbfounded as he tried to get into his bar. It was too crowded. Dave, Cece, and Tex watched the casino's security manager, his team members, and the Clark County Metropolitan Police handcuffing Harvey behind the sports bar as they read him his rights. The public, also, watched the bust go down right in front of everyone in the casino areas. The scene continued to unfold in front of a growing crowd watching from the other side of the race and sports bar. The keno crew and the Race and Sportsbook's crew had a bird's-eye view of everything. Customers were running up to the bar to see. Harvey was being disgraced and arrested in front of everyone in the casino, including his fellow employees.

The first thing Cece thought was how sickly Harvey looked. He was sullenly pale white. She was worried Harvey would have a heart attack right there behind the sports bar. Harvey looked horribly faint. The security team had to hold Harvey up to finish handcuffing him! Harvey looked like his knees were about to collapse under his own weight. He was taken away to be jailed at the Clark County Detention Center. They all passed by a still astonished Dave as he was trying to return to his station.

The next day Harvey wouldn't be coming into work ever again. All the bartenders told the same story. Harvey was busted for taking $2.00 daily out of his work's cash drawer funds for many years and placing a bet on company time with company money.

The recordings picked up Harvey putting on his jacket as he lifted his cash drawer's lid and discreetly slid $2.00 out of his cash drawer, under the protection of his bulky jacket. Then Harvey left his station unattended and walked around the far corner to the sportsbook betting windows. He placed a $2.00 bet on the horses with the hotel owner's money! It was all on film. Harvey apparently confessed after they handcuffed him. He said he couldn't make enough tips, so he was compensated by betting.

The hotel cut a deal with Harvey's attorney. If Harvey retired, didn't ask for unemployment, or cause any other problems, the owner would not press charges. It was very possible Harvey would have to go to trial and to jail if he did not agree. Harvey did not want to go to jail or trial. He agreed. He got lucky, finally.

Harvey is now retired and getting full benefits from his union and his social security. His wife of 50 plus years is still angry with him for being a thief who got caught and the fact he was now home all the time.

* * *

We know 'the downright stupid'. We will move on to 'the most stupid' before 'the very vulgar'.

* * *

PJ was a showman. He had to look perfect every night. He was fifty years old and married to a woman 20 years his junior. She didn't have a regular job. She had a full-time job at home caring for their four very young children. PJ kept running in and out of his bar's back 'pump and storage room' constantly. PJ did it often enough to have already caught the attention of undercover security before the cameras were even installed. Now the cameras were activated. Security wanted to know why he was constantly going in and out of the storage room behind his bar and not bringing out any supplies.

Cameras were secretly installed and were ready for the day of the sting. As the cameras watched and recorded him, PJ ran into the back-storage room and checked his teeth and primped into a miniature wall mirror. He primped worse than a woman. Security laughed, watched, and thought what he just did wasn't so bad.

PJ ran out to his front bar to serve a couple of drinks and hit on a set of 'big boobed' ladies at the corner of his bar. PJ needed tip money, so he hustled the customers. Once again, PJ went into the back-storage room and checked on his pump station and his bottles. Only one bottle needed to be changed. The confused security screeners thought there was nothing wrong about what he had just done. PJ went back out to his front bar and checked on his customers. A few hours went by and PJ was doing fine. PJ made sure everyone was all right. Security thought this bartender may be all right. Suddenly, PJ quickly headed for the bar's back pump and storage room.

If PJ called for a break, it might cost him tips. Those tips helped to support his bad habits and large family. He did not want to lose any of his very needed tips. Therefore, PJ never called for a break. PJ entered the storage room. PJ shut and locked the door and ran up to the sink inside the pump storage room. He unzipped his pants, pulled his penis out, and urinated into the storage room's work sink. He was in such a hurry to make money; he didn't wash out the sink, and he didn't wash his hands. He barely got his pants zipped back up as he left the storage room to go back to the front bar area.

PJ was called into the security office immediately. The owner was called as soon as PJ was caught on film. The owner was outraged! The owner and security did not want to wait until before PJ's shift was due to end or the next day. They did not want to wait because PJ committed a very serious health violation. The owner did not want any problems with the Clark County Health Department in Las Vegas, Nevada.

The owner's hotel, bars, public restrooms, restaurants, private rooms, the grounds, and pool areas always got excellent perfect 'A' ratings from the Clark County Health Department. The owner would walk the areas himself to make sure his property was always spotlessly clean. PJ was escorted out from behind his bar by a security team. The beverage manager was called in to shut down the bar right away. A cleaning detail team was immediately dispatched to go into PJ's bar, and his pump and storage room. The patrons were all upset to vacate their seats without an explanation. Their slot machines were being locked. They were all given four dinner comps to any of the finest restaurants of their choice in the hotel. The customers were suddenly appeased.

PJ was shown his recordings right away. He was asked if he would resign or if he wanted to fight his termination. Knowing he would be disgraced in front of all his fellow employees and his union, he resigned quickly. It's difficult to keep anything quiet in a casino. After their shifts ended, the other bartenders got off and found PJ drinking 50 cent drinks alone in a dark bar across the street. They got PJ more intoxicated, and the story was out.

The male bartenders made fun of PJ's situation saying at least he wasn't as bad as the kitchen porter, who got busted in the restaurant across the street, for 'peeing in the pickle barrel'. It was an old Las Vegas 'fable of a story' that was supposed to be funny, but it never was true and it never was funny, unless, you're a bunch of drunk bartenders, who just got off from their high-stress jobs.

* * *

Willy was one of the quickest bartenders anyone could ever imagine! His front bar was a real moneymaker. He made so many tips and was always on top of his game. He acted like a movie star. Suave, handsome, built, and masculine, Willy had some 'sure to please' jive lines. He could talk it up with the best of them! He didn't care if they were men or women. He could talk to anyone about anything. He took over conversations and made intoxicated people laugh and have fun. He had so many stories! No one knew which stories were real and which stories were imagined. Just looking at Willy made people wonder how he could continuously be so entertaining. Willy's customers got drunk and gambled heavily when they sat at his bar. Willy thought he was great for business. Customers always seemed to enjoy themselves at Willy's bar. Customers kept returning to Willie's bar to repeat their fun experiences when they came to town. They thought Willy was a high energy guy!

Every now and then Willy's bank didn't balance, and management was getting upset with the odd discrepancies. Plus, Willy was another 'back storage room jockey'. Management had the cameras on Willy and watched him. So far nothing was wrong with Willy. He was almost to the middle of his shift when he went into the storage room. He locked the door behind him.

Willy pulled out a small vial of what security thought was cocaine. He made out a line and took his pinky finger's long fingernail and gathered up the cocaine and snorted it into his left nostril. The next time Willy visited the back-storage room, the only thing he did differently was to use his right nostril. Hence, it was surmised cocaine was the reason Willy was such a high energy showman. Willy was called into the security office as his shift was about to end to view his recordings. He was informed if he resigned, management wouldn't have charges filed against him. The security teams thought they had seen it all, but little did they know what was around the corner!

* * *

Then there was Shafer.

* * *

Because of a very sudden high impact of unexpected downtown customers, and a lack of personnel on late night's shift, not all camera recordings would be scrutinized until later the next day. The few available undercover security people had to go onto the casino floor to watch and protect the casino crowds and control the thieves. It turned out to be an extremely busy night. Hence, you are about to be introduced to 'the very vulgar'.

* * *

A suspicious female undercover security guard targeted the casino's most sought after and very alluring bartender, Shafer. Women flocked to his bar. He was a smooth talker and extremely conceded. He was tall, well-built and so very handsome. He thought every woman wanted him.

Security suspected something, but they weren't sure what it could be. They were hoping he wasn't pimping out women from his bar! Security didn't think Shafer was pimping because the women were of different ages and there were hardly any male customers at his bar. That night an undercover security woman sat at the far-right end of Shafer's bar and watched him in action. She thought the man had some fine lines. He could 'razzmatazz' the lady customers with his compliments.

One very intoxicated female customer was making a fool of herself flirting with Shafer. The customer was staying at the hotel because she was signing room charges. The female customer was seated at the extreme left end of Shafer's curved bar. The undercover security female officer was watching them flirt but could not get a seat closer to them because of the growing crowd. The female undercover security guard reported she saw Shafer and the inebriated female customer walking around the small wall at the other far end of Shafer's bar as he was leaving for his break. The female security officer had to fight the busy crowds just to get off her barstool to follow Shafer. By the time she broke free of the crowds to follow them, they had disappeared.

The officer knew the female customer was staying at the hotel because she was signing room charges. The female undercover officer made up a story, showed the relief bartender her security ID, and she got the woman's name and information from the signed room charge slips. The female security officer called the security surveillance office and suggested checking to see if the cameras picked up any recordings of Shafer and the woman leaving together. She wanted the films from the guest elevators, and the guest hotel room's hallway cameras, right then! She thought they may have gone up to the customer's room, which was totally against the rules for employees. It was very late at night, and security was awfully shorthanded. All uniformed and undercover security officers were on the floor and were on alert. Security had no one to spare, but they did check Shaffer's front bar's films and saw nothing suspicious. Then security saw Shafer returning from his break. He was alone. They called off the alert. They thought nothing of the incident. The day shift security team manager would later wish the security guards on the last graveyard shift would have listened to the undercover female security officer.

At 8:00 am the next morning, the female customer who was last seen leaving with Shafer by the undercover female security officer, was filmed checking out before her vacation was over. The front desk manager approached her and was asking her if something was wrong with her room or with the service. The manager was wondering why she was checking out so many days early. The front desk manager was offering to change her room or do anything else 'the well to do' lady customer wanted.

The customer became extremely agitated. She cried copiously and sobbing like she was trying not to hyperventilate. She was visibly traumatized. She seemed hunched over as if she were sick. She was so distressed a front desk clerk called a female security guard to see if she could help calm the woman down.

The customer screamed in a shrill voice, "All I want is to pay my bill and get out of this disgusting hotel and casino forever!"

The woman did not wait for more security guards to arrive. She ran out of the hotel's front door and caught a taxi. More security guards finally arrived and called up to the film screening office. Everyone there was just coming in for their workday's screening of the former night's films, which included Shafer films.

Security realized by the room number and name; she was the female customer the undercover female security officer called in to report one hour after midnight that same morning. Security followed the female security officer's suggestions to search out the female customer and Shafer's appearances on any very early morning's recordings in several areas. Shafer was shown his recordings the next day when he came in to start his late-night shift. Once again Police and Security were present.

Instead of going on his break, Shafer had quickly guided the very helpless intoxicated woman around the small wall at the far-right end of his bar when he was supposed to be leaving on his lunch break. Shafer quickly unlocked his pump room door, which was accessed from around the back of the small wall. Shafer shoved the drunk female customer into the pump room, locked the door, and then barricaded the door from within with nearby bar supplies.

The female customer sat down on the bar supplies. Shafer crudely took all the female customer's clothes off with no harm to her clothing as she laughed and playfully slapped at him. Shafer swung her around, bent her over, and repeatedly raped and sodomized her. He held his hand over her mouth so strongly it appeared she lost her breath and fainted. When she reacted, she looked very frightened and was so astonished she struck at him, stood, and stumbled away from him repeatedly. The female customer was just too intoxicated. She continued to fight Shafer off, which made him furious. He repeatedly hit her body's midsection where it would not show, as he tried to control her. You could read the pain on her face as tears ran from her eye makeup down onto her smeared cheeks. Shafer continued to hold his hand over her mouth to stifle her screams. She vomited onto his hand and Shafer got markedly irritated. He punched her again, hitting her where the bruises wouldn't show.

After he was done with her, he hurriedly redressed her limp body, and he roughly cleaned her face up with a bunch of wet paper bar towels. She was like a rag doll. She looked like she was faint and in pain. He grabbed his black windbreaker and his black baseball cap. Shafer put his baseball cap on the female customer's head. Then he let her crumble slowly to the floor. He put the windbreaker on himself, pulled the collar upward over his work bow tie, and snapped the windbreaker closed. He forced her to stand upright as he put his arm around her waist. She sobbed in pain. It was difficult for her to breathe. He grabbed her shoulders, spoke sternly, and shook her roughly. The way it looked on film, security figured he was threatening her while telling her to stand and walk.

The back pump and storage room cameras caught everything. Shafer was leading the injured woman out of the pump and storage room through the congested crowds towards the guest room elevators. They looked like a couple partying. He looked like an embarrassed husband who pulled the baseball cap over his woman's face and was desperately trying to help his intoxicated wife to their room. Because of the black windbreaker jacket Shafer wore, you couldn't tell he was an employee; however, his face was very prominent.

The elevator cameras picked up the couple in the elevator alone. Shafer let her fall limp to the elevator's floor as she cried in pain. He grabbed her up off the floor of the elevator in case someone was waiting when the elevator doors opened. When no one was there, he let her fall limp once again. The guest room hallway cameras showed Shafer had pulled her halfway out of the elevators to continue to see if the guest hallway was still empty. The elevator's doors kept trying to close and were repeatedly hitting the woman's mid-section. Her face was distorted in pain. She cried more.

Tears spilled from her eyes. The hallway cameras filmed Shafer dragging her by the back of her collar from the elevator to the door of her room. Those same cameras caught him opening her room door for her. The cameras watched as he grabbed the do not disturb sign from the room's inside doorknob and placed it on the outside door handle. The guest hallway cameras showed him kicking and shoving her collapsed body into the guest's foyer area of her room. Shafer grabbed the cap from her body. Shafer looked around, making sure no one saw him. He threw her room key in after her. He closed her room door and trudged back to the elevators. Shafer quickly took off his windbreaker while entering the elevator. Shafer smoothed back his hair with a pocket comb and got into the elevator alone. The elevator cameras showed him adjusting 'Himself' as the elevator doors closed while he laughed.

The break bartender told Shafer not to take advantage of him ever again. He was mad Shafer locked the pump room door making it impossible for his break bartender to get needed supplies. He told Shafer it was only supposed to be a 60-minute lunch break and not 70 minutes. Because of loud music and crowds, the angry relief bartender had no idea of what Shafer had done right behind the bar. He left and Shafer smiled smugly to himself. He acted like he got away with it once again. The way it looked to the cameras; Shafer seemed like he was very adept at doing such things. Security wondered how many women were victims of Shafer over the 20 years he worked as a front bartender.

After watching the films of himself with the customer, Shafer's explanation was that the woman told him repeatedly she wanted his body and she would let him do anything he wanted to do to her. Management had the police present while showing Shafer all his recordings from every location. They took Shafer to the Clark County Detention Center. He was more than just fired. There was rape on film! The Police said the department would try to contact the woman for the next three days, if they could, and discreetly speak to her about pressing charges.

Shafer was held in jail.

The hotel's owner said the hotel's management and lawyers would try to contact the female customer to ask her about pressing charges. When the hotel's lawyers finally contacted the woman late the next day, she screamed at them to leave her alone because her husband would never understand. She hung up. No one ever pressed charges.

Management also wondered how many times Shafer must have taken advantage of female customers in the past. Shafer knew everything about his target. He knew a married woman wouldn't want her husband to ever find out what happened to her. He knew she was alone in her room. He knew she was a wealthy lady and vulnerable because she was intoxicated and alone. He knew her lady friends all had separate rooms and their rooms were not on the same floor as the customer's room. He knew everything. He got her drunk on purpose. He may have even slipped something into her drink, but without cooperation on the customer's end and blood chemical and urinalysis, they would never find out.

The police stretched it out for as long as they could. No one was pressing charges. The police needed proof the sex was not consensual. If no one would file any charges, the police had to let Shafer out of the infamous Clark County Detention Center. After four days passed, the police released Shafer at noon because he was threatening the police with charges of his own.

Shafer was a marked man, but he didn't know it. He was about to find out.

* * *

Paramedics arrived at the scene of a horrific accident in a private parking garage late the next morning. They found Shafer had miraculously survived a terrible fall down a steep flight of concrete stairs. It happened on the top floor of a well-to-do quiet area of town in an exclusive private condominium parking garage. When Shafer recovered after being on life support for two months, he could not remember why he was in the private parking garage or what happened. Someone somewhere knew. The parking garage conveniently had no security cameras.

All of Shafer's fingers had been bent all the way backwards. His fingers had been popped out of their joints and were badly crushed and broken. Shafer suffered from multiple broken bones in both legs. Almost all his ribs were broken. His once handsome face had severe traumatic damage and cuts. As soon as he could, Shafer got out of Nevada. He was smart enough to be terrified. He would have never made it out of state, but the hospital made a mistake and let him out a day earlier than expected. Whoever beat Shafer thought he was dead when they left him. They would not make the same mistake twice. Shafer realized someone was serious.

The mob is untraceable. They've had their hands in Vegas from way back. Las Vegas boasts about a glorified mob museum in the downtown area. They did not like bad publicity for their city. They would not put up with classless people. They knew women controlled a great deal of money in the United States. As soon as the Mob was informed Shafer was released from jail, he had become a hunted animal. He could never have anything again, that could be traced back to him, or the mob would find him, and matters would turn out worse. The mob didn't get the result they wanted regarding Shafer the first time they 'hit' him. He was supposed to take a long time to die after much suffering. The only thing Shafer had going for him was he did not look anything like the very handsome man who he once was. The mob didn't like friends losing business, even if they were presently called corporations.

To this day, Shafer is humped over a mess of scarred flesh and deformed bones. He only has the use of one of his eyes. He has a terrible limp and painfully walks with a cane he can barely hold with crippled hands. He wears rags, is very filthy, and lives on the street from towns to towns far from Las Vegas. Shafer lies to people as he begs on the side of streets. He declares his broken body resulted from war wounds. He never fought for his country, but he continues to fight for his life. He is very repulsive! Now his appearance matches his inner self.

* * *

What you think is what you become. Be careful of your thoughts.

* * *

Las Vegas safety has significantly improved for everyone since the Clark County Metropolitan Police Department, hotel and casino owners, and hotel and casino security officers were given the tools of surveillance cameras. Safety continues to improve daily as undercover officers dress in plain clothes, walk through the casinos, hotels, hotel grounds, the beautiful Las Vegas Strip, and the fun downtown areas. Look up in intersections and you may see the security cameras pointed at you. Our hats are off to all our heroes of our Las Vegas community. They remind us we are our first line of defense. We need to keep our eyes open and realize not to put our loved ones or ourselves in harm's way.

* * *

Have a fun life, Shafer! Remember to always look over your shoulder and never come back. Someone in Las Vegas is waiting for you to make a mistake. They are always watching and waiting.

* * *

Think and watch yourselves, too, Ladies, everywhere you may go! Be careful who you trust. Don't put yourselves in vulnerable positions. Stay in groups or with a trusted friend. Watch your backs. Be alert, be careful, be smart, think, be informed, and most of all, always be in complete control of yourselves.

To all of you, low lives, just try to bring it on. Our alert community is our strength. We have cameras everywhere. We are filming and watching because cameras promote safety.

* * *

'We are Vegas Proud, and We are Vegas Strong!"

Chapter 13

TOTAL LOVE

So much alike, yet they were so different. Ian portrayed a manly toughness ready to protect what was his own. Cece somehow had the ability to exude a feminine kindness full of love and positive feelings, however, there was no mistaking the fact she could be a wildcat if she were backed into a corner. She knew she could always use her wits to get the results she wanted, and that Ian had that ability, too. Cece had learned to be protective and hold her own since she was that little girl on the Miami news. Ian learned that lesson in his mother's bedroom.

They would get on an elevator, and the people inside the elevator would just stare at them. When the people stepped off the elevator, Cece would look inquisitively at Ian and ask him why those people were staring at them.

Cece wondered, "Do you know them, Ian?"

Ian would answer, "I don't know them, do you, Ce?" Perplexed, Cece would say, "No!"

Another passenger still in the elevator with them asked Ian and Cece why they didn't know the reason people stared at them. Ian told the other passenger they didn't know any of the people who were entering or departing the elevator. Ian asked the other passenger what he meant when he said that he knew why the folks were staring at him and his wife.

The passenger said, "It's pertaining to the fact you are two of the most attractive people whom they had ever seen in person. I heard them talking."

Ian and Cece were both tall and stunning. His glowing mane of hair was full and strawberry blonde. His very baby blue eyes twinkled when he was happy, but his eyes became pinpoints when he was angry or in a searching need for his woman.

Cece definitely had the Italian American look about her except her long brunette locks of hair showed natural blonde highlights left over from her little blonde girl childhood. Her eyes were a mysteriously dark brown color rimmed with a jade circle around the iris.

She was his woman, and he was her man. Cece had never seen a more handsome, protective, and moral man in her life. Ian knew he had never seen a more beautiful woman than Cece, and as far as he was concerned, he never would. Most importantly, Ian realized Cece's beauty extended deeply into her soul and her loving personality. Ian knew Cece put Ian and their sons, Scott and Aaron, before herself. No one would ever harm them as long as Ian was near.

He would go to her more often than she would come to him. He did because she was busier in their daily lives. When they came together, it was a hurricane of emotions. When he needed her, he felt a hunger deep down inside of him. The hunger was so strong sometimes he thought he would die. The insane lust for her had to be satisfied. Sometimes the hunger would cause Ian to become angry over nothing. It almost reminded Cece of a child throwing a tantrum over a toy the child could not get. It was then Cece knew he needed her emotionally as well as physically. It was time to take care of her man. Ian would never act so irrationally if he weren't in need of being satisfied sexually, emotionally, physically, mentally, and sprinkled with a little bit of love's own spirituality.

Cece would smile to herself and think, "Ok, I can fix this!"

Many times, the arguing over nothing turned into sexual bliss. Cece would just seem to disappear out of a room while Ian was still raving on about something totally off the wall. After a while of continuous raving, Ian would realize he was ranting away while he was all alone! He would wonder where and when Cece disappeared. He would search her out.

They were in the kitchen when he walked in the room blustering. He'd look in the garage. No Cece. He went to the back garden. No Cece. He'd walk through the house. No Cece. There was only one perfect place left. He opened their bedroom door. No Cece.

Wait. He heard water. He'd go into their bathroom and there she would be soaking naked and waiting with her long legs covered with glistening water droplets up on the side of the bathtub. Cece would cross her dewy legs one over the other and slowly smile at her husband, waiting for him to register what he was seeing before his eyes. Ian would start in again with his filibuster raving, but for the life of him, he couldn't remember why he was upset in the first place. She drove him crazy when he laid his eyes upon her sensuous body. She would tell him to come closer. Before Ian realized what was happening, he was also naked, wet, and in the tub with her. Ian loved the fact that his wife was a sultry sexual woman, and only for him.

Then suddenly, they somehow would be on their bed engulfed in each other's arms. She was bewitching! He couldn't even remember getting out of the bath. How did they get into bed? He knew he would never make it much longer. He picked her up and placed her higher onto the bed. He grabbed both of her ankles and spread apart her long gorgeous legs. Kisses were being placed up her inner thighs. His mouth found her loveliness. Her body quivered under the touch of his lips. His teeth grazed her delicate area ever so slightly. She jumped! He did it again! He knew his woman was ready. He was upon her body once more. Ian, studying his own mental control, had to be sure of satisfying his woman completely. Only then would he let go of his rush to enjoy hers beneath him. He would collapse down on top of her and nuzzle her breasts. Then a sly smile appeared on his face as she gazed at him with completed love. Turbulent sex was a wonderful game to them. It was backed up by tenderness. It was theirs for only each other.

It was a total love and desire that belonged to only the two of them. No one else would ever be allowed to share what they had together.

She could sense him when he walked into a room full of people before she ever heard or caught sight of him. She could feel his manliness before he spoke or laughed. She could find him from the other end of a crowded room. She would watch his eyes searching for her as she giggled to herself and enjoyed the hunt. Other people got in his way while he was in search of his woman. People demanded his attention, too. They felt important and happy when Ian would stop and acknowledge them. Cece could tell Ian wanted to locate her before he would feel comfortable enough to relax and talk to others. She enjoyed the show. At first Ian seemed to enjoy everyone else. However, when it took too long for him to find Cece, she could see his impatience. He would start glancing over their heads, while they continued to talk to him. He had no idea what they were saying.

When Cece stood so he could see her, he finally saw her loving gaze. He would smile and settle down a little, but he would still have a determination to get to her through the crowd. Cece and Ian could acknowledge each other across a crowded room with just a glance. If she felt devilish, Cece could make him work to find her, which turned out to be a lot more fun in the long run! Ian realized they knew what each other was thinking. It was not only sexual. It was an enjoyable and exhausting experience of loving exchanges that would last through their lifetimes.

Finally, people seemed to know he wanted to get to his wife. They watched when he got close to her and they saw the glow of love from his eyes to her eyes as they embraced. Cece hoped every woman in the world could feel that kind of attraction and love for a man at least once in their lifetime. Ian knew every man could not, unless they were lucky enough to earn it. If they were fortunate enough to find a good moral lady to fall in love with them, and if she was the one who would appreciate them, then they could be as blessed as Ian felt, but they still would not have Cece. She would forever belong to him, and him alone. He thanked God for letting him experience such an infinitely spiritual, intelligent, and balanced woman, who had become his own.

Many times, when they were alone, they would fall apart soaking wet. Two athletes, not in competition, but in a completion of desires for only each other's minds and bodies, which included the strong wonders of him and the firm softness of her. It could start with a knowing smile or maybe accidentally brushing by each other. They knew not only were they lovers for life, but, also, the very best of friends for as long as they lived. When true love is young, it doesn't realize how fast time goes by and how fast people age. When a person finds that kind of genuine love with a special someone, they will always be lovers. It doesn't matter what their ages are. Love will always be there. Young lovers will always be lovers, but sometimes they don't realize they won't always be young. True love is complete when it knows two people always want to be together in a moral situation no matter what their ages are.

So, it was that as quickly as time went by, these two young lovers enjoyed each other's beautiful strong bodies and each other's wonderfully moral minds as much as they could. Affections were always present between them, even if love making wasn't possible. A hug, a kiss, or a touch in passing would have to satisfy them until they could be alone. They knew that others would try to invade their private world, but they had no interest to share what they had. For their family, other opinions did not matter. They made their own decisions.

Other men were sometimes a recurring nuisance to Cece.

Especially men who would say things like, "So what if you are married? I'm married, too."

Cece thought them to be idiots. If they were trying to entice a woman, their statement was ludicrous.

Ian was a magnet for women. They were drawn to him. They had no chance because Ian would compare them to his Cece and in his mind there was no woman in the world who could possibly have all the attributes Cece possessed.

With a husband, two sons, a home, a garden, her chores, athletic workout time, and a full-time job, Cece barely had time for herself. There were strict rules for appearance where she worked. Being attractive was important. Customers enjoyed speaking to beautiful employees. The hotel management noticed things like that in those days. What really amazed management was Cece's reactions to the customers? They were never a bother to her. She actually loved talking to customers and helping them sort out their experiences. She didn't just cater to them. She enjoyed them. When Cece saw a pretty lady, she would extend a compliment to her. Being a lady herself, she knew how ladies enjoy genuine adoration.

Cece would declare, "When a lady gives a compliment to another lady, you can believe it. When a strange man gives a compliment to a lady, the woman wonders what he wants."

Most of all, when the female customer's husband or boyfriend heard the pretty cocktail waitress give their wife or girlfriend a compliment, they felt proud. It was all very sweet to see the male reactions. However, Cece felt she could only give compliments to ladies who truly deserved it. Such a customer and Cece's cherished friend was Barbara, who was always beautiful on the inside and the outside. Barbara was someone who Cece trusted, respected, loved, and enjoyed tremendously!

On the other hand, Ian trusted no one. They had to earn his trust. It wasn't just Viet Nam. His lack of trust started as a five-year-old child. He had a hard time with trust, but Cece understood. In the back of his mind, his greatest fear was losing Cece. She was his world. She was the only woman whom he would forever love. Without Cece, Ian knew he would wander through life not knowing what to do with his existence. She was his first and his last love. It was destiny. She held a great power over him, but he had a greater power over her. Losing Cece's love was the only thing on the planet that could break him. He loved and needed her more than he feared her. No matter what reassurances Cece proclaimed, Ian wholeheartedly feared Cece. Losing her love would kill him.

That's when Tony came into their lives.

Chapter 14

TONY

SAL, Jr., aka Sallie, was raised to be an absolutely awful spoiled brat. It wasn't because his parents didn't love him, but because his parents were always working to better their lives. They loved their baby boy more than they could express. Everything they accomplished was for him.

Sallie's parents, Salvatore, Sr. and his very proper wife, Sophia, were children of poor Italian immigrants. They were born in the USA. They worked long hard hours alongside their employees in their uniform clothing factories. Their full days caused them to overcompensate their son by giving in to every one of his fantasies and whims. Sallie got everything except his parent's time. Somehow or other during his lonely young teen years, he realized because of his lack of friends, he would have to act civil towards other people or he would be isolated for the rest of his life. But Sallie just could not do it! He would rather be solitary. After all, he knew his parents were very rich, so he felt superior to the rest of the world. He had to be respectful to his parents, only, because they were where his wealth would come. Sallie already liked money.

Sallie's parents expected Sallie to take over the family businesses someday. Sal, Sr. and Sophia, and their dear friends, were paying off prime vacant casino zoned property on the fabulous Las Vegas Strip in Nevada. They built a home in Las Vegas, which would establish a Las Vegas residence for them in the early 1960s, just off the Strip in an elite newer rural type area of town called Rancho Circle. They came to Las Vegas often. They would start using their home as soon as it was done. Their Las

Vegas contacts told them they would have no trouble being approved to build a top-ranked casino and hotel in the near future now that they were going to be residents. The finest lawyers helped them and their partners, Tom, Senior, and his wife to obtain their gaming licenses. Tom, Sr. was of Irish American descent. Sal and Tom were childhood best friends. They grew up together in New York. Tom left New York because of casino connections who offered him a new life. He learned the gaming business from the ground up. He was trustworthy. He made a very good living and his whole life changed by making his move out west. Tom and his wife, also, had a home in Rancho Circle. Sal's land was next to Tom's land. It was a lovely area with homes built on ranchero lots. Since it was 'the west' many of the residents had horses, stables, and farm animals. The homes were exquisite and had frontage on the foliage-covered long circular street named Rancho Circle. You couldn't tell there was an animal anywhere until you walked around the gorgeous homes to the back acreage of the home's plot. Since the very rich lived in Rancho Circle it was protected by armed security guards 24 hours a day.

Sallie's problem was boredom. While his industrious parents made all their wonderful plans with their best friends, he lived in a guarded and secure building in New York. He felt like a prisoner in the luxurious plush condo. His tutors came to him. If he tried to go out, he chanced being harassed, robbed, or beaten by juvenile delinquents. He was being raised by many nannies who didn't even like him because he was so spoiled. He made their jobs impossible, so they kept quitting. Sallie was a frail, small young teen who wanted to go outside to play.

He had nothing that gave him a thrill until he thought up his own little side business after a terrible near-death incident. The other boys could tell he was rich. They knew where he lived. They knew he always had cash money. They knew he was an easy hit, even guarded by a nannie. When he got away from his nannies to sneak outside into the real world, he became a target even in his early teen years. The boys would steal from him after they knocked him down, kicked, and beat on him. The young women, who Sallie knew, weren't nice young ladies. They were contemptible and street crude. They even helped to set Sallie up to be robbed for a cut of the action. The girls figured it was what Sallie deserved for buying them for sex for a few minutes and verbally degrading them. They didn't realize Sallie was not taught how to treat young ladies with kindness and respect. He treated them like they were a toilet and nothing else.

Sallie would never find one special young lady because of his lack of sophistication, manners, and his mother's strict evil eye. Sallie thought his mother would never approve of any woman. He didn't really care because at age 14, Sallie figured he could continue to just buy girls when he needed relief.

He was never taught respect for anyone except his parents. His parents didn't want Sallie emotionally involved with girls at a young age. They had their own plans for him. He was to eventually be groomed to run the many prosperous family businesses. If he wanted to marry and have a family at approximately 30 years of age or older, then they might consent if they approved of the young woman.

Real life just didn't work for Sallie even though he thought it would. He knew he would have to learn the family businesses but dreaded it. Sallie wanted excitement! He had a hard time communicating with people. He had already decided he would require a highly paid intelligent employee, an assistant. Someone who he could verbally abuse and someone he thought would not take the abuse personally. He could use his new "tough skinned assistant" to talk to his employees for him. Everyone, who knew Sallie's parents, could not understand how Sallie turned out to be such a spoiled, self-centered, immature person. Little did they really know the family. The family didn't even know each other.

After being a victim of a horrible street brawl, 14-year-old Sallie had lots of time to recuperate and think about being continually robbed outside his own home. Sallie was in the hospital for almost six months. He decided to come up with a teenage loan shark business just out of retaliation and spite. However, his idea was out of need, too. He was just tired of being chased down and chancing by another excruciating beating from street gangs. He was sick of the guys picking on him. He didn't like pain. Now he would enjoy seeing the guys, who he didn't care for, suffer through pain, too. Sallie's lack of confidence was because he had very little physical strength. If he tried to fight the bullies back, they could beat him to a pulp. He needed a strong arm for his new business and for protection. Sallie needed Tony.

Sal Sr, and Sofia suffered through the results of Sallie's last brawl when he had to be hospitalized because of his life-threatening and severe injuries. They would never understand that happening again. Sallie realized he needed protection because he couldn't even walk out on the New York sidewalk in front of his family's luxury condominium building. Sallie hated all the teenage boys in the surrounding neighborhoods except for the one who saved his life. He was the one who stopped the gang beating before Sallie died. He was Sallie's hero. He was the tough guy, 'Tony from the Bronx'.

The one friend, who Sallie seemed to keep, was his best and only friend, Tony. It was only because Tony felt sorry for him when the other boys picked on wimpy Sallie. Tony continued to fight the big kids off Sallie whenever he was around because Sallie rewarded Tony with money just like Sallie was rewarded with money by his parents. Tony enjoyed fighting. He seemed to become Sallie's bodyguard and best friend after saving Sallie from being killed by street gangs. Sallie wanted so much to be just like Tony, but Tony was huge, strong, handsome, and streetwise.

Who was Tony? All the women loved 14-year-old Tony. He was much older than his years. He could have any of them at any time he chose, no matter what the age of the female, and at no charge! When Sallie would say something rude to Tony, his best friend would only laugh at responding with the phrase, "Go fuck yourself, Sallie."

They were from the same neighborhoods and had a weird respect for each other because somehow, they both survived the places. Sallie had fun with his new secret loan shark business after he convinced Tony to do the collecting. Sallie told Tony he would get a percentage and be his partner. Tony loved the money and accepted their partnership.

Sallie knew he was the neighborhood wimp, but his friend, Tony, wasn't. Tony was everything Sallie wished he could be, except Tony was not rich. Instead, he was tall, dark, handsome, strong, and Sicilian-American. He was extremely well built. When Tony walked by people, men would stop talking and lower their heads. Women would bat their lashes, flip their hair, and feel the tingle. Yes, Tony was almost perfect, but money was the one thing Tony didn't have. Money was the one thing Sallie had and was a way for him to control Tony, or so he thought.

Tony, an only child, was raised by exemplary parents, but they were considerably poor. Tony's education was never important to his parents or himself. As a teenager, he was a poor playboy, who wanted to be a rich. He loved beautiful women, but he never met one he could respect. Tony wanted money because money could get him anything he wanted, except a righteous woman., which was okay since he wasn't too interested in good women. Tony would never get the money he needed to keep up his playboy lifestyle if he didn't put up with Sallie. Money was the reason Sallie had his best friend, Tony, "by the balls."

Sallie planned out how he could really get 'over on' the bullies, who made fun of him by calling him the little wimpy spoiled "Sallie kid" and put him in Intensive Care for months. He began by loaning out a few bucks. Before Sallie gave them money, Sallie would explain the rules. He made them sign an agreement to the rules of the loans. He would loan them money, and they had to pay it back with interest within a certain period. As the years went by, there would no longer be signed agreements. Sallie got older and wanted no proof of what he and Tony were doing. Sal, Junior's clients knew all agreements would be verbal, painful, or 'near to deadly,' if not followed.

As youngsters the neighborhood guys had laughed at Sallie, while they all agreed to the loans saying, "Yeah, let's see how Sallie makes us pay him back!"

The neighborhood didn't know about Tony being Sallie's 'Collector' when Sallie first started his little business. Sal got back at his enemies by loaning them money. Then Sallie watched and enjoyed how his 'Collector' got the money back from them when they didn't pay. For once in his life, Sallie was having fun! Sallie loved the excitement! It was as much fun as going to a big prize fight. No one ever reported who beat them because they knew Tony would return and do it again.

Without signed agreements, there was never any proof left behind connecting Sallie, Tony, or the borrowers. Tony was always sure of one thing. There were never any witnesses to his collections.

Tony considered bringing another collector along someday into their business, if he thought he could trust someone. In the back of his mind, Tony figured he could always kill a collector if the guy didn't get along with Sallie or him. It appeared Tony had no respect for human life. Money was his god. He loved easy money. Tony didn't have to have a regular job. He did not have to work at a certain time. There weren't any time clocks. He could work when he felt like working.

In the old days, Tony learned what every style of street fighting was. Tony had lived in New York, from Chinatown to the Bronx. Tony had to learn to survive his everyday life on the streets of whatever neighborhood his impoverished parents could afford. The time of Sallie's and Tony's adolescent years passed quickly after they started making their own money.

Sallie's parents eventually paid off their Las Vegas land for their future hotel and casino. Since Tony was Sallie's only real childhood friend, the family took Tony under their wing to Vegas when they left the old neighborhood. Tony was an already self-made 'nowadays tough guy'. If anything were to happen, Sallie would make sure Tony would be totally protected. Sallie's parents had Las Vegas family lawyers, and both the owners had close connections to the Las Vegas District Attorney. Sallie's parents thought Sallie just couldn't be without his best and only real young childhood friend. They didn't know why, but for some reason, they thought Sallie needed Tony.

In those years Sallie's parents treated their son's best friend, Tony, like another son. However, they expected Tony would have to work and earn his own way in their new casino, The Bella Ricco, just like Sallie would be expected to work. When they came to stay in Las Vegas, the family's hotel and casino was breaking ground. It was like being at a big happy Italian American family reunion party.

When the new place, "The Bella Ricco" was done, Tony would be given the cushy job of top Baccarat dealer in their new plush "High Roller" room. Tony grew into a very attractive 24-year-old man who looked like he wouldn't take any shit from anyone. He would make a very good living legally, but his 'under the table' collector's job would make him well to do soon. Las Vegas was the big time for loan sharks.

Tony may have been better suited for a security job, but that job was more strenuous, and Sallie wanted Tony to save his strength for their other ventures. Sallie did not want his parents to ever find out anything about his past business practices with Tony in New York. Sallie expected Tony to work for him after his regular job ended. Tony had to be in shape to go collecting. They were in the big time now!

Sallie wanted to develop a good loan shark business in Vegas and wanted Tony to stay in prime shape. Sallie was already working on the new business. Sallie would cover for any of Tony's absences from his new prime workstation. That is what regular people called having some 'strong juice.' Tony would still be paid, even if he were working out in the hotel gym. Tony could use the Bella Ricco's state-of-the-art gym and spa facilities for free. Sallie made sure Tony had the 'power of the pen' just like Sallie did. Anything Tony wanted; he could just sign for it. While Sallie was getting massages, manicures, and pedicures in the spa, Tony was sweating in the gym for hours every other day of the week.

Sallie thought he was getting over on Tony, but Tony did whatever he wanted and just gave Sallie 'the nod.' Tony had to make it look like he had to do what Sallie wanted, for Tony to keep his dealer's job at the new casino, and still get his percentage for collecting. Tony was not smart enough to stash more of his money because Tony blew money away on many toys. However, there was always plenty of money to save, too. Tony wasn't smart enough to get away from Sallie, and Sallie wasn't smart enough to get away from Tony. The two friends were a deadly combination.

Most hotel and casino owners in the early days had their own tough guys. The men were called security guards. They would never make the money Tony would make in Baccarat. Many of the security guards were old thuds who gave orders to, no question about it, younger thuds. It was as if every hotel and casino had their own police force. Some finer, more substantial casinos and hotels hired good retired career policemen.

Sallie's parents had no idea what he had been up to for most of Sallie's younger teen life. They thought their Sallie was such a good boy. After all, Salvatore, Jr. was raised right. He had no responsibilities and never had to work a day in his life. He had gone to all the finest schools and had the best tutoring. His parents gave him everything, or so they thought.

Sallie never had to know 'who fought back.' Tony always took care of those things for him. Sallie took care of the payoff money by investing. Their loan business could make very good money in Las Vegas. It was totally unnecessary for them to have to do, except for their own enjoyment. Thanks to the 'Bella Ricco', they were making excellent legal money, too. It was the excitement and thrill of their loan shark business that 'kept them happy' and excited. Power lust can backfire and hurt you. But they didn't think ahead. They didn't have good women enabling them.

If Sallie told Tony to make it look good, Tony did. Tony thought any idiot could deal with Baccarat, but not everyone could be a tough guy and a collector. Little did Tony know this was Las Vegas. Knuckleheaded tough guys outnumbered each other. The only difference was Tony was very street smart since he was a kid. He befriended people. He got them to trust him before he practically killed them to collect. He knew how to surprise them. He knew their families, their jobs, and all their schedules thanks to Sallie's spy, Woody. Tony enjoyed fighting and collecting. He got to make his own work schedule.

He never announced times or made a prearranged appointment related to his collection job. He had never met a challenge that could match him one on one in his life. Tony was conceited with the fact that he was big, strong, and the best. Whether it was hand to hand or weapon to weapon, Tony never met an adversary he couldn't beat.

* * *

The grandest and best new hotel and casino in Las Vegas, 'The Bella Ricco', would still be hiring up until the very last minute because they were waiting for someone. It was only days to go before the grand opening. Employees were doing orientation for three weeks, preparing to open the grand 'Bella Ricco'. Tony watched across the empty Baccarat room while the lucky young pit boss, Tommy, Jr. was preparing some empty games for the grand opening. Tommy was the son of Sal's best friend and partner, Tom, Sr. Tony thought, "Some guys just fall into it!"

Tony knew the two old guys went way back. He knew about them planning this outcome when he was still a young boy. The day after tomorrow would be the grand opening of the Bella Ricco hotel and casino. Tony noticed, from where he was standing in the high roller lounge, something interesting was happening near Tommy's games.

* * *

Tony continued to observe Tommy, Jr.'s area of one of the 21 pits. A tall, very handsome, well built, strawberry blond guy had walked up next to Tommy, Jr. and purposely bumped into the table where he was working. The two guys began laughing and talking fast. Tommy did a little jump up and threw down the cards in his hands and came out from his 21 pits. He grabbed the tall, attractive man in a big bear hug. Tony continued to watch them as they spoke for a while. Tony watched as the two men began laughing as they continued talking quickly. Tommy motioned towards the plush coffee shop as he grabbed some paperwork from his podium and stored the cards. The two men began walking towards the entrance of the new coffee shop. Shorter Tommy kept holding and patting the big strawberry blond guy's shoulder. Tommy looked like a midget walking beside the tall, well-built man. Tony could swear the area around the handsome man glowed. The two men disappeared into the coffee shop. Tommy, Jr. kept a firm grip on the big man's shoulder as if he wouldn't get away.

Tony thought, "Now that's Irish American!"

Tony felt somber. He wondered why he couldn't be best friends like Tommy and the handsome man. Whoever he was, Tony wanted to meet him. It would be fun having a best friend, who was the equivalent of himself! His 'so called best friend', Sallie, was rich, but Sallie was still a spoiled jerk. Tony felt a bit sad and as dysfunctional as Sallie. The smart little wimp tried to run his life, but Tony liked the money he was paid that allowed him to acquire his big boy toys and loose women. Tony knew he could do whatever he wanted with that money. Even though Sallie had a hand in his life, Tony knew Sallie couldn't have survived this long without him. Sallie would have never made it out of the old neighborhood alive without Tony, and Sallie knew it, too! They owed each other. They owned each other.

So, who was that 'glowing man'?

Tony wondered, "Could he be a best friend or worst enemy?"

Tony planned to somehow find out.

Chapter 15

Ian's New Job

It was tough on Ian and Cece when one of them wasn't working, but they always seemed to survive those hard times. Cece would tell Ian to take advantage of the time off to play with their sons. The boys would get a bit spoiled, but most of the time Ian was tough on them by being strict. Children need consistency, especially from their parents! Ian was sure it would make them better men. It was difficult for Ian to relate to his sons because of Ian's tough relationship with his strict ex-marine father. Ian realized he wouldn't always be with his sons, even though they were still very young. Ian wanted his sons to be prepared to take the world on head first. Ian wanted his boys to become very strong men and demanded a lot from the two boys. Then again, Ian would turn around and spoil his sons. Ian seemed to live a second childhood through his boys. Giving them wonderful childhood like he wished he had.

* * *

Ian started with a little motorized scooter. Once the boys mastered it, Ian bought a go-cart. Cece wanted a roll bar and seat belts installed on the go-cart. She feared it was way too fast. She was right. Their sons mastered the go-cart in no time. They were well-built youngsters and agile little athletes, but one of the neighbor boys flipped the go-cart going too fast into a turn. Ian looked at Cece when they saw it happen because they both had told the boy not to go fast. His mother gave him permission because the youngster was so excited to get a chance to ride the go cart. He had promised not to go too fast. They ran and checked the boy, who kept saying he was fine. Thank heaven he was because he scared the heck out of everyone.

In a very forceful tone, Ian said, "You were right, Ce, about that roll bar, the helmet, and the seat belts! Thank God, I listened to you!"

Cece finally looked at Ian and said, "I think it's time for you to stop playing with the children so much, and go see about another job. Isn't the Bella Ricco going to open soon?"

Ian smiled and replied, "I think you're right, but what about the motorcycle I just bought for them?"

Then Ian smiled lovingly as his eyes sparkled. He was so perfect in Cece's eyes. He could melt Cece's heart instantly!

Cece rolled her eyes at her husband and said, "Stop kidding around! I just can't believe you, Ian! Sometimes you act like one of the little guys!"

Ian nuzzled Cece around to the other side of the SUV, away from the children's view. He gingerly turned her around to face him. Then, he grabbed both of Cece's buttocks and pulled his woman towards his groin.

Cece rebelled, "Ian!"

Ian growled softly with a smile on his face, "I'm no little boy. Want me to show you?" Cece winked up at her 'hunk of man' as she smiled and purred in a sexy voice, "Later, Baby!"

Later wasn't good enough for Ian, but with children around, he would have to wait. The next day Ian slept in after his "Later" was well satisfied. Cece had just left. She was running errands and taking the boys to school. Ian couldn't keep it all straight. Thank God he had Cece. He still envisioned his wife's beauty after their very satisfying morning together.

The casino connection, whom he had, would go into work that evening on late swing shift or early graveyard. Ian knew Tommy, Jr., went to the newest place in town. Tommy's father, Tom, Sr., was one of the new owners of the Bella Ricco, and they were getting ready for their grand opening. Tommy, Jr. was Ian's connection. He was a congenial guy and knew Ian for many years since they were young and worked downtown while they broke into dealing together. Tommy, Sr. was their Instructor. Those were the days when there weren't any dealer's schools popping up all over Las Vegas. You had to know someone to get a dealing job.

In later years, those dealer schools would sucker people into paying exorbitant amounts of money to learn to deal live casino games in hopes of getting a dealing job. The trick was 'keeping' the casino job. You had to have nerves of steel and you had to learn not to let anything bother you. Yeah, right, huh?

Those were the days of "giving them the nod". That meant no matter what was said to you by customers or bosses, you kept your mouth shut, and your head nodding 'yes' in agreement. The 'Nod' could send you to another more wonderful place, other than a dirty, smelly smoke-filled casino. The nod made you feel you were just on auto pilot going through the motions of dealing. The 'Nod' could save a dealer from being fired by a loudmouth boss, who was a jerk. In the early days of casinos, some bosses would kick their dealer's legs, if they lost a hand. Actually, it was BWD (Before Women Dealt) in most Las Vegas casinos!

In the old days (pre-1960s) when some casinos needed new dealers, the casino's management would have some gaming tables set up in one of the empty hotel rooms. The management would pick out a few guys they knew and send them up to that room to learn to deal. They would practice for a week and go to work on graveyard until they got experience.

When they 'broke in' together, Tommy, Jr. would watch the crowds, as they formed around Ian's games every night. Beautiful rich women would be the first to sit down on the handsome dealer's game. They weren't just women. They were beautiful women with lots of money. Those women and their money drew rich men and more of a crowd. Tommy, Jr. already knew, when they were very young, that Ian would be a "House" money maker for any casino for which he would ever deal. Ian had been told many times he was a "draw" because of his appearance.

Ian really did not mind it, but he expected respect and compensation for his hard work because his tables were always full.

There were many stressful times when Ian put down his cards, took off his dealer's apron, threw it down on the 21 table's rack of chips, as he smiled at a boss and said, "I quit, you deal, Asshole!"

Ian was a man. He was a real man. He didn't take any shit from anyone, except for maybe a little from Cece. Cece never knew when he would come home unemployed.

After Vietnam, the casinos were cheap and wanted to cut their costs by hiring government compensated employees and women. Casinos have their tricks and their 'penny pinching in-house lawyers' working for them. The companies had no idea they would get what they paid for by hiring cheap help. They deserved what they got because they laid off many good, hard-working people. You want cheap; you get cheap. Some dealers would not even carry on a conversation with their players, or speak. Casino bosses never seemed to make up their minds about allowing dealers to have conversations with players or not.

In Ian's case, the casino management decided Ian mostly attracted rich female customers, who wanted Ian to respond to them. Ian seemed to get away with a lot because he was congenial and very pleasant for a woman to look at, while she lost all her money. Casino companies realized women controlled a lot of money. Ian's female customers would get up from his game and thank Ian for a delightful time while they lost. Ian amazed casino management.

When Ian walked into an area, men looked up and stepped back. He radiated an ambience that most men wished they had. Ian's smile, his mane of glowing hair, his mannerisms, his size and demeanor filled the area with the aura of a real man, who was comfortable, confident, and happy with himself. Ian made the ladies of every persuasion smile, old or young, rich or poor, it didn't matter, they always smiled!

A former casino where Ian had once worked, hired a government compensated dealer, who was supposed to be rehabilitated. The man was a reformed convict and a thief. The dealer always seemed to cough on the game. He would put his cards down after a deal and bring his hands up to his mouth while he coughed. One of the bosses wondered why the dealer's rack never balanced and why the dealer's cheeks were so red while he continually coughed.

The boss worked it out with undercover security to follow the dealer as he went on his break. He was followed into the restroom by 4 undercover security men. The dealer stood at the sinks and brought a large handkerchief up to his mouth. He started to cough and spit out something into his hand while holding the 'something' in his handkerchief. While cameras recorded the dealers in the casino area, there were no cameras inside the men's room. The dealer proceeded into a toilet stall, closed the stall door, and sat down. Undercover security guards hit the floor on all fours, to enable them to see what the dealer was doing by looking under the stall's door. Those undercover security guards watched the dealer pulling his pants leg up and sliding black chips down into his boot. That dealer had been in jail for pickpocketing up to the time of his rehabilitation, and for his retraining into his future government compensated employment with the casino, all thanks to Uncle Sam's stupid law makers. The USA Government's rationale was "ex-cons, who committed crimes of 'lower impact', could change, if they were just given a chance."

Mostly, it was not going to happen. You get what you pay for! Yeah, right!

The bottom line is a lazy thief does not want to work. The more he stole, the more he wanted.

Ian remembered some weird things Tommy, Jr and Ian learned. Tommy's Dad was a floorman where Ian and Tommy, Jr. broke into the dealing profession. Soon after Tommy broke in, his father put him on the casino floor as a floorman. There were big hopes for both their futures.

Late one night in their younger years, Tommy was closing down an empty game next to Ian's game. Tommy had his back to the game where Ian was dealing. It was three in the morning. Swing shift was closing down the empty games and getting ready for the graveyard shift to arrive.

The graveyard shift would take over at 4:00 a.m. Ian had one customer left. She was slumming downtown on swing shift for a thrill, and found this young, handsome dealer, Ian. She wanted a reserved high limit game for herself for Ian's entire eight-hour shift. She had played $1000.00 a hand on all six betting spots so she could have continued privacy with Ian. When he went on a break, she took a break, too. A reserved sign was placed on the table to deter anyone else from playing there.

Most people just saw the minimum bet sign of $1,000.00 a hand and were deterred quickly, but they wanted to watch the show! The big bosses would not close the game, because the lady customer was a real class act and an extreme high roller. She only wanted to play where Ian's dealt. The lady was a very wealthy widow from Beverly Hills. Tommy could hear the woman talking to Ian. She was offering Ian everything she had while she played her cards.

Ian smiled as they spoke, and the cards flowed. Ian just kept raking in her thousand-dollar chips. She didn't care. Ian had a way with women. Ian could say "no thanks" in a roundabout friendly way. Ian had a talent of politely saying 'no' without embarrassing or offending a lady's feelings.

This customer had been persistent, but it was getting close to the time for Ian to leave to go home for the night. She gave up. She pushed the remainder of her chips out to Ian. There were only five chips left. She looked at Ian and said the rest of her chips, which were worth $5,000.00 totaled, were for him to drop into the dealer's box for a tip. She got up and leaned over to declare a few sweet nothings into Ian's ear before she retired to a suite management comped for her. The woman's expensive skimpy silk top fell forward as she leaned over to whisper into Ian's ear. Her large full pendulous breasts were totally exposed in front of Ian's blushing face. Ian couldn't possibly miss a thing. Even Tommy, Jr. got an eye-full from a distance behind the 21 table. She looked at Tommy and said that she wouldn't gamble the next day if Tommy allowed Ian a day off. She walked away towards the room elevators to go to bed alone.

Tommy closed down Ian's game when Ian said with a big grin, "Thanks for forgetting about my 'early out' I requested when I first started my shift tonight."

Tommy, Jr. looked at Ian with his mouth agape and said, "Stop busting my balls! I still have to take your day off tomorrow away from you. I've got to have you here. You made a ton of money for the house today. I'll make it up to you, Ian! You should be happy. All the eyes in the sky are noticing you. Besides that, Ian, you know she won't bet on anyone's table but yours! She would rather go home to Beverly Hills and keep her money! We don't want that to happen, right?"

Ian patted Tommy's shoulder and said, "I understand, Buddy, but I'm just running out of excuses to give to her."

Tommy shook his hanging head and said, "I wish I had your kind of problems and constantly had to beat off rich beautiful women!"

Time went by, but Ian and Tommy would always remain good friends no matter how many years had passed. Tommy still missed seeing Ian. Tommy, Jr. knew he was going to work for his Father, Tom, Sr., in their new hotel and casino, The Bella Ricco. Tommy, Jr. would be Swing Shift Boss, but his Dad was to be the casino manager and an equal owner. Sal, Sr. and Tom, Sr., were old friends, and equal partners in their share of owning "The Bella Ricco". They completely trusted each other with everything, including their lives.

Tommy thought, "This new hotel and casino will be a first-class joint! We will treat our employees right! How long has it been since I have seen Ian? Where is Ian when I need him?"

Tommy, Jr. continued working to prepare the tables for the grand opening, as he rehashed the old days over again in his mind. Tommy never forgot the money Ian could pull in for a casino wherever he worked. Tommy thought to himself, 'Ian would make any boss look good'. Tommy thought this new hotel and casino would be a very good job. Tommy, Jr and Tom, Sr., would hire Ian on a dime anytime!

With that thought in mind, Tommy spread some cards on an empty gaming table while he continued contemplating the past. He missed Ian and couldn't figure out why Ian had not come in to see him for a job of a lifetime! He had so many happy memories of their younger years breaking into dealing together. Those were decent days when they broke in as dealers. One of the older bosses, with a lot of experience, would teach the guys "the ropes". If you were any good, the boss would know right away. If you weren't smart enough, quick enough, or any good with cards, you were told to leave. The training bosses, along with Tommy, Sr. and Tommy, Jr. watched as Ian could make his cards fly in the air, turn, and land perfectly in front of the correct player. All the trainees were mesmerized at how beautifully Ian's cards could float in the air and land in front of the designated players in complete alignment with the player's other cards. Tommy, Jr., was fascinated by Ian's work performances.

Anyone could tell Ian had a special talent with cards. Ian was fast or slow, depending on what the bosses wanted, or the players preferred. Most of all, Ian was smart. He could add in a split second and since he learned the old school ways he could catch cheaters, card markers, thieves, and counters. Tommy, Jr. admitted he had training from his father before he and Ian started downtown training class together. However, Ian never had exposure to casinos or friends, who could teach him his natural talent with cards and his quick control of his calculating mind.

When men asked Ian how he learned to handle cards so beautifully, Ian would laugh and say, "I've never played with cards. I just treat the cards like a beautiful woman, ever so gently."

Even Ian's first old Cowboy Boss employer would ask Ian, with his Texas accent, "How'd you do that, Boy?"

In the old days when the training boss thought the guys were ready, he would put them on the graveyard shift to get experience. That experience included handling the cards, the experience with all the strange people, who the new dealers would be exposed to, and to the strange conditions the new dealers would have to work under. It seemed Ian had the strangest experiences of all the new dealers. Tommy was sure it was because of his looks.

As the two young friends got to know each other, Tommy, Jr's father, was getting experience in casino management. He had an incentive. He knew he would someday be running a great casino and hotel with his dearest friend from New York, Sal, Sr.

Tommy, Jr. knew how the crowds loved Ian. How could anyone not like Ian? Ian was such a cheerful person. It was as if Ian was a glowing star behind his 21 table. His strawberry blond hair and blue eyes caught every woman's attention. Ian was just way too handsome, but he had a completely normal personality. Many women told him every week just how handsome he was, but Tommy knew Ian was a happy person because of his woman. Sure, Cece and Ian were married young, but when Ian spoke about Cece, Tommy could watch Ian's eyes twinkle. Ian was in love, and because of Cece's love, Ian stayed grounded.

Yeah, Tommy really missed seeing Ian. Tommy wondered what Ian had been up to these days. This new owner from New York, Sal, Sr., and Tommy's father needed expert help in their new grand casino and Hotel, The Bella Ricco. Sal, Sr. would like Ian a lot, just like his father, Tom, Sr. did. They would soon open this beautiful "Bella Ricco". There were not that many experienced employees who have a personality and a smile, too. Their employees would be treated right. Tom, Sr. and Sal, Sr. were not cheap. They wanted the best employees. Sal, Sr. was a class act. He would be bringing in a lot of New York money on junkets. Those customers would gamble so much money that they would become 'R (room), F (food), and B (beverage) Comps (Complimentary)'. That meant they would gamble extreme amounts of money and they weren't expected to pay for anything, and because of that, they would tip heavily when they won! All "R, F, and B" customers had to do was sign for whatever they got, be it a room, food, an ice cream, a beverage or a piece of pie and a cup of coffee. The main reason they got free R, F, and B complementary privileges was because the hotel and casino owners wanted to keep those customers happy and to stay in their hotel and casino to do all their gambling. Those guests were known as "High Rollers". An employee never wanted to piss off a high roller, because if that happened, they could be fired, and it could cost the casino millions of dollars in revenues. Therefore, any intelligent employer wants only the best dealers.

In the long run, the hotel and casino will make more money than if they tried to cut corners on salaries.

Tommy, Jr., thought maybe he could entice Ian to come to work for them if Ian would just show up and say he wanted a job!

Tommy, Jr. thought to himself, "Where are you, Ian? I know you moved into a new home two years ago, but I never got your new unlisted phone number! We're running out of time, Buddy!"

* * *

Some guy walked up to the closed 21 game where Tommy, Jr., was working and reminiscing about Ian. Tommy continued ignoring the person as he worked. Tommy was too busy concentrating on the decks of cards and thinking of where Ian could be.

Tommy continued thinking, "I put the word out that I'm looking for Ian, but no one knew where Ian was. Hopefully, someone will see Ian around and tell him. Ian knew my Dad would be building the Bella Ricco someday."

Tommy stayed deep in thought and ignored whoever was standing at the table while he concentrated. Tommy continued to think, "Ian had to know the news and who owned the Bella Ricco! Ian knows my Dad's name, even if he doesn't know the New York owner's name. Damn, Ian, we're running out of time. Where are you?"

The person who had just walked up to the game, where Tommy had his head down while deep in thought, tired of being avoided and rudely shoved the table on purpose. Tommy's disgusted face frowned as he looked up right into Ian's eyes! Ian laughed and said something while showing Tommy his huge smile. Tommy threw his arms into the air as he did a small jump up and smiled from ear to ear. Tommy was guffawing. Ian was trying to talk.

Tommy held up his hand in the STOP position and said, "Don't bother, you're definitely hired! If you would like to be, that is! Where the hell have you been? All the employees have been in orientation for the last three weeks! I've been waiting on pins and needles for you to show up! It's just like you to wait until the last minute! How's Cece and the boys?"

Tommy couldn't talk fast enough as he ran around the 21 table and grabbed Ian in a big bear hug as Tommy was saying, "Come on. I'll buy you lunch and we'll talk about everything!"

Ian said, "It's 4:00 a.m.! Make it breakfast, and you got a deal."

After a little more conversation, Tommy grabbed Ian's shoulder as they walked towards the new plush coffee shop entrance. They were already laughing out loud! At that point in time, no one else in the world existed but the two best friends. They were boisterous as they walked to breakfast while remembering the past and laughing.

The two new Bella Ricco owners, Tommy's Dad, Tom, Sr. and his partner and best friend, Sal, Sr. were still at the other end of that same 21 pit watching the young men walking towards the new plush coffee shop.

Sal, Sr. asked, "Who's that, Tom?"

Tom, Sr. said, "Tommy's best ma, Ian, is back, Sal! Tommy's been anxiously waiting for him every day to show up! Ian will probably start working tomorrow. I'll introduce you when he comes into work. He's one of the best out there. A good man, husband, and father. One of the best draws we've ever seen. Can't beat the rich women off of his games, and that draws the men, too! Then, it's like they are all at a party while they are having fun losing all their money. He's unbelievable!"

Sal, Sr. was nodding affirmatively and broke out in a big smile of his own. He enjoyed watching the two young men, who were best friends, laughing and entering the coffee shop together.

Sal, Sr. said, "There's nothing as good as an old friend. Right, Tom?"

They laughed together and reminisced about the old neighborhood. They spoke of when they were young on the rough streets of New York, and how they made it all those years by sticking together, being honest with each other, trusting in each other, and working long hard hours. They appreciated how they finally made it to the jackpot of "Las Vegas,

Nevada" in the great country of the USA! The two Seniors made it all happen together because they had values, were good moral people, and knew the satisfaction of what hard work can do for a 'real' person.

Meanwhile...

* * *

Other more envious dark black eyes watched the two young men walking towards the coffee shop. Those same jealous dark eyes observed all the women employees turning to watch the tall, strawberry blonde, handsome, well-built man walking by them while Tommy, Junior's grip was still on the tall man's shoulder. Tony felt a pang of jealousy. It was an unfamiliar emotion for Tony. As far as Tony was concerned, no man was ever better than he was.

Tony thought, "Who is that glowing good-looking guy? Why can't I have a normal best friend like that? All I ever got is screwy Sallie. I gotta meet that guy!"

Oddly, Tony did not know he was not normal either, in any way.

Chapter 16

THE SET UP

BEING the new guy at a casino job was always awkward. The Bella Ricco employees had been practicing for a three-week period before the hotel was due to open its doors. Ian procrastinated way too long when he should have been going to speak to Tommy, Jr.

The other employees thought Ian must have had some powerful connections because he strolled in at the last minute and got a great job. For that reason, Ian didn't know any of the other dealers or where he needed to go for food, lockers, relaxation, or restrooms. Ian did not go through any orientation procedures at all, only because he didn't think it was necessary.

Ian thought to himself, "Why waste three weeks of my life in orientation when I had a chance to spend it with my boys and my beautiful wife? We had fun! I guess I cut it short though, getting here the day before the grand opening! Lots of these people would have never made it when I started dealing. Hell, management asked you to get on a table so they could see how good you were at dealing. If they liked your style, they told you to go to the office and tell them you were hired. While you filled out an application, the time office called the casino manager and asked him what time and shift he wanted you to start at work. Then the time office told you when to start. What's Orientation? What the heck? Good grief, why waste your time?"

Ian would soon find out... because times were changing!

Ian laughed and thought he'd have plenty of time to learn, eventually. Cece claimed Ian had the best sense of direction than anyone she ever met! The day before the grand opening, Ian went in for processing. After Ian completed processing, Tommy asked him to stop by the 21 pit so they could meet up for lunch. After a delicious lunch Tommy, Jr., took Ian to see his father, Tom, Sr. and to meet Sal, Sr. With all that done, Ian told Tommy he was going home to be with his boys after school while Cece had to go get some work clothes for him.

Tommy laughed and asked, "Who's the boss around here? I think it's me! Sure, ok. Of course, Ian! You are going to show up on time for work, right?"

The grand opening was at noon the next day. Ian was there at 'clock in' and went to Tommy's 21 pit. As he walked into the pit, he was getting looks from the other dealers. The guys just nodded and kept their eyes lowered, but all the women had different reactions. Some women nodded. Some women smiled. Some more forward woman licked their lips with their pointed tongues in a circular motion or stuck out their chests and posed. Ian smiled in return and thought of his gorgeous wife. As far as Ian was concerned, there would never be another woman who could attract his attention like Cece. She would never accept an extramarital affair. He never wanted to lose Cece. Ian loved Cece with all his life and love. He only wanted peace at work and 'no girl friends', unless they knew their relationship with Ian would be platonic.

When it was time for Ian's first break, he didn't know where he was going. He decided to follow the group of dealers leaving the pit who were getting the same break time as him. Ian followed them patiently, but they started splitting up into different directions.

He heard two female dealers walking behind him, commenting on the nice view in front of them. One was an attractive blond woman, who was named Dolly. The other attractive woman was dark headed, and her name was Tina. Ian asked if they could direct him to the dealer's room. They looked at each other and giggled between themselves. Together they smiled and said to just follow them. Ian dropped in behind them and followed along. They walked up to a doorway, opened the door, and descended stairs. Tina led the way. Dolly was behind her. Ian was behind Dolly. As soon as the two women heard the door close behind Ian, they stopped and turned around. They were looking up at Ian.

Dolly, the woman immediately in front of Ian, suddenly turned around, and grabbed his crotch with one of her hands and said nonchalantly to Tina, "See, I told you he was hung! It's that Viking Norsemen thing!"

Now, this was a first for Ian! He never expected it to happen!

Ian let out a shocked, "AHH!"

As soon as he found his voice, Ian stopped on his stair. As Dolly's aggressive grip loosened, Ian gave the women one of his looks!

Ian chided, "OK, now you both know for sure! Let go of me or you will pick each other up at the bottom of this lengthy flight of dark stairs. You are not going to remember how you got there. Understand me?"

Dolly commented in a Draconian matter, "You can't prove anything so don't bother reporting this to anyone because there's two of us and we will deny it. There are no cameras in here. You hear? We'll reverse the tables on you and make you suffer."

Ian yelled out as loud as he could, "Lady, I said let go of my balls!" Dolly's hand dropped to her side as her eyes seemed to grow. Ian walked backwards up the stairs to the doorway behind him, while keeping his eyes on the two female dealers.

Before Ian departed through the doorway, he turned to face both women and warned, "If you ever do anything to harm me or my family, you will have Hell to pay! Now, do you two understand me?"

Both women had pie eyes and stood dumbfounded while they shook their heads in agreement.

As Ian walked out the door, he could hear them saying, "Wow, that really backfired on us. Guess we better leave him alone."

Ian surmised it was the strangest seduction he had ever had in his life.

Ian let the door slam shut behind him. He turned around and saw a men's restroom across the aisle in front of him. Ian entered the men's room and saw his very red face in the mirror. He didn't know if his color was from embarrassment or if it was from the fury, he felt inside. He was angry.

Ian walked over to the sink and threw some cold water onto his face as he was thinking, "That woman had a forceful grip."

Ian heard some guy walk up beside him asking, "Are you alright?"

Ian looked up. Ian could tell unmistakably the man was a very handsome Italian American dealer.

Ian answered, "Yeah, I'm ok."

The dealer smiled and asked, "Are you sure?"

Ian recanted the story to the handsome dealer, then Ian introduced himself.

The handsome man said, "Oh, yes, I've heard Dolly has made a lot of boyfriends that way in the last three weeks. The word is already out about those two women."

Ian said, "Thank God my Sicilian American wife doesn't know what happened. She'd come in here hunting! I'll go home today and the first thing she will ask me is, 'How was your first day, Honey?' I just hope I can keep a straight face. My woman can read me like a book. She seems to know things will happen before they do happen. Her Grandma tried to explain it to me once, but I had a hard time trying to understand her broken English/Italian/Sicilian accent and something pertaining to "The EYE". I'm making a mental picture right now. I need to remember to turn around when I answer her question later today, so she won't be looking into my face. Cece can read me like a book."

The handsome Italian American dealer laughed loudly and said, "I'm Sicilian American, too. We are the mean ones. During World War II, the Sicilians never turned their back on the USA. We welcomed the Americans and helped them as much as possible to establish a base in Sicily. I've heard about "The Eye". Rare Italian women are like that. It's as if they have an extra sense. You're a very lucky man. Italian women aren't only 'HOT' looking, but they can cook, too! Just don't touch their men or their children. They will kill you!"

Ian said, "I didn't know you knew my wife!"

Both men started laughing out loud together and Ian's tensions felt somewhat abated.

Tony thought to himself, "I like this guy! He was smart enough to find a righteous woman. I've been trying to think of a way to meet him. This is a perfect accidental meeting!"

Ian said, "Yeah, Cece's something else. On top of everything, she's a real lady. I am a fortunate husband and father."

Ian's natural color seemed to return to his face as he toweled off.

The dealer said, "Well, there you go. You've finally returned to your normal complexion and have already forgotten about those two sluts. See what a good woman can do? Can't imagine any guy taking a chance on touching either of those two girls with a ten-foot pole. It's a new hotel and casino and the word's already out. Dolly and Tina are already on the 'Ho' list. By the way, my name's Tony. Glad to meet you, finally. Haven't seen you around the last three weeks for orientation."

Ian said, "Yeah, I sort of put it off as long as I could. Glad to meet you. I'm Ian. I don't know where anything is around here."

Tony said as they were shaking hands, "Break's over. We better get back! Meet me on our next break here and I'll fill you in quickly!"

Tony didn't have to worry about setting things up to look natural while meeting Ian for the first time. It just happened like it was meant to be. Tony was delighted. He knew Ian was the guy who he observed with Tommy, Jr. in the early morning hours of the day prior to the grand opening. He even thought maybe there was camaraderie starting to develop between them after this accidental meeting. He felt like he was making a new friend. He longed for a real good friend. One he could trust and one who was his equal. Maybe Ian could be a potential business partner someday, if Tony played his cards right, just like Tony dreamed of since he first laid eyes on Ian.

Tony thought to himself smugly, "This guy, Ian, could fit my mental request."

They were quite a match. They were both tall, well built, and very handsome in their distinct ways. They were walking back to their workstations. People were turning their heads to watch the two tall, striking men walk through the crowd. Tony liked the notoriety. He noticed people's reactions to them. He, also, noticed Ian couldn't care less about the crowd's reaction.

As they hurried back towards the pits, Tony asked, "Hey, Ian, do you snow ski?"

Ian said, "Both my wife and I love to ski!"

Tony asked, "What are your days off?"

Ian told him, "Both my wife and I are off on Wednesdays and Thursdays."

Tony laughed and said, "Yeah, that's a dealer's weekend! A large group of us really good skiers are going up for a two-day ski trip at the end of our work week. It would be on Wednesday and Thursday at Brian Head, in Utah. Do you think you and your wife would like to come up to the 'Brian Head Ski Resort'?"

Ian answered, "Cece's a better skier than I am, and I'm told I'm an excellent skier. Cece's on her hotel's ski team! She's been practicing, as much as possible, for the 'Hotel Challenge'. She's a downhill racer and absolutely loves it. I'll ask her. I'm pretty sure she would love it."

As they parted, Tony headed for the Baccarat room.

Tony looked back over his shoulder and said, "Ok, let's plan on it. We'll talk more about it later."

Since everything Tony just told Ian wasn't really planned, Tony had a lot of work to do to organize a big ski trip for Wednesday and Thursday.

Tony thought to himself, "Ian's wife, Cece, sounds exceptional, and she skis, too! Wow! I'd like to check this situation out."

Tony smiled to himself as he thought and hoped for the future. Tony might 'set up' this new friend, Ian, as a partner in Sallie's and his side business. He would have to feel the situation out to see if it were comfortable. He had to find out if Ian was "The Type". Maybe Ian would like more money, drugs, or extra women on the side. Money entices many men!

Tony thought, "Ian appears to be tough, but is he really? Could he have a bad side or only a good side? After all, some men can be tough, but only if they had to be."

Tony laughed because so many good guys had to have a cause.

Tony had no idea of the powerful causes in Ian's life. Ian learned to be street wise in in the outskirts of Los Angeles. He was in the Vietnam war and became jungle smart quickly or die. Ian did his duty. Army Rangers never ran away from confrontation. Ian chose his causes carefully. Ian's causes were the love of God, the love of Country, the love of Family, and the one true love of his good woman.

Ian's causes were not necessarily always in that order.

Ian walked in that evening from work and headed directly for Cece. She was cooking in the kitchen. She was dressed in short shorts, a tiny sheaf top, and sported bare feet. Ian could feel his needs by just looking at his beautiful wife. His magic touch was felt on her arm and she twirled around with a surprised wide smile on her face. Ian kissed her mouth and pulled her to him before she could ask him any questions. Ian felt her trying to free herself so she could ask how his first day went. Ian turned off the stovetop. Cece was giving in during the long, sensuous kiss from her man. As soon as their contact broke, Ian quickly turned around. He opened the refrigerator door and stuck his head deep into the refrigerator, as if he were looking for something.

Cece asked, "Wow, Honey, nice kiss! How was your first day? Don't start eating things because dinner is almost ready."

Ian prayed that his upper body wasn't turning bright red because he could feel the hairs standing up on the back of his neck after their kiss.

Ian answered, "Oh, you know, just the normal first day things that happen. I'm not looking for food. I just need something to 'ahh', to drink. I met a guy who has a bunch of friends going up to Brian Head, Utah, to ski on our days off. It'll be an overnight trip. Sounds like fun. Do you want to arrange for your folks to keep the boys so we could go?"

Now Ian had Cece's attention, and he got her to completely think of skiing instead of what happened on his first day at the Bella Ricco.

Cece said, "There's water on the refrigerator door, Honey. Oh, yes, I would love to go up and ski! I need to practice for the Hotel Challenge. I'll make arrangements with Mom and Dad. They are so good to us, and the boys love spending the night with them. Grandpa tells them stories of the old days. He's still so entertaining, like when I was his baby 'Cara Mia'."

Ian closed the refrigerator and stood up with his water.

He grabbed her while he pulled her to him again and said, "Yeah, but now you're my baby girl and Dear One."

They were still kissing when their boys, Scott, and Aaron, ran into the house after playing outside in front of their home. Their sons giggled while they were both saying, "EW, they're at it again! Kissy kisses!"

The boys yelled out, "How was your first day, Dad?"

Cece's eyes flew open during Ian's long sensuous kiss. Cece wanted to know that answer, too.

Ian continued kissing Cece long enough for the boys to run through the house and outside to their back-garden pool area where the boys, also, had a half basketball court set up for them. Their Rottweiler, Max, ran out behind the boys while wagging his entire body. The commotion grabbed Cece's thoughts! The boys and their best friend shot baskets as Max did figure eights around and between their legs, just like he was one of the basketball players.

Cece and Ian finally stopped the kiss and watched out the gigantic kitchen window as the boy's happiness unfolded in their back garden. They observed the playful interaction of the children and the dog. Ian and Cece laughed as they spoke of how Max did the same thing in the pool. Max loved his entire family. The dog was taught by an Army Ranger. The dog possessed a lot of love for his family, but the protective animal could turn vicious in an instant if he must, just like Ian.

Cece asked, "So, tell me how your first day at work went!" Ian thought, "DRAT!"

Ian turned away from her while he pretended to drink his water, "Oh, you know. It was uneventfully peaceful and serene."

Even from his side view Cece caught the blushing of her husband's skin and a twinkle in her husband's eye as he finished drinking the water and walked toward the back of the house saying, "I'm going to take a quick shower. I'll be out shortly."

Cece returned to her cooking and yelled out after him, "Ok, Honey, glad it was a calm day. It'll be time to eat in approximately thirty minutes."

Ian thought it went quite well as he smiled to himself and stepped into the shower. Ian thanked Heaven Cece didn't notice the blush on his face. How would he explain the Dolly and Tina incident? He just didn't want to go there. He never lied to Cece. She could read him like a book. Maybe it was the 'The Eye' thing that Cece's Grandma Angie proclaimed she and Cece both possessed! He didn't want to shower right then, but Ian would rather be safe than sorry, plus he needed to shed the smell, thoughts, and filth of the casino environment.

Meanwhile, as Cece was finishing up the cooking, she judiciously wondered what was up with that twinkle in Ian's eyes. She was sure she saw his face blushing, and the hairs on his nape sort of standing up. She figured she'd find out, eventually. Right then she had to get dinner on the table. After she needed to get ready for her swing shift.

Cece thought, "Wow, time's flying. I better get in a hurry. I have lots to do yet!"

Finally, their days off arrived…

The drive up the mountain through the town of Parowan, Utah, to the ski slopes at Brian Head, and to the lodge was beautiful. It took four hours one way to drive up to the ski area of Utah from Las Vegas, but worth the effort. The Utah snow was almost always of great volume, powdery on the mountain surface, and had a nicely packed base.

Las Vegas did have Mount Charleston in Lee Canyon, which was about a 45-minute drive outside of town. It was their only local ski mountain. 'Ski Lee' was where they both learned to ski when the Las Vegas valley had a very wet winter and snow was plentiful, but many years the snow wasn't as plentiful as the Utah snows. Mount Charleston was the only ski area near Las Vegas. Las Vegas has always loved their Mount Charlie, no matter if the snow was good or bad. Cece was tough and learned to ski the hard way. Cece could not afford ski lessons so she just stood up and flew down the mountain and stopped into the side of a tool shed at the bottom. She did not know how to stop yet, but she was determined to figure it out. She realized soon after to sit down when she was out of control or it would hurt when she fell or crashed into a tool shed to stop!

Eventually, the ski patrol guys got to know Cece and one of the men asked her, "Aren't you the girl who didn't take lessons?"

Cece just smiled at him.

He continued, "You know, people should really take ski lessons, but I got to tell you, you are one of the best skiers on the mountain today! I don't know how you did it, but you can really ski!"

Cece said, "Because I love it!"

Meanwhile, as they looked forward to a fun day, Cece and Ian hydrated by drinking water, coffee, and hot chocolate on the trip up to Utah and listened to good music. They laughed and talked. They enjoyed just being in love with each other. They both felt very secure in their marriage and with their love. They pulled into the parking area near the condos. A man was over to the side of the road. He recognized Ian and immediately looked over to the passenger seat at Cece.

Suddenly, the man seemed to stand up straighter and puffed his chest out. Ian thought only to himself, "Tony looks like a horny rooster while he's checking out my wife!"

Ian didn't like Tony's reaction to seeing Cece for the very first time. It was a mental note Ian would keep forever.

Cece saw the same reaction from a stranger at the roadside.

After Ian jumped out of their SUV, Cece prepared to leave the vehicle. Tony was thinking to himself, "I would have never guessed, as handsome as Ian is, that his wife and mother of their two young sons, would be so stunning. OMG, Mother Fucker! How did he rate and get so lucky?"

Ian thought to himself while watching Tony, "What the fuck, Tony, stop acting like that! It's so blatantly evident!"

Cece innocently asked out the window to her husband, "Do you know that guy?"

Ian answered, "Yeah, that's the guy who invited us up. His name is Tony."

Cece looked at her man and asked, "Why is he acting weird?"

Ian knew Tony spotted Cece, and Tony liked what he saw. Ian didn't want Cece to think badly of his new friend right away. Ian was still figuring out Tony's personality, Tony's reactions, and soon Ian would determine Tony's future intentions.

Ian answered, "Probably excited to see we made it up here on time. Now he can tell us what rooms we are all in, so we can get settled in quickly. We can all hit the slopes early!"

Ian wanted to keep his wife busy. He didn't want Cece to leave the vehicle yet, or to notice what would happen next.

Ian asked, "Honey, can you please dig my gloves out of my things in that bag on your floorboard, so I can unload?"

Cece did one of her 'wondering frown things' with her pretty face, and said, "Oh, ok, sure, Honey."

Ian wanted to keep Cece very occupied while he had a word with Tony. Ian quickly walked over to Tony.

Ian looked at Tony as he approached Tony and said, "Tony, you're acting like a love-struck horny fuck head! She's my wife! Stop being so obvious!"

Tony snapped out of it and said, "Oh man, I can't help it! I'm sorry. She's gorgeous! You should have warned me! Will she still look that good when she gets out of your SUV?"

Ian said, "I won't have this, Tony! She's a lady and we've been together for many years since we were very young. She will not accept this kind of reaction. Take a few deep breaths and calm down or else we'll get back into the SUV and go back to Vegas, now."

Tony sarcastically laughed and asked, "Yeah, right. What would she think after you guys just drove 4 hours straight to get here?"

Ian grabbed the front of Tony's jacket and pulled Tony around and began walking away while switching over to pull Tony's arm. Ian was heading away from his SUV and Cece.

Cece took her time exiting their SUV after she dug Ian's gloves out from the bottom of his big ski bag.

She saw her husband speaking to Tony. They were still walking away. Ian seemed upset over something. Cece wondered what happened. She felt almost frightened of Ian's new friend's appearance and the way he kept catching glimpses of her over his shoulder. She was sure of one thing. If she noticed it, so did Ian. She did not get a good feeling from her husband's new friend, but she would be polite if she ever got to meet him. She thought maybe she was mistaken, but her feelings were extremely powerful. Cece watched as Ian kept grabbing the guy's arm and pulled him away from the road. Ian walked with him into a snowy field with bushes and small trees. They walked for a while. Cece was wondering what they were talking about when the 2 men disappeared around some bushes.

The men finally returned by walking toward Cece. Cece took a big breath. She exhaled and did it again. She saw the man's demeanor and recognized his reactions. She had seen it many times before from men. Cece had been excited about this trip and she wanted Ian and her to have fun because they had both looked forward to it for their entire work week. She knew her man, though. If he said they were leaving, Cece would understand.

Cece said out loud to herself, "Gee, the snow looks so great, too. I'd be sorry to leave. I really need to practice for the hotel challenge! I hope we can stay."

Cece stayed next to the SUV with Ian's ski gloves back in her hands. The guys were still a good distance away from her. Cece put Ian's gloves on his driver's seat. Cece decided to start unloading. If Ian had other plans, Cece knew Ian would inform her and he would help her load their gear back up.

Tony stopped dead in his tracks, staring at Cece while she unloaded her skis. His mouth fell open.

Ian shook him and said, "Damn it, Tony! You better act normal or I am going to kick your ass! She's my wife! STOP IT!"

Tony turned toward Ian and asked, "How tall is she? About 5'8"? Wow, She's something else! She has a perfect body for everything, especially for sex, skiing, and whatever!

That did it. Cece's back was turned to them. Ian shoved Tony hard, and he landed behind another large bush and onto a pile of big rocks covered with enough snow to disguise the boulders. Tony got up, still hurting.

Tony looked up in amazement at Ian and said, "What the fuck's wrong with you?"

Ian said, "That's it, Tony! We're going home! She's my woman and I demand respect for her! She's a respectable lady! Got it?"

Tony scrambled up off the ground and said, "Oh, wow, man, I'm sorry. I didn't mean anything by it."

Tony was almost running to keep up with Ian's long strides as he walked back towards his wife. Tony ran up to Ian and grabbed his arm to stop him.

Tony said, "Please, stop!"

Ian stopped and stared into Tony's black devil eyes.

Tony continued, "You know how many beautiful women we see daily. I guess it's just a shock to see the one in a million. I've never seen a prettier Italian American woman! Listen, man, I'm really sorry. I'll behave. Really, I'm sorry, but your wife is so damn beautiful."

Ian turned away and continued walking towards his vehicle and away from Tony. Tony ran up to Ian a second time as he was brushing snow and dirt from his hands and both of his bruised buttocks.

Tony said, "Please, man, I'm sorry. I'll behave, but you should have warned me about her."

Ian turned on Tony with his hands of fists and said, "She's not a piece of meat, Tony. She's a total woman. She's MY wife! Got it? If she were ever hurt in any way, I would kill the guy. It wouldn't be the first time I had to kill. Got it?"

Tony was impressed by Ian's words. He heard Ian was an Army Ranger because he heard the talk at work. He decided to kiss up to Ian for the time being. He really needed this friend. They paused and spoke some more. Tony held out his hand and patted Ian's arm with his other hand. They shook hands. They walked diligently towards Cece.

Cece noticed they had walked very far away while having an active conversation, but she didn't notice Ian shoved Tony onto the rocks and snow because she couldn't see them clearly from her position. She had been terribly busy unloading her ski equipment and the things for the trip when the guys started to walk towards her.

When she turned to face them, she put forth her best effort and gave them one of her beautiful smiles. She watched Ian stop in his tracks as he glared at Tony. Tony quickly stepped up to her. Tony realized Cece was even more beautiful up close.

Tony said, as he took Cece's gloved hand into his own hands, "Hi, I'm Tony! I am thrilled to finally meet you!"

Ian thought to himself as Cece eyed Ian's reaction, "Good, that was quite respectful."

Cece returned the introduction and commented, "Glad to finally meet you, Tony. I am Cece. Ian was happy to meet a new friend who invited us up for a weekend of skiing. We have been looking forward to this trip!"

Ian was proud of his wife. She was a good sport and a terrific lady. Ian noticed Cece tried twice to pull her gloved hand out of Tony's hands. Tony was gazing into her eyes as he finally let go of her hand. Ian realized Cece had that effect on men, but Ian thought Cece was naïve to that fact.

She wasn't. Cece knew.

Cece wondered what her man would do. Ian often told Cece she was gorgeous, but she would shyly brush it off and would always comment he felt that way because he was in love with her. Ian knew she didn't think of herself as gorgeous. Ian knew she never thought she appeared beautiful because Cece felt a person's genuine beauty came from deep inside their soul and not how their body appeared to people. She constantly strived to be a good woman, who could exude beauty from deep within her spirit only because it was natural for her to do it.

She knew many women with whom she had experiences. Those women considered themselves to be beautiful, but some of those women had cruel, greedy, envious, and money hungry personalities. In Cece's eyes, those women were hideous and evil.

Cece 'feelings' sensed some uncomfortable and ominous emotions emanating from Tony even though he was a very handsome man. She could tell Ian was giving him a chance at something, but she couldn't totally figure it out. She thought she needed to give Tony a chance, also, for Ian's sake. She wanted to be nice to Ian's new friend even though she felt a dark ominous aura around him. Cece was determined to try because she thought it was what Ian wanted. All Cece ever wanted was for Ian to be happy. Tony was his new friend from work, and Cece loved her husband with all her heart. It was nice Tony invited them up for a fun weekend. She made a mental note to ask Ian more about Tony when they got a chance to be alone.

Tony helped them to finish unloading and get to their room. Tony left to go to his own room to prepare for the mountain. Everyone was to meet in 20 minutes at the chair lift line. It was Cece's chance to speak in private with her husband.

Cece tried to calm herself, and once she did, she asked, "Honey, what was going on between you and Tony when you two took that long walk?

Ian dreaded making up stories to his wife. He never would lie to her on purpose, but to Ian, Tony was trivial and nothing important right now. If anything substantial were to develop out of his new friendship with Tony, that was of any importance, he would confide the information to his wife, but only if he had to protect her. As far as Ian was concerned, Tony was not of any importance, but Cece was all important.

Ian turned his back on Cece and acted like he was checking out his ski gear as he replied. "Oh, you know, he has girl trouble. Stupid stuff."

Cece felt like it wasn't her business and replied, "Oh, is that all?"

It wasn't meant to be a question. It was meant to be a nonchalant dropping of the subject. Tony's girl problems weren't her concern, but Cece sensed there was an attraction. Tony was making a fool of himself. Cece, also, knew no man could win her heart away from Ian. As long as Ian was all right with things as they were, Cece didn't care about anything else.

Ian didn't feel like he lied to his wife because it was the truth in a hasty manner. He loved her. He really didn't know Tony well, but in Ian's heart, Ian thought he would always be around to protect Cece, and what Ian called 'her little girl innocence'. Ian wasn't too concerned with Tony after their confrontation, and, if Tony remained respectful to Cece, Ian was appeased.

They had a wonderfully cloudless day of snow skiing on the powdered snow-covered mountains of Utah. The group of 15 skiers were all just becoming acquainted because they were all new employees of the Bella Ricco except for Cece. Cece was the only outsider in the group. Tony liked that idea. Cece was accepted immediately after the group watched her ski just one time. They asked her questions, and she gave advice. Tony followed her like a puppy. Tony's actions were obvious to Ian. Ian watched Tony's every move. Ian was relieved Cece was preoccupied with their group and didn't notice Tony noticing her. Cece was having an enjoyable time with all the other people in their group. She looked like she didn't have a care in the world. Ian loved to see his wife having fun. Ian knew skiing made Cece happy.

But Cece felt it, she knew. Cece wanted Ian to enjoy himself, too.

The group made it to the bottom of the mountain and were lining up to get back onto the chair lift for another run. Ian noticed suddenly Tony wasn't there. All he cared about was Cece at his side. She was smiling, laughing, and happy. Everyone was calling out to each other and yelling comments to Cece and Ian pertaining to the nice-looking run down the mountain. Even bystanders on the lodge's sun deck were yelling out comments and waving at the group. Ian looked over to his smiling, lovely wife. He was happy she was enjoying herself so much because it made him happy, too.

Ian thought to himself, "Cece works so hard. I want her to have a great time, and she is!" Ian remembered her comment once when Cece said, "Skiing is like being close to God and Heaven!"

Ian thought, "Cece is having the time of her life, especially because she has the 'peace of mind' knowing her wonderful parents, Sammie and Carmella, are caring for our boys."

The group was waiting at the mountain's top until everyone arrived so they could take off in a large formation. The leaders were waiting for Cece and Ian to get off the chairlift. The group was waving for Cece and Ian to come to the front of the formation. Cece surpassed the other female skiers in ability and strength. The group was proud to put her up front. Cece kept up with the men and loved the feeling she got from skiing. She felt like she was in flight. The scenery was spotless and beautiful. The air was clean and not like the hot blowing sandy desert.

Cece felt close to God when she skied. She was close to Heaven. Ian looked at his woman's joyful face and smiled. Cece looked at Ian and did the same.

The group pulled over about halfway down the mountain and stopped to take pictures.

Ian skied up to Cece's side and spoke to her, "You will meet a lot of dealers today. Most are normal, but some are not normal at all. If you feel uncomfortable with anything or anyone, just let me know, and I will fix things, or we can take a break. Ok?"

Cece replied, "Honey, I meet abnormal people every day at work. I think I'll be fine. I know you always have an eye on me. I am not concerned, ok?"

Ian smiled at her and gave her a wink. He took off, and she followed him elegantly down the mountain. Crowds of people on the lodge's outdoor balcony watched and pointed at the lead skiers with delight as they descended the big mountain together with a long line of skiers in a long graceful formation following them.

People on the chair lift going up the mountain were clapping and yelling, "Way to go, great run, you guys!"

Ian noticed Tony finally joined the back of the group just in time to keep up. Ian wondered where he had been and what he had been doing when he missed the last two runs down the mountain.

As the group gathered at the mountain's bottom, everyone was saying maybe it was getting close to time to eat a good dinner.

Tony yelled out, "I've got it all arranged. I made reservations for 15 people. The restaurant workers said it would take them at least thirty minutes to set up a huge table down the middle of the restaurant. If you guys want to take another run, we have plenty of time. Don't worry, I tipped them for the group."

Ian thought it was strange that Tony would say something like that. They all lived on tips. They knew how to tip. It wasn't necessary for Tony to tip for everyone. Ian didn't understand, but Ian sensed Tony was up to something and didn't want Ian to know what it was. Ian was determined to find out.

Everyone decided to take one more run and then go eat dinner. Jacob's was a cool place to eat. The food was great, but so was the ambiance. It felt like being in a huge log cabin with all your very best friends. There was a great round fireplace in the middle of the dining area. It felt warm and inviting after skiing all day. There was a huge long table set up for 15 people right next to the grand fireplace. The tables were covered in crisp white tablecloths. Someone had fashioned pinecones and small pine boughs with red ribbons right down the middle of the tables. Tony was already seated at the head of the table when Cece and Ian got there after they had changed for dinner. There was a seat to his right with a red rose surrounded by small bits of ferns in an exquisitely delicate hand carved ribbon vase. Cece's eyes grew wide.

Cece said to Ian, "Wow, I hope the food is as great as the atmosphere. Why are you seated on the other side of the table from me?"

Ian questioned himself mentally, "Is the seat to his left is mine? The son of a bitch put me on the other side of the table from my wife. That's why he tipped! I will show him!"

Ian walked up to Tony and said, "Get up!"

Tony looked at Ian and said, "Come on, I want to sit between my two favorite new friends!"

Cece put her hand on Ian's wrist and said, "It's ok, Honey. We can talk better this way and I can see your handsome face across from me."

They sat down, and the rest of the group greeted them.

Cece apologized, "I'm sorry, everyone, if I took too long changing."

People were saying things like,

"Don't worry about it."

Or, "We didn't even bother to change."

Or, "Sit down and relax."

Or, "Everything's fine."

Or, "We ordered rounds of drinks."

Or, "No problem!"

Ian fumed. He planned on taking Tony aside later for another talk, but Tony was feeling his booze already.

The ski trips would continue that season, but Ian's wife would be seated next to him anytime there was a break.

Cece was the only female on her hotel's team. Her three male partners were so worried about her winning, they almost screwed up. Cece always came through with flying colors. Cece's team won first place in the "Hotel Challenge". Cece won her gold medal.

Tony wanted to know everything was to be known about Cece. Tony would use Sallie, Jr.'s spy, Woody.

There was a bit of winter left and Tony planned on making the most of it.

Soon the season would be coming to an end, Tony was determined to get Cece back up on the mountain and away from Ian's protective eyes. Cece would be his someday, or else!

Tony coveted Ian's wife.

Chapter 17

The Spy

Tony realized he better stop making comments to Ian pertaining to his wife. Ian was giving him threatening looks and would become suspicious of him if he continued. Ian could make it impossible for Tony to be around his wife, and he did not want that to happen. Tony absolutely knew Ian could 'hold his own' against him. He opted to pursue Cece on his own. Tony knew Ian would not easily allow his wife to be around him. He wanted all the information that could be collected on her. He decided to use 'The Spy'.

Woody was Sallie's best man as far as spying went. Since Woody had the nasty habit of gambling, he always wanted to work on the side, but he feared repercussions from Sallie, Junior. Tony and Woody were not planning on telling Sallie that Tony was using Woody to watch a woman. Salliehad an explosive personality, and people who worked for him learned not to tell him everything. Woody would never think to rat on Tony. It wasn't only because Tony could do him extreme harm. Woody would never chance suffering pain. Woody was a wimpy small skinny rat fink, but he was excellent at what he did. Besides, Woody knew Tony was cool when you did favors for him. Tony was generous when he got what he wanted. Tony would give Woody extra tip money for a job well done. Tony paid better than Sallie, with Sallie's money.

Woody was one of the original old Italian compadres. He was slight and cunning. Tony pay Woody more money for his talents to cover

Woody's work for following this new female mark. Tony didn't tell Sallieeverything. Tony had no respect for Woody. Tony just knew Woody was the best spy in the business. It may have been a talent, or it may have been because Woody was a nondescript small person in stature who could never look like a real threat. The best part was Sallie wouldn't even realize he was paying for something he didn't order. Sallie was so wealthy he never noticed what Tony did with the payout money. That payout money was controlled by Tony. Tony oversaw the distributing payout money as he saw fit. Sallietrusted Tony completely. Tony had saved his life, after all.

Woody wondered about this assignment, "Why was this woman so important? Tony was tight-lipped about her, but Woody dared not ask Tony for fear of his reaction to the question."

The surveillance began. Somehow, as spies do, Woody had gathered the basic information on Cece. He knew she had graduated from Western High School on Decatur Blvd. in Las Vegas. She had excellent grades. She had a Florida driver's learning permit when she was attending Southwest Miami High School and was given a Nevada Driver's license when she entered the State of Nevada. Her nickname was Cece. Woody thought the nickname was a little different. She was gorgeous and of Sicilian-American heritage, just like he was, and he felt a strange commonality towards her. Woody began to like her the more he followed her.

Woody thought, "She's so beautiful! She's smart and nice, but mostly, she is good!"

Cece's family was connected on her Father's side, but they preferred not to get involved doing business with their mob relatives. The mob, especially relatives, expect payback. They did not want the responsibility of owing a favor for a favor, plus the mob relatives were a bit crazy.

You never knew what could happen. People died from 'mob mistakes on purpose' often. Cece's parents and relatives were extremely strait-laced Sicilian American Catholics and preferred it that way.

Cece had mediocre jobs after she completed Western High School in Las Vegas and entered the casino business when she became of age. Her first casino job was a 'Carousel Girl' position. She had a good honest reputation for money handling. After that, Cece got a nonunion job in a downtown casino cage in a nice hotel. While she worked there, she somehow transferred into a day shift cocktail job. She was married four years before her first son was born. She worked at her first hotel job for two-and-a-half years, while she continued her education studying real estate law. She loved and visited with her elderly parents often. They were a very affectionate family. She had two other sisters and three brothers. She loved skiing.

Ian hardly ever visited his parents in the Los Angeles area of California because he worked odd hours and was called into work at different times on the ever changing 21 Pit schedule. He would need at least 3 days to drive to LA and back for a decent family visit. When the family did get to visit the Los Angeles area, their two small sons enjoyed theme parks and the beach areas. Cece visited her extended family in LA when she was able. Her favorite cousin, who was her maid of Honor, lived there. Cece loved her dearly. Woody followed the family and the woman for many months. Woody couldn't believe how normal they were and living in Las Vegas.

Woody thought, "This woman is a devoted wife and mother. She has no bad habits. She does not gamble but saves what she earns to pay for her family's needs. She goes to all her son's games and practices. She doesn't frequent bars or fancy lounges. She drives straight home every night after work. She doesn't 'fool around' with her marriage or her life. She is determined in everything she decides to accomplish. She is a very moral lady. She's an easy report. She is a dutiful wife and mother."

That was the bottom line. She met her present husband when they were very young in high school together. They became the best of friends for three years. They married at young ages when her husband was stationed at Fort Bliss in El Paso, Texas. That was about the sum of her information. She was an exceedingly loyal wife, mother, daughter, sister, relative, friend, and employee.

The next day Woody reported to Tony to tell him what was going on with Cece.

Woody told Tony, "It's another exciting late Wednesday afternoon of tailing Cece. She's grocery shopping because all of you aren't skiing this week. Cece's sons are with their coaches until later this evening for basketball practice and pizza later. I saw the boy's coach picking up the boys before Cece went to the grocery store. She just arrived at the market at 5:00 p.m."

Tony said, "Give me the grocery store's address!" Woody told Tony the store's address.

Tony surprised Woody by saying, "Ok. I will meet you at the grocery store very soon for a complete report while Cece is shopping."

Before they hung up, Woody timidly told Tony that Cece took none of the flowers home Tony had been sending to her place of employment for the last three months. She was giving the flowers away to any girls at work who wanted the flowers. If the flowers were delivered to the beverage office, Cece would leave the flowers there for all the ladies to enjoy. Woody told Tony to stop wasting his money because her husband never found out about any of the flowers. Therefore, his efforts to make Ian jealous and upset weren't working. Woody surmised Ian did not find out because Cece would never allow anything to upset their marriage or family.

Woody found out Cece's customers had sent her beautiful bouquets of flowers many times in the past. Through one of Woody's bell desk connections, Woody found out, 'that over the years', the bellmen were told to throw any flowers away that were being sent to Cece from other men. Finally, Cece told the bellmen to take the flowers home to their wives and/or girlfriends, and definitely not to deliver the flowers to the cocktail office. Cece would tip them for doing it. It was one of the reasons Cece was so popular with her bellmen acquaintances. Her flowers made a lot of their wives and girlfriends delighted in the past months, and that made the bellmen happy, too. Cece was well liked and respected at work. Everyone, with whom she worked, admired her. Most of them liked her, apart from some of her jealous fellow cocktail waitresses.

Woody let out a deep breath and thought, "Good, I'm glad I got to tell Tony all that on the phone before he gets here. It will give him time to cool off."

Tony knew the group was not going skiing on their days off that week. He had Sallie schedule Ian to work on this Wednesday evening.

Tony called Sallie and told him to take him off the schedule for Baccarat that night because he needed to follow a lead. The day before, Tony had asked Sallie to have Ian called into work on Wednesday. Sallie wondered why Tony wanted Ian to be called into work. Tony made up a story and told Sallie he heard Ian needed the money. Sallie said he would take care of it. Tony lied to Sallie all the time, but he never got caught. Tony knew Salliewould make sure Tony was still paid and still got a full share of tips even though Tony was not working in the casino. Tony loved his power.

Tony thought, "If I get lucky, maybe I can convince Cece to go out for a bite to eat after I accidentally, on purpose, run into Cece at the grocery store."

Tony headed toward the west preppy end of Las Vegas. It was where all the honest, hardworking younger people lived. He pulled up in front of the grocery store and saw Woody watching through the big plate-glass windows of the supermarket. Tony exited his red corvette convertible and headed for Woody. Woody was concentrating on his job when Tony walked up and touched his shoulder. Woody jumped.

Tony laughed and asked, "What's wrong with you? Don't pee your pants!"

Woody answered, "Hell, man. Have you ever seen the size of her husband? I've been paranoid ever since I found out about him. If he ever caught me, he could hurt me!"

Tony laughed, "Yes, we're friends. Don't worry about him. They called him into work and told him they needed him tonight so he's at home probably getting ready for work right now."

Woody said, "Hell, that must be the reason Cece's not in a hurry to get done with her shopping like she usually does. Her husband's going to work, and her boys are with their coaches."

Tony said, "I arranged it. I'm sure she already knows Ian's going into work tonight."

Woody asked what Tony wanted.

Tony said he wanted the latest report on Cece.

Woody told him everything else he had on Cece.

Woody ended by saying, "She is so pretty and 'straight arrow'! Please don't hurt her. This has been one of the easiest assignments I have ever had. Hey, she's a real looker alright! Men make fools out of themselves when she's around them and she doesn't even notice them.

She's boring and moral. She doesn't do anything wrong. She's totally devoted to her family. She cares for her aging parents, her children, but mostly, she cares about Ian. She's really in love with him. What's your interest in this married woman anyway, Tony?"

Tony snapped, "That's none of your business! This was an assignment for you. That's all, Woody! Just remember to keep your mouth shut! Got that?"

Woody held his hands up in the air in front of his frightened face and said in a shaky voice, "Ok, Ok, Tony! Sorry. I didn't mean anything! You know that I'll be quiet! Please don't hurt this Lady though. She's a really good person."

Tony got the information he wanted. Cece was everything he could possibly want in a woman. She would be his woman someday. He had paid enough dues in his lifetime to deserve to have Cece.

Tony handed Woody a thousand dollars for a tip in one hundred-dollar bills and told him, "Your assignment is finished. Give me all the paperwork on Cece that you have. I'll pay you another $2,000.00 plus expenses within 3 days. So be quiet and get lost for now."

Woody profusely thanked Tony. Tony just looked at him blankly like he was piss ant. A frightened Woody left quickly!

Tony walked into the grocery store. He saw a fresh-brewed coffee station. Tony walked up and down the aisles until he saw Cece shopping. He admired her body, especially her long legs. She was perfect. She was tight and strong. He felt a sensation in his groin and shook it off. He wanted to walk up to her and feel her breasts as he pulled her to his chest. He wanted to grab two handfuls of her perfect buttocks. Instead, he acted innocently as he approached her sideways while he pretended to be looking on the aisle shelves. Through his sunglasses, Tony could see her notice him.

Tony asked, "Cece, is that you?"

Cece was surprised to see him and said, "Wow! Hi, Tony! This is the last place on Earth I thought I would ever meet you! Do you live around this area now? I thought you lived on the Strip."

Tony looked at her admirably and answered, "I drove up to Mount Charleston to see if we had enough snow up there to ski. You can never trust their hotline. I seemed to get turned around because I'm not familiar with this side of town. That's when I saw this grocery store and I thought I'd buy some mushrooms for sauce tonight. After walking by that coffee station though, now I think I need a hot cup of coffee instead. Would you like some coffee when you are done?"

Cece looked at him so strangely that Tony thought he may have been too obvious. Tony pulled off his sunglasses, smiled widely, and asked, "Did I say something wrong?"

Cece felt a sensation as their eyes met. It was as if she saw a flash of darkness. She should have paid more attention to the feeling, but she felt comfortable on her home ground.

Cece didn't want her feeling to show, so Cece said, "I was just thinking coffee sounded good. I know what it feels like to crave coffee, especially at this time of day. I'm almost done. I usually get a coffee when I'm done grocery shopping, anyway."

Tony said, "Ok."

Tony asked Cece for the kind of coffee she would prefer. Tony heard Cece tell the bag boy she needed two bags of water softener salt.

She turned to look back at Tony and told him, "Just black, thanks. I'll meet you at the coffee station's seats as soon as I pay for my groceries."

Tony was waiting at a table with 2 coffees when Cece arrived. He helped her to position the grocery cart near their table so it would not be in the way of the other shoppers.

Cece smiled and said, "What a nice treat! I love having a coffee after the chore of grocery shopping! Thank you."

Tony replied, "This is such a pleasant surprise."

Tony just looked at her. She was gorgeous! She had no idea just how beautiful she was standing there. He thought of her perfectly proportioned body; her flowing long hair of many highlights, her long legs, her beautiful face, and the fact she was of his heritage, also, made him feel absolutely satisfied that she should be with him. He would give her everything. He would make sure her sons had everything. They would go to the finest schools and be picked for the finest colleges and graduate schools. Whatever she desired for her sons; he would make sure she had it.

Tony just did not realize how a woman, as special as Cece, could be simply satisfied. He didn't realize she didn't need much, as long as she had her family. Cece just wanted her family to be happy, healthy, and safe. That wish included Ian, who she loved with all her heart.

Tony hated Ian even though he admired him.

As Cece sat down she said, "I never expected to see you way out here on the west end of town in a regular family neighborhood. What a surprise!"

Tony smiled really big and said, "There's something to be said for being lost!"

Cece looked at Tony and felt a strange feeling. She not only sensed it, she felt it deep in her heart. She was giving warning to herself, but she was inadvertently shaking the feeling off as if it were nothing. After all, this was her husband's new friend from work. He had been friendly with Ian and did favors for him. In many ways, they were a lot alike. In many other ways, they were totally different. Cece felt confused.

Cece said, "Thanks for the delicious coffee again, Tony."

Tony raised his handsome face to study hers. He just stared at her.

She saw "The Warning" flash in her mind's eye again.

He thought to himself, "Did I give myself away?"

Cece thought to herself, "What's that supposed to mean? Did I just read his thoughts?" Cece felt uncomfortable. Something wasn't right. What could be wrong with such an accidental meeting in a grocery store? She changed the subject.

Cece asked, "What's up with the ski group? Looks like we may have enough snow in Utah to ski, but not here locally. I need to practice for the hotel sports challenge. It's coming up soon. Hope we get snow up on Mount Charlie! Nothing local usually compares to Brian Head, though."

Tony knew he'd have to play his cards right.

He replied, "I know! You're right. Snow's better up in Utah. Mount Charlie didn't look good at all to me today. Too much junk coming up through the little bit of snow we've received so far. Maybe in another month it will be ski worthy, but not now. Hopefully, by the time of the Hotel Challenge, we will have enough snow up there on Charlie otherwise you're going to have to go to Utah."

He could sense Cece was disappointed about Mount Charlie, but Tony wanted to get her away from the Las Vegas area for his plan to work. He needed to get her alone and away from Ian. He needed to make her his woman. His tricky mind was already formulating a plan. He knew a girl who was pretty good at scamming, and that girl needed her drug money all the time. He knew it would be a difficult task to pull off, but he would do it, if it meant he could have Cece. Right now, he needed to change the subject. He needed to be patient.

Tony asked, "So I take it you are off tonight?"

Cece answered, "Yes, I'm still on the same shift I was on when we all went skiing for the first time, Day shift with Wednesdays and Thursday's nights off. Ian's usually off then too, but he got called in tonight. Guess they're short on staff."

Tony said, "Ok. Tell Ian I'll book the same condos for Wednesday night next week. Everyone from the different hotels needs the practice for the hotel ski challenge. I'm going to go ahead and book those rooms later today before they get booked up."

Cece said, "Ok, I'll tell him, and I'll arrange it with my folks for babysitting the boys. My folks are so good to us. I thank God for my family. I really need to practice for the hotel challenge. You know it's in March, right? Hope we have snow in Charlie by early March."

Tony looked at her. He needed to touch her. He needed to caress her face and her body. He needed it now. This interaction with her was way too difficult for him. This encounter was getting to his senses.

Tony took a deep breath, and shook his head as he looked down at his groin and asked, "Where's Ian now?"

Cece answered, "He's getting ready for work now. Probably sick calls. He'll be on his way there shortly. It's likely he's driving by right now."

Tony asked, "Do you want me to help you with the heavy bags of water softener salt? Everyone in Las Vegas needs a water softener."

Cece laughed and commented, "Every woman with long hair in this desert certainly needs one."

He loved her laughter.

Tony laughed, "I'm hungry. How about you?"

Cece smiled, "I better not eat. I don't have to cook tonight. The boys are eating with their coaches after their practice this evening and I don't need food. I have to be good."

Tony looked at Cece and said, "You always look good."

Cece blushed and said, "It's a constant endeavor for a woman to look good, but it's even more difficult to be healthy."

Tony said, "Wow, I'm glad guys don't have to think about those things."

Cece giggled and said, "Oh, you will when you get older."

Tony said, "I don't plan on getting old."

Cece replied, "You better plan on it before you get there!"

There was another sudden flash in Cece's mind's eye. Then Cece had a feeling Tony was right and he would never get old. Cece wondered why and how, but she couldn't concentrate while talking to Tony.

Tony said, "I really don't think I'll ever see 30."

Tony asked her once again to go grab a bite to eat.

Cece felt a little irritated and said, "No, I have too much to do!"

Tony said, "It's only a bite to eat."

Cece answered, "No, Tony, I don't do that!"

Tony frowned and asked, "Do what?"

Cece said, "I don't go out even innocently with other guys."

Tony said, "You've got to lighten up. It's only a bite to eat!"

Cece knew she wouldn't win this conversation. She stopped and stood up to ready herself to leave.

Ian was waiting at a red light on the corner where the grocery store was located. He knew Cece was probably getting done there about that time. When the light turned green, Ian did a double take as his vehicle moved forward. He thought he saw a beautiful red corvette just like Tony's red beauty 'The Babe'. Ian drove on while thinking to himself some lucky neighbor must have hit a jackpot because most vehicles in this family neighborhood of growing families were SUVs or Minivans. He thought an expensive car like Tony's wasn't often spotted in a neighborhood of young parents with cars full of children. A strange feeling came over him for Cece's safety. Ian made a mental note to call Cece when he got to work.

Cece's and his favorite song came on the radio and his mind went to a happier memory of their teenage years. He drove to work humming to their first song, 'I wanna hold your hand'. He laughed and remembered when they were in California and it was playing at school as he grabbed her hand for the first time. To this day, he still held her hand when they were together.

Cece arrived at her SUV. Tony was right behind her. She felt uncomfortable.

Tony said, "At least let me help you with the heavy salt bags." He did so and turned towards Cece.

Cece thanked him for putting the heavy bags into the back of Cece's SUV along with her groceries. She walked around to the driver's side to get into the vehicle. That's when she felt the grip on her arm. She felt frightened. She turned on him instantly. He felt her piercing eyes warning him off.

Tony couldn't help himself as he said, "Cece, you've got to know how I feel about you."

Cece bluntly said, "That's enough, Tony. I'm going home now!"

Tony said, "Ok, look. Here's my personal information and the code to get into my luxury condo complex on the Strip. Just come over anytime if you ever need help or have to get away. You are already on my personal guest list. You will not have any trouble getting into the complex even if I'm not home. They've been instructed to hold a key for you and to let you enter my private residence anytime."

Cece replied, "That's not going to happen. Never! I'm not comfortable with you talking to me like this. Just stop!"

Tony pleaded, "You've got to know how I feel. You've got to feel it, too! Since the very first moment when I saw you, I was in love. I have never been in love before. I feel like I'm going to explode. Please try to understand."

Cece said, "You're my husband's best friend at work. He likes you. This would devastate him. Just stop this!"

Cece pulled her arm from his grip.

Tony continued saying, "Cece, I am getting very wealthy. I have accumulated a fortune because of wise investing. I can give you and your sons whatever you want from life. You deserve all the wonderful things life offers. You are everything I have longed for all my life. I adore you and I need you with me."

Cece was trembling as she said, "I am leaving now." Tony begged, "Try to understand, please."

Cece could feel herself shaking uncontrollably. She pivoted and got into the SUV. Her head was spinning. Cece drove away without saying another word to Tony. She left Tony standing alone in the parking lot, staring after her vehicle.

When she arrived home, she quickly hit the garage door opener and drove in. She brought all the groceries into the house; the phone rang. She was hoping it wasn't Tony.

Cece answered, "Hello."

Ian spoke, "Hi, Honey. Got to work early and just wanted to check on you. Is everything ok?"

Cece knew this was not the time to upset him. Ian was preparing to go into his workstation. Tony did not follow her home. Maybe Tony got the message!

Cece said, "Yes, Honey, I'm just putting groceries away, but can you get the heavy water softener bags of salt out later. The boys are just getting home. I love you so much, Ian!"

Ian said, "Ok, Honey, I will do that tomorrow. I love you, too! Will give you a kiss when I get home tonight even though I know you'll be asleep."

Cece said, "Wake me if you want. I'm off tomorrow. I love you, too! I look forward to you getting home. Be careful!"

Ian said, "Good night, Baby. Sleep soundly."

As they hung up, Cece knew 'sleeping soundly' was not going to happen. Her mind was spinning. She did not want to upset the man, who she loved above life itself, especially while he was at work.

Cece prayed to sleep many times before in her life. She did not want anything to happen to her beloved man, her children, her family, or to herself, "Please. God, put your white light of protection around my loved ones and me."

Cece fell asleep exhausted!

Then it was morning, and Cece saw the calm, handsome face of her husband next to her as he slept. It was time to get up with the children!

"Thank you, God!"

Chapter 18

Ian's Lesson

Tony kept after Ian to go out with him after work. Tony wanted to achieve certain things with Ian's help. Tony wanted to undermine Ian's good marriage, as well. Ian kept making excuses because, more than anything, he wanted to go home to be with his family after he finished working daily.

The next day, Ian and Tony were sitting in the dealer's room. The other dealers kept their heads down around Tony. Ian sensed they knew something about Tony. Something Ian had yet to learn. He could tell the dealers were cautious of Tony and were trying to make themselves invisible. Ian picked up on the dealer's reactions to Tony but couldn't figure out why. Ian had his own strengths and feared no man after he left Vietnam. However, he noticed the way the dealers kept fearfully respecting Tony. Ian knew Tony had a lot of 'juice' with the other owner's son, Sallie, Jr, but he did not know why.

Ian thought to himself, "So what? I do have some 'juice' of my own. Even though I never plan on using it."

There were dealers who pretended to read the newspaper, but secretly peeked over the top of the papers to look at Tony. There were dealers who pretended to catnap but were secretly checking out where Tony sat. Ian learned to be observant in Vietnam. It could have meant his life, or someone else's life. Ian wondered why the other dealers acted so strange when Tony was walking towards them. Ian wanted to know why, or did he? Ian was sure he was not imagining what was happening. Ian was never one for gossip, so he wasn't privy to what they said about Tony. The dealers knew Tony was friendly with Ian. Ian prided himself on learning, for himself, what a person was like. Ian kept to himself most of the time. At break time Tony always managed to sit next to Ian, even if someone had to move to enable Tony to have a seat by Ian.

The dealers were easily moved with a 'shake' of Tony's head while Tony's eyes were aimed at theirs. When Ian was on a break trying to relax and Tony wasn't there yet, Ian seemed to know when he would arrive when other dealers started acting nervous. Ian was puzzled and wanted to know what was going on with his fellow dealers.

Tony finally tricked Ian to get him to do what he wanted him to do. Tony knew Ian did not go out after work often. Ian made that fact perfectly clear. He was loyal to his wife. Tony would just 'ask a favor' of his new buddy. Tony was walking towards Ian, when three dealers quickly got up and move.

Ian looked around and thought, "I bet Tony's approaching."

Tony arrived next to Ian within seconds holding two cups of strong hot black coffee.

Ian looked up, accepted the coffee, and said, "Thanks."

Tony said, "Ian, I need a favor."

Ian felt like he knew better but asked anyway, "What's up?"

Tony explained he needed some help to move a heavy cabinet after work. Ian noticed everyone around them kept moving away from them. Ian had definitely decided the other dealers did not want to be noticed by Tony. Ian explained Cece was off that day and he better call Cece to tell her not to come to the Bella Ricco to pick him up after his shift was over.

Tony asked Ian, "Can you just explain to Cece I need help moving some furniture and I will drop you off after we're done, which should only be a couple of hours at the most."

Ian did as Tony requested. Ian said goodnight to Cece and told her he loved her and to explain to the boys what was happening.

Ian said, "Tell the boys I'll see them tomorrow, OK?"

Cece said, "Ok, Honey, but be safe!"

After their shift was over, they met in the dealer's room. Tony told Ian to walk with him. Ian was puzzled because Tony was heading to the regular parking garage and not to the employee parking lot, which was 'a four block long walk away' behind the hotel and casino. What Ian didn't know was Tony didn't have to park where all the other employees parked.

Ian asked, "Where are we going?"

Tony said, "To the parking garage."

Ian asked, "What gives you the right to park there?" Tony said, "I know someone."

Ian and Tony arrived at the parking garage within a minute. When they arrived, Ian noticed a beautiful new very shiny red corvette with vanity plates that read 'My Babe'. Ian had seen her in pictures, but finally got to see Tony's sports car in person.

Ian couldn't believe what was happening when the attendant ran up to Tony with his car keys and said, "I've got her warmed up for you, Sir."

Tony handed the valet parker a ten-dollar bill and said, "Thanks, Martin. See you tomorrow."

Ian was standing to the side watching the interaction in awe. Ian had already heard about the car with the "MY BABE" plates, but she really stood out!

Tony pointed to the flaming 'fully decked out' beauty of a car and yelled to Ian, "Come on, jump in. The top's down so we are ready to roll."

Ian asked Tony, "Who are you? You had an SUV when we went skiing?"

Tony laughed and said, "Yeah, I have an SUV, too. Damn Ian, I'm a bachelor. I have no one to spend my money on since my parent's death, but myself. You haven't seen my place. It's a large high-rise luxury condo with all the toys. I don't have a wife or any children, who I know of, anyway."

Ian smiled and said, "You don't know what you're missing."

Tony chided, "Yeah, sometimes I think you are right, especially when I see your wife."

Ian shot a stern look, "I've warned you."

Tony said, "I'm kidding, man, ok?"

Ian solemnly said, "You better be."

Feeling the need to change the subject, Tony excitingly said, "Come on, man. Jump into 'My Babe'. See how good she feels."

Ian said, "Why are we taking a beautiful hot rod red corvette convertible to go pick up furniture?"

Tony was a fast thinker. He knew why, but he wasn't taking any chances telling Ian. Tony explained, "Oh, there's a truck there to use. It's parked out in front of the place." The ride over to the mysterious destination in the beautiful red sports car was an experience. Tony could handle the vehicle with the skill of a race car driver. The City of Las Vegas had just completed their new I-15 freeway with access to the Strip. Ian enjoyed the ride. It took about 15 minutes, but only because Tony was showing Ian what his 'Babe' could do. The destination turned out to be closer to Swenson, near the Strip. At that time, Swenson was not a fully developed congested area. The house was in the middle of a ten acre sandy desert parcel. It was surrounded by a chain-link fence. The front area had a double-gated chain-link fence where the owner could park his vehicles in a secured area. There was a big truck parked inside that area.

Tony pointed out the house as he drove by and said, "See the truck!"

Ian said, "Well, where are you going? There's room to park next to that big truck."

Tony said, "Hell, look at that dump! I'm not parking the Babe on to all that deep sand.

She'll get filthy, and she could get stuck in that shit."

What Tony said made sense to Ian. It was a 'Babe' of a car! Tony continued to look for an area he preferred to park. Ian thought it was ridiculous to take such an attractive fast car on an errand in a dirty location. The house looked deserted as Tony had mentioned earlier. It was almost 9:00 p.m.

Ian thought, "It must be a special cabinet to go through all this trouble after working all day!"

Tony finally found a place where he wanted to park. It was a secluded area surrounded by huge salt pines. The desert was somewhat firmer to park on, but it was 4 blocks away from the house. Ian looked at Tony as he drove between the salt pines and parked.

Ian said, "These trees are full of bugs and who knows what else. You are new to the desert!"

Tony parked and said, "I'll put the top up, and Babe will be fine here."

Ian said, "You are out of it. This is all sand, too! I thought you didn't want to get the Babe dirty."

As Tony parked, he said, "Well, there's less congestion here." He pulled a satchel out from behind the passenger's seat.

Tony said, "There's no one around and the Babe will be safer here. Here are some gloves, a black knit cap to cover your head, and a black windbreaker to wear over your clean clothes. The place is filthy. You'll be glad you have them to wear."

Ian looked a bit puzzled and Tony hoped he would just follow his lead as Tony put on a black knit cap and a windbreaker. Tony handed Ian his pair of gloves and put something into his windbreaker's pocket along with his own gloves.

Before leaving the Babe, Tony dug deeper into the satchel he used to carry the caps, windbreakers and the gloves. Tony pulled out a burlap sack, and they casually walked over to the place. When they arrived, Tony pulled out a big meat covered bone from the sack he had been carrying.

Tony explained to Ian, "My friend has a big dog and I feel sorry for the poor animal left out here all by itself for long periods of time to guard this dumpy looking property, but my friend does not want to have to deal with vagrants around here."

The large dog ran up wagging his tail and seemed to recognize Tony but was a bit skittish about Ian.

Tony explained, "The dog knows me and loves all the bones I give him every time I come over. The dealer's break room attendant loves dogs, too, and gives me all the bones I want for the dog."

Tony didn't mention the tips he gave the attendant. The guard dog wagged its tail and jumped in the air, happily accepting the delicious bone. Then it ran away to a safe spot to enjoy the treat for a few hours, which was plenty of time for Tony to accomplish his mission.

Ian thought, "People, who love dogs that much, have to have a good heart." Little did Ian know!

Tony walked up to the back door and said, "Damn, I forgot my keys."

Still holding the burlap sack in his hand, Tony folded it and doubled it. Tony covered his left hand and quickly hit the small pane of glass, next to the back-door's knob. The small glass pane broke and Tony reached in and unlocked the door.

Ian said, "Why the hell are you breaking into your own friend's house?"

Tony said, "I'll call and get it repaired tomorrow. I forgot my key. He'll never know. It's easier than us having to come back another day. We're here now. We might as well get it done."

Ian thought Tony spent too much money uselessly.

Ian said, "Hey, I hear music. You could have just knocked on the door and he could have let us in."

Tony was quick and said, "He always leaves the radio on as a deterrent. It helps to keep out unwanted guests. Come on, just follow me."

Unfortunately, Ian did.

They walked through a kitchen. They entered a dark hallway after leaving the kitchen area. The music was getting louder. The hallway looked like they were heading toward a back bedroom doorway.

Tony didn't look at Ian as he said, "It's here. Follow me."

Ian thought, "It's about time!"

Ian asked, "Why are you creeping down this hallway?" Tony said, "Shhh, I hear something."

Ian felt confused. He assumed the house was empty. Did Tony just hear something else beside the music?

Ian wondered, "What the heck is happening?"

That's when Tony ran up to the doorway as he was pulling something out from under his windbreaker. Ian saw the gun in Tony's hand. Tony suddenly fired two shots into the ceiling!

Ian yelled out, "What the fuck are you doing?"

Ian ran up to Tony's side and saw a naked woman jump out of a bed as she began screaming. A naked man was reaching under his pillow.

Tony yelled, "Don't do it, Gerrie, or you're dead! Shut that bitch up or I'll shut her up myself!"

Astonished, Ian stood very still.

Tony continued, "Both of you put your hands up! Sit up, Gerri, now! Don't even try to figure out a way to get your dumb ass hands under that fucking pillow, Gerri. Do you hear me, Man?"

Gerri shook his head affirmatively.

Tony continued, "Where's the money you owe Sallie? Shut up, Bitch!" Gerri was having troubles coming out of his sleepy dope filled stupor. Ian yelled out, "We better get out of here! Who are these people?"

The woman started screaming at the top of her lungs. Tony walked up to her and punched her right in the jaw, while keeping his pistol pointed at the fat man in the bed. Ian heard bones crunching and cracking. She crumbled to the floor silently. The man made another move and Tony shot off another bullet that went within inches of the man's temple as it hit the bed's headboard. Ian was shocked and flabbergasted. Tony looked like a madman! A stunned Ian had flashes of Vietnam war memories! Ian recovered his thoughts while trying to think of a way out!

Tony seemed irrational and acting crazy. Ian wondered if Tony was insane or was it an act? Ian was afraid for their lives and the lives of the bedridden man and the unconscious woman. Ian stood perfectly still. He waited. Seconds felt like hours. Ian wished he could vanish, but he tried to think. It was difficult to focus. Ian knew from war experience he had to be very careful. He didn't want to catch a stray bullet from either man. Ian wondered what Tony was asking Gerrie about. Sallie's money, what money? Who was this man and this woman? Who was Sallie? Another woman?

Tony said, "Get your fat ass out of bed and get the $10,000.00 pay back money now. If you don't, I'll kill your girlfriend!"

It was the first time 'Big Gerrie' spoke as he said, "She's not my girlfriend. Go ahead and shoot her. She's nothing but a whore!"

That really pissed Tony off royally. He became apoplectic! Tony walked over to the unconscious woman and up to the big man. Tony began using the fat guy's face as a punching bag. Blood spurted out of the lean naked man's nostrils. Blood flowed quickly as Tony worked the man's face over with the gun. Gerrie was no match for Tony and the deadly gun.

Tony put the gun to Big Gerri's forehead and said, "Get up. I like to look into the eyes of the men I kill."

Big Gerri was sweating profusely. He tried to talk but was stuttering so badly he couldn't speak.

Ian could smell urine.

Tony said, "I said stand up!"

Ian saw the naked man's urine all over the sheets and the bed. Urine was still dripping from his penis. Gerrie was having difficulty trying to manage getting out of bed without using his uplifted arms. Tony's gun was pointing to his temple. The woman began to stir and whimpered.

Tony screamed, "Shut up, bitch, stay down or you're dead!"

The naked woman started screaming in panic again as she staggered and stood up. She went down very hard the second time Tony's fist connected with her chin. Ian heard more cracking noise. Things were happening way too fast. The woman was totally knocked out this time.

Tony's neck and facial veins were sticking out as he yelled, "Stupid bitch. That oughta fix her for a while."

Ian was still. He watched, he waited. No matter what, Ian never wanted to see any woman suffer like this prostitute was. He hoped her jaw wasn't broken, but he was pretty sure it was. For all he knew, an enraged man like Tony could easily aim the gun at him if he said something Tony didn't want to hear. Tony was completely out of control.

Tony waved the gun and looked at Big Gerri and asked, "Where?" Gerri didn't want to answer. Tony began to pistol whip the man again.

Ian was still frozen watching the confrontation. Ian saw enough carnage in Vietnam. He didn't have time to be killed. He had a wife and two sons, all of whom he loved dearly.

Tony beat Gerri's face hard. Ian was sure the man's nose was fractured after hearing more crunching noises.

Ian had to step in as he said to Tony, "Come on, man, he can't take anymore. What if he has a heart attack?"

Ian said, "Come on, Gerri, tell him. He's nuts! No amount of money is worth the beating you're getting."

Tony began punching the big man again.

Ian yelled, "Stop it! You're gonna kill him! He's having a hard time breathing with you continuously slugging him like that. He'll pay up. Let me help him stand."

Ian helped the big man stand up. Blood was running down Gerrie's face and onto his extended belly as he looked up at Ian and said, "Thanks, Mister."

Tony looked at Ian like he was pleased. Tony smiled wickedly.

Ian took the bloody man's arm and helped him steady himself.

Ian said, "Mister, he's nuts. You better give him what he wants before you really get hurt."

Big Gerri tried to focus on Ian, but Ian could tell he was having a hard time seeing. Gerri weakly replied, "Thank you, Mister."

Ian said, "Sure, Buddy. I want out of this, too."

Tony yelled, "Where's the 10-grand?"

Gerri pointed to the doorway. Tony waved his gun at the naked man insinuating, he should start walking. Gerri stumbled but quickly recovered when he felt the gun in his back. Tony grew impatient.

Ian said to Tony, "Give him a chance, man. You worked him over pretty hard." Gerri said to Ian, "Come with me, Mister. Help me make it into the hallway."

Ian helped Gerri make a right turn into the hallway and they slowly walked up to a shabby-looking picture hanging off center on one side of the hallway's wall. Gerri removed the picture, exposing a safe. He began using the combination. He was having a difficult time. When he finally opened the safe, Tony shoved him aside. Tony told Gerri to put both of his hands high on the hall's other wall, and to spread eagle. Gerri looked even more frightened. Ian helped to balance Gerrie. Gerrie got to the position Tony ordered.

Both men's eyes were trying to focus on Tony as Tony opened the safe slowly with the tip of his gun and jumped to the side. There was no booby trap. Tony held the gun pointed toward Gerri as he reached into the safe and pulled out another loaded gun. Tony nodded at Ian. Ian sensed there was a gun in the safe, but Tony still impressed him. Ian thought Gerri was too weak to even focus and aim a gun at that point.

Tony said, "So were you going to reach in the safe and shoot me, huh, skinny Boy?" More urine ran down Big Gerri's weak shaking legs to puddle around his flat feet. Gerri was having an awful day. He was sure Tony would kill him now that he had the money. Ian watched as Tony gestured for Gerri to put his hands down and said, "Stay cool."

Gerri looked at Ian and said, "Thanks, Buddy."

Tony nodded affirmatively and told Ian to get him the burlap sack he used to break the pane of glass on the back door. Gerrie's eyes grew wide. Ian did as he was told without a word. Ian wanted to save the whore's and Gerri's lives and possibly his own life.

Tony gave the sack to Gerri while ordering, "Empty the safe!"

Gerri, still shaking and extremely weak, emptied the safe. The men watched carefully. All the money was in smaller bills. Some of it was filthy. Some was wadded up. Some was neatly banded. Gerri completely emptied the safe and stood helplessly leaning against the wall with a full sack. Tony heard the woman stirring. Tony backed up towards the bedroom door and shot into the bedroom ceiling. The woman moaned and tried to talk. She couldn't do it. Her jaw was hanging down so far she couldn't do anything but make moaning sounds.

Ian figured her facial bones and jaws must have been badly broken.

Tony said, "Just stay down, Bitch, and everything will be ok."

Tony pulled the sack from Gerrie's grasp. He put Gerri's two guns into the burlap sack with the money. Ian helped Gerri to a chair. Tony waved the gun at Ian to leave. Ian gave Tony a worried look. Ian feared for Gerri's life. Tony just smiled and waved the gun at Ian to leave.

Ian reiterated, "Stay cool."

Once out of the house and headed back to 'My Babe', Ian unloaded on Tony, "You fucking prick! What was that all about?"

Tony said, "I just wanted to see how you would handle yourself. I loved the 'good guy bad guy thing' you had going on."

Ian said, "I don't ever want to hang out with you again. You're a crazy bastard! What about the police? They could have showed up at any minute. They would never believe I was suckered into all of this. I don't have time to go to jail and lose my family. Cece would never believe this!"

Tony said, "He won't call the police. He's a fucking drug dealer! He borrowed 'start up' money from Sallie. Gerri doesn't want to pay it back. I collect for SallieHe wants his money back with interest. Now he'll get it and more because Gerri was too greedy."

Ian was flabbergasted and asked, "Sal, Junior, the Bella Ricco owner's son? He's a loan shark? He's rich! Why would he risk doing this? His Dad's wonderful to him. He has everything a guy could want. How did you get involved in this kind of situation?"

Tony began running quickly to his car.

Fuming with anger, Ian started running after him.

Tony took offense to what Ian had asked and once they were in the car he answered, "We were kids together. Hell, Sallie got beat up and robbed in the old neighborhood daily. I felt sorry for him and I began to protect him. That's how it all started. We only had each other. Sallie's good parents were working hard all the time to become rich. Sallie never had any love. He had nannies. My parents never could get work and were always poor. What the fuck! It's none of your business. I wanted to share with you. I wanted you to be my best friend. We could take you in. You'll become rich. You'll have everything, just like me."

Ian looked at Tony in amazement as he drove. He didn't want to walk twenty miles home to the edge of town. Ian's mind was running through possible quickly. Ian didn't want to be walking or catching a cab while Tony could be doing harm to his wife or family to keep him quiet! Ian knew he had to remain calm. He knew Cece should never hear about what just happened.

Ian thought to himself, "At least not right away."

Ian said, "I want to go home."

Tony said, "Just tell me where."

Tony knew all he wanted to know about Ian, Cece, and their family already. He knew where their home was. Hell, he knew how much their home cost and how much their taxes were.

He knew all the family schedules. Woody's complete spying report on Cece contained all kinds of information.

Tony had already decided he was going to take Ian's precious woman, even if his new best friend, Ian, had to die.

Chapter 19

Last Ski Trip

It was the last ski trip of the season! This weekend was anticipated to be two days of fun. Everyone was elated. The hotel challenge was over and favorite teams had won. Cece's team came in first. The three men on her team did great. The one girl on the team, Cece, won honors in her division. Their hotel secured all the snow skiing competitions with the highest scores ever made. The team was honored at their hotel and casino.

A jealous few had comments to make, but Cece wasn't interested in pettiness. Rivalry is something team members, whoever they may be, are accustomed to confronting. Cece thought many of the girls, with whom she worked, could practice, workout hard, and train to become competition skiers. Athletes are only as good as their health, strengths, skills, determination, and positive minds.

Many of the cocktail waitresses did not want to do any more exercise, other than what their strenuous profession required. Las Vegas cocktail waitressing is a laborious work, if not done correctly.

People can get washed along in the tides of life without control, because of terrible choices or vanities. Cocktailing could eventually take an emotional, mental, spiritual, or physical toll on a more genteel woman. The determined women, with inner positivity, intelligence, and strength, learned to handle it. If a person doesn't have self-control, no matter what their profession is, they are doomed.

Before her weekend was due to begin, Cece came into the cocktail office to get her correspondence. On the countertop, overwhelming golden trophy was standing. Attached to the trophy were ten colorful lines of ribbons leading to ten bright streaming balloons!

The balloons kept bobbing and bellowing over the trophy's top as they swayed to and away from the ceiling of the cocktail office! Girls could hardly get in or out without balloons trying to escape into the hallway. All the women were giggling and enjoying the balloons! The congratulations were for their cocktail world to see, and for their department to experience the pride of 'One of their own' winning a hotel challenge competition.

At first, Cece didn't realize it was her trophy. A manager announced it to the office full of women after she entered. Cece knew how much arduous work was involved in her accomplishment. She was proud to do it for her cocktail department, the hotel's owner for sponsoring their team, and for herself! The manager handed Cece her trophy. Cece smiled and thanked her. The classier ladies congratulated Cece and she thanked them humbly, as well. As she turned to leave the office, while carrying her trophy to her service bar for clock-in, she heard cocktail waitresses walking behind her.

One of the more pessimistic cocktail waitresses following Cece said, "She's lucky she didn't break a leg."

Cece thought to herself, "That's very true, but stop and think. People could exist all their lives fearful of being hurt. Nothing would ever get accomplished, and people would certainly miss out on a lot of fun!"

It's just like love, you have got to take the chance to find it! Go out and look for it in the right places!

Another cocktail waitress replied, "I wish she had broken something. At least we would have less competition on the casino floor without her."

Cece thought, "Ouch! How mean!"

A third cocktail waitress said, "Too bad she didn't fall on her face."

Cece thought to herself, "Wow! Talk about negative! I fell on my butt a lot in learning to ski!"

Cece acted like she did not hear their tainted comments. Cece had to work with different and difficult personalities from customers, managers, and fellow employees.

Luckily only a few of the girls were cruel, sly, jealous, greedy, and devious. The most frightening women were the ones who practiced all five foul habits! They could ruin relationships with their cruel insinuations and false accusations, because, unfortunately, some of the more trusting women believed their lies. Until the lies ricocheted back to them, and they quickly wised up. Cruelty hurts everyone, especially the person doing it! Usually in cocktails, when a person lies to extremes, it is caused by their personal greed of some sort. Cece was grateful there were many normal ladies at work, too! She admired most of the women with whom she worked, and considered them her friends, but she was always aware of the weasels whispering.

Cece thought to herself, "Women should be each other's very best friends! Don't they realize I know what they are doing? How stupid are they? Negative people's thoughts will only eat away at their own minds, their own bodies, their own families, their own relationships, and their own hearts."

Cece focused on thinking positive, living positive, praying positive, and eating positive!

* * *

Ian and Cece's special weekend ski trip fast approached. They were going to Brian Head, Utah, to celebrate! As Cece continued to walk to clock-in, fellow casino employees passing from the opposite direction kept congratulating her on her trophy. Cece smiled and thanked them. Cece heard the girls behind her snickering. She did not give it a second thought because she would do it again for her love of snow skiing!

Cece concentrated on the upcoming weekend, thinking, "One more day to work, and then I'm free for two days of fun with my wonderful man!"

Cece thought she should have been overly excited to go have fun with Ian, but she was suffering a bit of anxiety with a touch of apprehension. She did not want to face Tony after their last standoff. She had a perfect life with the man, whom she loved so completely. But, for some reason, Cece feared an oncoming retaliation!

Being negative is a spiral downfall! It's 'self-inflicted' harm on oneself! It only hurts the ones who are negative, live negative, act negative, or those who use any form of negativity to harm the innocent, the naive, or the pure of heart.

Cece questioned people's thoughts as she pondered to herself, "Do they actually enjoy being obstinate? It is so much more fun to be happy, productive, and positive. It is what God wants for us, how we are meant to be, and for us to learn 'when we share' it comes back a hundredfold!"

Cece often wondered, "Why do I go through so many strange experiences in life? All I ever wanted was to be left alone, with my good honorable man and our two sons, to enable us to accomplish four happy, healthy, wonderful, and productive lives."

Cece understood her premonitions because she lived with them constantly. She sometimes wondered if the cocktail waitresses spoke out loud or if she could 'pick up' on their thoughts, or 'read' their mannerisms after working with them many years. Upon entering her service bar, Cece observed 'Weasel' at the other end of the station. Weasel had a disparaging reputation with the other cocktail waitresses and for that reason she was nicknamed 'The Weasel of weasels', by the waitresses! She knew Weasel was slandering her to another cocktail waitress.

When the other waitress left, Cece walked up to 'Weasel' and asked, "Why are you lying to her about me?"

Weasel's eyes flew open. Weasel was astonished Cece could tell what she was doing. Cece knew it was all about money.

Cece asked, "Is money worth losing a friend?"

A shocked Weasel replied, "I don't want her to ask you to watch her area, because I want to give her breaks to make extra money."

Cece replied, "Knock yourself out!" (In other words, go for it!)

Weasel had a vicious ability to 'turn things around' about something someone might have mentioned innocently. Weasel's gossip kept a few waitresses constantly mad at Cece. What disappointed Cece was, she thought the waitresses were her friends. Cece really liked the other woman, and they had a long history together before Weasel entered the picture. Cece couldn't understand how anyone could believe Weasel's blatant lies, except only a 'so-called friend' worth losing.

As the Weasel finished counting her coveted tip money, she said to Cece, "I really don't know why you want to be my friend. If I were you, I wouldn't want to be my friend."

Cece walked away shaking her head as she thought to herself, "Wow, I can't believe what she just said! I feel for her. She enjoys being negative, cutting good people down behind their backs and stretching the truth, all because of money! I wish her the very best, and I wish her very far away from me in peace and never to be seen again!"

Cece refused to let lies hurt her. She figured if people believed gossip, it was their problem. She would still be kind but Cece never spoke to the Weasel again unless she had a work-related reason. It improved her life and work environment tremendously.

Other waitresses, who knew Weasel, asked Cece, "What took you so long? We all had her number for a year now! None of the women like or trust her, except the new naive ones, and they will learn the hard way."

Cece always tried to find the good in people, but weasels are in every profession. They are called pathological liars. In the years to come, Weasel burnt many bridges. She became an outcast at work. Weasel sent Cece a text a year later. It read: "I miss you." Cece never answered. It's called self-preservation. Cece learned to handle dysfunctional employees, but now, Cece had a much more serious problem, Tony.

The Next Day in Utah:

No one knew Tony had his own plans for the weekend, except Connie. Tony had it all worked out. He was bringing Connie up for the ski celebration weekend. Her nickname fit her. Connie was a well-paid con artist. She could get anyone to do anything, and she got paid the big bucks to do it. Because of her affiliation with mobsters and gangs, Connie had more business from thuds, than a hooker would have, if the hooker didn't charge. Connie, which was not her real name, liked 'conning' people a lot more than being a hooker. Connie adapted to her new way of life easily.

Between spies and con artists, Tony was on a roll. Tony had the big bucks to pay Connie, and Connie liked bad habits. She would do anything for drug money. Tony told Connie her job was to keep Ian busy and away from his wife for the next two days. Connie never realized how painfully cold, wet, and difficult that task would be.

When Ian and Cece arrived in beautiful Brian Head, Utah, they checked into their rental. Later, when they were unloading their ski gear, they laughed, giggled, and lovingly joked around. Suddenly Tony's SUV came to a screeching stop in the parking space next to Ian's vehicle. She cringed. Ian caught her reaction. Both became solemn. Tony exited his vehicle and was laughing and saying his hellos like nothing had ever happened at the grocery store, or at Gerrie's house. Cece and Ian looked at Tony incredulously. They were amazed at Tony's congeniality, considering what he had recently put them both through. Tony walked around to the other side of his vehicle, talking and preparing to help a woman out of his SUV.

Ian was somewhat relieved as he thought, "Tony brought a date up for the weekend." Cece wanted to feel relieved, too, but she sensed she shouldn't let her guard down. She did not tell Ian what she went through when Tony 'accidentally on purpose' ran into her while she was grocery shopping. She knew she should have told her husband, but she thought she could wait until after their fun weekend ended. She knew Ian had a lot on his mind and she didn't want Ian to be upset over nothing. Ian and Tony had to work together. Tony was the best friend of Sal, Jr. who was the son of one of the Bella Ricco hotel and casino owners. They had been best friends since they were preteens.

Cece thought, "Wow! that is some 'strong juice'! It had to be, for Tony to move out west to Las Vegas to work."

Cece could imagine the cruel things Salliecould do to people if he wanted, like terminating their lucrative jobs! No wonder employees were afraid of Tony! She really had no idea just how evil the repercussions could be. She only cared about her family's safety and well-being.

Cece thought to herself, "Ian is a best friend of Tommy, Jr. and Tommy is the other Bella Ricco hotel and casino owner's son. Tony's friend, Sallie, has lots of pull and could probably get almost anyone fired on the spot, but so could Tommy, Jr. Why did Ian say all the Bella Ricco employees feared Tony? I wonder if there's another more pertinent reason people fear Tony. Tommy, Jr. does consider Ian part of the family, and the two Seniors like Ian. I don't want to have to force Ian to take advantage of his 'Juice' to preserve his job. Plus, I am sure Tony got my point!"

Cece's kindness caused her credulity, but now her 'Italian Eye' was trying to warn her, and she was unconsciously pushing it away! She needed to pay more attention to her infinite intelligence, but she was looking forward to a wonderful fun filled weekend with her husband and making excuses for not paying attention to her inner warnings!

In the old days, if things went sour between two men because of a woman, the casino bosses would fire one man to stop the dissension. It was the easiest solution. Casino managers had a difficult time trying to understand why men went head to head, over what they considered, a dumb 'Broad'. Women were unimportant to casino men. Many casino men carried on a very machismo characteristic way of thinking, even into the late 1980s and beyond. A lot of it was because women of the past let it happen, instead of standing up for themselves. In later years, women fought back! All Hell broke loose in the casino business, especially because hotels and casinos started new departments titled, "Human Resources".

Cece did not think it would have to come to someone being terminated, but she just wanted to 'forget about it' for a while and enjoy her husband and their special weekend together. Cece thought she had made things plain enough to Tony. She was not interested in any kind of relationship with him, and she never would be!

Ian also planned on telling Cece about Tony and Sallie's side business after the ski weekend ended. He wanted his wife to have fun and not worry about anything. Ian knew how strenuously Cece worked for her 'Hotel Challenge' accomplishment.

In the back of Cece's mind, something was telling her to beware. Cece always had a great regard for her premonitions, but she was ignoring her feelings because she felt happy preparing for this weekend alone with Ian.

Grandma Angelina had always insisted on Cece respecting her mind's eye or beware! Cece prayed, "Please, God, Ian worked so hard for this good secure casino job. Ian deserves it. Please let us be ok and happy. How much plainer can I make it to Tony without getting Ian involved? I don't want any trouble! Please protect us! We love each other so much."

* * *

God helps those who help themselves.

* * *

Ian was planning to go back to school after the ski season. Cece didn't want to put any more stress on him. Ian needed some fun, too. There was enough stress constantly on casino employees just to go into work every day, let alone, trying to rest when they were off. Twenty-one dealers putting up with drunks is ridiculous enough! When you have a live 21 games with intoxicated 21 players, they can flip into foul moods in an instant. No one likes to lose money, especially when it is their own fault for gambling when they cannot afford it. Twenty-one dealers were expected to referee fights between players. Bosses got mad at dealers when players started fighting at their game. Casino dealers do not practice psychoanalysis! Dealers are not therapists or doctors.

For example, a reason could be: A person is playing 21 on a live game with five other players. The person 'takes a hit' (card), when the person should 'not' have asked for the card, or cards. The hit causes a win for the house (dealer), and the five other players lose a lot of money. Suddenly the five other intoxicated players start verbally attacking the one player, who asked for the hit. It could be a very serious problem, if the one player asking for the hit card was a lady alone, and the five other players were intoxicated people, who bet big money, and lost! Foolish or serious, the dealers always seemed to be blamed because most floor persons didn't want to take the blame, and chance losing their own jobs. They would rather see a dealer get fired. Most dealers were damned if they did and damned if they did not.

Cece was trying to make things as easy as she could for the man, with whom she shared a wonderful love. She truly felt the need to be happy at this wondrous place and extraordinarily loving time in her life. She prayed her happy feelings were not interfering with her inner warnings.

Cece looked up at Ian with a skeptical look in her eyes! Ian had been watching Cece's concerned face. He knew Cece had been involved in some deep thoughts. Ian smiled really big and winked at Cece. Ian's loving reaction caused Cece to come back to reality. She smiled at her wonderful man. Tony caught their interaction. Tony was poutful getting ready to introduce the woman, who drove up to the mountain with him. Connie smiled coyly at Cece while sizing up her competition. Cece felt Connie's eyes scanning her while Connie remained seated in Tony's vehicle.

Cece thought, "She's checking me out! They're up to something!" Tony was saying, "This is Connie, my girlfriend."

Connie automatically said, "Tony said many gracious things about you both."

Tony acted overly congenial and happy. Connie was playing up her girlish helplessness. Cece just looked at Tony. She knew her alert was apparent to Ian's ever watchful gaze. Ian could pick right up on Cece's moods. Ian wondered why Cece looked at Connie doubtfully when Tony introduced Connie as his girlfriend. Ian had never seen Connie. Ian doubted Tony met her at work. Ian couldn't resist it.

Ian asked, "So, how did you two meet?"

Tony hurried up to answer, as Connie looked flabbergasted and at a loss for words, "We met at a gas station!"

Connie came to mentally and should have stayed silent, but said, "Yes, I couldn't get the fuel cap off of my gas tank and then a big brawny man came along and helped me."

Cece wondered, "What did Connie do when she had to get gas for her car, before Tony 'came along'? Ian will never believe that one!"

Trying to change the subject, Connie blurted out, "I hope I don't put any of you out today. I'm just learning to ski. I heard Ian is the best instructor on the mountain."

Both Tony and Ian watched Connie's eyes running up and down Cece's body as if Cece was serious competition.

Ian thought, "Why is she appraising Cece that way?"

Tony thought to himself, "Don't blow this,Connie!"

As Connie finally stepped out of Tony's SUV, she wobbled and leaned forward towards Ian as she stood up. She jiggled her female assets back and forth. She smiled sweetly up into Ian's face.

Connie asked in a singsong sexy voice, "Is it true, Ian? Are you the best instructor on the mountain?"

Ian looked stunned and at a loss for words.

Cece said, "He is the most patient man, whom I have ever met."

Ian seemed to blush a little but finally said, "It's best to take lessons. It's well worth the cost, and Tony can afford it!"

Connie said, "I doubt I can afford it."

Tony blurted out, "Lessons are not worth the cost!"

Tony was ready to carry their overnight bags, and Connie, into the office to check in. Connie looped her hand through Tony's other empty arm. Connie swaggered weak kneed in four-inch stiletto high heels on the icy sidewalk alongside Tony. Connie struggled not to fall. It did not look like they were going to make it 30 feet to the office. It was pathetically comical.

Cece looked at Ian and asked, "Do you believe them?"

Meanwhile, Ian observed Cece did not believe Connie's explanation either.

Ian said, "Connie sure could use a good pair of snow boots! It will be nice to get Tony's mind off of my wife for a while. Don't you agree?"

Cece was surprised at Ian's question as she smiled and answered, "You are the only man for me, Big Boy!"

Ian said, "Come on, let's go have some well-earned fun together!"

* * *

The late spring skiing in Brian Head was great. Snow powder covered the groomed advanced skier's trails. Ian and Cece had a lot of fun chasing each other down the big mountain. The day was still, bright, and beautiful. Ian and Cece were in love! Cece met up with other skiers, who she had skied with during the season's competitions, and they all had a good time visiting.

As the day progressed, Ian and Cece noticed Connie was alone on the big mountain's most difficult advanced runs instead of learning on the beginner's bunny hill. They could not understand why Tony was not with her.

Tony was watching all of them through binoculars from the lodge sun deck. Tony wondered if Connie was going to earn her money. Connie wondered when Tony was going to give her the thousand dollars, he had promised to pay her.

Connie thought, "I am already in the hole for the hundred dollars bill I tipped the lift operator to let me carry these skis onto the chairlift. I never skied! I had to lie by telling my boyfriend is waiting for me at the mountain's top to help me! That was all the money I had."

Ian and Cece made several afternoon's trip up and down the advanced mountain's trails. They kept seeing Connie sitting on her skis while she faced parallel to the bottom of the mountain. Each time Cece and Ian went up, they checked on Connie's well-being.

Connie would say, "I am trying. I will eventually get down the mountain, especially if Ian could help me!"

Ian constantly offered to get ski patrol for her assistance.

Connie refused saying, "Oh, I really don't want to embarrass myself!"

Connie seemed perturbed with them. Cece thought Connie should be upset with her own date, Tony.

Cece asked Ian, "How did she get up on the mountain carrying her skis, instead of wearing the skis? That is impossible and against the rules!"

Ian answered, "I have no idea!"

Every time Ian and Cece made a run, Connie kept insisting she could do much better if Ian gave her a few pointers.

Finally, Cece told Connie, "It is a special weekend for us to be together before Ian must return to school and work, but we would be happy to get ski patrol for you. Where is your date? Why hasn't Tony checked on you?"

Connie shrugged and flashed hateful looks at Cece. Cece was used to all kinds of looks from women. Hate could not hurt her, or could it? Cece did not want to give it another thought. She felt something was amiss. Cece just smiled and kept offering to get ski patrol to assist Connie.

Cece wondered, "Why are my ski patrol suggestions irritating Connie so much?"

Finally, towards the end of the chilly day, Ian and Cece decided to stop and take a break to warm up before dinner. Ian skied down towards the restaurant and looked back to see if his wife was behind him. When Ian did, he saw Cece smiling back at him. At the mountain's bottom, they took their skis off, propped the skis up on the ski racks, rested their poles and straps over and against their skis, and went into the restaurant for hot coffees. Cece followed Ian inside the crowded restaurant's entrance as he held the door for her. Ian turned into the restaurant's bar area where there were still a few available bench seats under the massive windows. Ian ordered two black coffees from the waitress, Cindy, who was at her cocktail pickup station. Cindy handed the coffees to Ian. People constantly moved around in the bench areas. Ian was on his way back to Cece when he saw her move over one seat so another couple could sit down together. Ian smiled admiringly at his beautiful wife.

Other envious eyes watched Cece and Ian from the far end of the curved bar.

Tony thought, "It's about time they showed up."

Ian bent over and kissed Cece's forehead and said, "Here you go, pretty Lady, hot coffee! The manager said they'll set up a table for our romantic dinner, when we are ready. I saw you move over for the couple who couldn't get seats together."

Cece said, "Of course! It's only right. I want to sit next to you. Why wouldn't they want to be together, too?"

Ian asked, "Are you having fun?"

Cece answered, "I always have fun when we're together. I love you, Ian."

Ian smiled as he lovingly viewed his wife's face and said, "I love you, too!"

A kiss followed their interaction.

Tony's envious and angry eyes flashed back and forth. He watched them.

Tony thought, "They are thrilled. I'll fix them."

Cece could see the concern in Ian's eyes.

Cece had an idea why, but asked anyway, "What's wrong, Honey?" Ian asked, "You've seen Connie?"

Cece only said, "Yes."

Cece knew her good gentleman would continue.

Ian said, "That jerk has gone off on his own. Tony just left her to fend for herself all day alone on the mountain's most advanced slope. She should have been on the bunny hill. It's getting darker, like it may start snowing any minute."

Cece said, "Did you ever think it could all be a ploy?" Ian said, "Wow, Cece, really?"

Cece diverted her eyes, almost feeling ashamed, but she wasn't!

Ian continued, "I'm just saying Tony has plenty of money. Why would he allow a woman up there when she's only a beginner? It's an advanced skier's mountain and not a bunny hill. Tony can afford to give Connie lessons. Every time we passed, she was sitting down on her skis. She may have walked down another ten or fifteen feet. Connie never had her skis on! She's shaking from the cold and she's soaking wet. She doesn't have proper clothing. I just don't get Tony's way of thinking! It's going to take her forever to get off the mountain. She looks cold and tired, too. Why would Tony just go off and leave her? The Sun's going to set soon. How can a guy do that to a woman?"

Cece said, "He has reasons. I do not trust him."

As if Ian didn't hear her, he said, "You just don't do that to a lady. I know we cannot trust him."

Ignoring the second part of Ian's statement, Cece said, "Maybe she's not a lady."

Ian looked at Cece incredulously and said, "Oh, Honey, I would have never believed you could say something so derogatory."

Cece sincerely looked up into Ian's eyes and persevered, "Ian, we don't know her. We don't know why Tony is treating her that way. Something's going on. If you're worried, tell ski patrol to get her off the mountain."

Ian replied, "I don't want to embarrass her."

Cece said, "I don't think much can embarrass her. She came up here with a jerk." Ian asked, "Cece, what's got into you?"

Cece wanted to tell Ian what happened at the grocery store, but she didn't want to ruin their dinner. For that same reason, Ian wanted to wait to tell Cece what happened at Gerri's house. Ian planned to tell Cece about Tony's collection job, and what happened the night he was supposed to be moving furniture. Ian didn't want anything to interfere with Cece's ski competitions or ruin their well-deserved celebration weekend together.

Cece said, "I don't trust them. That's all. Something is wrong. I feel it and you understand my feelings more than anyone!"

Ian answered, "Yeah, something's wrong. Tony left her up there alone. She's cold, tired, and shivering wet. She needs help."

Cece said, "Ok, I'll report it to ski patrol. They'll bring her down right away."

Ian said, "That will really embarrass her. How about I go up and help her?"

Cece said, "I don't think that's a good idea. I don't want to be alone. We don't know what Tony is up to, or where he is! I am terrified of Tony."

Ian asked, "What does that mean? Why would you say such a thing? I will always protect you, Ce! Look, it's starting to get late, and it's starting to get dark. How about I go up and lead Connie down? When I get back, we'll have cocktails and our romantic dinner. We can go to our room for an early retirement and have peace of mind when we make love. Would you like that? I'll explain to the hostess our friend is stuck up on the mountain and needs help. I'm sure they'll hold our reservations until I get back."

Cece looked at Ian and begged, "Please don't leave me alone, Ian."

Ian said, "You're surrounded by lots of people in this bar and restaurant, Honey. What could go wrong? I'll be back very soon."

Cece looked at Ian imploringly and asked, "Where is Tony? We haven't seen him all day. Please, Ian!"

Ian lovingly kissed Cece's cheek, "I'll be back within minutes, before you will even notice it!"

Ian headed toward the hostess, then out the crowded front door.

Cece sat there and watched through the giant windows as Ian snapped on his skis, grabbed his poles, and headed for the chairlift. The evening was getting inauspiciously cloudier, darker, and colder. People were starting to quickly come down off the cold mountain for their dinners. Cece saw Ian catch an empty lift seat, and he was off. Cece had an ominous feeling about what was happening. She felt something was about to go terribly wrong.

Cece thought, "Please, God, help me."

Tony smiled. He watched the gallant Ian go to his so-called girlfriend's rescue!

Cece thought, "We left to come up to the mountain early this morning. We ate breakfast at approximately 4:00 a.m. before our four-hour drive up to the mountain. That was over twelve hours ago. We were supposed to have dinner and go to bed early. We wanted to get home and spend some time with our boys. Wow, I feel like I'm starving."

Cece thought maybe another coffee would sedate her stomach for a while. The waitress, Cindy, was very busy with the crowd. Thirsty and hungry skiers trailed in and out of the crowded restaurant and bar areas after they had spent all day on the mountain.

Cece went up to Cindy's empty cocktail service station and asked the bartender, "Can I get another black coffee from you, George? Cindy's so busy."

George said, "Hi, Cece! I just started brewing a fresh pot. I'll have Cindy carry a coffee over to you as soon as it's finished brewing."

Cece thanked him, went back to her seat, and stared out the window.

Tony continued watching everything Cece did. He was dressed entirely in black. He wore an oversized jacket with a large hoodie over his head which covered half his face. He wore dark sunglasses and was slumped over a drink in front of him. He could see Cece's every move. Ian and Cece would not have recognized or noticed him sitting at the back corner of the ski lodge bar. He was dressed in dark street clothes. Tony didn't even look like a skier.

Tony knew Cece's business better than anyone. Sallie's spy, Woody, had filled him in on everything about her and her life. Woody begged Tony, "Please don't hurt her, Tony! She's such a good woman!"

Tony snapped, "Bullshit! I'll finally be able to do what I want to her."

Tony determined his scheme had finally started to work. It just took all day! Tony was very happy his plan was unfolding.

* * *

Tony thought to himself, "Now, if I can continue things along. I'll watch and wait a little while longer. You are mine, Miss Innocent Cece! I got the means and I want you. I want to take away your 'little girl' innocence. You're so damn good and way too beautiful. You're just what I have always wanted. I didn't think it was possible to ever find a woman who would be as perfect as you."

Tony's head continued to purposely hang low. He had watched Cece approach the bar to speak with George. Tony saw George point to the coffee brewing and to Cindy. Then George pointed to the cocktail waitress pickup station. Tony figured Cece ordered another coffee. He could see Cece was tired, dehydrated, hungry, and, hopefully, weak.

Tony thought, "This is working out better than I ever thought it would. Now if it will only continue."

Tony watched Cece return to her seat. She stared out the giant window.

Tony got excited as he saw a drunk stand and stagger away from the barstool next to the cocktail pickup station.

Tony jumped up and thought, "I've got to move fast!"

Tony put some cash on the bar where he had been seated. It would reserve his barstool, so he could get up and move around. He felt for a pill inside his right pocket. Tony's binoculars and black knit ski cap were in his left side pocket.

Tony kept thinking, "I have to get over to the empty barstool quickly before someone else sits there. I think George will put Cece's coffee cup in the pickup station for Cindy to deliver. I better hurry. This place is so busy. No one is even noticing what I am doing."

Tony pulled his hoodie down as he slipped a big black knitted cap over his head. Tony walked towards the cocktail pickup station. He immediately readjusted his sunglasses and tugged the cap down tightly over his face and hair. Tony moved over to the vacated barstool and sat down next to the cocktail pickup station. Tony's left gloved hand grabbed onto the empty dark beer bottle left by the drunk. He watched. He waited. Tony felt for the pill with his right gloveless fingers. He waited patiently. He didn't want the bartender to notice he had moved. The bartender brought a large Styrofoam cup of coffee to the cocktail station, but George couldn't get Cindy's attention. Tony kept his head down low. A customer yelled out for the bartender's service. The frustrated bartender put the cup of coffee on the delivery station, but George couldn't find any plastic lids for the cup's top.

George yelled out, "Cindy!"

Cindy looked at him. George placed a small cocktail napkin over the top of Cece's styrofoam cup.

George yelled out again as he pointed to the cup, "Hey, Cindy, could you deliver this to Cece now?"

The busy waitress nodded as if she understood. Cindy was finishing writing up a large dinner order. Cindy held one finger up behind her, as if to say to George, "Ok, one minute, and I'll be there!"

George saw Cindy's reaction. George's other customer yelled out again for service. A flustered George did not notice the quiet man wearing the black knitted cap with his head hung low. The bartender checked to make sure the napkin was in place. George turned and left to go to his yelling customer.

Tony slyly thought, "Excellent!"

Tony watched Cindy finishing up her order. He saw Cece was staring out the window looking for Ian. The bartender was getting the screaming customer a beer. Everyone was busy in their own worlds. No one noticed as Tony took a deep breath and blew out toward the Styrofoam cup covered only with a cocktail napkin. The napkin gently fell off the top of the cup. He passed his right hand over the coffee cup like he was reaching for the fallen napkin. A tiny pill fell from his fingers into the hot coffee. He picked up the napkin and replaced it back on top of the coffee. If anyone did see him, it would look like he saw the napkin fall and he replaced it.

Tony got up, left the barstool, and the empty beer bottle. He started back toward his original barstool. As he walked, Tony lifted the hoodie back up over his head. He pulled the knit cap off his head from under the hoodie. He stuffed the cap into his jacket's pocket next to his binoculars. Tony went back to his original barstool, picked up his cash, and replaced it in his pants pocket. He sat down where he had waited all day to accomplish what he had just completed doing. He was very proud of himself! He watched Cindy return to her station. The waitress quickly found a cap for the coffee cup on her side of the pickup station. Tony watched Cece hand Cindy money and a tip. Cece removed the coffee cup's cap. Cece took a long drink of her coffee. Tony smiled and waited patiently for things to start going his way. It would not be long!

Minutes went by, and Cece seemed to swoon. She put her fingers to her forehead. Tony watched and smiled.

Cece thought to herself, "Wow, I must have a very empty stomach. I feel so dizzy. I almost feel sick. I need to get to our room fast. I can make it. It's just out that door over there. I can see it from here. If I'm not here, Ian will know I went to our room."

Cece stood up and walked to the restaurant's back door. She didn't realize it was an emergency exit. The door's alarm was not set, because the door faced the condo rentals. She opened the door to leave and stepped out. She held onto the door's frame as she helped herself down the icy steps. Then the security door slammed shut behind her. As Cece completed reaching the ground, she felt her stomach turn over. She sat down on a snow pile in the bleak area behind the restaurant. Cece felt disorientated. Her stomach lurched. She vomited.

Cece thought, "This isn't normal. I need to get to the room now!"

* * *

Ian eventually found a cold, wet, and freezing Connie still halfway up the mountain sitting on her skis.

Ian thought, "It's odd ski patrol isn't insisting Connie should get off the mountain! What kind of cheap jerk is Tony, anyway? No one deserves to be this cold and wet. Wow, it's getting dark fast."

Ian had hoped to motivate Connie quickly to get down the mountain, but she kept procrastinating. Ian was realizing something wasn't right.

She should have been ecstatic to get off the mountain. She was shivering, and her lips were blue. The woman didn't seem to care if she did not have to do anything quickly. Connie did everything she could do to distract Ian and not cooperate with him. Finally, ski patrol came by and Ian flagged them down.

Ian told them, "This shivering and soaking wet woman needs help. She's been sitting on her skis all day and needs to get down off the mountain before it gets any colder and darker."

Ian quickly left to go back to Cece.

Ski patrol looked at Connie and asked, "Lady, what are you still doing up here? You kept telling us your boyfriend was coming up to get you! We're taking you to the medics!"

Connie answered while shivering, "I didn't think things would be so difficult."

Ski patrol just looked at Connie like she was strange as they prepared their tow carriage. Ian skied down the mountain thinking, "Connie was uncooperative with me. She was not in any hurry to leave! Where 'has' Tony been?"

The sun had set. Ian stopped. He noticed darkness was setting in quickly. Ian looked at his watch. It was almost 40 minutes since he left Cece. He never thought he'd be gone for more than 20 minutes. Ian had to stop to check the slopes. The darkness was encasing the mountain, as it played havoc with the snowy surfaces. It was difficult to see the contours of the mountain's mounds, edges, and runs. Ian didn't want to end up with a broken leg, or ankle, or worse.

Ian's thoughts went back to Connie, "Cece was correct. Something isn't right about Connie. It was as if Connie didn't want me to leave. I asked her where Tony was, and she acted like she didn't know. Their relationship is very strange, unless maybe something is up."

Ian immediately took off skiing and started to get extremely worried. Had he put Cece in jeopardy somehow? Ian flew down the darkening mountain trails.

Ian thought, "Damn shadows, if I could just see more clearly!"

* * *

Tony thought everything went well and smiled. Tony stood and nonchalantly worked his way through the packed crowd of people to exit through the restaurant's front door. No one seemed to notice Cece went out the back-emergency door into the darkness, but Tony did not want to take the chance of someone seeing him following her out that same door. Not when things were finally going his way.

Tony thought, "By now, Cece will be helpless out there in the dark icy night!"

* * *

Cece sat on the snow struggling, to get up. She wanted to cry out but felt so sick to her stomach. Her head started spinning and pounding.

Cece thought to herself, "What happened to me? I was surrounded by people! They were in their own worlds and having fun with their friends and loved ones. I didn't know any of them. How could I possibly get this ill so quickly?"

Cece felt cold and faint. She was disoriented. She stood to walk and fell onto the snow once again. She crawled. She could see people in the well-lit restaurant, but they could not see or hear her in the darkness where she struggled. She could see her room's door, but she couldn't stand up to walk to it. She took her room key out of her pocket and pulled the key's attached elastic band twice around her wrist. She was determined not to lose it. She felt the key with her fingers. She knew she had a weapon. She vomited again but she continued crawling.

* * *

Ian was having a difficult time. The Sun was done setting, and the darkness was working against his determination to get off the mountain. He felt for the ski patrol trying to help Connie, when suddenly they quickly passed right by him towing Connie down the mountain! She didn't procrastinate at all with them! She was sitting straight up inside the tow carriage and smirked at Ian as they passed.

Connie's demeanor let the cat out of the bag. Ian knew.

Ian thought, "What was I thinking? Cece is alone and unprotected!"

He proceeded to fall in behind the ski patrol towing carriage. The tow carriage left a nice smooth path behind it. Ian was making great time getting back to Cece. Ski patrol knew all the good paths down the mountain. Ian would travel behind them for as long as possible. Connie didn't like the fast progress Ian was making. Connie became visually upset. Ian was flying down the mountain following the ski patrol carriage. They were moving fast towards the medic's office. Ian left the smooth tow carriage trail to cut across the mountain's bottom to get to the restaurant.

Cece sat again and swayed gently. She checked her room key to make sure it was secure. She left the tight elastic band around her wrist. She did not want to lose her key! She needed to get to the room. The key was the only weapon she could think of to protect herself. Cece looked once more for their room's door. She could see it. Her stomach was turning over and over. Her head was pounding, and she thought she would faint from the pain. The frigid air helped her to focus. She picked snow up and put it on her face and the back of her neck. She was determined to get to her room as she crawled. She made it to the restaurant's back border wall and leaned up onto it. Cece crawled over the three-foot-high stone wall and fell to the snowy ground on the other side. She figured their room was only about 30 feet away from the rear of the restaurant. Her key was ready. She was sure she was more than halfway there.

Cece prayed, "Please, God, I know it's coming. Give me strength."

Tony hurried as he rounded the restaurant. He was astonished when he could not see her! He looked around frantically. She had to be there! She could have never made it alone! Then Tony saw movement. Cece was pulling herself up onto the other side of the short wall located along the restaurant's back border. The first guest condominium rentals were right behind the wall. Tony had to hurry. Cece was close to her door!

Tony thought, "Damn, Cece climbed over the wall by herself! She's a very strong woman, but I got her now!"

Cece was sick to her stomach again. She kept falling back against the other side of the wall.

She wondered, "What is wrong with me? Vomiting is probably the best thing that could happen to me. If breakfast was bad, I'm sure I would have felt it sooner and not after skiing all day!"

Cece was perplexed. She realized this wasn't normal. She tried to push away from the wall again. She noticed no people were around to help her. She turned to look at her condo's door.

She thought, "It's only maybe 10 feet away!"

She noticed the door next to her room was slowly opening like people were quietly saying their goodnights.

Cece was too weak to ask for help! Tony ran up to Cece who was quietly crawling. He violently grabbed her around the waist and began striking her. Tony did not notice the other door opening.

One woman, in a group of three couples, who came out of the condo next to Cece's condo, started screaming, "Look! That man's slapping a helpless lady!"

All three couples started yelling at Tony repeatedly, "Let go of her! Put her down! Stop slapping her! Help, we need help, here! Someone calls the police! Help! Help! Help!"

People started coming out of both floors of the condominiums.

Three men were trying to pull Cece out of Tony's grip. Tony's sunglasses fell as his huge hand came down out of nowhere trying to slap her. She ducked clumsily out of the way just as one of the men snatched his Tony arm aside. She looked up to see a black hooded head and a set of cruel black eyes.

Cece thought, "NO! Tony is holding onto me!"

Tony was so strong. Cece's world was spinning out of control. Things started to get very dark. She tried to scream, but no sound escaped her lips. Cece heard people yelling! Tony broke free of their hold on him.

Suddenly, another hard slap painfully grazed the side of Cece's head. She forced herself to hold on to consciousness. Blood ran down onto her face. Her painful world was spinning. She fought to recover. She used one of her oldest tricks and pathetically tried to kick between Tony's legs. It made him angry. He moaned slightly in pain, but he didn't lose control. Cece was suffering. Tony's other hand retaliated and forcefully slapped her cheek. Cece tasted her own blood.

Cece worried, "I have to fight back! I taste my own blood! Please, God, don't let this happen to me. Tell Ian I love him and our boys."

People were yelling for help! Multiple men were trying to stop Tony. Tony was strong. He was kicking, punching, and winning. Cece had to begin her attack. She remembered the key on her wrist! Another slap hit her cheek as she struggled. Tony was too strong. She drooped helplessly. The elastic band clung to Cece's wrist as the key dangled freely. She was being thrown over his shoulder as he was slowly running through deeper snow away from the fighting crowd. She could feel her stomach muscles tighten and felt them bruising. People were yelling for the Marshall as the crowd followed Tony again!

Cece thought, "Am I dying or almost dead? My head's pounding! I need my key. Is it still dangling from my wrist? Good! I am losing control, but I can try to stab!"

Cece grabbed for the hoodie on Tony's head. Cece reached under the hoodie and stabbed, and stabbed, again and again, toward Tony's eyes, face, and head! Finally, Cece pulled his hoodie down and regurgitated all over Tony's upper body.

* * *

Ian skied quickly closing in from the mountain's bottom. Ian visually found the restaurant location. It was getting dark quickly. From out of the shadows behind the restaurant, Ian saw someone trying to carry a body over his shoulder as he darted towards the rear of the condominium rentals. Ian could see the person being carried away was trying to hit the man's head with weakened fists of rage. Ian thought the carried person was dressed like Cece! A screaming crowd followed them. The person clumsily clawed at her abductor's face with something small and shiny.

The abductor kept trying to run away while carrying his prey! She looked very weak, but she kept trying to get the abductor down as he kept hitting into the carried person's side with his free hand. Ian saw the abductee purposely pull back the man's hoodie and vomit on his head, his neck, and into his face. People were yelling for help for the woman!

Ian prayed, "Please, dear Lord, help me! Please let my skis fly! If Tony's got her, then the person must be Cece! He's built like Tony! He is as strong as Tony! That is Tony! Look how the person on top is fighting him off! She is.... my Cece!"

Tony was furious with her for purposely vomiting on him. What a weapon! He couldn't see through stinging bloody eyes! Cece was using whatever means she could muster to fight back. She finally started connecting better with the room key as she struck at Tony's vomit covered face and head repeatedly. It repulsed Tony more than she thought she could hurt him, but she gave it her best try. She had a plan to go for his eyes. Tony started screaming and kept trying to strike into Cece's side with his free fist. Even though she was weak, she was taut and muscled. Her thick ski jacket and sweaters padded her body! She kept wiggling and stabbing at Tony's eyes with her room key connecting perfectly.

Tony was outraged as he thought, "Cece is strong for a girl. I should have used two of those rape pills. What the hell is she trying to strike my eyes with? She's killing my eyes!"

Tony's cheeks started running with blood from his eye wounds.

The growing crowd of people kept trying to catch up again with Tony to fight him off. They yelled for more help for the wounded woman!

Ian skis seemed to fly across the snow. He had to figure out the direction Tony was taking, and where Ian could ski into him and hurt him the most, without letting Cece get harmed by his skis. After Ian left the path behind the ski patrol, his skis were dangerously flying along chunks of snow, ice and rock. One of Ian's skis caught an edge in the dark mountain's snow behind the restaurant. Ian didn't care what happened to him. He had to get to Cece. As Ian's skis caught the edge of grooved ice, Ian threw his ski poles to the side. Ian bent his knees, threw his arms up into the air, and jumped. When Ian leaped up, his skis broke loose off the ice edge as he landed and stayed in his crouched position. Ian started gaining speed quickly.

Ian screamed out loud as he prayed, "Please God give me strength. She's so good! Please protect her. She doesn't deserve this! Let me just get to Tony!"

Suddenly, Tony fell to his knees. Ian was astonished! A group of people still struggled to get to Tony through deep snow drifts. The group helped by causing a commotion and calling for help to get the Ski Marshall through the crowd. They continued shuffling through the deep snow towards Tony. Tony dropped his beautiful prey. People were yelling at each other to hurry and let the Ski Marshall through, but the high snow drifts hindered all paths towards Cece, except Ian's! Ian felt like he was flying! The crowd persevered and so did Ian!

Tony held on to one of Cece's arms as he screamed out, "My eyes, my eyes! She's killing me!"

A woman in the crowd was screaming back, "You deserve it, you dirty scumbag!"

Cece was slurring her words and struggling to scream.

Ian thought, "What's happening?"

Cece was in slow motion caused by Tony's drug. Ian saw her struggling to be free of Tony's hold! Her strong fingers were jabbing into Tony's eyes. Ian saw Cece inflicting something into Tony's eyes causing him as much pain as she could! Ian figured it was their room key! Ian could tell Cece was not herself as she tried to fight Tony off. Ian realized somehow Tony must have drugged his wife. Ian became enraged as he flew to his wife's aid as fast as his skis could fly!

Ian was finally involved! It all happened so fast, like he was still in the jungles of Vietnam! No one in the screaming crowd knew what had truly happened. The Resort's Ski Marshall and the crowd were still stumbling through the 5-foot snowdrifts to come to Cece's aid. Ian figured if it worked once, it would work again.

Ian swung his arms as he jumped up, leaving no ski trails near the scene. Ian drew his knees up to his chest, while gliding through the air. As Ian was losing momentum, he extended his legs quickly. Forcefully landing, Ian slammed his skis down onto the right side of Tony's rib cage. Then Ian jumped to an abrupt stop on top of Tony's back. As Ian kept his balance, Tony's bloody face and chest slid along the top of a huge snow-covered boulder, smearing it with red blood and skin. Tony tried to scream in pain, but it hurt too much. Tony fainted. Bloody eyed Tony never saw what hit him. There was a strange morbid satisfaction when Ian felt Tony's broken ribs starting to crack more under the weight of Ian's skis. Ian immediately jumped off Tony's back, disconnected his skis, and singly threw the skis as far away as possible. Not knowing what he was going to find, Ian ran through the huge snowdrifts to his wife's aid.

Finally arriving at the scene, the police couldn't believe the damage Cece had done to the perpetrator with her room's key! Everyone in the crowd was screaming and gathering around Tony's body with the police. All tracks were wiped out. The crowd was not sure what really ended the confrontation! They just knew Tony was abducting Cece, but somehow, Tony had been stopped by a bloody boulder next to his body.

Ian repeated to Cece, "It's ok, Cece, I'm here now! I'm here now, Baby!"

Cece feared Ian killed Tony, even though she had already given it her best shot. She gave up struggling when she heard Ian's voice and fell helplessly ill into his arms. Tony was unconscious. The Marshall called for immediate medical emergency backup. The police began asking questions and checking to see if Tony was alive. Tony was still breathing. Witnesses were staring at Tony's bloody face, head, and ribs were smashed onto the snow-covered boulder next to him due to his hard-running fall and caused him to drop the captive lady.

The Police report stated Tony must have fractured both sides of his own ribs when his binoculars smashed between his breastbone and the boulder. Ian did not correct them. Eyewitnesses were filling out reports stating Tony forcefully tried to abduct Cece, while assaulting her, when a group of people and a snow skier came to her aid.

* * *

An unconscious Tony would not know he was under arrest, until he recuperated. Tony was carefully taken by stretcher to a holding cell inside the medic's station. Connie got an eyeful! After the initial medical care was rendered, an unconscious Tony was retained in the medic's holding pen for emergency transport to the nearest hospital emergency room's crime ward. Tony would have to face charges of kidnapping and battery in front of a group of more than twenty witnesses. Tony's ribs were taped, and bandages were wrapped around his head and over his eyes and face, Tony looked like an ancient petrified mummy!

A policewoman took pictures of Cece's bruises on her body, the bloody head wound, and the stitches on the side of her head. The medic told Cece there would be no permanent damage to her face, her head, or to the side of her body where Tony had punched repeatedly, but Cece needed to rest because her ribs were bruised. The medic recommended Cece see her regular doctor as soon as possible upon her return to Las Vegas.

The medic, also, told Cece, "You are bruised, but I do not think anything is broken. The x-rays look good! Thank Heaven, you like big puffy down filled ski jackets! I'm going to tape up your ribs where the perpetrator was punching, and send you home, if you promise to get checked out as soon as you get back to Las Vegas. We will send copies of your photos, lab work, x-rays, eye witness accounts, and all of the complete medical reports to your attorney, to you, and to the Clark County District Attorney, and the Clark County Metropolitan Police Department, Ok? I think somehow this guy, 'Tony Something Italian', must have slipped you a date rape drug. I believe the drug was in the cup of coffee you drank in the restaurant, because it is all you ingested since your early morning breakfast. You are going to feel lousy, but you will get over it.

All I can say is you are very lucky this attack was not any worse. You are a strong, young woman, who is in excellent shape physically and mentally. You will eventually be just fine. The bruising will take a while to dissipate."

A female medical assistant was happy to report the good news to Ian as she led him to Cece's room. She, also, congratulated Ian for having such a feisty wife.

The assistant said, "Wow, you should see the other guy! We have a long list of witnesses volunteering to go to court. It seems the whole crowd of witnesses wanted to volunteer! They loved your wife and how she fought back!"

Ian smiled and commented, "She's Sicilian-American! What can I say?"

The female assistant said, "Oh, that explains a lot! They're tough! I am married to one myself!"

Ian smiled and shook his head as if to agree.

The assistant smiled, too.

After they arrived home, Cece feared the repercussions they would suffer after Tony recuperated. A week later, Tony finally reported into the Bella Ricco and Sallie. Tony's recuperation would take many months! Tony reported he had a very severe skiing accident, and he would probably be in the hospital for a couple of months. Tony reported he suffered from severe wounds around his face, his eyes, and both sides of his ribs were badly broken. Tony said he had to remain stationary until his bones healed, and he had to be constantly medicated with drugs for severe pain. Tony, also, reported he needed facial plastic surgeries.

Salliewas totally pissed off! He was raging, "Tony never told me he was going out of town to ski! I didn't even know where Tony was until he called in after a week's absence! Now Tony needs hospitalization and surgeries for an unknown amount of time! What the hell am I going to do?"

As far as being Sallie's bodyguard, Tony wouldn't be any good in his current physical condition. Without Tony, Sallie had no muscle!

Secretly Sallie was thinking, "What's going to happen to me when the mob figures out, I can't deliver in time?"

* * *

Cece missed work, too. Cece was on a three-month medical leave, but the medic was right. She was going to be fine.

Ian finally had to confide in Tommy, Jr. about what really happened in order to obtain some extra time off to help with Cece's initial recuperation. Tommy, Jr. became absolutely furious. He reported the news to his father, Tom, Sr., and asked him to keep it private unless it had to be divulged to help protect Ian's employment as Ian had requested.

Tom, Sr. became even more furious! He told Sal, Sr., who told Sophia and Sophia told Tom's wife before Tom got home from work!

Of course, Sal, Sr. came down on Sallieabout his no-good friend. The wheels were set in motion. Tony was immediately fired from Bella Ricco.

Sallie didn't care! Tony would be his employee if they were still both alive.

* * *

The police heard through the nurse's grapevine Tony was mumbling constantly in Southern Nevada Memorial Hospital. Tony kept saying he was going to get even when he got out of the hospital, but the staff didn't understand "with whom," since he hurt himself. Tony was confined in Ward 700, where the mentally ill and insane criminals were hospitalized. Nurses were under constant guard by security officers when they had to go into Ward 700 to treat patients.

Cece found out how horrible Tony could be, and how he loved to inflict pain on his innocent, helpless victims. Ian already knew because he blamed himself for Cece's condition! She constantly feared for her beloved husband's and son's lives, as well as her life. She couldn't even imagine how many people Tony had beaten much more severely than he hurt her. It was three months before her bruises vanished.

Tony's charges were pending, but Sallie got the best possible crooked lawyers that money could buy. Tony's case would be delayed many times. Sallie knew he would take care of his childhood buddy, even though he thought Tony's foolishness over a broad was stupid. Sallie was angry because Tony caused this mess to happen when Sallie had a big dope deal coming up. Sallie was trying to figure out how to tell his fellow dealmakers he had to wait for his partner to heal so his partner could protect Sallie from them! Because Sallie was stalling around, the deal-makers became extremely angry and called Sallie unprofessional. 'They' would do whatever it took to get even if Sallie stalling on this big money transaction if it failed!

For the first time since Tony rescued Sallie from death as a preteen, Sallie was really scared! He began living on the top private floor of the Bella Ricco under twenty-four-hour surveillance with constant rotating security guards.

Sal, Sr. started asking Sallie, Jr., "What the hell is going on with you and Tony?"

Sallie squirmed out of answering but only time would tell.

Ian reported to Tommy, Jr. and explained Cece's progress. Tommy, Jr.'s family loved Cece, too.

Tommy said, "That son of a bitch! I would have killed him if he did that to my wife! Don't worry, Ian, we'll get through this. That stupid son of a bitch! Poor Sal, Sr. and Sophia! They were so embarrassed over their son's affiliation with Tony, that Sal, Sr. personally fired Tony immediately."

Ian surmised Salliewould most likely be hiring Tony as his full-time collector for Sallie's growing loan shark business. However, Tony could not do that kind of work until he recuperated. No one knew how long Tony's recuperation could be! Ian realized Tony wouldn't look like his old handsome self ever again unless he went through many surgeries. Tony's face looked like chopped hamburger the last time Ian saw him.

Ian knew Sallie liked his Loan Shark business because of Tony's big mouth. Ian's concern was for Tom, Sr., and Tommy's family losing their business for having an affiliation with Sallieor his illegal affairs. Ian confided in Tommy, Jr. about what happened at Gerri's house. Ian told him to be careful of Sallie and Tony in the future. Ian, also, reported Sallie's parents knew nothing about Sallie's adventurous life, his side business, his deals, or why he always wanted Tony with him. Tommy, Jr. was perplexed, and saying, "I dread telling my father! Maybe Sallie will go straight because of what happened, but if Sallie's involved with the mob, they may have other plans. Maybe Sallie and Tony will stop their foolishness. They certainly don't need the money! I need to speak with the two Seniors and our lawyers!"

Stoic Sallie planned to enable Tony to remain in Vegas. Tony never mentioned Ian's name, or Cece's name to Sallie, but Sallie's Spy, Woody, could figure things out if he made a connection. Tony didn't need Sallie any more pissed off at him.

Cece worried, "What is going to happen to my beautiful little family? What will Tony do to me? What's next? It is only a matter of time until he recuperates."

Ian looked forward to Tony's recuperation being over but didn't mention it to Cece. Ian kept telling Cece everything would be fine. Tony would recuperate someday. Ian knew the real Tony now. Ian would be waiting and ready for him the next time. Ian was taught to be a savage in the Vietnam jungles by Uncle Sam and by South Korea's Captain Joe and his troop of sixteen jungle Tae Kwon Do warriors. They killed silently, without any weapons except their bodies. They taught Ian their martial art because they liked him. Ian paid them back by teaching them to walk on their hands, buying them the American cigarettes they cherished, and by letting them beat the shit out of him until Ian learned to be a Master.

Tony never paid Connie.

Connie thought, "Women remember things like this! ....and freezing our wet cold asses off all day for nothing, except catching pneumonia. Plus, I lost one hundred dollars of my own money! Then I had no way back to Vegas, no money in my pocket, and I had to hitch a ride! That stupid Tony! He will be sorry! I am so 'pissed off'! I plan to get even with him someday!"

Do not underestimate the power of a woman.... especially a bad woman!

Cece knew Tony was not out of her life, and he would never be without someone's death involved. They would hear from him again.

* * *

Cece thought, "What is going to happen to my beautiful little family? What will Tony do to us in the future? What's next? It's only a matter of time! I'll do anything to save my family!"

* * *

Ian bought a six-month-old male Rottweiler Pup. His name was Max. Max really loved his family and vice versa! Max slept on the floor next to Cece's side of their bed.

* * *

Carmella and Sammie could not get over the television news report involving Cece once again. She was on the local TV news as a child in Miami, a teenager in Las Vegas, and as a young mother, wife, and beloved daughter.

* * *

The Finale

Four months later, at the Employee of the Month Luncheon festivities…

Cece seemed to be on autopilot even though she was a healthy, fully recuperated young woman. She sat in the beautiful ballroom trying to enjoy all the luxuries offered while Ian held her hand.

Ian was so proud of his wife. She was a fighter. He swore to himself he would do whatever he had to do to protect her, their sons, and their future. She and Ian got to invite their two best friends to the festivities. Cece's parents, Carmella and Sammie, were also there smiling greatly as their daughter was praised for her good work and her ethics.

Everyone stood and applauded when Cece was announced as Employee of the Month! Her happy tears flowed. She was awarded an all-expense-paid round trip to Maui for two for a week, plus spending money. Everyone gathered around her to congratulate her. It took over an hour to get through all the greetings, well wishes and hugs from her fellow employees.

When It Was Over…

Cece thought, "It was a wonderful event. It's something we needed right now. Getting out of Vegas for a week of tropical relaxation will help us clear our minds and try to figure out what we need to do to prepare for Tony's next intentions."

* * *

A flash entered Cece's mind….

Glossary of Casino Terms

Back of the house	Where only hotel and casino employees can go
Broad	An unfortunate nickname men once called women.
Casino chips	Vary in colors. The color determines the amount. Example: Yellow chip= $1,000.00 Black Chip=$100.00 Green Chip=$25.00 Red chip=$5.00 and Blue=$1.00(most common) Pink=$5,000.00
Casino Shift Boss	Manager in charge of all the live casino tables for an entire shift
Comp slips	Slips signed by bosses to give high rollers what they want. High Rollers are usually given free Room, Food, Beverage. (may vary) RF+B Comps
Craps/Dice	Crap pit or dice pit
Day shift	Day hours ex. 8am to 4pm or 10am to 6pm or Noon to 8pm.
Fish hooks	It is said that a non-tipper has fishhooks in his pockets, which make it difficult to get the money out of their pockets

Floorman	Managers, who watch over a certain amount of tables
George	A generous tipper, one who tips with cash, tokes, or chips
Graveyard shift	4am to Noon (Hours may vary)
High limit	Any table or area where the limits are set high
High Roller	Anyone who plays in or on high limit areas
Hooker	Prostitute
John	A person who favors prostitution
Juice	When someone has a friendly or family connection, who usually watches over them. Could have had a mob connection, also.
On a roll	Winning and cannot seem to lose.
Out of Line	Doing something wrong
Pit boss	Higher up Manager in charge of an area of tables
Stiff	A non-tipper
The Strip	Las Vegas Blvd South in Las Vegas, Nevada. Where many of the fine Hotels and Casinos are located.
Swing Shift	Evening hours to early morning (most common is 8pm to 4am)
Tokes	Many of the tips given in casinos were tokens made by Hotel management. Tokes meant tips. (To Insure Proper Service)
Tom	A non-tipper
VIP	Very Important person

About the Author

Phyllis Carver was raised in Las Vegas, Nevada, from her teen years. Many of the *Bet On You* experiences are tantamount to Phyllis' own life.

Several of Phyllis' occurrences throughout her adult life had been revealed to her early in her childhood. First, that she could always be counted on as a loving and serving daughter and sibling. Secondly, that she would marry her amazing "Glowing Man," who showed up repeatedly in her youthful daydreams. Thirdly, that she would raise two wonderful, handsome and highly respected sons. Lastly, that she would become a Las Vegas cocktail waitress.

Phyllis' fairytale-like marriage and motherhood faced serious challenges upon the return of her Glowing Man from the Vietnam War. It seemed as though he, and all of America, fell into a depressive state. Because of those difficult years, Phyllis swore all three of her men would become well educated to avoid any future possibility of the draft.

Her loving husband worked as an Electronics Engineer before his death in 2015. Her first born, Scott, earned a PHD in Biochemical and Biomedical Engineering. He is a loving husband to Claire and doting father to Annie, Gigi, and Carmela. Second born, Aaron, became a Structural Engineer, who loves his guitars. He is a loving husband to Cristi and doting father to Grace and Clark.

Phyllis still resides in Las Vegas, where a favorite pastime is snow skiing on Mt. Charlie. Her rescue dogs, Skipper and Benny are great little companions, leading Phyllis to declare that they have actually rescued her! Diva, a gorgeous German Syrian Rottweiler pup, recently entered Phyllis' household to offer lots of love and protection, and to receive a lot of love back from Diva's new family.

Made in the USA
Coppell, TX
12 August 2020

33065717R00187